Lady Killer
Miasma

Elisabeth Sanxay Holding

Stark House Press • Eureka California

LADY KILLER / MIASMA

Published by Stark House Press
1945 P Street
Eureka, CA 95501, USA
griffins@northcoast.com

Text set in Adobe Garamond. Heads set in Champion and Dogma.
Cover design and book layout by Mark Shepard
Cover art by Campbell Shepard

PUBLISHERS NOTE

First Stark House Press Edition: October 2003

0 9 8 7 6 5 4 3 2

LADY KILLER

Perhaps Honey hadn't married Weaver for love, but it wasn't entirely for money. When he had proposed to her he had been so attentive, the perfect gentleman. Now he quarrels with her all the time. And by the time they embark together on a cruise ship to the Caribbean, she begins to have serious doubts about their future together. So it really is quite a welcome distraction to find that the newly-wedded woman who shares the cabin next door with her handsome husband, Captain Lashelle, seems to be in need of her help. Poor Alma has victim written all over her. Soon Honey becomes convinced that Alma's husband is planning to murder his new bride! So why wouldn't anyone listen to her? Why did Mr. Basingly seem so hostile to her suspicions? Why did Mr. Perez warn her to be quiet? And why is her own husband suddenly so afraid of her? Nothing makes any sense. But it all leads to murder.

MIASMA

Dr. Dennison is finding that a career in medicine is more challenging than he expected. After several months in business, he still doesn't have any patients. So when wealthy Dr. Leatherby offers him a position as his assistant and asks him to move into his fine house, Dennison is certain that his troubles are all behind him. But as soon as he arrives, he finds a mystery at every turn. Why does the pretty, young nurse, Hilda Napier, ask him to leave? Who is the mysterious patient that arrives one evening, only to die the next day of a sudden heart attack? Where has his predecessor, Mr. Folyet, disappeared to and why does everyone at the house seem to hate him? And what is the strange drug that Dr. Leatherby keeps in his safe for his special patients? A miasma of doubt and suspicion assails Dr. Dennison, and he will stop at nothing until he can discover its cause— even if it costs him his reputation, and perhaps even his life.

ELISABETH SANXAY HOLDING BIBLIOGRAPY

Invincible Minnie (1920)

Rosaleen Among the Artists (1921)

Angelica (1921)

The Unlit Lamp (1922)

The Shoals of Honour (1926)

The Silk Purse (1928)

Miasma (1929)

Dark Power (1930)

The Death Wish (1934)

The Unfinished Crime (1935)

The Strange Crime in Bermuda (1937)

The Obstinate Murderer [aka No Harm Intended] (1938)

Who's Afraid [aka Trial by Murder] (1940)

The Girl Who Had to Die (1940)

Speak of the Devil [aka Hostess to Murder] (1941)

Killjoy [aka Murder is a Kill-Joy] (1941)

Lady Killer (1942)

The Old Battle-Ax (1943)

Net of Cobwebs (1945)

The Innocent Mrs. Duff (1946)

The Blank Wall (1947)

Miss Kelly (1947)

Too Many Bottles [aka The Party Was the Pay-Off] (1950)

The Virgin Huntress (1951)

Widow's Mite (1952)

INTRODUCTION

We have the Depression to thank for Elisabeth Sanxay Holding's career as a mystery author. Until 1929, she had been writing serious, mainstream novels like *Rosaleen Among the Artists, Angelica, The Unlit Lamp* and *The Shoals of Honour.* She published six novels before the Depression, starting with *Invincible Minnie* in 1920, and ending with *The Silk Purse* in 1928. Early critics noted her expert characterization, and in the *New York Times* review of *The Silk Purse*, the reviewer said: "They are as real a collection of peoples as ever said yes when they wished to heaven they could say no."

So when the Depression hit in 1929 and she was no longer able to sell her leisurely character novels, Holding turned to writing mysteries. Or, more properly, suspense novels. Because, simply put, Elisabeth Sanxay Holding is the precursor to the entire women's psychological suspense genre, and authors like Patricia Highsmith and Ruth Rendell owe her a very large debt of gratitude.

Holding was one of the first to write mystery novels that didn't so much ask whodunit, but *whydunit.* In fact, we know whodunit because it's quite often the main character. It's the "why" that is always the most important part of her books. The psychological underpinnings of her novels form the basis of the mystery. Her characters always act from a very determined point of view. Whether from guilt, discontent, deception, misconception, or even pure altruism, they act out their dramas with very little consideration for other points of view. And therein lies the conflict. They have all got blinders on, seeing just what they want to see, each with their own misguided agenda. They lie when it will get them in the most trouble and tell the truth when it's in their own worst interest. In other words, her characters feel very real to us—we believe in them.

A rich, alcoholic husband grows tired of his well-meaning but lower-class wife. Everything she does irritates him. He decides he must get rid of her but his drinking is making him delusional and easily annoyed. Who can he trust? As he rushes from one hidden bottle, one seedy bar to another, the answer is clearly "no one." When his chauffeur comes to him with a plan to catch his wife with another man, he jumps at it. After all, sooner or later you've got to trust somebody.

This is the basic plot of *The Innocent Mrs. Duff.* What makes the book so compelling is the degree to which Holding gets under the skin of this self-deluded man. She wrote the story in a crisp, staccato style and makes the reader feel every bit of the scheming husband's mounting alcoholic mania. Though casual drinking was more a part of the daily lifestyle in Holding's day, she wasn't afraid to shed some light on its darker aspects. In fact, she had previously explored the theme of the alcoholic male in the The Obstinate Murderer—albeit more sympathetically—and clearly knew this personality well.

The Innocent Mrs. Duff and The Blank Wall (filmed twice, as The Reckless Moment in 1949 and The Deep End in 2001) are arguably two of her best works and the only two novels of Holding's that remain in print, thanks to Academy Chicago. Dell published several of her novels in paperback in the 50's, and Mercury published a few in digest form as well. And back in the 1960's, Ace Books published twelve of her books as Ace Doubles. But since then she has almost entirely gone out of print. A sad state of affairs for an author whom Raymond Chandler called "the top suspense writer of them all" in a letter to his British publisher.

All in all, Holding published eighteen suspense novels in her lifetime, beginning with Miasma in 1929, and ending with Widow's Mite in 1952. Many of these novels were also serialized in national magazines, and almost all were published in paperback and foreign editions, as well as by mystery book clubs. She also published quite a few short stories in magazines ranging from McCalls, American Magazine and Ladies Home Journal to Alfred Hitchcock's Mystery Magazine, The Saint, Ellery Queen's Mystery Magazine and The Magazine of Fantasy and Science Fiction. She even wrote a children's story, Miss Kelly, the story of a cat who could understand and speak human, and who comes to the aid of a terrified tiger.

Elisabeth Sanxay was born in Brooklyn in 1889, the descendant of an upper middle class family, and was educated in a series of private schools, specifically Whitcombe's School, The Packer Institute, Miss Botsford's School and the Staten Island Academy. She married a British diplomat named George E. Holding in 1913 and together they traveled widely in South America and the Caribbean, settling in Bermuda for awhile where her husband was a government officer. She also raised two daughters, Skeffington and Antonia, the latter of whom married Peter Schwed (until his recent death the executor of Holding's estate and a retired author and publisher with Simon and Schuster).

Holding was thirty-one when her first book was published. Right from the beginning she introduced the theme of discontent that she was to use so often in her mystery books. *Invincible Minnie* starts off slowly—telling at first when it should be showing—but evolves into a fairly lurid tale, the compelling story of a headstrong woman who uses sex to control men and get her way. There's no pat, happy ending either. Minnie runs roughshod over everyone, including her sister and children, and prevails through sheer determination. Holding's lean 40's style was only seen in glimpses in this first effort, but her characterizations were already taking shape in the relentless actions of Minnie and the various people she controlled.

With her second novel, Holding lets the story tell itself, vastly improving over the style of her first book. *Rosaleen Among the Artists,* a bit less melodramatic than *Invincible Minnie,* tells the story of a self-sacrificing young woman struggling to survive and find love in New York City. Though polished off with a sweeter ending, there is much travail as Rosaleen hits rock bottom before finally being united with her soul mate, Mr. Landry. In fact, the two are so matched in the stubbornness with which they hold onto their ideals—tenaciously sacrificing their own happiness at every turn—that they almost wear each other out by the end of the book. Ironically, it is their own principles that almost kill their only chance at love.

In 1929, when the Depression killed her mainstream career, Holding had to do something to help support her two daughters. She could have started writing nice, cozy romantic mysteries. But she just didn't have it in her. The characters she was creating were too contrary, too impulsive—too flawed—and not particularly romantic. They didn't act in their own best interests, holding onto ideals that invariably precipitated trouble. It's as if they felt compelled to do the very thing that caused the most havoc, even if for all the best reasons.

As a consequence, the mystery novels Holding began to write were dark affairs, having more in common with noir than standard detective fiction. It's easy to understand why she was such a favorite of Chandler's. Murder and mania are always lurking in the wings—and the menace doesn't always exist from the outside, but is quite often found from within. These are characters with something to hide. Sometimes there is a happy ending, sometimes not. Sometimes there is a detective, but he's usually as clueless as everyone else. You might say that Holding's characters are quite often lucky if they can make it to the last page with their health, if not their sanity, intact.

In *The Virgin Huntress* we follow young Monty on V-Day as he meets an older woman, Dona Luisa, and is brought into a world of class and culture he had always dreamed of. He is a charming if somewhat insecure young man, somewhat expedient—perhaps too expedient—in his past dealings with women. In fact, he is constantly nagged by secrets from his past, secrets that begin to fracture him as Dona Luisa's niece Rose begins to pry into his past life. By the end of the short novel, Monty has become completely unraveled, the victim of his own expediency. It's not a pretty portrait.

Another of Holding's favorite themes involves fractious family relationships and domestic disputes. *Dark Power* is a perfect example. In the first chapter we meet a young lady, Diana, who discovers that she is quite penniless and soon to be out on the street. Before this happens, however, she is suddenly rescued by an eccentric uncle she didn't know she had. He happily escorts her back to the family home, where she meets such a thoroughly dysfunctional collection of relatives that by the end of the book she barely makes it out alive.

Holding also loved to examine the way stress works on characters, particularly middle-aged men, and would combine this with her theme of domestic disharmony. *The Innocent Mrs. Duff* is an obvious example, but *The Death Wish* is another in which a man, Mr. Delancey, who had always thought himself happily married, comes to a moment of crisis in which he discovers that he actually hates his wife. She has slowly been emasculating him by controlling his purse strings, but when his best friend reveals a similar domestic situation and announces his plans to kill his own wife, Delancey is plunged into a world of self-doubt. At first he is shocked by his friend's confession, and when the wife is found drowned, he hopes that it is the accident that it seems to be. But a seed has been planted, and nothing in his formerly phlegmatic life will ever be the same.

Holding's deft hand at characterization makes all these situations ring true, giving them a psychological perspective that not only presents all her characters' foibles sympathetically, but creates the tension that propels her story along as well. Their actions are understandable, given the circumstances, and all the more frustrating because they are so identifiable. In *The Death Wish*, we watch Delancey try to convince himself at first that his wife is simply moody and a bit insecure. He wants to think the best of her. But the reader knows that his wife's insecure nagging is stifling him, her words little barbs that sink in and latch Delancey to her side, subtly but firmly controlling him. We feel his weakness and frustration, his mounting domestic horror, and nothing that proceeds from this realization seems anything less than inevitable. Not even murder.

This is Holding's true forte, that she can make the commonplace, the ordinary, so horrific and so suspenseful. But make no mistake, whether writing about dysfunctional families or failed marriages, her books are full of mystery. In *Lady Killer,* a young recently-wedded ex-model named Honey is on a cruise ship in the Caribbean with her older husband, who is turning out to be a fussy, fault-finding old crab. At the same time that she begins to realize that a life with this man will be completely intolerable, she also becomes aware that the man in the next cabin might possibly be trying to kill his wife. She begins to set about a campaign to protect this poor, plain and unfortunate woman, who doesn't really seem to want her help. In fact, no one on board seems to feel that Honey has any business stirring up trouble.

But the more Honey finds out, the more mysterious her fellow passengers begin to seem to her. Even her own husband begins to seem alien to her. And when she finds a body, even that isn't quite what it seems. But still the little mysteries pile up, and we are swept up in Honey's suspicions and doubts until even we begin to believe, like her, that *no one* is to be trusted.

Miasma presents us with another set of mysteries. A young doctor named Dennison has just about reached the end of his financial resources when he is contacted by a wealthy older doctor in town who wants him to take up residency in his house and assume the care of his patients. All well and good, except that the doctor's young nurse immediately warns Dennison to leave, mysterious patients come and go in the middle of the night, and his predecessor has gone missing. And then there is the weird drug that the older doctor prescribes to certain of his patients, one of whom is now dead from an apparent heart attack. Holding keeps the mysteries coming until both we and Dennison are wondering what the hell is going on here; daring us to put the book down no matter how late it is and how early we have to get up the next morning.

There is a reason that Dorothy B. Hughes said that "connoisseurs will continue their rush when each new Holding reaches publication." Her books are first and foremost very readable. Not only are they excellent examples of psychological suspense and first rate character studies, they move along at a nice, brisk pace. Holding was never one for overwriting. Her dialog always sounds just right, all the doubtful pauses and self-serving/self-deceptive lies in place. We may not always like these characters, but Holding makes us feel compelled to keep reading about them.

Elisabeth Sanxay Holding's mystery novels have been out of print far too long. Until her death in 1955, she was one of the best, and it is a pleasure to be able to bring her books back into print again, many of which have been unavailable in any edition for well over sixty years. In fact, none of our first four reprints were published by Ace Books in the Sixties, and are considered to be some of her scarcer titles. It's time to rediscover Elisabeth Sanxay Holding. Her books may have gone out of print, but they have never gone out of fashion.

Gregory Shepard
Publisher, Stark House Press
September, 2003

LADY KILLER

Elisabeth Sanxay Holding

ONE

They got into the elevator and the bell-boy began putting in the hand luggage, Mr. Stapleton's cowhide bag, Mrs. Stapleton's hat-box, a big suitcase, a smaller one.

"That's enough! That's enough!" said Mr. Stapleton. "There may be other people getting in. That's enough."

He was nervous about elevators being overloaded; he was worrying now, standing in a corner, hat in hand, slender, grey-haired, ineffably distinguished.

He's a pain in the neck, thought Mrs. Stapleton. I'd almost rather stay home than go anywhere with him. But you have to be sorry for the poor goon. He never has a happy moment, fussing the way he does, and being so jealous of me.

Well..., she thought, looking at herself in the mirror. *Spirituelle* type, Mr. Handy had called her; she had seen that written down in his book under her photograph, with all her measurements. A tall willowy blonde with pale misty hair and dark-blue eyes, a sad, beautiful mouth, she had been lovely even when she had bought her clothes on Fourteenth Street. But now, in a mink coat, a hat with a black velvet bow behind her soft pompadour, black nylon stockings and twenty-dollar pumps on her arched, narrow feet, she was something to look at.

The elevator stopped and she stepped out, with her gliding model's walk, one foot almost straight before the other.

"Sit down, Honey," said her husband. "I want to speak to them at the desk."

She sat down on a sofa and looked after him as he crossed the lounge, very erect, in his very full overcoat. He sort of toddles, she thought. There he is, being so important, and it's only about holding his mail. It would be just too bad if he missed one of those catalogues from the museum or one of those things about Save Our New England Trees. That's all he ever gets. And I never get any mail, any more, except from Mother.

Well, you can't eat your cake and have it, too, and I've got a lot to be thankful for, she thought. It was cute of Weaver to think of this trip. He's certainly generous to me and I certainly appreciate it. Only, being married gets on my nerves sometimes. If only we didn't have to be together all the time, it wouldn't be so bad... I couldn't know he didn't have any friends or anything to do. He's so different from what I thought that sometimes—it almost scares me.

But it was not her nature to be scared. She knew how to look after herself. She had made a lot of mistakes, but mostly things came out all right. So would this. As time goes on, she thought, I'll get kind of more settled down. It's not like me, to be so nervous. But this trip will help a lot. It's certainly an experience, going to the tropics.

Weaver was coming back now; he beckoned imperiously to a bell-boy, who did not see the gesture. "Boy!" he called, affronted. "You may take the bags out to the car now. Are you ready, Honey?"

Why wouldn't I be? she thought as she rose. Jeepers! The ship sails at eleven and we had to get up at half-past six. Room service didn't open until seven, but Weaver had arranged the night before; breakfast was to be sent up to their suite at six-thirty promptly. It had not come. It's funny, she thought, the way everything goes wrong for Weaver. I guess he sort of defeats his own ends, fussing so much.

"Oh! It's snowing!" she cried, as she came out of the revolving door.

"Come! Come!" said Weaver, taking her arm and hurrying her along under the portico to the car.

"I just love the snow," she said. "I'd love to walk a little way, even a couple of blocks—"

"Come!" he cried, in a sort of panic, and his hand tightened on her arm. "Honey, get into the car! "

"Hold everything!" she said, mildly. "What's the hurry?"

"You can't go tramping the streets in a snowstorm," he said, in a fury. "You have a certain position to consider now. Get into the *car,* please."

She got in, with a loud, weary sigh. "Whatever is the matter with you, Weaver?" she asked. "This isn't a snowstorm, it's only a few flakes, and I've got a warm fur coat on. I don't understand—"

"Naturally," he said.

"I suppose you mean that to be spiteful," she said. "But it's just foolish."

"No doubt any sort of dignity seems 'foolish' to you."

"Will you kindly tell me how it isn't dignified to take a walk?" she demanded.

"We won't discuss—"

"Yes, we will," she said. "I'm getting pretty tired of you always finding fault with everything I do—"

"I—am—not—going—to—discuss—this," he said.

"Oh, nuts!" she cried. "Discuss *what,* may I ask?"

He did not answer; there he sat, looking so aristocratic, and he's really such a pill, she thought. I hope to God there'll be somebody a little bit interesting on this trip. If there is, *I'll* give Weaver something to discuss. I mean, not anything serious, but I'd just like to have some fun. Honestly, when I think how it's been, all the seven months we've been married... How I've stood it, I don't know.

And how would it be for seven years? For seventeen years? I'm twenty-three now, and he's fifty-one. In ten years even, he'll be old. I mean really old. Suppose he gets funny, so he can't walk or anything? Oh God! Then I'll just *have* to be nice to him.... I'll have to take him out for walks and all like that couple I saw at Atlantic City.... Just crawling along... It would serve me right...

She was suddenly convinced that this was her destiny and it terrified her. But it serves me right! she thought. *I knew* I ought to wait for real love.... I knew ever since I was little, that there was one in the world for me, and one for him, and we were bound to meet some clay. I didn't really exactly marry Weaver for his money. I honestly liked him. I thought he was a gentleman in every sense of the word. Well, I guess he is. But it's very different from what I thought.

They were down near the docks now, and hemmed in by towering trucks, there was one keeping along beside them loaded with chickens in crates. You have to feel sorry for them, she thought, watching them compassionately. But Weaver had started fussing. He took out his wallet, and was examining the tickets, the passports, the travellers' cheques.

"Where do you suppose those chickens are going?" she asked, just to make conversation, just to be nice.

"Chickens?" he repeated. "I don't know what you're talking about."

"Well, I'm talking about those chickens right beside us," she said. "I wonder where they're going."

"Good heavens!" he said, looking at her in a way that cut her to the quick. "No. I'm sorry I don't know where the chickens are going."

He said nothing more, not a word. He fussed and fussed about getting the luggage out of the car; he gave the porter a lot of directions and then he told Edwards the chauffeur all the things he had told him before. "We'll be back on the twenty-third," he said.

They went up in the elevator with some other people who were not interesting-looking. But it's beginning to sort of get me now, she thought, walking along the pier with Weaver with her languid, gliding, model's walk. That woman was certainly staring at my coat. Let her! I'm going to have some fun on this trip, and if Weaver doesn't like it, that's just too bad. He's mean. Spiteful and mean.

They went up the gangway, and for the first time she was on board a ship as a passenger.

"I'll leave you here for a moment," Weaver said. "I'll have to see the Purser—several things to attend to."

She sat down in a wicker chair and looked about her. Not much of a cabin, I must say, she thought. Of course, Weaver told me it was a small boat, but he generally likes things to be so grand.... The times I've been to see people off, going to Europe, their cabin was certainly a lot better than this. Even when Gladwina was going over to Paris... It was fun that day. The whole crowd of us, and Beck brought champagne. Glad's cabin was simply like a bower of flowers.... And I haven't one. Yes, but I've got three fur coats, and those pearls, and the sapphire bracelet... Only I wish there was even one person to see me off, and send me some flowers.

"Er... Excuse me! " said somebody, and turning her head, she glanced up backwards to see who was standing in the doorway. Very handsome he was, slim and debonair, with a little dark moustache, and smiling dark-blue eyes. Attractive.

But Mrs. Weaver Stapleton was dignified. "Yes?" she said, raising her brows a little.

"Well, y'see," he said, "I understood this was my cabin."

"My husband'll know when he comes along," she said.

"Of course, they do make mistakes sometimes, don't they?" said the handsome stranger. "But anyhow we're going to be fellow travellers, aren't we? May I introduce myself? Hilary Lashelle."

A cute name, thought Honey. "I'm Mrs. Weaver Stapleton," she said.

"Will you have a cigarette, Mrs. Stapleton?"

"No, thank you," and at that he threw his own into the wastepaper basket.

"If you don't mind," he said, "I'll just wait until your husband comes, and then we'll see..."

"There's something burning," said Honey, and he hastened to the wastepaper basket. "I'm *sorry,*" he said. "But it's just a few scraps of paper. Stupid thing to do, isn't it?"

"Honey?" said Weaver's voice trembling with anger.

"This is Mr. Lashelle, Weaver, and he thinks maybe this is his cabin."

"What?" cried Weaver. He looked at the number on the door, he looked at the tag on a suitcase. "You're mistaken, sir!" he said.

"Well..." Lashelle said, apologetically, and held up a little brief-case. "This label has the number of this cabin on it."

"We must see the Purser at *once!*" said Weaver. "If you'll kindly come with me, sir.... Honey, wait here. No matter what you're told—by anyone. I intend to get to the bottom of this. Wait here!"

He moved the bags the steward had set down, pushed them a little with his foot, he looked about the cabin for something to set right, he found nothing. But then as he turned toward the door, he saw smoke rising from the wastepaper basket.

"Good God!" he said, and filled a glass of water and threw it over the tiny conflagration. "It's—criminal. It's—criminal—to be careless about fire on a ship! Criminal!"

"So sorry," said Lashelle, earnestly.

Honey could hear Weaver still talking out in the alleyway. "They shouldn't permit smoking in the cabins.... Nowhere but the smoke-room... I've travelled a good deal, and I've seen—"

"What have I done?" Honey thought. "It's going on and on like this for ever. It—scares me.... I don't know if I can stand it. I'm not going to wait here, sitting in this chair.... I'll take a look around the ship, or something, to kind of take my mind off things."

She rose and took up her fine purse; one of her white gloves was missing, and she lifted the chintz cushion of the chair to look for it. The glove was there, and a folded sheet of paper which she opened.

> "Darling little Sleepyhead:
>
> Here I am on my way back to my little wife. I'll send this air-mail just before we sail, and you can expect me in a few weeks' time. I'll send a cable from Trinidad to let you know.
>
> Your last letter was adorable. I carry those sweet letters with me everywhere—over my heart, and I only hope you think of your Hilary only half as much as he thinks of his Dormilona."

So it's Hilary, she thought, smiling to herself. He must have been in here writing letters. I bet he threw that cigarette in the basket on purpose, to burn up what he'd been writing, and probably he didn't know he dropped this down behind the cushion. She went over to the wastepaper basket and looked into it; nothing there but a little charred paper soaked with water. She put the unfinished letter back behind the cushion, and looked at herself in the mirror, adjusted her hat a little, and turned toward the door. Weaver was returning, followed by a steward.

"Utterly inexcusable mistake!" he said. "I regret that I ever undertook this trip. There you are, steward. There! This way, Honey."

He grasped her arm, painfully tight. You've got to be sorry for him, she thought. So upset—about a little thing like this. The new cabin was only next door. "And it's just as nice, Weaver," she said. "I think it's bigger, even."

"That's not the point," he said. He closed the door and sat down on one of the brass beds. "We were given Cabin Number Forty-one. It's distinctly marked on our ticket. And now the Purser informs me that it was an 'error.' "

"Listen, Weaver! Don't get so upset. This cabin's—"

"I will *not* be—flouted!" he cried. "I don't intend to let this matter drop. I'll take it up with the manager of the line."

"Weaver, this is the first trip I ever took—"

"A fine start!" he said. "If it were possible, I'd cancel our passage."

"Oh, Weaver, come on! Let's enjoy ourselves. Let's go and look around—"

"No!" he shouted.

She went over to the port and looked out; people were going past along the dock, and beyond them the snow was falling fast, with no wind. She wanted to be out there with the other people. I couldn't ever do that, she thought, Weaver'd carry on so. He'd talk about how I don't find his company sufficient. Well, I don't.

The steward brought their trunks in then. "We'll unpack now," Weaver said.

"What's the hurry, Weaver?"

"Always unpack what you want for the voyage *immediately,*" he said. "The weather may turn rough. The thing to do is to have everything ready."

He rang for the steward to open the trunks, and they both began to unpack, taking things out of the wardrobe trunks, out of the suitcases. She always felt better when she was moving around, her natural cheerfulness revived, and she wanted to talk. "When'll it start to get warm, Weaver?"

"Impossible to say."

"The time I was down in Florida I was just crazy about it. I bet I'm going to love the West Indies, Weaver."

"That man you were talking to...." he said. "You'd arranged to meet him on the ship."

She put the armful of silk underwear she was carrying down on the bed.

"Weaver," she said, "I never set eyes on the man before. Let's get this straight before we start."

"My dear girl," he said, "you take me for a bigger fool than I am. The whole thing, the mix-up about the cabin and so on were obviously pre-arranged."

"Weaver," she said with a sort of sternness, "you *are* talking like a fool. We've been married seven months now, and you ought to know me better. When we went into that church, and I took those vows, I *meant* them. I'd *never* cheat on you."

They faced each other; his face was white, his eyes narrowed.

"No?" he said with a faint smile.

"No," she said. "But if you go on like this—all the time accusing me—well, I won't stand it."

"My dear girl," he said, "you didn't marry me for love."

"Well, I've had enough of this," she said. "If you can't be nice to me, and have confidence in me—all right. I'll walk right off this ship, here and now, and you'll never see me again."

"That's not likely," he said.

"Weaver," she said, "you're so mean and spiteful to me that sometimes I think you hate me."

"We're a nice couple," he said, "an ideally happy marriage, isn't it?"

"All right," she said, "I'm through."

She picked up her hat from a chair and put it on; she got the mink coat out of the wardrobe.

"Don't forget your pearls," said he. "A mink coat and a string of pearls—that was what you wanted."

The color rose in her cheeks; she threw the mink coat on the floor, and kicked it into a corner.

"All right!" she said, turning toward the door, straight and tall in her black dress.

"Where are you going?" he said, seizing her arm.

"I'm getting out," she said, her blue eyes blazing. "To hell with your mink coat."

"You can't... You can't go out in the snow—"

"Can't I? To hell with the snow!"

"You're not going, I tell you!"

She pulled away from him and ran to the door, and he caught her again, by the wrist. "You're—not—going!" he said.

"You'd be surprised," said Honey.

Then she looked at him, and she was afraid. His face was horrible.

"Let me go!" she cried. "Let me go!"

"Honey..." he said, and that horrible look vanished, "Oh, Honey, for-give me!"

She stood like a statue, and he raised her hand to his lips.

"Don't!" she said, but he kissed it, bowing his grey head humbly.

"All visitors ashore!" cried a voice. "All ashore! All visitors a—shore..."

"Honey... Forgive me. For God's sake, forgive me...."

"All right," she said, slowly.

He put his arm around her shoulders, and pulling off her hat, he stroked her shining hair back from her forehead.

"I'm so sorry, Weaver. Forgive me, please."

The people on the deck above were stampeding, laughing, calling to each other. And here she was, shut up with Weaver, for ever and ever. No escape. Oh, what have I done? she thought.

TWO

"Have you got a headache, Weaver?" she asked.

"Migraine," he said. That was a special kind of headache he had, different from anyone else's, worse than anyone else's, if you believed him. He did look bad now, leaning back in a chair with his eyes closed.

"Lie down, why don't you, Weaver?" she said. But he never would lie down in the daytime; he never would do any of the little things other people do to make themselves comfortable, like taking off his coat if it was hot, or putting his feet up on a table. Honey admired this discipline of his. She had no name for it, but it was part of that quality she called gentlemanliness.

"Would you like a cup of tea, Weaver?" she asked. "Or some brandy maybe?"

"No, thank you," he said, still with his eyes closed.

"Weaver, would you like me to rub your head?"

"No, thank you, I'll be quite all right presently, if you'll—er..."

He let his voice trail away, but she knew what he meant. He wanted to be let alone. It was easy for her to forgive; it was fatally easy for her to forget; all her anger and her formless dismay had left her and she was only sorry for Weaver.

The cabin was chilly, she got up and went on tip-toe to get her mink coat from the wardrobe. That made her feel worse, remembering the day they had bought that coat, and how generous Weaver had been. She glanced at him, and saw the stamp of pain on his face, and she regretted with all her heart that she had thrown the coat on the floor and kicked it. And I said to hell with it, she thought.

It grew darker and darker, but it would not be right to turn on the light, she thought, recrossing her knees. Well, here I am at sea.... I'd like to look around, only I don't want to be mean. She moved again and the wicker chair creaked.

"Honey," said Weaver, and his voice sounded hollow and spent in the dusk, "why don't you go and get a cup of tea for yourself?"

"I don't want to leave you alone, Weaver."

"I'll do very well," he said. "There's no sense in your sitting here in the dark."

There was a dreary impatience in his tone; he really wanted her to go.

"I'll be back soon, Weaver," she said in a hushed voice; she stooped to kiss him lightly on the temple, and then went on tip-toe out of the cabin.

I'm not so good with sick people, she thought. Mother always used to tell me that. I'm kind of irritating, Mother always said. Only she didn't get really irritated. A lovely disposition, she's got.

Out in the alleyway she paused. All the cabin doors were closed; it was silent and deserted here—where's the tea room? she thought. I wonder if you pay extra for it? What are all the other people doing now, I wonder?

A door opened beside her, and from the cabin next to theirs came Mr. Lashelle. He closed the door and came toward her.

"Mrs. Stapleton," he said. "Could we have a cocktail?"

She reflected a moment. "Well, thank you," she said. "I wouldn't mind."

It's all right to talk to anybody on a ship, Gladwina had told Honey, and she had noticed for herself that people did that in the movies. Lashelle was handsome and gay, and, she thought, sophisticated. It would be nice to have a drink with him. And if he got too enterprising, she was perfectly capable of coping with that.

They went up the stairs and into a vast lounge panelled in dark wood, lit gloomily by electric candles in wall brackets, and furnished with massive leather armchairs, octagonal tables with heavy columns. Lashelle led the way to an enormous sofa before the towering mantelpiece, where on the hearth an electric fire glowed steadily among artificial logs.

"Cosy..." said Honey with amiable irony.

"Odd, isn't it, that there's nobody else here at this time?" he said.

Maybe it was odd; she didn't know. A steward in a dark-blue uniform stood beside them.

"What's yours, Mrs. Stapleton?" asked Lashelle.

"An old-fashioned, please," said Honey. And at that moment a whistle blew in a monstrous bellow, the ship shivered and stopped. "What's that?" she asked, startled.

"Fog, or snow. Thick weather," said Lashelle. "Smoke, Mrs. Stapleton?"

The whistle bellowed again. It is odd, thought Honey. Sitting here in this big, huge room, nobody but us. And it's cold. The unwinking, silent electric fire seemed to give out no warmth, she drew the mink closer about her.

"Have you been down this way before, Mrs. Stapleton?" asked Lashelle.

"No, I never have," said Honey. "Have you?"

"Oh, lord, yes. Any number of times."

That reminded her of his letter, and she was amused. Dear little Sleepyhead... I'll bet, she thought, that he's not going to mention that he's got a wife.

"I suppose you know a lot of people in the islands," she said, tentatively.

"A great many," he said. "I've been down there on business, y'know."

No, she thought, still more amused. He's not going to mention dear little Sleepyhead. She glanced at Lashelle, and caught him looking at her with ardent admiration; she lowered her silky lashes and put her two middle fingers to her temples, pushing up her hair a little.

The steward came then with the drinks, and a check which Lashelle signed.

"Here's to our voyage !" he said, raising his glass of whiskey and looking straight into her eyes. "I hope it will be—perfect."

"There's nothing perfect in this life," said Honey.

"Sorry. I don't agree with you," he said, still looking at her.

The sound of voices made her turn her head; she saw two men come in and sit down at a table, two grey-haired men, one of them with a grey moustache, one portly and clean-shaven. She was glad to see them; they made the atmosphere more normal. She sipped her drink and she felt better in spite of that gloomy and direful whistle. Mr. Lashelle's got a kind of cute line, she thought. He's a man-of-the-world, and he's certainly good-looking. But he's not the type I'd ever fall for, some way. Too smooth. You could feel sorry for that wife of his. It's just too bad for her if she's a sleepyhead. Anyone that was married to him ought to be pretty wideawake.

Somebody else came into the smoke-room then, a tall, fair-haired boy with almond eyes and a gentle smile. He sat down at the table with the two middle-aged men, he caught sight of Honey, and he was interested at once.

Gladwina always said there was nothing like a sea trip, thought Honey. She always said you meet so many new types, it's an education. Of course, I've travelled plenty on trains, but there you have to be careful with those salesmen and men going to conventions and all. I can see how it's different on a ship.

"Let's have another drink?" said Lashelle.

"Well, thanks," said Honey, "but I've got to get back to my husband. He's got a bad headache."

"Sorry," said Lashelle. "It would be too bad if he were laid up for any length of time. Wouldn't it?"

"He won't be," said Honey.

The almond-eyed boy was looking at her, for an instant their eyes met. *I like him,* Honey thought. You could *talk* to him. And you couldn't talk to Lashelle. You had to be on your guard with him every minute. I never did like those double meanings, she thought. Now, how was it my French teacher told me to say it—*Double entendre*... I'd certainly like to be able to speak French like a native. I'm going to keep on with my lessons when I get back, with *all* my lessons, dancing and everything. I want to get to be... She sought in her mind for a word. Not 'cultured' exactly, she thought. But accomplished. Gracious, I guess.

"A quick one?" said Lashelle.

"Well... thanks," she said, and he turned to call the steward, but something he saw made him rise, and Honey turned her head, to see a woman coming toward them. A dark and solidly-built woman this was, and wearing a mink coat, superior even to Honey's. She approached unsmiling, straight as a dart.

"Alma!" said Lashelle. "Mrs. Stapleton, my wife. Alma, Mrs. Stapleton."

"How d'you do?" said Alma Lashelle briefly, and sat down on the sofa beside Honey.

Your *wife?* Honey thought. But what about the other one, the little Sleepyhead one?

I knew he was a smoothie, she thought, but I didn't know he was this bad. *Two* wives... Well, of course, only one of them can be legal. Is it the one he wrote the letter to, or this one? Maybe this one knows he's married to somebody else, and she's just taking a trip with him. Those things happen.

She glanced sidelong at Alma sitting beside her on the sofa. She was handsome in a way, and she had made the very best of herself, her black hair was brushed up from the temples to give length to her square jawed face, her skin was good, her make-up was good; her shoulders were a little heavy, but she carried herself well, and everything she wore was very expensive and very carefully chosen, the mink coat, the black dress, the suede pumps. And a necklace that looked like real pearls.

Thirty-five, about, Honey thought. Well, she's certainly not any too friendly. Jealous maybe. Didn't like to find her husband here with me. I *wonder* if she knows about Sleepyhead? Or is he cheating on her?

"What will you have to drink, Alma?" asked Lashelle.

"Tomkraut," she said, briefly to the steward.

"Pardon me, madam?" he said, anxiously.

"Well, carrot juice, then," she said.

"I'm sorry, madam, but..."

"Bring three champagne cocktails," said Lashelle. Alma frowned and looked at him, and he smiled at her. And her heavy sullen face changed; she smiled with a reluctant and half-shy tenderness. All right! I'm sorry for her, Honey thought. "Too bad Mr. Stapleton isn't with us," Lashelle went on. "But he's laid up with a headache. How—"

A bugle began to blow.

"What's that?" asked Alma.

"Dressing signal," Lashelle answered. "Half an hour before dinner."

"Well, I don't see what I can do about dressing in the circumstances," she said.

"Oh, nobody bothers, the first night out," he said.

She's never been on a ship before either, thought Honey. But *he's* travelled a lot, from what he told me. I wonder...

A silence fell upon them, the fog-horn bellowed, the electric fire glowed, unwinking, the ship was not going anywhere. And there's Weaver lying down there in the dark, Honey thought. It's—gloomy. It was cold, too; even the first drink had not warmed her. She was pleased to see the steward coming with the champagne cocktails. He laid the chit on the table face downwards, but Alma took it up.

"Hilary!" she said. "This can't be—"

"Alma," he said, smiling at her. "What does it matter—*this* evening?"

"Well, you don't want to be overcharged at any time." she said, sternly. But his smile vanquished her, she looked into his eyes, looked and looked.

Oh lord! Honey thought. There was something almost horrible in that look of Alma's, something helpless and lost, all her solid strength dissolved.

"It doesn't matter *this* evening," he said.

"Hilary!" she said, warningly.

"Oh, Mrs. Stapleton's guessed our little secret, darling," he said. "Haven't you, Mrs. Stapleton?"

"Do you mean," said Honey, "that you're on your honeymoon?"

"We don't want it known," said Alma, curtly.

"*You* don't," said Lashelle. "But I'm the proudest man on earth."

Alma believed him.

"I—wish you the best of luck!" Honey cried with desperate heartiness, and jumping up she knocked her glass off the table. "Oh, how clumsy!" she said, in the same hearty tone. "Only I just remembered I had to give my husband some medicine. I'm terribly sorry. Thanks a million."

In her haste, she forgot her gliding walk until she saw that almond-eyed boy looking at her. She recalled it then, and went across the wide floor with that gait artificial and graceful as that of a Chinese woman with bound feet. It was almost automatic with her; she had had her fill of admiration ever since her babyhood, she had no doubts about her beauty, and remarkably little vanity. She was pleased with being beautiful, and she would make use of it for anyone.

That sense of haste was still upon her. I just couldn't stay, she thought. I couldn't drink his cocktail. If he knows I spilt it on purpose I don't care. No... I knew he was smooth, but this... On his honeymoon with that poor Alma, and he writes a letter to another 'little wife!' I call that going *too* far. Honestly, I'd like to tell Alma.

And then she thought, it wouldn't do any good. He could fix it up, and she'd believe anything he told her. It's—awful to see a woman like that. Without any pride.

At the foot of the stairs, she had to ask a steward where her cabin was, and she went in that direction quickly and willingly. Anyhow, Weaver's a *gentleman*, she thought, and he has *respect* for me.

She knocked politely on the cabin door. "Come in!" he called, sharply and, as she entered, "You've been gone nearly an hour," he said. "Where have you been?"

He really looked terrible, so white and drawn. But he could not be allowed to speak like that.

"Don't you wish you knew?" she said airily.

He made no response to that, and she went over to the mirror to inspect her hair. And in the mirror she saw Weaver glaring at her like a lost soul.

Oh, whatever have I done? she cried to herself.

THREE

Weaver was taking some of his little pills in the bathroom.

"Haven't you taken some already?" Honey asked.

"I know what I'm doing," he said.

I'm going to get those pills away from him somehow, she thought. The doctor said, only every three hours, and never to take more than twice inside twenty-four hours. But he gets sort of frantic with these headaches.

"Honestly, Weaver, you shouldn't try to come down to dinner," she said.

"It will do me good," he said. "I've arranged for us to sit at the Purser's table. I'd expected, I admit, that we'd be asked to sit at the Captain's table, but the Purser explained the situation. On this run, the Captain is more or less obliged to cater to the local people who go back and forth all the time."

She listened to him, as she listened to everyone, wanting to learn everything. But as soon as he stopped speaking, that gamine attentiveness was switched off, like a light, leaving her in a curious twilight of distress. I didn't know it would be like this, to be married to Weaver, she thought. Of course, I know I wasn't madly in love with him, but I thought... I thought it would all be—sort of gracious. He was certainly crazy about me—then. I never met anyone that was so thoughtful and attentive as Weaver was.

He treated me like a queen. I remember Mother said these very words, that he treated me like a queen. He was terribly nice to Mother, too, while she was in New York. Every time he'd bring me orchids, he'd bring her a corsage, too. He took us both to the Horse Show.... But Mother was dead against my marrying him, right from the start. Wait for romance, she said.

And I'm not the type to fall in love, I mean, I *have* been in love but I never was swept off my feet, and I never want to be, either. God! I'd rather be dead than like that poor Alma.... I could have been happy with Weaver, if he hadn't got—like this. Honestly, sometimes I think he almost *hates* me....

She was sitting before the dressing-table brushing her pale hair, and it flew out after the brush in bright threads.

"You look like an angel," said Weaver behind her.

"Well, I'm not one," she said, briefly. "Weaver, I think we ought to get things on a different basis."

"I don't know what you mean," he said.

"We don't get on the way we used to."

"Naturally," he said.

"What's natural about not getting on?"

He did not answer that, and Honey did not press the point. She could, and did, lose her temper now and then, but she did not nag. Leaning forward, she began to make up her face, rouging her beautiful, rich mouth, smoothing her eyebrows with a little brush, delicately fluffing powder on her clear skin. The floor beneath her feet began to tremble, the electric fan on the wall rattled, everything began to rattle and shake.

"What's the meaning of *that?*" she asked.

"We're getting under way again," said Weaver. "If you're ready now, we'll go down to dinner."

There were other people in the alleyway now, and that set her thinking.

"Weaver," she said. "Weaver, where I really was. I was having a cocktail with Mr. and Mrs. Lashelle."

"You *did* know that fellow before, then?"

"I did *not!* Only I met them while I was looking for a tea-room, or something, and I had a drink with them."

"My dear girl," he said. "this is a very small ship, and we're going to be on board for three weeks. I sincerely hope you'll use a little discretion about whom you pick up."

"I always do," said Honey; and it was true.

"I don't care to become involved with that fellow," he went on. "He's a type I don't care for. What's more—" He frowned. "We had to wait before we could see the Purser, and he talked... He didn't mention any wife. I certainly got the impression that he was travelling alone. I'm not sure he didn't *say* he was travelling alone."

"Well, far from it!" she said. "He's on his honeymoon."

"Honeymoon!" Weaver repeated, and he was undoubtedly mollified. "What is his wife like?"

"Oh...!" said Honey, vaguely. "She's very quiet."

"I hope," Weaver said, "we'll have congenial people at our table. I imagine we shall. The Purser—Basingly's his name—seems very agreeable."

They went down the stairs to the dining saloon, and there were quite a lot of people going down with them. But there was nobody who looked very interesting; on the contrary, everyone seemed chilly and preoccupied, most of them wearing coats. It's different in the pictures they have of cruises, Honey thought. Everybody's always dressed up in pictures, and having a wonderful time.

The Second Steward came up to them. "Mr. Stapleton..." he said. "Mrs. Stapleton... This way please!" And he led them to a table where four people were already seated. Two of the people were Mr. and Mrs. Lashelle.

What d'you know! thought Honey, dismayed. She glanced at Weaver, but his thin, fine face showed nothing except a blank fatigue.

"Mr. Basingly," he said, "my wife. Honey, Mr. Basingly."

The Purser was a stout, dark man, buttoned neatly into a navy-blue uniform, his clean-shaven face had a look of faintly cynical good-humour. He rose, and with him, Lashelle. "Miss Bewley, Mrs. Stapleton. Mr. Stapleton..."

"How do you do?" said Miss Bewley.

She's somebody, thought Honey. She's so funny-looking, in that special way. A very spare woman, she was, in a dress of dark purple wool with a queer little vest of pleated white chiffon; and a curly frizz of dyed red hair beneath which her dark eyes looked bright and pleading. Kind of like a monkey, thought Honey.

The purser was interested in Honey; she saw that at once, and she was pleased. He began to talk to her in the way she liked best in the world, with a deferential gallantry, and with the worldly wisdom she so profoundly admired.

She had a wisdom of her own; she had a knowledge of a world, but not *this* world. But she was going to learn it. I do like him! she thought. I like that English way of talking, his voice going sort of up and down. He starts his questions high. *Do* you care for bridge, Mrs. Stapleton? She practiced that inflection in her mind, she noticed the words he used, she noticed how he ate, what he ordered.

"Your first trip to the islands, Mrs. Stapleton?... Very nice little trip.... But one of these days you ought to try our South American run..."

He had been everywhere. He knew everything. She asked him questions and listened to him with her violet-blue eyes fixed upon his face, and they were both extremely pleased.

"Who is at the—er—Captain's table, Mr. Basingly?" asked Weaver.

He was evidently extremely displeased, and Honey turned her head to look at the table at which he was looking. The two middle-aged men she had seen in the smoke-room were there, and the almond-eyed boy, a grey-haired little woman in pince-nez, a thin horse-faced girl, desperately animated, and the Captain, a calm and burly man with a fringe of ginger hair about his bald pate.

"There's Mrs. Plaudy from Barbados," said Basingly. "And Miss Fellows—English girl. Mr. Homer from New York, and Mr. Nordstrom and his son, Mr. Michael Nordstrom."

"I don't know the man," said Weaver, frigidly.

"From Minnesota," Mr. Basingly explained.

"I see...!" said Weaver.

"Probably *Swedish,*" said Miss Bewley. "I'm *very* fond of Swedes. My uncle had a Swedish cook for years, when he lived on Twenty-third Street."

"On Twenty-third Street?" said Weaver. "West? Did you happen to know a family named Hanniford who lived there?"

"Oh, yes!" said Miss Bewley, and they were off. Honey was about to give all her attention again to the fascinating Mr. Basingly, when Alma spoke in her toneless voice.

"This meat tastes funny, too."

"Funny?" Basingly replied, instantly alert.

"It tastes bitter," she said. "And so did the soup."

"Steward," said Basingly. "Bring Mrs. Lashelle something else. Some chicken, Mrs. Lashelle?"

"Well... All right," she said. "But what makes everything taste bitter like this?"

"Can't imagine, Mrs. Lashelle. But we'll see what we can do."

"Even the cocktail I had before dinner—" said Alma.

Honey saw Lashelle and Basingly exchange glances.

"Sometimes the motion of the ship—" said Lashelle.

"No," said Alma, flatly. "It's got nothing to do with the ship. They're using some chemical, some preservative."

"Oh, but I can assure you, Mrs. Lashelle . ." Basingly began.

"Taste it for yourself," said Alma, pushing the plate toward him.

"Alma, my dear girl!" her husband protested. But Mr. Basingly took the plate, and a bit of meat, and chewed it, while everyone at the table watched him.

"I don't notice anything wrong, Mrs. Lashelle," he said, earnestly. "But the steward's bringing you some chicken. You may like that better."

She lapsed then into a sullen silence; when the chicken was set before her, she pushed it about with a fork in a scornful fashion. Lashelle leaned toward her across the table, murmuring something; she looked up and gave him a grudging little smile, and began to eat. She refused dessert.

"Suppose we take a turn on deck?" Lashelle suggested. "Get a little of this good salt air?"

"All right!" she said, pushing back her chair, and they went out of the dining-saloon and up the stairs; he so slim and elegant, she so solid and stubborn.

"A—rather difficult lady," said Weaver.

"Very," said Mr. Basingly.

"To be candid," said Weaver, "there's nothing I dislike more than being at a table with someone who complains about the food."

"So many people *do,* don't they?" said Miss Bewley.

"It's—disgusting to me," Weaver said, unsteadily. "Makes it impossible for me to eat. This talk about chemicals, and preservatives and so on."

"Nothing to worry about, Mr. Stapleton," said the Purser. "We have rather a name for our food, y'know. Nothing but the best."

"I'm *really* enjoying my dinner," said Miss Bewley. "But I think that poor Mrs. What's-Her-Name is *nervous.*"

"Very likely," said Basingly. "She's lost all her luggage, y'know."

"Lost it?" said Weaver, appalled.

"It's very odd," said Basingly. "Of course we're making a thorough search of the ship, but I'll swear it never came on board. I mean to say— we do make mistakes once in a while—get the luggage into the wrong cabin, or into the hold sometimes. Not often, but mistakes do happen, what? But two big wardrobe trunks, hat box, shoe box, etcetera. Couldn't mislay all that, could you?"

"Lost it?" Weaver repeated.

That's his nightmare, Honey thought. That time we went up to Quebec by train, on our honeymoon, he nearly had a fit worrying about the trunks. He said he'd never go on a train again. It's bad for him to hear about this; he'll be worse than ever now.

"I don't see how such a thing is possible," he said.

"Oh, probably the fault of the trucking company," said Basingly. "Y'see, they sent the stuff on by truck, the night before. Lashelle admits he didn't see it on the pier when he came on board, but that was early. And apparently Mrs. Lashelle didn't understand that she should have looked it up when she came later. I don't believe the things ever got to the pier."

"Incredible!" said Weaver. "Two people—simply walking on board a ship without even taking the trouble to ascertain if their luggage was there."

"Oh, his things came on board all right," said Mr. Basingly. "Trunks— everything. Only Mrs. Lashelle's things that are missing. And she herself was very nearly missing'." He laughed a little.

"How was that?" asked Honey.

"The gangway was going up when she arrived. There she was, as cool as you please—people yelling at her, but she didn't even notice it. She'd made some mistake about the sailing time—didn't have any idea she was late."

"But wasn't *Mr.* Lashelle quite *frantic?*" asked Miss Bewley.

"He thought she was on board. Some steward told him she was."

"Incredible!" said Weaver, again.

Mr. Basingly turned again to Honey, but her flattering interest in all he said had vanished. She sat quiet, a little pale, looking down at her plate.

There was that letter he wrote, she thought. And her luggage, and her getting here so late... I don't believe she was meant to come at all.

FOUR

Mr. Basingly lit a cigarette for her, to smoke with her coffee. But Weaver did not drink coffee at night, it kept him awake, and he began to grow restless now.

"Well, shall we go and take a little walk, Weaver?" she suggested.

He rose, and with a polite bow to Miss Bewley, he went out of the dining-room with Honey.

"It'll be nice to get some fresh air," she said.

"It's positively *dangerous,*" he said, "to take exercise after those tablets. I'm supposed to rest. I've told you that."

So they went to their cabin. The beds were turned down, their night clothes laid out, and it was all very tranquil. And very stuffy. I'd give *anything* to get out in the air, she thought. But I've got to be nice to Weaver if he doesn't feel well.

They sat down in the two little wicker chairs that creaked every time you moved. I'm not generally so nervous, Honey thought. Only that Mr. Lashelle and Alma worry me. He didn't ever mean her to come. And it's their honeymoon. What's he up to, anyhow?

"What d'you think of Mr. Lashelle, Weaver?" she asked.

"An adventurer," said Weaver, shortly. "And his wife's a woman of no breeding. But Miss Bewley is a woman you might cultivate. Her father was a Portness."

"Well, what's that, Weaver?"

"A Portness," he repeated, exasperated. "It's a name, a family. The Bewleys are a very good old family. Boston people."

"Didn't you think it was pretty queer about Mrs. Lashelle losing all her baggage?"

"No," he said. "I found her very objectionable. That talk about the food being bitter, and so on... "

"Weaver, I think there's some funny business going on."

"Very likely," he said. "I'm not interested in those people. Miss Bewley, though, is quite an asset. The sort of person you might well cultivate."

She reminded herself that Weaver had that migraine. But, just the same it's a mean way to talk, she thought. Practically telling me I might learn something from his precious Miss Bewley. I wanted to tell him about that letter I found, and all. There's something *queer* going on. But I'll have to wait till Weaver's over his headache.

He shut himself into the bathroom to undress, and she heard him lock the door. Silly, she thought. I don't feel like going to bed at this hour. It's the first night I've ever been at sea, and I haven't even seen what it's like out on deck.

She got the mink coat out of the wardrobe and put it on, and sat waiting in the wicker armchair until Weaver came out of the bathroom in his clean blue pyjamas and his dark purple silk dressing-gown and his black leather slippers.

"I'm going on deck, Weaver," she said looking straight at him. "I want some fresh air, and some exercise."

He stared back at her, and this was a fight. Not a quarrel such as they had had before, but a fight, a duel. She was defying him, and he yielded bitterly, sullenly, without a word. He sat down on the edge of his bed, and took off his slippers; she left the cabin with that image in her mind. It hurt her. She did not wish to see her gentleman defeated.

But I can't *help* it! she cried to herself. I'd just go crazy shut up in there. I'll only take a little walk. and then I'll go back. She went along the alleyway to the square where the Purser's office was, and behind the wicket she saw the bland and cynical face of Mr. Basingly.

"How do you get out on the deck, Mr. Basingly?" she asked.

"The door behind you," he said. "But it's a nasty night, Mrs. Stapleton."

"I don't care," she said, with a little smile, and opened the heavy door.

She stepped out into a new world. Rain drove into her face; the unshaded little lights shone upon wet, glittering planks, the rail seemed to slide back and forth. And beyond it was the hissing black water.

This was not the sea you saw standing on a beach, or even from a motor or a sail boat. That ocean had a horizon and a shore. But this black sea had no limits. She stood at the rail looking at it, and she felt that she could look at it forever. Here and there a white crest showed, and along the ship's side there was a pale stream of foam running past; the rain fell steadily, not icy now but faint and cold, the sky was all darkness.

I just don't know, she said to herself. I didn't know it would be like this. She had imagined only a sort of Gladwina ocean, a background for a glittering social life, blue and sunny water, or perhaps a touch of moonlight, and music playing. Oh, but this was better!

A confused and passionate elation filled her. I'm alone! she thought, and it seemed to her that never before had she been really alone, never before had had time to think. Only she was in a hurry to think—about something, and could not grasp it. Life...? she thought. I mean, what are we here for? I mean...

"Will you have a cigarette, Mrs. Stapleton?" asked a voice beside her; and she turned with a little gasp.

The tall almond-eyed boy was standing beside her, in a raincoat, bareheaded.

"No, thank you," she answered, politely enough. But she wanted him to go, she wanted with all her heart to be alone. She turned back to the sea, dreading to hear his voice again, longing to escape. But he did not speak; he stood there a few feet from her, leaning on the rail, and he was quiet. Glancing at him, she found his blunt-featured young face blank, his grey eyes steadily regarding the darkness.

And, after a time, her nervous dread of being disturbed was gone, she felt sure that he was not going to speak, and she was willing to let him be there. He was sharing this; he was lost in this as she was. The rain came down on her head, on her hands, against her face; she breathed in the primeval smell of the sea, and she tried, in haste, to think about life while she had a chance. This was the moment to understand everything.

If it were a long moment or a little one she could not tell, for there was no measure of time now but the beat of her own pulse, and the broken chaotic motion of the waves that tumbled over one another. The Flood, she thought. Noah's Ark, with all the animals—and it rained like this...

"Hello!" said Mr. Basingly's voice behind her in mild surprise.

He was wearing an overcoat and a vizored cap, and he looked different, burly and strong.

"You people don't mind a little rain?" he said, coming to Honey's side.

Nobody answered him, and he too, was silent for a moment.

"I came out," he said presently, "to hide. My God! What d'you think's happened now?"

"What?" Honey asked, with an effort.

"Mrs. Lashelle has lost her jewels," he said.

"Oh! Anything much?"

"Much?" he repeated. "It's the greatest tragedy of the age. A diamond ring, a ruby ring, a pearl necklace."

"Well, but that's pretty bad," said Honey.

"It's insured," said Mr. Basingly.

"Yes, but you hate to lose things like that," said Honey.

"So it seems," said Basingly.

Honey had a deep respect for jewelry; she and her mother had lived in a world where a really good ring meant not only a financial asset, but prestige. A man really thought something of you if he gave you anything like that, and to wear it was a proof that you were cherished, and not broke.

"Mr. Lashelle wants the whole crew searched and questioned," he said. "I don't think she'd object to a spot of torture. As a matter of fact, her steward's an absolutely trustworthy man. And as for Mrs. Doakes, the stewardess... Even the Gestapo would think twice before annoying *her.*"

"Still," said Honey, "nobody likes to think there's a thief around."

"Mrs. Stapleton," he said. "If you knew how many times, how many passengers—especially ladies—have said they were robbed, and then found the missing articles down behind a cushion."

Like that letter. Honey thought. Gosh! That poor Alma... There's her husband with another wife, or something, and now her jewels gone. Some honeymoon.

"What's Mr. Lashelle doing about it?" she asked.

"What can he do?" said Basingly. "He came along with her to report the loss—but she was so—extreme. I think he was a bit embarrassed."

"It's too bad about him," said Honey, briefly.

"Well, he's retreated to the smoke-room now, to play bridge," said Mr. Basingly.

"And where's she?"

"Mrs. Lashelle? I don't know, Mrs. Stapleton."

"I think I'll go and find her," said Honey.

"Mrs. Stapleton..."

"Yes, Mr. Basingly?"

"I'm afraid I'll have to tell you that Mrs. Lashelle's suspicions are pretty far reaching. I shouldn't trouble myself if I were you."

"You mean she thinks maybe I took the jewels?" Honey asked. "Well, after all, she doesn't know anything about me, and our cabin's right next to theirs."

"You're very forbearing, Mrs. Stapleton," said Basingly.

"You're very understanding," said the almond-eyed boy.

She liked him to say that, she looked at him with a smile as she went away.

"I think I'll just see if I can find her," she said.

Her mood of exaltation still lingered, she felt an immense good will toward everyone, an eager sympathy for Alma. She went along the alleyway and knocked at the door of the cabin next to her own.

"Who's that?" asked Alma's low-pitched voice, toneless and hostile.

"It's me. It's I. Honey Stapleton," she answered, remembering that it was not etiquette to call yourself Mrs. Stapleton.

"What do you want?" asked Alma.

"I'd like to see you a moment," said Honey.

"Come in, said Alma, and Honey opened the door.

Alma was wearing a kimono of flat black crepe, and with her black hair, her smouldering black eyes, and her pale olive skin, she had the look of a figure in a tragedy. She was sitting in an armchair, smoking a cigarette; she did not rise, she did not smile, she gave Honey no welcome at all.

"I just heard that you've lost your jewels," said Honey. "I think that's *terrible.*"

"I think it's a damned outrage," said Alma, curtly. "All that Purser says is that I should have put them in his safe. Are you expected to run out there to his office every time you take off a ring?"

"How did it happen?" asked Honey.

"I took off my necklace," said Alma, 'and I took the rings out of my purse. I put them on the dressing-table while I went in the bathroom to wash. When I came out they were gone."

"Someone came in your cabin right while you were in the bathroom?"

"Yes."

"I think that's terrible," said Honey, and she meant it.

"Well, you're the only one," said Alma.

"I've got some pieces of my own, and I know how *I'd* feel if I lost them," said Honey. "Just getting the insurance for them wouldn't make up for it. It gives you the funniest feeling, to have something stolen, doesn't it? I mean—it's as if you had an enemy."

Alma looked at her with her straight black brows drawn together.

"Yes," she said. And after a moment, "D'you want to sit down and have a smoke?"

"Thank you," said Honey.

"That's just how you feel," Alma went on. "Somebody's put something over on you. And that doesn't often happen to *me.*"

Well, your fine husband's putting something over on you, Honey thought, with compassion. It's a shame. "I don't suppose you locked the cabin door?" she said.

"No. I didn't want to lock out my husband in case he came along. I thought I could leave my things there for fifteen minutes without any danger. I'm not careless about things."

Honey lit a cigarette, one of her own, for Alma did not offer her one.

"It's been a damned queer day altogether," said Alma. "I almost missed the ship, to start with. When I get home, I'm going to take—that—up.

Somebody's going to pay for that."

"What happened?"

"The sailing time was on the ticket all right," said Alma. "And I was ready in plenty of time. I always am. Then the telephone rang and my maid answered it. I don't know whether it was her fault or not. She may have misunderstood what she heard. She's a dumb German. If it wasn't that, it was..." She paused. "Anyhow," she said. "Trudie told me it was the steamship company calling, to say the sailing had been postponed until four o'clock. I didn't have any reason to think there was anything wrong, and it's just lucky I didn't wait till too late. I thought at first I'd run down to my office—but then I changed my mind. I thought, well, I'll get on board a little early. If I'd been ten minutes later, I'd have been left behind."

Honey lowered her eyes, not to betray the pity and astonishment she felt. She never was meant to come at all, she thought. That's plain.

"Captain Lashelle thought I'd come on board," Alma went on. "Some fool told him so. Then, as soon as we'd sailed, I found out that my luggage wasn't here. And everybody acted as if it was my fault. My God!" she cried, "I've travelled plenty. Not on ships, but I've been around the United States plenty, on trains, and airplanes. And I've never lost a thing."

"I think it's terrible," said Honey.

"Captain Lashelle's very nice about everything," said Alma, "but he's got funny ideas about women." A faint reluctant smile came over her heavy face. "He thinks women are all sort of capricious and unreasonable. He likes them that way."

"Men get funny ideas," said Honey.

"It's a funny way to think of *me,*" said Alma. "I wouldn't be where I am if I was as helpless and dumb as all that." She paused again. "Do you ever use any of the Mimosa products?"

"Sure!" said Honey. "I used to get the cold cream and the powder."

"That's *my* line," said Alma.

"Oh, you work for them?" Honey asked.

"Nope," said Alma. with another faint smile. "They work for me. All the Mimosa products are made from my formulas. I started that business, and I own it."

"*Do* you?" said Honey.

She was greatly impressed by this information. The Mimosa products were famous; they were advertised in magazines and newspapers, and over the air. That takes brains, she thought. Alma must be smart, very smart. Only not about that husband.

"I'm opening a salon when I get home," said Alma. "On Fifth Avenue. I'm going to give beauty courses and different treatments. I've made a study of all that. I've got the most up-to-date methods." She was silent for a time. "I could have opened my new salon last week," she said. "Only Captain Lashelle wanted to take this trip. I wish to God we'd gone to Florida instead. I never took a trip on a boat before, and I certainly never want to again. Of course, Captain Lashelle's travelled a lot, and I guess he takes some things for granted. That food, for instance. Why, it was bitter as gall! Didn't you notice it?"

"No, I didn't," said Honey.

"Well, what *I* had was bitter," said Alma. "And I don't imagine things. It couldn't have been just my food, either. It must have been something they did in the kitchen. I wonder if they use salt water?"

"I don't know," Honey said, absently.

It gives me the shivers, she thought, to hear her talk about that. But her husband *couldn't* be such a fool as to try anything—like that. Unless he's crazy.

That was a very unpleasant thought to her, sitting here in his cabin.

"You just got married yesterday?" she asked.

"Yes," said Alma, briefly.

"Did you have a nice wedding?" asked Honey.

"We were married by a Justice of the Peace, in the country," said Alma. "I didn't want anyone to know."

"Oh..." Honey began, but she stopped. It might be tactless, she thought, to ask questions.

"On account of my business," Alma said. "I didn't tell anyone I was taking this trip, either. I just told them I'd be away for three weeks. Captain Lashelle helped me to keep it secret. He stayed in his hotel last night, and he didn't tell anyone, either."

"Well, would it be bad for your business, d'you think?"

That faint, grim smile came over Alma's face again.

"No." she said. "It was only that I'd feel like a damn fool. I mean, I've got a reputation for being pretty hard-boiled. And if they thought I was a bride..."

"I see," said Honey.

There was a silence.

"Well, it was nice of you to come in like this," said Alma. "Nobody else seems to care a damn about my jewels. That Purser treated me as if I was a prima donna, trying to get some publicity. And even Captain Lashelle's taken it pretty lightly. I don't mean that he isn't sympathetic and all. Only he won't believe they've been stolen. He kept saying I'd 'mislaid' them. Well, I don't 'mislay' things. He got on my nerves, wanting to hunt around in the cabin for them."

"Well, but the chambermaid—I mean the stewardess or someone might have put them away."

"I've spoken to her, and the steward. They both swear they never saw the things."

"But then—*haven't* you looked around for them?"

"I—have—not!" said Alma, ominously. "I know where I put them. I don't 'mislay' things and I don't forget things. I put my jewels on the dressing-table, and somebody's stolen them."

"Listen!" said Honey. "Won't you let me look for them a little?"

"No," said Alma.

She undoubtedly meant no. Honey rose.

"Well," she said. "I certainly hope you get them back. "

"I'm going to, said Alma, and rose too. She was not hostile toward Honey any longer; she was almost friendly in her grim and grudging way. "Thanks for coming in," she said. "Good night!"

"Good night!" said Honey, and went out closing the door behind her. But before she had reached her own cabin the door was opened.

"Come here a minute, will you?" said Alma, and Honey returned.

"I was just getting out my cold cream," said Alma. "Look!"

One of the little top drawers in the dressing-table was open, and in it, lying on some pairs of folded silk stockings, lay a pearl necklace and two rings.

'I'm *terribly* glad!" cried Honey.

"I didn't put them there," said Alma. She stood staring down at the jewels with no sign of pleasure in their recovery. There was a curious look on her handsome, heavy face. "There's something funny going on," she said.

FIVE

"It's seven o'clock!" Weaver said, shaking her by the shoulder.

"Well—what?" she protested. "I don't want to get up at seven o'clock."

"It's the best part of the day at sea," he said.

"You can have it," said Honey. For a moment she sulked, lying flat on her back without a pillow—better for your figure—with her silky blonde hair spread out, her shoulders white as milk above her blue satin night-dress.

"If you'd listen to me," said Weaver, "you'd reap some advantage from this trip."

She gave a sigh that turned into a yawn, and then she saw how very blue the sky was outside the port.

"Is it tropical yet, Weaver?" she asked, sitting up.

"To some extent," he said. "But it's a beautiful morning. The best part of the day. If you'll get *up*—"

"All right Weaver," she said, resigned. "Only I'd like a cup of coffee first."

"That's a disgusting habit, that eating in bed." he said.

"Weaver," she said. "I just don't know what ever has come over you. You find fault with every single thing I do these days. When we first got married, I *always* had my breakfast sent up, and why not? It's one of the things I looked forward to when I didn't have to get up and go to work. And what's more," she added, "they say it helps you keep young.

"Bah!" he said.

"Bah yourself!" said Honey with spirit. "Now, I won't get up."

He went into the bathroom, slamming the door behind him, and Honey rang the bell by the head of the bed. The stewardess came promptly.

"*Good* morning, madam!" she said, looking at Honey's night-dress and Honey's hair. And upon her sharp nosed and suspicious face was an expression which Honey interpreted to mean that she thought the night-dress was too expensive to be respectable, and the hair too blonde to be natural.

"Er..." said Honey languidly. "I think I'll have coffee and toast and grapefruit."

"Yes, madam," said the stewardess, and retired.

She took a pillow from Weaver's bed and made herself comfortable; the air blowing at the open port was balmy, the breakfast came quickly, and she was happy. Weaver came out of the bathroom all dressed, and went past her out of the cabin, without a word, but that didn't bother her now.

Honestly, you've got to be sorry for Weaver, she thought. I never heard of anyone who got less out of having money than he does. She lit a cigarette. Now, if I only had a morning paper! Gladwina said that on ships she had been to Europe on, they did have a sort of little paper they printed. But of course, they were much more de luxe boats, in every way. Not that I care. I *like* this.

That boy... I don't even know his name, but he's nice. I'll see him today. I'm bound to. I'd sort of like to talk to him. And then she thought with a queer dismay that was almost fear: I mustn't be interested in him. I mustn't ever be interested in any other man—not ever. Only Weaver.

She began to think about Alma. That was a very queer thing last night, about Alma's pearls and rings. Of course she could have been mistaken, only she doesn't impress you as the kind of woman who'd make mistakes. I mean, if she's developed that whole Mimosa business, and if she's opening a new salon on Fifth Avenue, she's got to be good. She's got a very definite personality. If she says she left the things on top of the dressing-table, well, *I* think she did. And if she said her food tasted bitter...? But that's different. You might imagine that, if you were getting a cold, for instance. I wouldn't take much stock in that if it wasn't for the other things. But when you take them all together, her losing her luggage, and nearly missing the boat, and the message she got about sailing time... It adds up to something.

Something funny going on. She said that herself. And she's darn right. She doesn't know about the letter to little Sleepyhead, his other little wife.... I haven't any use for that Lashelle, but I like Alma. I've got a kind of respect for her.

Because she's done what I wanted to do. She's made a career for herself. She's somebody. And me, I'm nobody. I quit. I got so sick of working. And I was getting forty a week. I might have got on. Mr. Garstein said he'd let me work into merchandising. That was a nice little apartment I had with Annette... It was so pretty looking up Madison Avenue when the lights were on. It was—

"Oh hell!" she said aloud. "Here I am, being sorry for myself when I'm sailing to the tropics. I guess I need some exercise."

She rose and bathed and put on a yellow linen dress and a yellow sweater, she put two little yellow bows in her long hair, and a pair of blue and yellow play shoes on her bare feet. Cruise clothes, she thought. When I used to model them, I always wondered if I'd ever get a chance to wear them.

She went out into the alleyway, and it pleased her to walk in these heel-less shoes. She felt so very well, so light, so nimble. She opened the door and went out on the promenade deck.

She stepped into the world she had dreamed of; *this* was what she had wanted. The blue sky, the blue and sparkling water, the fresh breeze, plenty of people, lovely clothes. She had the most perfect day of her whole life.

The boy's name was Michael Nordstrom; she played ping-pong with him. He was nice to her; everybody was nice to her. At lunch, even Weaver was nice; he said he was glad she was enjoying herself. After lunch she sat on deck with Weaver, and when he wanted to take a nap, she put on one of her new bathing suits and went into the little pool. Michael was there, and Lashelle and a few other people, the sun had grown hot now; they had tea sitting on the hatch cover.

"Early dinner to-night," said a thin, chic, dark woman called Mrs. Pruitt.

"Why?" Honey asked.

"We're getting into St. Jeff's at eight, my steward told me."

"Into port?" Honey cried.

"It you can call it a port," said the heavy man with pale-blue eyes called Mr. Lake. "We'll just lie out in the harbour for a couple of hours, send the mail ashore, and go on. Nothing there."

"You mean you're not going ashore?" Honey asked.

"I am," said Mrs. Pruitt. "I'm going to have a moonlight swim. The beach there is *too* perfect."

"If there's anything repulsive and eerie," said Mr. Lake, "it's a moonlight swim."

"It charms me," said Mrs. Pruitt.

"Very good," said Lake. "Then we'll get up a party. Mrs. Stapleton, d'you think you and your husband would care to sign up?"

"Oh, thank you!" she said. "I'll ask him."

She had to ask him that instant; she was in a desperate hurry to settle this. She wanted this moonlight swim more than anything in the world, and she was so very much afraid it would not appeal to Weaver. She opened the cabin door and entered, and she saw, with dismay, that she had waked Weaver from a nap.

"Oh, I'm terribly sorry, Weaver," she said. "Only—did you know dinner was going to be early?"

"That's only for the people who want to go ashore at St. Jeff's," he said.

"Well, let's us go, Weaver."

"My dear girl," he said, frowning impatiently, "there's nothing there, especially at night."

"Well, but some of the people are getting up a party to go swimming by moonlight—"

"That's out of the question!" he cried. "It's dangerous. I've known people to get really serious chills from this idiotic bathing in the dark—without the sun. What's more, there are sharks and barracudas and God knows what. It's out of the question."

"Well, we could just go to the beach, even if we didn't go in swimming."

"Honey," he said, his voice unsteady with rage, "it-is-out-of-the-question. It's a long row ashore, and in the dark it's extremely unpleasant. Some of the boats leak. Some of the boatmen are entirely unreliable. I don't think you can say, with any justice, that I don't do everything possible for your pleasure. I lie here alone all afternoon, feeling considerably ill, while you amuse yourself, and I don't—"

"I didn't know you felt so ill, Weaver."

"You never came near me, to make any enquiry," he said.

Well, you win, thought Honey. She was cruelly disappointed, but she accepted the disappointment with resignation, because she felt guilty. Maybe Weaver really was ill; he looked tired and grey. And it could not be denied that she had completely forgotten him for hours.

There'll be other ports, she thought. There's another one tomorrow. Why not make the best of things? And back came her golden happiness. She sat in front of the mirror doing her hair, having fun with it. When I get a really good tan, she thought, I'll start to wear white. Honestly, I think a blonde with a good even tan, in a white dress, is stunning. But to-night she wore a black dinner dress with long full sleeves; she looked slight, delicate and wistful. With a little blue eye shadow.

Weaver, she thought, looked very nice in his dinner jacket; she was pleased when he suggested a cocktail before dinner. Only she was a little sorry when he caught sight of Miss Bewley sitting by herself in the smoke-room, and asked her to join them. Miss Bewley was unmistakably a Weaver kind of person, a nice friend for him; Honey admired their talk in a way, their mention of well-known names; but it was boring. She had nothing to contribute, and sitting silent, she looked around the room. This is more like it, she thought, pleased to see the other people in evening dress.

Then she saw Michael Nordstrom, in a grey suit. He was sitting at a table with his father, and the stout, grey-haired Mr. Carlow, and she liked his looks. She liked his high cheek bones, the sharp angle of his jaw, she liked the gentle and almost worn look he had. He's not wearing formal— she thought, and smiled to herself at the word. Michael glanced up then, and saw her smiling; he raised his hand in a sort of salute.

She liked everything, she liked going down to dinner, she liked the look of admiration in Mr. Basingly's face as she appeared at the table. But it disturbed her not to find Alma there.

"She has a bit of a headache," Lashelle said.

"She's resting."

He was very lively. He had come down early, and he finished early, and left.

"I was very glad to hear that the poor woman had *found* her jewelry," said Miss Bewley.

"Yes. So was I," said Mr. Basingly, drily.

"Has she found her *trunks* yet?"

"No, Miss Bewley."

"That's very *odd,* isn't it?"

"Very," said Mr. Basingly.

There was an implication in his tone that Honey resented.

"Mrs. Lashelle has the worst luck—" she said.

"Oh, quite!" said Basingly. "Some people do, y'know."

"Psychologists *say* that you lose things because you subconsciously *want* to lose them," Miss Bewley remarked.

"Well, she didn't want to lose all her luggage, or her jewelry, either," said Honey.

"But she didn't lose her jewelry, did she?" said Miss Bewley. "I had an aunt who lived in Staten Island—a charming place *then,* and completely different to what it is *now.* She had a gardener she *detested* and time after time, when she made out a cheque for his pay, she mislaid it."

"Well, I don't think Mrs. Lashelle is psychological," said Honey.

The engines stopped.

"Oh, we're here!" Honey said. "Oh, let's go and have a look! Weaver, let's go—"

"My dear girl," he said, briefly, "there's nothing to see."

"I'll go with you," said Miss Bewley, rising. "I do get such *a kick* out of tropical islands, as my nephew used to say."

There was something endearing about her brightness, something very pleasing in her friendliness.

"I'll be back, Weaver," Honey said. "I just want to take a look."

She and Miss Bewley went up the stairs, and out on the promenade deck. And it was raining and black as the pit. But even that didn't daunt Miss Bewley.

"Here!" she said. "Here, my dear! Now! Look *straight* ahead of you."

They stood together at the rail, the rain blowing against their faces, and Honey could discern a darker mass and a cluster of blurred and twinkling lights moving toward them slowly across the black water, the warmer orange lights of oil lanterns in row boats. The rain fell hissing straight into the sea; there was no wind, no stir, no noise. Nothing was happening.

"Well..." Honey said.

"There's a new passenger," said Miss Bewley.

A row-boat had come up to the grating at the foot of the accommodation ladder, and a sailor standing there helped a woman to disembark; she started up the ladder, a big girl, broad-shouldered, dark-haired and pert— looking leisurely, indifferent to the rain, hatless, and wearing a transparent raincoat. A bashful Negro followed her, carrying two small pieces of airplane luggage; she reached the deck and waited for him looking about her with nonchalant curiosity. Then she paid the man and went off into the saloon, her raincoat rustling like paper.

"D'you suppose she lives there on that island?" Honey asked.

"Possibly," said Miss Bewley. "There's quite a lot of visiting around from one island to the other, you know."

What could it be like, Honey thought, to live there, on a dark hill in the middle of the ocean? Maybe it was a wonderful life.... Her heart beat fast with a great longing to know, to understand this other world; something like grief oppressed her breast, it was so utterly hidden from her.

Mrs. Pruitt and Mr. Lake and Michael were at the head of the ladder.

"Don't you want to come along, Mrs. Stapleton?" asked Mrs. Pruitt.

"Certainly she doesn't," said Mr. Lake, with bitterness. "Who would want to go ashore in an open boat on a night like this?"

"You're going to love it," said Mrs. Pruitt, gently.

"If I get a tropical fever," said Lake, "there may be an investigation."

Lighthearted and most fortunate people; free people, going off to look at the world. I'd give *any*thing, Honey thought, just anything, if I could go.

She watched them down the ladder, and into one of the boats that were clustered around the grating; she watched the boatman begin to row in a strong leisurely rhythm, she saw the yellow lantern light on Michael's face that looked drowsy and happy beneath the turned-down brim of his felt hat.

"Mistake," said Mr. Basingly's voice behind them. "And I'd advise you ladies to come in out of the rain. Mistake. Foolhardy to get wet in this climate."

They went up into the smoke-room and sat down. *I feel* like being foolhardy, Honey thought. Who wants to be so darn sensible and careful all the time? More than anything in the world, she wanted to be with those others rowing across the dark water toward the unknown, that unimaginable island. Now maybe, I'll *never* see it, she thought. If we go home a different way, I'll never, never see it.

She no longer felt guilty about Weaver. It seemed to her that somehow the score was evened. She had forgotten him while she had a good time, so it was all right to stay away from him. He could come up here if he wanted, she thought. Even if he doesn't feel well, he doesn't have to stay shut up all by himself in the cabin.

The ship's whistle blew, a frightful blast, another and another echoing through the damp air. "What's that?" she cried.

"Calling the boats *back,*" Miss Bewley explained. "It's half-past ten."

"I think I'd better see how Weaver's getting on," she said.

But first she wanted one more look at that dark shore that she was never to know, the forbidden land, more enticing, more wonderful than any other could be. She stepped out on to the boat deck and moved away from the area of brightness outside the smoke-room windows. She went to the rail, stood there without shelter from the steady rain, she could see the light of a lantern in a boat drawing nearer and nearer, but she could no longer see the island. It was lost in the rain and the darkness.

It seemed to her that this had some special meaning for her, something infinitely sad and grave. There'll be other things like this, she thought. Things I can't do, places I can't see. Well, that's life I guess. That's—

And then, as if in mockery, she heard Weaver's short, nervous laugh. She turned her head quickly, but there was no one in sight on the rain-swept deck. Just imagination, she thought. But she heard it again.

Then she was afraid. Weaver was hidden here somewhere, laughing at her with spite, with cruelty, glad she could not see that island. Weaver, out here in the rain...?

There was a block of cabins aft looking like a cottage, with chintz curtains at the lighted windows. Was he there, watching her? She moved hesitantly toward those windows, and she heard a woman's voice, husky and slow.

"So we threw him out of the taxi and left him there on the Bois."

"Rather drastic, wasn't it?" said Weaver's voice.

"We were feeling pretty drastic by that time," said the woman's voice, someone Honey did not know.

She went close to the window. The curtain was drawn, but not quite all the way. By standing flat against the wall of the cabin, she could get a glimpse of the sitting-room of the suite, and she could see that big girl who had come on board this evening, sitting slouched in an armchair, smoking, her long legs crossed.

She was wearing a dress of thin, white wool, the neckline cut square from shoulder to shoulder, and fastened on one side by a silver coin. It was an original and a beautiful dress, and it was grimy; there were runs in the girl's stockings, lipstick had been smeared on her mouth with extraordinary carelessness, when she smiled her teeth were stained red with it. Weaver in there, talking to her?

The ship's whistle blew again.

"If you'll excuse me," said Weaver. "I'll have to be going. But I'll see you to-morrow."

"Sweet dreams," said the girl.

Honey ran down to the cabin, and began taking off her own clothes. It wasn't anything, she told herself. Weaver'll explain that. I just didn't want him to start fussing about my getting wet.

She was sitting on the bed taking off her shoes and stockings when he opened the cabin door and entered.

"Oh, you're here?" he said. "I've been writing letters in the library."

She looked up at him, too astonished to speak. He met her glance with a smile, a smile of the strangest triumph. And he himself was a stranger to her. She knew nothing about him. and she was afraid.

SIX

Honey waked early the next morning of her own accord, and sitting up in bed she looked at Weaver asleep. A fresh breeze blew in through the port, the sun was up, and Weaver didn't look strange at all. He was just Weaver.

Maybe he's met that girl before somewhere, she thought. Of course it's funny that he lied about it, but that could easily be one of his ideas of being gentlemanly. I mean, sort of to protect her or something. Or he might think I'd be jealous and make a scene.

She sighed. Of course, she thought, I couldn't feel jealous of Weaver, no matter what he did. But if he doesn't know that, so much the better. I'd honestly be glad if he was having a little flirtation with somebody. It might build him up. If he thinks he's got a great secret, well, let him go on thinking so.

He opened his eyes at that moment.

"What are you doing?" he said. "Why are you staring at me?"

"I just waked up," she said.

"I had a poor night," he said, severely.

"I'm sorry Weaver. What was the matter?"

"I still have this indigestion," he answered. "It may be simply the change of food. But it's very distressing."

He told her all about it, *all* about it. He had slept very badly, he had a pain.

"Weaver, let's go and see the doctor," she said.

"That might be a good idea," he said, obviously pleased.

There was no one at their table but Miss Bewley, very cheerful and lively, in a dress of thin white material with a pattern of purple lilac and a queer little frill at the neck.

"I don't know..." Weaver said. "I don't know what I'd better take. Something very light."

Miss Bewley took her cue at once.

"Don't you feel well, Mr. Stapleton?" she asked.

"Oh, it's nothing, thanks," he said. But all of breakfast was given up to a discussion of indigestion, his, and that of other people.

The doctor's office hours began at ten o'clock, and on the dot of ten, Weaver and Honey were in the alleyway outside his cabin. But someone had come before them; they could hear the doctor's voice.

"She's been dosing herself with something," he said.

"But she told me—" said Lashelle's voice.

"I don't care what she told you, my dear sir, or what she told me," said the doctor in his irritable and unpleasant voice. "Your wife's been dosing herself with something. And if she doesn't stop, I'm not going to take any responsibility for the case. I'm not going to treat her unless she puts herself entirely in my hands, and you can tell her so."

"I'll tell her, Doctor," said Lashelle, in a subdued and anxious tone, and he came out.

"Good morning!" he said, and hurried on past them.

"I'd rather you didn't come in with me, Honey," said Weaver.

"All right! I'll wait out here."

"There's no necessity for that," he said. "I can tell you everything later—if there's anything to tell."

Then I'm going to see Alma, thought Honey. That talk about Alma's 'dosing herself' made her uneasy; she wanted to see for herself how that unlucky bride was getting along. She went along the alleyway and knocked at the Lashelles' door. There was no answer.

Maybe she's gone out on deck, Honey thought, and knocked once more and then tried the handle. The door opened and she looked into darkness.

"Alma!" she said, sharply.

"Yes?" said a dull, faint voice.

A heavy dark curtain was drawn across the port, the fan was not running, the air was hot and still. Honey went over to the bed, she could see Alma lying on her back, her face indistinguishable.

"I'm terribly sorry you don't feel well, Alma."

"I'm as sick as a dog," said Alma.

"Is the doctor helping you any?"

"No," said Alma. "He's a damn fool."

It was so hot in here, so airless. So unbearable.

"Don't you think you'd maybe feel better if you had some fresh air?" Honey asked.

"I don't know," said Alma. "I'm cold."

You're cold in here? Lying here, so sick, in the dark? I won't have it.

"Listen, dear," said Honey. "Doctors can be wrong. If you're cold, let's have some sunshine in here. It'll do you good. It'll cheer you up."

"No," said Alma with her flat uncompromising negative. "It would upset Hilary. He wants me to do what the doctor ordered. It wouldn't help anyhow. I'm sick."

"Well, you'll get better."

"I don't know about that..." said Alma.

"Listen Alma," said Honey. "You've got to fight this."

"I don't know..." said Alma. "It's all gone so wrong. Right from the start—losing all my new clothes—on my honeymoon."

"Listen Alma! You *mustn't* give up. You can buy more clothes, the different places we stop."

"All the other things," Alma went on. "My God! I wonder if I *am*—queer?"

"No, you're not," said Honey briefly, and going to the port, she drew back the curtains. A flood of glittering, sunny air streamed in; she had a glimpse of the brilliant sea before she turned back to Alma.

And Alma looked ghastly, in a black night-dress with a lace yoke, a black mesh cap over her black hair, her face white and pinched, with a greenish tinge about the nostrils.

"Listen, Alma," Honey said. "Just *how* do you feel sick?"

"I've been as sick as a dog," said Alma.

"What have you been taking, Alma?"

"Nothing."

"Well... Just some aspirin?"

"Nothing, I said."

"Hasn't the doctor—or anybody—given you anything?"

"What's the idea?" Alma demanded ominously.

"Well, I mean, it seems all wrong not to do anything to help you if you feel so miserable."

"Medicine's no good," said Alma. "I never take any. I'm never sick."

"You're lucky—"

"It's not luck," said Alma. "It's sense. I know how to live and how to eat. If I have to be away from home, where I can't get the right things to eat, I take my Vitalixir."

"What's that?"

"I'm putting that on the market next Spring," said Alma. She looked better now; perhaps it was the freshening of the air, perhaps it was her interest in her subject. "I got a refugee chemist to work on it for us for the last two years, and I've been taking it myself, ever since he worked out the first formula. Vitamin A, B, C, and D, in a syrup of phosphates."

"Did you take it to-day?"

"Yes, I did," said Alma.

"Did you take it before you began to feel so miserable?"

"Look here!" said Alma. "What are you trying to get at anyhow? I've had a control group of fifteen people taking my Vitalixir every day for over six months. Every ingredient in it is tested and checked. I'm no fool. I—"

The door opened and Lashelle came in; he went straight to Alma, not even glancing at Honey.

"Better, dear?" he asked.

And Alma looked up into his face with that look that so disturbed Honey; that lost, helpless, rapt look.

"A little, maybe..." she said.

"Still cold, darling?"

"The sun feels good."

Then he looked at Honey.

"Mrs. Stapleton's a fine little nurse," he said. "Nurse, may I have a word with you—outside?"

"Certainly!" said Honey looking at him.

"Really," he said, "you mustn't bother, Mrs. Stapleton."

They were still looking straight into each other's eyes.

"It's no bother, Captain Lashelle," said Honey.

"The doctor's given me full instructions, Mrs. Stapleton. I'm only too happy to look after Alma."

"I'll be very *glad,*" said Honey, "just to keep an eye on Mrs. Lashelle."

He was silent for a moment. Then he gave her one of his quick and dazzling smiles, and went back into the cabin and closed the door.

I know what he means, all right, Honey thought.

A cold and thoughtful anger filled her. It seemed to her that what she was witnessing was the most atrocious form of cruelty, without panic, without recklessness. Alma was simply to be got rid of; she was nothing more than a nuisance. She had been robbed and deceived and discredited, and even that was not enough. Lashelle had not meant her to come on this trip, but she had come, entirely disarmed, blind, unfriended. With all her tough, stubborn vitality she was so terribly vulnerable, she had no suspicion, not because she trusted other people, but because she trusted herself and her own strength and intelligence.

And she's just so dumb, Honey thought, standing in the alleyway. She'd lie there all alone in the dark and die, before she'd even guess what was happening to her. Captain Lashelle put something in that Vitalixir. He could just feed it to her with a spoon and she'd swallow it. The doctor's not worrying about her. He just isn't interested in her. Nobody is. Captain Lashelle's got them all believing that she's a queer, half-cracked sort of woman, always complaining about something.

Well, I said I'd keep an eye on her, and I will. Captain Lashelle's not going to get away with this. So help me God, I'm going to stop this.

SEVEN

Weaver was in the cabin waiting for her, and he was a little aggrieved.

"What did the doctor say, Weaver?" she asked, making a painful effort to turn her mind toward him and his indigestion.

"I don't think much of that fellow," he said.

"Don't you, Weaver?"

"No. He's a pompous ass," said Weaver.

"What did he say, dear?"

"Nothing. Nothing of any significance," said Weaver. "He's a fool! Suppose we go up on deck?"

He was moving toward the door, but she stopped him.

"Weaver, I'd like to speak to you seriously," she said.

He looked at her with a smile. "Silly kid..." he said. "You're quite pale. Take my word for it, Honey, there's nothing to worry about."

Oh, lord! she thought in dismay. He thinks I'm worrying about *him;* and he'll be all upset when he finds it's something else. I really want his advice, but I'll never get it if he's in a bad mood. I'll have to sort of play up to him.

Well, that's marriage, I suppose, she thought. Mother always had to be careful with Mr. Dell, not to rub him the wrong way, and I guess she was the same with Father while he was alive. I've been tactful with men plenty of times. But when you're married, there's no let-up, I guess.

Weaver sat down and lit a cigarette; he was smiling, he was so pleased. He held out his hand, and she came and sat on the arm of his chair.

"You mustn't worry, Honey," he said.

"Well then, tell me exactly what the doctor said."

"He told me to take things easy, and cut down on smoking."

"And what else?"

"That's all."

"Weaver, tell Honey," she said, leaning her cheek against his neat, grey head. "I want to know."

"Silly kid..." he said with his arm around her. "You mustn't worry. There's nothing wrong with *me*. Little run down perhaps, and this trip'll do me all the good in the world."

"Maybe we could find another doctor in one of the islands."

"It isn't necessary," he said.

"Well, if you haven't any confidence in *this* doctor..." She waited a moment. "Weaver, you heard what he said to Captain Lashelle."

"I didn't notice," he said.

"It's... The doctor didn't seem to realize... Weaver, Captain Lashelle has been giving something to Alma."

"Alma? Who's Alma?"

"That's his wife, Weaver—"

"Too bad," he said, getting a little restive.

"Weaver, anybody could see there's something queer going on."

"Possibly," he said. "It's getting on for eleven, Honey. Suppose we go on deck and have some bouillon?"

"But, Weaver... I think he's doing it on purpose."

"Who's doing *what* on purpose, my dear girl?"

"Weaver, I think—Weaver, I'm *sure* he wants to get rid of her."

"Honey!" he protested. "You mustn't say things like that."

"Weaver, I've got a lot to go on. A lot of little things. When you take them all together... Weaver, listen. You remember when we got in their cabin by mistake? When I was waiting there while you went to see the Purser? Well, there was a letter there. I didn't know who it was for, or anything. I just happened to find it lying around. *He'd* written it, Weaver, Captain Lashelle had, and it was to some other woman he called his wife—"

He pushed her away and rose.

"This is—" He swallowed. "This is—*disgusting!*" he said.

"That's a funny word to use," she said.

"It's the only word." He moistened his lips and swallowed again, trembling with the effort to master his disgust. "My dear girl, we'll drop this if you please."

"Weaver, if I think that man's trying to get rid of his wife, d'you expect me just to do *nothing* about it?"

"Do? If you try to 'do' anything—if you go running around making these—these preposterous accusations, you'll get yourself—and me—into God knows what trouble. You—"

"I wasn't 'running around,' "she said briefly.

"I was trying to tell you, my own husband, that's all. If you'll help me—"

"Help you?" he shouted. "What are you talking about?"

"You could stop shouting and listen," she said.

"I don't intend to listen. And you're not to mention this—farrago of disgusting nonsense to anyone, d'you understand that?"

"Weaver," she said sternly, "that's no way to talk to your wife."

Her tone and her words impressed him. "I'm—er—sorry," he said. "We'll drop the subject, if you please."

"That's no way to *act* to your wife. If I'm worried about something, and I want to talk it over with you—"

"I'm sorry," he said again, stiff and chilly. "I'm perfectly willing to talk over anything that concerns you, at any time. This doesn't concern you. And I'm not going to sit down and gossip about strangers."

"Okay!" she said.

"What do you mean by that?"

"I mean okay."

He sat down in the chair, heavily.

"I can't stand much more of this," he said. "It makes me—positively ill."

"That's just too bad," said Honey.

But he did look ill. He just can't stand anything, Honey thought. He just can't take it. There had been times in the past when she had more or less respected this fastidious sensibility, when she thought he was somehow finer than herself. But not now. She felt almost arrogantly aware of her own young vigor and courage; now, for the first time, she felt that she could not count on Weaver.

"Want to come and get that bouillon now?" she asked.

"No, thank you," he said.

"Is there anything I can do for you?"

"No, thank you."

"Then I'll see you at lunch," said Honey.

And I wish I didn't have to, she said to herself. She sat in her deck chair and closed her eyes, so that nobody should speak to her; and with the world shut out, she faced for a moment a desolation that made her cold. It has to go on and on like this, she thought, for years and years, and it never will get any better. I can give in to Weaver about a lot of things, and I can kid him along. But what's that? That's not a life. I don't hate him. I'm sorry for him. I like him in some ways. But I wish to God I never had to see him again.

That was a dreadful thing to think. But it's better to face things, she thought. I've gone and got myself into this; and this is the pay-off. I was twenty-three years old, I knew what I was doing. I knew I wasn't in love with him. Only I thought there'd be something else—a kind of companionship, or something. And there isn't. There isn't anything.

"Your flying fish are here," said Michael, beside her.

He was about the only person she didn't mind talking to just now. Ever since that first night when he had stood near her on the deck not speaking, she had had a queer feeling about Michael. As if they were old friends; as if she could be sure of him.

They went to the rail, and there were the flying fish, skimming like scraps of silver in the sun.

"It's a shame to think they're not getting any fun out of it," Honey said, regretfully.

"Who says they're not?" Michael said.

"Well, somebody told me they only do it to escape from the big fish that are after them."

"But not all the time," said Michael. "It's a funny thing, isn't it, that they've learned to fly, and none of the other fish have? They evolved themselves into this, to survive. But the other little fish that haven't learned to fly seem to survive, too."

"Yes, it is funny," Honey said, very much interested.

She liked the way he talked; he was sort of serious, but he wasn't ever pompous or boring; he had background, a lot of it, you could tell that, but he didn't seem to be thinking about it. She liked his looks; a little too thin maybe, but tall and well-made, and that gentle, tired look on his face.

"Are you taking a holiday?" she asked.

"Yes..." he said. "I suppose you'd call it that. I was shot, a few months ago."

"Shot?" she cried.

"I think it was a mistake," he said. "We'd been having some trouble at the mine, but I didn't think anyone had it in for me, especially. I was riding down the hill rather late one evening when someone got me."

"Were you much hurt?"

"It was pretty bad," he said. "My horse bolted and threw me, and I smashed my shoulder."

"Where did this happen?" she asked.

"Guatemala," he said.

He was not shy or reserved; he just didn't seem to think that he could be particularly interesting. But when she asked him questions, he answered willingly. He was a mining engineer; that was, she thought, about the most attractive thing a man could be; he was twenty-seven, and that was a nice age. He had been to a prep school that was a little fabulous to Honey, and he had been to Harvard and to Columbia. He's got every bit as much background as Weaver, she thought, and he's much more interested in things.

She was surprised to hear the bugle blow. I told Weaver I'd see him at lunch, she thought, and I'm not going back to the cabin even to wash. I don't want to fight with him. 'Disgusting,' he called it, when I tried to tell him.

And for all that time she had forgotten about the thing she had tried to tell Weaver. How *could* you forget a thing like that? I've got to do something about Alma, she thought. I've got to warn her, some way. But I know darn well that if I ever tried to say anything against her precious husband, I'd be out on my ear before I was half started. That's what makes it so horrible, the way she adores him.

I did want to talk to Weaver about it. But he wouldn't listen. He's never going to, either. All right. I'll have to think out something to do without him.

"Would you like a cocktail before lunch?" Michael asked.

"Well... Thank you," she said. "A glass of sherry, maybe."

Maybe I'll tell him about Alma, she thought. Weaver had his chance and he wouldn't help me, or even listen to me. Yet, she could not quite decide to do this, for reasons she had no intention of analyzing. It was a comfort to think she could tell him if she wanted. He was there. And Weaver wasn't. Weaver was shut up in his cabin, with his grievance....

They went into the smoke-room, and there was Weaver sitting in a corner with that big girl, with tall drinks before them.

"Well!" she said aloud, stopping in the doorway.

Weaver saw her then, and rose and came toward her with the little frown she knew so well.

"How d'you do?" he said curtly to Michael. "Er—Honey... I've been looking for you."

"Oh, have you Weaver?" she said, ready to laugh.

"If you'll—er—join us..." he said, with an annoyed glance at Michael.

"Thank you," said Michael, mildly, "but..." He moved away.

Weaver led Honey over to the corner.

"Honey," he said. "this is Mrs. Condy. Mrs. Condy, my wife."

The big girl looked up at her with a vague and wandering glance. She was wearing a grey linen dress, superbly tailored, but far from fresh, her abundant dark hair had a dusty look, her lipstick was smeared on with that same carelessness, red polish had been put on her nails anyhow, streaking her finger tips, the buckle of her broad grey suede belt was broken and mended with a scrap of black ribbon. Yet, careless and even slovenly as she was, she was handsome, and she had what Honey immediately conceded to be Class.

She was amiable too.

"Honey..." she repeated. "That's a cunning name."

"We've been—er—discussing Paris. As it was," said Weaver.

"I don't believe it's changed," said Mrs. Condy, in her slow, husky voice.

"But my dear lady, I'm afraid the facts—"

"Well, I don't know any facts," said she. "I never look at newspapers."

Weaver laughed indulgently.

"Mrs. Condy's had some extraordinary experiences in Europe," he said. "She escaped at the last minute."

"That's what they tell me," said she. "But I never saw any Germans."

"And consequently you didn't believe in them?" Weaver asked.

Simply doting on her, Honey thought. The situation entertained her, she felt a liking for this big, careless, amiable girl.

"I wanted to ask..." said Mrs. Condy. "Can I come tagging along with you when you go ashore this afternoon?"

"I'd be very glad," said Honey, and meant it.

"Miss Bewley has already suggested joining forces," said Weaver. "But I'm sure she'd be more than pleased, Mrs. Condy.... Another drink?"

"God..." she said, sadly. "I don't know how to say no."

He laughed again and beckoned to the steward, Mrs. Condy had another Scotch and soda, and Honey ordered a glass of sherry. And Weaver had another Scotch. He never drinks before lunch, Honey thought. But if it makes him happy....

Mrs. Condy began to tell of an adventure she had had in Cairo, a fantastic tale of an elderly French general who had been very, very enterprising in his efforts to win her favor. It was a ribald story, told without a smile in her slow and amiable way; it was the sort of story that Weaver would naturally disapprove of strongly. But he laughed at this one. It was half-past one before they went down to lunch, and he was in fine spirits. Mrs. Condy walked off to her own table, and Weaver and Honey went to join Basingly and Miss Bewley and Captain Lashelle.

"How is Mrs. Lashelle?" asked Honey instantly.

"Oh, quite a bit better, thanks," he answered.

And she is going to keep on being better, Honey thought. Other things and other people diverted her again and again from that grim business, but not wholly, and never for long. This was the thing that could not wait. I think I scared him, she said to herself, a little, anyhow. But you can't count on that.

"I'll stop in and see her after lunch," she said looking straight at him.

"You'll find her on the boat-deck, Mrs. Stapleton," he said.

"Oh! So she's that much better?" said Honey.

"She has a wonderful constitution," said Captain Lashelle.

She did find Alma on the boat-deck after lunch, lying back in a deck chair, all carefully made up with mascara and lip stick and powder, handsome and curiously complacent.

"This sickness has been an experience," she said. "It came on so suddenly.... Captain Lashelle was almost frantic. He sat beside me for hours."

"Oh, did he?" said Honey.

"I never saw anyone like him," Alma went on. "I never had anyone make such a fuss over me. It's an experience." She glanced at Honey. "I suppose you've had plenty of people fussing over you," she said.

Well," said Honey, "my mother was always very sweet to me if I was sick."

"And I guess you've always had plenty of men around," said Alma.

"Well... Sort of," said Honey.

"My life's been different," said Alma. "I started helping out my family when I was fifteen and believe me they were willing to take all the help they could get. I never had any time for men, I never had any of the good times other girls have." She paused. "Why, d'you know," she said, "I never even learned to dance till a couple of years ago."

"Well, anyhow, you've got somewhere," said Honey. "You amount to something."

"That's true," Alma admitted. "And you certainly get a kick out of that, out of getting the things you always dreamed of. I mean, like a penthouse, and a couple of good rings, and a good dark mink."

Then you bought your own mink coat, Honey thought. "All I ever got for myself," she said slowly. "was a squirrel jacket I was buying on time. But I'd have lost that. if my mother hadn't helped me out. I just—never struggle enough."

"I made up my mind when I was a kid that I'd get to the top," said Alma, "and I did. I did it alone. too. No help from anyone. I don't mind saying I'm proud of it. But you have to pay for it. You have to give up a lot. You have to be plenty hard. If you'd done more struggling, you wouldn't have the nice little ways you've got."

"D'you think I've got nice little ways?" Honey asked, anxiously.

"Yes. Only there's one thing... Captain Lashelle's got it into his head that you don't like him."

"Oh... What makes him think that?"

"I don't know. But he's very sensitive," said Alma, and was silent for a time, leaning back against the pillow, happy and serene, thinking of her captain.

"Alma," said Honey, "you'll be careful what you eat and drink, won't you?"

"I'm not a fool," said Alma.

Oh, aren't you, thought Honey.

"I hope you won't go back in that stuffy cabin, Alma," she said.

"I'll see," said Alma, with impatience. "Captain Lashelle'll look after me."

A little shiver ran through Honey, even here in the bright sun. It seemed to her that Alma was the most unfortunate woman in all the world; if she learned the truth, it would so shake and undermine all her pride, all her faith in herself, she would be so utterly bereft to lose this happiness that had come to her so late. And the only thing that could keep her from learning the truth about Lashelle, sooner or later, was death. I don't know . . she said to herself, looking at Alma.

But that doubt was alien to her, and she dismissed it. Her blood told her that life was good in itself. She went down the ladder to the promenade deck, and there she found Michael standing by the rail. He was waiting for her; she knew that.

"This way!" he said seriously⁻, and she went with him forward, and to the other side of ship. "There!" he said.

Before them lay an island, a green hill rising from the sea, casting a dark shadow upon the quiet water. The ship seemed to glide through a world of ineffable peace and jewelled color, sapphire and emerald, and a plumy line of white where the long rollers broke gently on the shore.

"But, it's so—quiet!" she said with tears in her eyes.

"I knew you'd like it," he said. "I was waiting to show it to you."

She turned toward him, and there was a look on his face that she could read. He had wanted to be the one who was with her when she first saw this. He was the one she wanted with her. They were sharing this.

She turned her head away, and he said nothing more. She saw his hand on the rail, lean and brown and young, and she turned away from that too. Tears ran down her cheeks and she let them flow. She knew he wouldn't say anything about her crying. He would just stand there.

Only now she knew what she had done. She had bartered away her life, she had willingly and eagerly taken the things she did not want and lost all this. All this mysterious and beautiful quiet world.

"Well..." she said, and dried her eyes and smiled. "Thank you, Michael," she said and went away to look for Weaver.

He was standing by the rail, watching the lowering of the accommodation ladder, and Miss Bewley and his precious Mrs. Condy stood on either side of him.

"I've ordered a launch," he said. "I don't like row-boats."

"Oh *did* you?" said Miss Bewley. "I think I get the *feel* of a place better, if I approach it *slowly.*"

"How would you like flopping down in a place in a parachute?" asked Mrs. Condy in her vague way.

"Er—have you had that experience?" asked Weaver.

"God, yes," she answered. "I've done everything."

A flock of row-boats was coming up to the ladder, jostling one another; the boatmen yelled and howled, the quartermaster standing down there took charge.

"Here you! Get back there."

"Sah! Sah!" cried an anguished voice. "I friend here, sah! Captain know me, sah!"

"Push off!" said the quartermaster, unmoved.

Some of the passengers were going down the gangway now, to get into the boats. Then a launch put off from the shore, coming smartly toward the ship.

"Here we are!" said Weaver. "Are you all ready ladies? Honey, where's your hat?"

He was fussing, as usual, but he was happy; this was the way he liked to do things.

"Ready?" he said again.

"I've got to take off my shoes," said Mrs. Condy. "I can't go down ladders in shoes."

"I'll help you," said Weaver, amused and indulgent. And what would he say if I talked about taking off my shoes? thought Honey.

It was quite a spectacle to see him helping Mrs. Condy down the ladder, and it took a long time; Honey and Miss Bewley watched from the deck.

"My dear," said Miss Bewley, "I've met that girl before."

"Oh, have you?" said Honey, interested. "Where?"

"My dear, in a gambling joint in Mexico," said Miss Bewley. "An *adventuress.*"

This was a new and fascinating idea for Honey, and she would have asked more questions, but the launch was alongside now, and Weaver beckoned to them. But just at that moment the Captain began to descend the ladder followed by a man in a white uniform carrying a briefcase, and they waited.

Weaver was starting to help Mrs. Condy into the launch, when the quartermaster stopped him.

"Sorry, sir," he said. "But this is the company's launch, sir. For the Captain, sir."

"Very well," said Weaver, annoyed.

The Captain got into the launch and off it went. Honey and Miss Bewley went down, and they all stood there. More and more passengers came down and got into row-boats and went off, and there was no sign of another launch. Oh dear! Honey thought. It's another one of those things that happen to Weaver.

Mrs. Pruitt and Mr. Lake and Michael came down the ladder.

"Aren't you people going ashore?" asked Mrs. Pruitt.

"I've ordered a launch," said Weaver.

"Oh, I see," said Mrs. Pruitt politely, and got into a row-boat.

"Can I go along with you people?" asked Mrs. Condy.

"Oh, yes!" said Mrs. Pruitt.

"Very pleased!" said Lake.

She got into the boat.

"See you later, people!" she said. "Somewhere."

Weaver turned away.

"Weaver!" said Honey.

He mounted a couple of steps and looked down at her; there was a dark flush on his face, his mouth twitched.

"I shan't be going ashore," he said.

"But, Weaver—"

"I shan't be going ashore," he repeated, more loudly. "It's—this is the most *disgusting* example of—gross mismanagement. No consideration whatever for the convenience of the passengers." He paused, trying to control his voice. "If Miss Bewley will be kind enough to let you accompany her... " he said, and went on up, surprisingly fast.

Impossible to let him go like this in his furious, trembling humiliation. Honey went up the ladder after him and caught him on the deck.

"Weaver..."

"Kindly—kindly—let me alone," he said. "I don't feel well."

"Well, then I'll stay with—"

"Kindly—go!" he shouted. "I don't *want* anyone to stay with me. I want to be *let alone!*"

But, still she went after him, worried by that flush on his face. In the cabin, he turned at bay.

"Honey, kindly go away," he said. "Here..." He took out his wallet. "Here..." he said. "Kindly take this money I expected to use ashore."

She looked at him for a moment, as if she had never seen him before. This was the way he felt about her. If he gave her the money, that was enough.

But, because she was so sorry for him, she took the money. It was all he had to give.

"Well... Au revoir, Weaver," she said.

EIGHT

Miss Bewley was still waiting at the foot of the ladder, and Basingly was with her. He went ashore with them, to engage a particular driver, he told the driver where to take them; he helped them into the car, and they set off through the narrow streets of the old town. A dead town of blank-faced stone buildings, of dim shops without fronts.

"It's the siesta hour," said Miss Bewley. "Quite *charming*, isn't it?"

The driver, a thin and gentle Negro with mournful eyes, pointed out everything, explained everything in English with a Spanish accent. "The preeson... The princi*pal* street of shopping... The market..."

It was not colourful or gay; it was strange, Honey thought, kind of sinister. The resi*dence* quarter, said the driver, and they entered upon a wide road. Two cars passed them, bearing some of their shipmates who waved as they sailed by.

They left the town and started up a steep hill, and in a moment they were in a forest, in a jungle of dark trees and tangled creepers. At the top of the hill in a clearing stood a stone ruin. The old fort of Castille, the driver said and stopped the car and opened the door. Miss Bewley and Honey got out, and he led them conscientiously, too conscientiously, through what had long ago been rooms, carpeted now with grass and weeds, roofless to the burning blue sky. "Here is the hall of banquet."

Honey was entranced; she followed their guide down some stone steps to a cellar. "The chamber of torture," he said. "You see yet the chains. In here was for gunpowder. Here for wines." So dark and still and ancient...

"It's fascinating, don't you think?" she asked Miss Bewley.

"Oh, *very!*" said Miss Bewley, veteran inspector of how many ruins all over the world. In her peasant dress, with an enormous hat on her frizzy dyed hair, and low-heeled sandals on her feet, she went amiably along after Honey. They came up the steps again and into the hall where the walls had crumbled, but an archway stood, frame for a view of matted hillside, and below it the sea. A lizard ran over the stones.

> "They say," Miss Bewley quoted, "the Lion
> and the Lizard keep,
> The Courts where Jamshyd gloried and
> drank deep
> And Bahram, that great Hunter—the Wild Ass
> Stamps o'er his Head, but cannot break his Sleep."

Honey listened to her with anxious intentness. "That's lovely!" she said, "and it's so suitable for here."

"It's suitable for a great many places," said Miss Bewley, somewhat ruefully. "I'm *afraid* I go all over quoting the Rubaiyat in a very dreadful way."

"Do you know any more, Miss Bewley?"

"Oh, my dear, yes! My father used to offer *prizes* to us for memorizing it."

"Will you recite some more, Miss Bewley?"

"Some of it is very melancholy," said Miss Bewley.

"I don't mind that, Miss Bewley."

They sat on the stone wall, and Miss Bewley recited verses from that most ancient philosophy.

The leaves stirred in the hot dry breeze, the driver stood respectfully aside, smoking a cigarette.

"But we haven't much *time,* my dear, if we want to get back to dinner. If you want to see the old Cathedral…"

"I like it here, Miss Bewley, if you do," Honey said.

She could not have put into words the enchantment of this place and this hour. It was, somehow, the thing she most needed; it was a respite from her life that so dismayed her.

"But my dear, we really *must* go," said Miss Bewley. She lowered her voice. "Mr. Basingly told me about this *place*—a *dive.* Everyone goes there for a drink, and I thought we might stop there, don't you think?"

The prospect of going to a dive alone with Miss Bewley had no attraction for Honey. She had very definite ideas about that sort of thing; never in her life had she gone into a bar without a man. It looked forlorn, she thought, it didn't look right.

But if Mss Bewley wanted to do that, it was a small enough concession in return for her peerless amiability. They got back into the car and Miss Bewley gave the driver his directions.

"And lately by the Tavern door agape," she said,
"Came shining through the Dusk an Angel Shape
Bearing a vessel on his Shoulders; and
He bid me taste it; and it was—the Grape."

There was no dusk here, only the fierce sun in the burning blue sky, the dust the wind stirred in the road, and the dark jungle that lined it. They passed a group of workers, barefoot and ragged, in wide straw hats, carrying machetes; sometimes they passed a little hut among banana plants. It grew hotter as they descended, and when they reached the town it was alive, the narrow streets crowded.

Miss Bewley's dive was on the waterfront, opposite the wharf, a dim little place entirely open to the street, with a bar and a dozen small tables. A squeaky phonograph was playing, and the place was well filled. And there were familiar faces there, people from the ship; the doctor was there with a party, and sitting at a table with a young man was Alma.

"Hello!" she said, unsmiling and challenging. "Miss Bewley and Mrs. Stapleton, this is Mr. Perez."

Mr. Perez rose, small and finely finished, slim and young, with long black eyes, and a brilliant smile.

"I am charmed," he said. "I make the trip to Trinidad on your ship, ladies. I see it shall be a wonderful trip."

He brought chairs up to the little table and they sat down, very close together, Mr. Perez next to Honey. "I think I must be seeing an angel," he murmured.

"Me?" Honey asked.

"You're not an angel?"

"Yes, I am," said Honey. "Definitely."

"I think the sky here was blue," he said, "until I saw your eyes. Now I think I am drowning, to look into them."

She closed her eyes.

"*More* beautiful," he murmured. "That is how you look when you are sleeping." He sighed, and she opened her eyes.

He's pretty Latin, she thought, and you have to keep them in their place. But he's a gay little fellow. Sort of fun.

"I'm awfully glad to see you so much better, Alma," she said.

"I've been shopping," said Alma. "I got one of these mantillas and some stockings, and there's some hand-made underwear that's not so bad. And I got—but I'll show you later."

She was sipping some sort of long drink with fruit in it, and she seemed entirely composed and matter-of-fact here in the dive with the enterprising Mr. Perez.

"Captain Lashelle's gone back to the ship to get me a coat," she said. "As soon as the sun goes down it gets pretty chilly, he says."

From where Honey sat she could see the ship and tiny figures on the deck. And Weaver's there, she thought. Just sitting by himself, I suppose. You have to be sorry for him..

"What will you have to drink, Miss Angel?" asked Perez.

"It's Missis Angel," said Honey. "I'd like a Planter's Punch, please."

"And Miss Bewley?"

"A gin tonic, thank you," said Miss Bewley. "I heard that there have been three murders in place."

"Oh, who knows?" said Perez, shrugging his shoulders. "At night time if there are many ships here, many sailors—who knows?"

"Do you live here, Mr. Perez?" asked Miss Bewley.

"Dios!" he cried, smiling from ear to ear. "I come this morning by airplane to catch the ship. I travel much in the islands to buy and sell, you understand. Puerto Rico, Cuba, Martinique, Trinidad, all the islands. But live here! I? I live in Caracas; very gay."

The drinks came, the squeaky phonograph was playing a milonga, the warm air was thick with smoke and strong of rum; there was a confused loud sound of voices. It was dim in here, and incredibly bright outside where the little white ship lay.

"I like it," Honey said to Miss Bewley.

"I always like native dives," said Miss Bewley, contentedly.

Alma turned her back on the rest of them to watch the door.

"They are love-birds, those two, eh?" said Perez.

He was amused, but Honey was not. All that fear and dread anxiety came back to her, and more heavily than ever. Even in the midst of a crowd, Alma was helpless. She remembered very vividly how Alma had looked only twenty-four hours ago, lying in the darkened airless cabin, sick as a dog. Captain Lashelle got away with that, she thought. Nobody but me thought there was a thing wrong. Now he'll think he can get away with—

The expression was getting away with murder. But he knows *I'm* suspicious anyhow, she said to herself. That might stop him. Only I want tell somebody else. Miss Bewley, maybe? Or Mr. Basingly? Or would they just be like Weaver, and think it was a lot of, what did he call it? Farrago...

Michael Nordstrom was the one not to tell; the one not to be thought about.

"What do you think about?" said Perez, softly.

"You'd be surprised," said Honey.

"I would be interested, I tell you that."

"My dear," said Miss Bewley, "it's getting late. I think we'd better be going."

Honey rose. "Anybody else coming?" she asked.

"We're going to have dinner on shore," said Alma.

"Mr. Perez with you?" asked Honey.

Mr. Perez took this as a sign of most flattering interest, he was delighted.

"Why don' you stay?" he asked. "You two ladies?"

"I'm sorry, but I have to get back," said Honey.

She was very glad that he was going to be with the I.ashelles; it would be some protection for Alma. And later on, she thought, I'll think of something better, something permanent.

It was dark already. Mr. Perez went out with them and into the waiting car; they drove off to the jetty through streets that were stirring with life now. It was pure magic to get into a row-boat with a lantern, to cross the stretch of dark water toward the lighted ship.

"Miss Bewley, I've had a *wonderful* time," Honey said.

"My dear," said Miss Bewley, "you're *a delightful* companion."

A launch went past them toward the ship, and the row-boat rocked in the swell. Poor Weaver, Honey thought. It was pretty mean of that Mrs. Condy to walk out on him like that; but she couldn't know he'd mind *that* much.

"Mrs. Condy's a sort of an interesting type, don't you think?" she asked Miss Bewley.

"A dangerous woman," said Miss Bewley.

"Dangerous?" Honey repeated, startled. "You mean, because she's so attractive?"

"I mean," said Miss Bewley, "because she's completely reckless. You can see that even by looking at her. Reckless—and lost."

"Well... How do you mean, 'lost,' Miss Bewley?"

Miss Bewley's voice sounded grave, almost stern in the darkness.

"She's obviously a woman of some breeding and education. She must have had a very good deal, once. But she must have thrown it all away."

"But there's *something* about her..."

"My dear," said Miss Bewley. "I noticed that her neck was *not* clean. When a woman, a young and good-looking woman comes to that, she's lost. Well, here we are!"

A sailor helped them out, and Miss Bewley paid the boatman, and they went up the ladder. On the deck, the young Assistant Purser came toward them.

"Oh, Mrs. Stapleton," he said holding out an envelope, "could I trouble you to give this to Mr. Stapleton? I've been looking for him, but I can't find him."

That worried Honey; she took the envelope and hurried to the cabin, she knocked on the half-open door, and getting no answer, she pushed up the hook and entered. The room was lighted and hot, and empty. She knocked at the bathroom door and opened it.

Then she went up to the smoke-room, and he was not there. She looked into the library, she went all around the promenade deck, she went down to look into the dining saloon, and it was closed, she went up on the boat deck. But Weaver never goes to any *queer* places, she thought. You always know just about where you can find Weaver.

Then she remembered where she had seen him the night before, and she stopped short. Mrs. Condy went ashore, she thought, but she could have come back. Weaver *could* be in her cabin again. He was in a terrible rage at her about the launch, but maybe she got around him.

She had to find Weaver. The memory of his darkly flushed face and his twitching mouth came back to fill her with an indefinite alarm. Weaver's capable of awfully foolish things, she thought. He's so nervous.... If he *is* with Mrs. Condy, all right, but I've got to know.

There was no light in the window of Mrs. Condy's sitting-room but standing close to it Honey could see a door half-open into another room where there was a light. She must have a suite, she thought. Well, Weaver *could* even be in the bedroom.

She knocked and got no answer. She tried the handle, and the door opened, and she stepped into the dark room.

"Mrs. Condy?" she called.

Nobody answered. She stood in the dark room looking toward the lighted one, doubtful, hesitant, frightened. They wouldn't be in there, and not answer, she thought. It's silly to think that. She took a few steps toward the half-open door, and her hand flew to her mouth. There was a horrible little brown head there, hanging up by its long, ropey, yellow hair.

It's nothing, she thought. It's—I guess it's a coconut.

"Mrs. Condy?" she said again.

Of course there was no answer, because there was nobody there. All right! Take a look and be done with it.

She pulled the door open, and Mrs. Condy was there after all.

She was lying on her back on the floor with her big black eyes wide open, and there were ashes and cigarette stubs and matches all over her white face. Her beautiful narrow feet were bare, and the toe-nails were a deep jewel-like red. There she lay, with ashes over her face and in her dark hair, and caught like dust in her thick dark lashes.

For a moment she was heart-breaking to see. And then, looking down into those big black eyes, terror rose and rose in Honey, and she ran, slamming the door after her.

NINE

There was nobody in sight on the boat deck, and she leaned against the rail, unable to move, unable to think.

She's dead. She's dead. She's dead. I must tell somebody. I mustn't leave her like that. Leave her. Leave her... It sounds like Weaver—weaver—leave her—leave her... Quit that!

I've got to find Weaver. I've got to tell him. It's—it's natural for me to go and tell my husband first.... Ashes. Dust and ashes... As if somebody had— Nobody's do that... Nobody'd throw ashes in her face.... It was an accident....

Oh God! I wish I was crying—or something . . I wish I knew—what to do.... I can hear people down on the promenade deck.... Let somebody else come—and find her.... I don't want—to be the one.... But if I have a little time I'll—pull myself together all right.

"Er..." said a deep, gloomy voice to her. She gave a gasp, and looked up to see a tall form in white. "Looking for Mrs. Condy?" asked the voice.

She gripped the rail to keep from sliding down on the deck in a heap. She could not make a sound, and if he spoke again, she could not hear. He went away; she saw him for a moment under a light, tall, thin, in a white suit and a queer floppy white hat. Someone she had never set eyes on before, coming up to her in the dark—to ask *that*....

But this second shock had done her good; it brought her back to a certain balance. She was not thinking clearly, but she began to act, to move, by instinct. She went along the deck and down the ladder; she was looking for Weaver, and she was getting away from that cabin.

Somebody said, *"Good* evening, Mrs. Stapleton!" and she said "Hello!" in a bright and rather loud voice, and went on looking for Weaver. And that was irrevocable. Her course was set now; she had met someone, and not told. She could go on not telling.

Someone else would go into that cabin; someone else would spread the news. It could make no difference to Mrs. Condy who did this, or when. There was no hurry. There was time to think and there was something to think of, something dire and dreadful. The one important thing was to find Weaver.

She went back to their cabin; she went into the library again. The dining saloon was open now, and she leaned on the rail and looked down; nobody at Mr. Basingly's table. She went out on the promenade deck again, she tried not to hurry. Other people spoke to her and she could answer them. But she did not tell anyone she was looking for Weaver. He wouldn't like that.

At any moment now it could happen. There would be a cry from the deck above, running footsteps. Oh, if only only she could find Weaver first; before that happened! Where could he be? There are so few places to look on a ship.

What if he was—*there?* The suite must have a bathroom, and that door had been closed. What if Weaver had been in there all the time? Still there...? What if he, too...?

"Honey," said Michael stopping her with a hand on her arm. "What's the matter?"

"Nothing," she said. "Nothing."

"You can tell me," he said.

That seemed very reasonable. She could tell Michael and the time had come to tell.

"Listen..." she said. "I went up to—Mrs. Condy's cabin, and—she's in there, dead."

"What cabin is it?"

"She's dead. She's lying on the floor—with *ashes* all over her face. She's dead. She's in there, dead."

"Take it easy, Honey," he said. "Here. This way. Go into my cabin and sit down, where nobody will bother you until I come back. Here's a cigarette, Honey. Just sit in here, and have a smoke until I come back."

The cigarette did her good, and it was very safe in this snug, brightly-lighted little cabin. There seemed to be a great noise of trampling outside in the alleyway, as if herds and herds of people were shoving and pushing past. Maybe something was happening. Maybe they were carrying someone along with them. A very hot night, this was. No air.

Michael came in without knocking.

"The door of that cabin's locked," he said. "I couldn't get in."

"I slammed it. Maybe that locked it."

"Maybe it did. Now, the next step is to tell Mr. Basingly."

"No," she said, flatly. "I can't."

"I'll tell him, if you want," he said. "That'll give you a little extra time to—rest."

"No," she said again, with a queer, blind obstinacy. "I don't want to—be the one. Somebody else will find her."

"That isn't a good idea," he said. "Miss Bewley's just gone down to dinner. Suppose you go down and join her?"

"Dinner?"

"Yes. And in the meantime, I'll see Basingly."

He was very quiet, but he wasn't gentle now. He expected something of her, something better than this stubborn vagueness.

"Yes, I will," she said. "I will go down and join Miss Bewley. I—I'll— I'll go."

"That's the idea," he said.

He just took it for granted that she would pull herself together and go down there with all those people. Maybe he even thought she would eat a good dinner. It was too much to expect.

"My—teeth are all chattering," she said.

"You'd better order yourself a cocktail," said Michael.

She got up and he put his hand on the door handle.

"Of course," he said, "Basingly will have to ask you some questions, later on. The police, too."

"Why do you—*say* that?" she cried.

"You're young and strong," he said. "You can take it."

There was mighty little sympathy in his tone now. He was ignoring the luxurious and delicate Mrs. Stapleton who must be shielded; he was addressing that other Honey who knew how to look after herself.

"I *won't* take it,' " she said.

Their eyes met, and she was surprised by the hardness of his glance.

"All right!" he said. "What do you want to do?'

"I'll go," she said, coldly. "I'll go down—and sit at the table."

"Very well. I'll get hold of Basingly," he said, and opened the door for her. "Just a minute," said as she was going past him. "You dropped this."

It was the envelope the Assistant Purser had given her, one of the ship's envelopes, addressed to Mr. Weaver Stapleton. She put it into her purse and went on along the alleyway. A very strange thing had now happened to her. She was no longer concerned about Mrs. Condy, she no longer felt any pity, or any fear, she was scarcely interested. She went down to the dining saloon, and there was Miss Bewley, alone at the table.

"My dear!" said Miss Bewley. "The red snapper is *delicious!*"

"Well, I'll try it," said Honey.

She could eat. She didn't need any cocktail, even. While waiting for her soup, she glanced about the saloon that was almost empty. And sitting by himself at a small table in a corner, she saw a tall, thin man with a heavy black moustache, and a lugubrious face tanned like old leather.

"I—wonder who *that is,* over in the corner..." she said.

"His name," said Miss Bewley, "is Smith. I was talking to him. Very *mysterious.*"

"Well, how?"

But as Miss Bewley was about to answer, Honey's eyes widened; she sat looking at the stairway, and Weaver, who was descending, in his white dinner jacket. He was frowning; he looked annoyed, and nothing more.

"Good evening!" he said frigidly. "I'm very much relieved to see you here, Honey."

"I—was looking for you," she said.

"Indeed!" he said, raising his eyebrows. "I was having a chat with the Chief Engineer in his cabin for a while, and when it was time for dinner, I couldn't find you. The steward assured me that you had come on board, but where you went I can't imagine."

"I'm sorry, Weaver." she said. "I was just around..."

How could she ever for a moment think that Weaver was involved in anything violent or tragic?... *I did* think that, she said to herself. That's what was in the back of my mind. He was so humiliated and so furious about Mrs. Condy—but he's like that about somebody so often. Why, just look at him! How could I ever, ever imagine anything so crazy?...

"*I had* thought," said Weaver, more and more affronted, "that we might go ashore this evening for an hour or so. I'd planned, in that case, to leave the ship promptly at eight-fifteen."

Oh, lord! Honey thought. When he finds out what's happened—and me mixed up in it—he'll be so upset, I don't know what he'll do. They won't let me leave the ship. The police will be asking me questions maybe for hours. And what I did is going to seem so—queer. Running away, and not telling anyone.

"If you'll be kind enough," said Weaver, "to let me know whether or not you care to go ashore...? If not, I'll countermand my order for a launch at eight-fifteen."

"Oh yes, I would like to," she said. politely.

"And will you join us, Miss Bewley?" he asked.

"You're *very* kind. Mr. Stapleton," said she, "but I really think I'd better *not.* I believe I'll go to bed early. Mr. Stapleton, *do* try the red snapper! Caught fresh this morning."

"Thank you, Miss Bewley. I believe I shall," said Weaver. "I'm very fond of it. I remember when I was down this way before—"

He told Miss Bewley how he had eaten red snapper, and relished it, and how he had been disappointed in the eating of angel fish, and Miss Bewley listened as if absorbed.

"Steward," said Weaver, "you might bring me an order of that red snapper, but without the sauce."

"Sorry. sir," said the steward, "but the snapper's all gone, sir. Some very nice flounder, sir...?"

That started Weaver.

'No *excuse* for this sort of thing... Your commissary department knows the number of passengers. There's no excuse for inadequate supplies." On and on, so entirely unsuspecting of what was about to happen.

It'll be bad, Honey thought. Very bad. If I'd acted with any sense... I wish the police would come now, and get it over with. What's happening now? Were these people in that cabin now, this moment...?

She was not able to think about that cabin, and what had been in it. A matter-of-fact briskness was taking possession of her; she began to think about what she would say to the police. It's a phony story, she thought, and I can't make it anything else. I'll just have to be feminine about it. I won't say I was looking for Weaver. I'll say I wanted to speak to Mrs. Condy, and that when I found her like that, I lost my nerve, and this one won't be like Michael. Even Weaver could understand it, if I lost my nerve. Older men make more allowances for a girl. I wish they'd come and get it over with.

And now she saw Mr. Basingly coming down the stairs, running down sideways, as if it were a ladder. Now! she thought, and her heart sank like a stone.

"Evening, ladies!" he said. "Evening, Mr. Stapleton! Your launch is waiting."

He sat down and took up the menu and studied it with care; there was nothing to be read in his face, cynically good-humoured as usual. Then *didn't* Michael tell him? Honey thought. Why didn't he? What's this *mean*?

She couldn't take her eyes off Basingly. When he had made his careful choice, and given his order, he looked at her and smiled; he glanced at Miss Bewley and Weaver, who were talking about hotels in Boston, then he leaned toward Honey.

"Don't worry, Mrs. Stapleton," he said, in a low and soothing voice.

"What do you *mean?*"

"She's gone—you know."

"Gone?"

"I went up to take a look, Mrs. Stapleton. Nobody there."

"But I saw—"

"I'm afraid Mrs. Condy was a little—well, a little the worse for wear this afternoon," he said. "You must have seen her when she was sleeping off the effects. But she's gone now."

"Gone? You mean you didn't find her there?"

"Not a sign of her," he said cheerfully. "She's gone ashore, luggage and all."

"Mr. Basingly... She was—" Honey lowered her voice. "She was dead, Mr. Basingly."

"Well, yes," he said smiling again. "In a way. But don't worry any more. She'd decided to leave the ship at this port, y'know, she went ashore and then she came back, collected her passport and so on, a rebate on her fare."

"Mr. Basingly... If you'd seen her."

"My dear lady, I've seen so much," he said.

The dining saloon began to revolve in slow and sickening spirals, and Honey went round with it, being sucked up to the ceiling. She gripped her hands onto the edge of the table until that stopped; then she sipped her glass of water.

"Mr. Basingly," she said, her voice still very low, but quite strong. "*I know* she was dead."

Mr. Basingly smiled.

TEN

"Now, if you're ready, Honey..." said Weaver.

"I'm all ready, Weaver."

"You'll have to take a wrap."

"All right, Weaver," she said, and went to the cabin to get one.

No. It can't really be like this, she thought.

It did not occur to her to doubt her own senses. She had never yet seen visions, heard mystic voices. She *knew* she had seen Mrs. Condy lying on the floor dead, and if a hundred people had told her otherwise, she would have believed them mistaken, or lying; all of them.

Could Mr. Basingly have been lying? she thought. I mean, to keep this from being any scandal on the ship? She remembered that story, told so unconvincingly to her by Gladwina, about the mother and daughter in Paris. The daughter had gone out, and when she returned to the hotel, her sick mother was not there, the names were gone from the register. Only years later had the heartbroken daughter learned the truth; that her mother's illness had been the plague, and that doctor, hotel manager, police, everyone had cooperated in spiriting away the poor woman the moment she drew her last breath. What if Mrs. Condy had died of a swift tropical disease?

Or if she had been murdered? Murder had been the first, and the only idea Honey had had. She had taken it for granted that Mrs. Condy had been killed. And she still thought that. I'd like talk to Michael, she said to herself.

That would come later. First, there was this to do, to go down the ladder after Weaver, down to the grating where a launch was bobbing up and down, shaken by its racing engine. And there people were getting into row boats, other people were coming back to the ship; they seemed so gay and careless in the warm night.

They reached the wharf, and Weaver stood still.

"Weaver, let's get a taxi?" she said.

"These drivers are damned independent," he said, affronted. "In most of these little ports, they're after you like a pack of wolves."

But the drivers of Puerto Azul sat in their cabs and waited and smoked their cigarettes. Some of them had proud Spanish faces, some of them were Negroes, some of them had a slant-eyed Oriental look; but they all showed the same fatalistic aloofness; there was no importuning, no eagerness. Weaver did not like that, but in the end he was obliged to walk up to a cab.

"I'll pay you a dollar an hour," he said to the driver, a boy in a peaked cap.

"Two dollars," said the boy, with a soft smile.

"Oh, no!" said Weaver, with his own smile. "I'm an old hand. I know—"

Honey moved away a little, because she never enjoyed Weaver's bargaining. I remember how mad Mother was with that man from Boston, she thought, the man who took her into a florist's to get a corsage, and then started fussing about being overcharged. She never would go out with him again.

Weaver had approached another driver now, and this time the affair was settled and they got into the cab.

"Let's stop at the hotel Mr. Basingly mentioned," said Honey.

"If you like. What's it called?"

"Well, he didn't say, but there couldn't be very many here, d'you think? Let's just tell him to stop at the best hotel."

"If you like," Weaver said, resignedly.

As the cab set off through the little town she became enchanted. You could look in through the lighted windows and see people sitting in their rooms, a group of people in rocking chairs in a big, high-ceilinged room, three old ladies in black, fanning themselves; the lanes off the main street were so dark, so narrow, so foreign.

"Weaver!" she said. "I heard somebody playing a guitar!"

"Oh, yes. Yes," he said.

There really are places like this, she thought. Courtyards, and high walls, air with this softness, stars like these, and the thrumming of a guitar. Oh—think what life could be like—if you just went ahead and lived it... Not afraid of anything, not hating anybody. Just living...

The cab stopped before a cramped little building, dimly lit, with a sign on the entrance. Grand Palace Hotel. It made her laugh.

"This couldn't be the best hotel, could it, Weaver?"

"This the *very* best 'otel!" said the driver. "'Otel Gran' Palace."

"Let's go and see what it's like," said Honey. "But I don't think this can be the place."

"What place?" asked Weaver.

"The one Mr. Basingly meant," she said. No sense telling him I want to go hunting Alma, she thought. It would just irritate him, and he'd say he wouldn't do it.

They entered a little tiled hall, very gloomy, and on the right there was a sort of cafe, equally gloomy; there was nothing at all in it but chairs and small tables, a bare floor, bare walls, jalousies across the front that was open to the street, a chandelier in the ceiling casting a harsh white light. Yet it was popular, it was filled, it was the right place. Honey saw Mrs. Pruitt and Mr. Lake, she saw the doctor with his middle-aged ladies. And she saw Alma sitting at a table with her husband and little Perez. And the sight of Alma gave her a curious shock.

"Godforsaken hole!" said Weaver. "Let's go somewhere else."

"Oh, let's have a drink as long as we're here," she said.

"Very well," he said with a sigh. "I suppose all this is a novelty to you."

"Let's sit over there, Weaver... I'd just like to speak to Alma, and ask her how she is."

"I can't understand what you see in that woman," he said.

"She's got a lot of character," said Honey.

"That's a good thing," said Weaver. "She hasn't anything else."

"She's pretty smart, Weaver. She owns the Mimosa products; she built the whole thing up herself."

"And what *is* it?"

"Oh, cosmetics and so on."

"Mimosa..." he said. "The sensitive plant... "

"Come on!" she said, smiling up at him, and he went along with her. Thank the Lord he's in such a good humour, she thought. I hope Alma is, too.

The two men rose and there was a polite exchange of salutations, and then Weaver withdrew to the next table.

"Won't you join us?" asked Lashelle.

"Well, thanks, but we've got a taxi waiting," said Honey.

"I'll bring my drink over to your table if you like," said Alma. "These two have got so much to talk about."

"Oh, Meeses Lashelle!" cried Perez.

"I'll be back," she said with a half-scornful indulgence, and took up her glass.

"Hello!" she said to Weaver, casually.

"Good evening, Mrs. Lashelle," said Weaver.

She didn't even try to make herself agreeable to him; she began talking to Honey about a watch she had seen in a shop window. "I might buy it," she said, "if I can get it for my own price."

Behind her, Honey could hear Lashelle and Perez talking in low voices, and very fast, talking a foreign language.

"That's Spanish your husband's talking, isn't it?" she asked.

"Yes," said Alma. "He speaks Portuguese and Dutch, too."

"Did he and Perez know each other before?"

"No. But Hilary can make friends very easily. He's travelled around so much; he knows how to get on with people."

He's certainly getting on with Mr. Perez all right. Honey thought. And suddenly that talk began to worry her, that low rapid stream of talk going on, going past her like a river, never to be recaptured. She glanced at Lashelle, and in profile his handsome face looked sharper, looked wolfish, she thought.

He did it, she thought, without surprise, without emphasis.

There was not one thing known to her that connected him with Mrs. Condy's death. But that seemed to her of no importance. She knew what he had done to Alma, and that was enough. He did it, she said to herself. He killed her, and then he got rid of her somehow. If I could only tell what they were saying, I might hear something. 'Muchacha,' Perez said. I know that word, it means 'girl..' If I could—

"Is this your first trip to the West Indies, Mrs. Lashelle?" Weaver asked.

"It's my first trip anywhere on a boat,' said Alma. "And it'll be my last, too."

Oh God! Don't say that, Honey cried to herself.

"Perhaps if you tried a larger ship..." said Weaver.

"Captain Lashelle likes small ships," said Alma. "He ought to know, he's travelled so much."

There! Honey thought. 'Hombre,' Mr. Perez said. They're not just talking like two strangers; they're saying something that's important to them. If I could *only*... She opened her purse and got out a little pencil and a folded piece of paper on which she had written a shopping list. You can't get hold of much in a foreign language; you don't even know where the words begin or end... But I've got good ears. I can catch something...

"What's that?" Alma asked. "Shorthand?"

"Yes," Honey answered. "I like to jot things down about this trip. For my diary."

"Not much *here* to jot down," said Alma. "The next island's going to be English, and maybe I can find *something* there. Even a couple of little cotton dresses."

"I certainly hope so," said Honey, trying to catch another word from the conversation behind her.

"Here's the waiter, Honey; what will you have to drink?"

"Oh... Beer, thank you, Weaver."

"Mrs. Lashelle?"

"Nothing more for me. I've had too many drinks on this trip. It doesn't do your figure any good, or your complexion either."

They say 'ja' like Germans, Honey thought. 'Dios,' that's another word I know. If I just put down what I hear—how it sounds.

"Our electric fan is out of order," Alma was saying. "There's certainly a jinx following me this trip."

"Too bad!" said Weaver.

I've got to rescue him, Honey thought. This is a little too much for him. Alma won't even try to be nice to him....

"Are you going on somewhere else after this, Alma?" she asked.

"Not me!" said Alma. "Perez wanted to show us around, but not for me. I told Hilary he could go if he wanted, but he'd have to take me back to the ship first. There's nothing *I* want to see in this place. I want to get my sleep."

"I'm afraid Weaver and I'll have to go now. We've got a taxi waiting."

"Well... See you some more," said Alma.

The young Assistant Purser came to the door-way and looked about the room anxiously; then he came over to little Perez.

"Oh, excuse me, Mr. Perez," he said. "But can you tell me where Mrs. Condy's gone?"

"Oh, I theenk," said Perez, lowering his lashes.

"Come, Honey!" said Weaver taking her arm.

"Wait..." she said, very low.

"If you'd be good enough to give me her address here—"

"She has went off from this island," said Perez. "By plane, she has went."

"Do you know where, Mr. Perez?"

"Curacao."

"You're quite sure, Mr. Perez?"

"I am aw'fly sure," he said. "She tell me herself."

"D'you happen to know what time she came ashore, Mr. Perez?"

"Oh... Seex o'clock, little more or less."

"Did you *see* her come ashore, Mr. Perez?" the young A. P. asked.

"Me? Oh yes, in a rowing boat."

"Honey!" said Weaver. "What are you doing?" He pulled at her arm, and she went along with him.

"Things like that..." said Weaver. "Standing in a public place listening to a conversation that has nothing to do with you.... Things like that make a very poor impression."

"I know," she said with a humility that surprised him.

"Well, there's no harm done," he said, magnaminously. "Where would you like to go now?"

"Suppose we go back to the ship, Weaver?"

"Nothing would suit me better," he said, and they got into the taxi.

She took his hand and held it, but not even to herself would she admit what made her cling to him, what forgiveness she asked of him in her silence. He's *a gentleman* through and through, she told herself holding his hand tight.

"What an appalling woman that Mrs. Lashelle is," he said.

"She hasn't got much tact, I admit; but she's got good points, Weaver."

"They must be very subtle," he said. "I *cannot* see what you find in that woman."

"She's—sort of lonely, Weaver."

"Who isn't?" he said. "My God! Who isn't?"

ELEVEN

The ship was strange to-night. One or two people sat in their chairs on the lighted deck, very quiet, facing the shore, like spectators waiting for a play to begin; the alleyway was empty and quiet, even their cabin had a blank look, so hot, so bright, so tidy.

I can't lie down here and go to sleep, Honey thought, in a sort of horror. Where's Mrs. Condy?

She sat down on her bed and began to take off her shoes and stockings. "Honey!" said Weaver sternly. "The curtain!"

"There's nothing out there but the ocean, Weaver," she said mildly.

"A boat could come past," he said, and jerked the curtain across the port. Then he went into the bathroom to undress, as he always did. Honey sat where she was in a sick daze. Why did Perez lie like that? she thought.

He had lied in such a careless way, so blithely, almost at random. He had said he knew where Mrs. Condy was going, he had said he had seen her come ashore. It had been a dreadful thing to hear. Where was she now?

Honey thought she knew. There was, she thought, only one grave for Mrs. Condy, one place where she could be hidden and cause no trouble, make no mute accusation. It was not far from her cabin to the rail; the boat deck was dark and there were times when it was deserted.

And there was one person, she thought, who had the cruel bravado for such an act. Laschelle, who played his monstrous game with Alma under the eyes of a shipload of people.

There was in Honey no abstract passion for justice. She had never expected it for herself; she took it for granted that some people were bad, and would treat you badly. She was not concerned with avenging the poor dead woman; that would have seemed to her impossible. She and her mother had many little phrases they used to express that point of view. What's done is done, they would say. No use crying over spilt milk. Mrs. Condy was gone and nothing could bring her back, nothing could help her now.

But what had happened to her could happen to Alma. If Captain Lashelle gets away with *this,* Honey thought, nothing will stop him. He had to be stopped.

It's a job for a man, she said to herself. I don't know how to cope with this. I've got to have help.

The bathroom door opened, and out came Weaver in his dressing-gown.

"Honey?" he said. "What's the matter? Don't you feel well?"

She was a little surprised herself by the sudden chill that seized her. Her teeth chattered, her feet were cold as ice, she put her shaking hands to her temples in an unconscious gesture of despair.

"I can't—go to bed," she said. "I can't—lie here... I can't do it, Weaver!"

"What's the matter with you?" he cried in a panic.

She couldn't tell *him*. Only she could not lie down in the dark. Not ever. For then she would see Mrs. Condy again, with ashes scattered over her white face. She had seen that, and had been able to walk away, to talk, to eat and drink. But now the whole shock and the whole horror came upon her.

"I can't *do* it...!"

'Do *what?*" Weaver shouted. "What's the matter with you? Are you crazy?"

He rang the bell, but she didn't care what he did, as long as he did not turn out the light. Doctor Lovejoy came and asked her questions.

"I'm c-c-cold," she said. "I feel—sick... I feel—queer..."

"Nervous chill," he told Weaver.

"She's not nervous!" Weaver said in a rage. "There's nothing for her to be nervous about. It's malaria."

Mrs. Doakes was sent for, and she came, sweet as sugar, and helped Honey to get into bed.

"You've been overdoing, madam," she said "In this hot weather.... There...! Comfy now, madam?"

Doctor Lovejoy came back into the cabin. "I'll give you a hypodermic, Mrs. Stapleton." he said with a sort of distaste.

She began to weep, because he was so disapproving, Weaver so angry, Mrs. Doakes so false. Never, never had she felt so friendless.

"Then I'll put out the light—" said Mrs. Doakes.

"No! No! Please don't!" said Honey.

"You can't expect the hypodermic to take effect while you're sitting up like that in all this glare of light," said Weaver.

"It's not—ever going—to take effect...." she said, with tears running down her face. "I—just—can't—lie down here—in the dark."

"Very well!" said Weaver, loudly, "You needn't wait any longer Mrs. Doakes. Very kind of you to get up and come here at this hour."

"I'll be *glad* to stay, sir—"

"No. No, thanks. I'll look after Mrs. Stapleton."

I can't close my eyes, Honey thought. Because then I'll *see* her. No...

When I feel better—I'm going to tell the Captain. They can still—find her....

The tears were stopping at last.

"Weaver," she said, trying to speak steadily. "Weaver, I've got to speak to the Captain."

"What?" he said.

"Please, Weaver, send for the Captain."

"Honey," he said, "you're out of your mind."

"Listen, Weaver... Weaver, please listen. Mrs. Condy's been *murdered.*"

He rose straight as a poker in his dressing-gown.

"This—will have to stop!" he said.

"Weaver, I *saw* her! Weaver...!"

He was standing by the bed looking down at her. The top of his head was rising to a point, he was growing taller and taller and taller; he was turning white like a candle, shooting up to the ceiling, thinner and longer and thinner. It was absorbingly interesting to watch; she let her eyes follow the elongating figure right up to the ceiling and then she began to float up after him. So pleasant...

When she opened her eyes, she knew that a long time had gone by, a very long time. But she was nicely rested. She stretched out her long legs with a sigh of comfort. There was a breeze blowing, and the sky outside the port was a deep, rich blue.

Only something was happening, something that must not happen. What was it? What was it? Something to be stopped....

The ship was moving.

She sat up, and saw Weaver's bed empty; she rang the bell, and waited with a fast-beating heart, and presently Mrs. Doakes entered.

"*Good* morning, madam! Did you have a good night?"

Honey forgot to answer; she stared blankly into Mrs. Doakes' face. The ship was moving, sailing smoothly and steadily ahead, away from Mrs. Condy.

"Are you ready for your breakfast, madam?" asked Mrs. Doakes, so sweetly.

"Yes, thank you," said Honey.

She felt very well this morning, and entirely composed. She looked back upon her miserable collapse of the night before with wonder. Weaver was right, she thought, I'm not nervous as a rule. But when he said I didn't have anything to be nervous about....

She could think of Mrs. Condy without that terror now; she thought of her with pity and a stern amazement. I've told three people, she thought, Michael, and he told Mr. Basingly, and I told Weaver. And nobody's done anything. But *I'm* going to do something.

Mrs. Doakes brought her a very appetising breakfast, grapefruit, coffee, toast, bacon and eggs; she ate it leisurely, she lit a cigarette with the second cup of coffee. But where's Weaver? she thought, suddenly.

Her watch showed a quarter past ten. He was always an early riser, he would surely have finished his breakfast long ago. It was queer that he didn't come to see how she was. And how did it happen that his bed was made up?

Well, I can bear to wait, she thought. He was so mean last night. Better not to remember how mean he had been. Better just go ahead and think what could be done without counting on him.

Count on Michael then? She narrowed her eyes, watching the smoke of her cigarette. She knew that she could count on Michael, could turn to him if she wished. And she knew what it would mean. If she were to think of Michael as her ally, her partner in this affair, it meant a repudiation of Weaver.

She thought about that. Nope, she said to herself after a while, I'm not going to do it. Weaver didn't turn out to be what I thought he'd be, but probably I'm not like he thought, either. I went into this thing with my eyes open, and I'm not going to let him down. If he just *won't* help me about Alma, I'll have to find somebody sort of official.

The Captain would be the right person. But the Captain, with his fringe of ginger hair and his gnome-like smile, was strangely intimidating. You couldn't impress him, she thought. He wouldn't care if you were— nice-looking, or anything like that. I wish there was a detective, I mean, one of those sympathetic men that understand character, like Charlie Chan, or Sherlock Holmes, or that one I saw in that movie. That English one, with a moustache. Well...!

She sighed and got out of bed; she ran a bath and got into it, and lying in the warm green water she thought again how queer it was that Weaver hadn't appeared at all.

There was a knock at the door while she was dressing, and Mrs. Doakes entered.

"Oh, are you up, madam?" she said, her eyes flickering up and down observing the twelve dollar, hand-made, ivory satin slip. "Mr. Stapleton told me to let him know when you were ready to see him, madam."

"Where is he?" asked Honey.

"He's not so well this morning, madam, I'm sorry to say."

'Where is he? On deck?"

"Oh no, madam! He's not feeling at all fit. He's lying down."

"Lying down where?"

"Oh, in his cabin, madam."

"I see," said Honey.

I'm not going to give *you* any satisfaction, she thought. I'm not going to ask you questions about my own husband. If he's gone and got a cabin for himself, fine; he can stay in it.

But back came the familiar doubt. Maybe he really was sick; you never could tell about Weaver. Maybe his meanness came from some mysterious malady, maybe he suffered more than she could imagine.

She finished her dressing slowly, waiting for him to come. She put on a dress of ice-white sharkskin, she played with her hair, doing it this way and that way. But he did not come, and she grew impatient. I want to see Alma, she thought. She seemed all right last night, but—

Then she remembered the shorthand notes she had taken. It was not to be expected that Lashelle had said anything of especial significance in that public place, and it was not likely that she had caught anything intelligible either. But there could be something in it, she thought, even just a word. Because I bet that Mr. Perez is mixed up in it somehow. Saying he'd seen Mrs. Condy come ashore.

She opened her purse to look over these notes, and there was the envelope addressed to Weaver. Oh my gosh! she thought. It may be something important. It had no stamp on it, it must have come from someone on the ship. Mrs. Condy? Why ever would she write Weaver a note? But you never can tell. They did get on together—and I can't think of anybody else on board....

She went out on deck, and the brilliant sun and the air, the people, startled and dazzled her. Here was the world, going on with the business of living, cheerful and gay, Mrs. Condy entirely forgotten. Mrs. Pruitt and Mr. Lake were sitting side by side, and standing before them was the man she had seen on the boat deck outside Mrs. Condy's cabin; the lean, tall Mr. Smith, in a loose-fitting white suit, and a queer limp white hat lined with green. As Mrs. Pruitt waved her hand to Honey, he took off the queer hat, and looked at her with a lugubrious and mistrustful gaze.

She stopped short, remembering everything for a moment.... But she was able to recover herself and go on, looking for—somebody, for the person to whom she was to tell everything, and from whom she was to get the counsel she so needed.

On the other side of the deck she found Michael, leaning back against the rail, his ankles crossed. He straightened up, and waited for her.

"How are *you?*" he asked, politely.

"Fine, thanks," she answered.

They stood at the rail together in silence; in unsmiling and almost severe silence.

"Do you know any Spanish?" she asked, after a moment.

"Yes," he said, "quite a bit."

"I took down some notes," she said. "Some words. I don't know if they make any sense..."

"Well, let's have them," he said. "We can go into the Social Hall."

They sat down side by side in chintz-covered arm-chairs, in full view of everyone who went up or down the stairway; both of them tall and fair, both with an air of business-like coolness.

"Some of the words I know," she said, looking at the notes. "I know muchacha, and dinero and hombre.... But what is 'vi-oo-da'?"

"Widow," he said.

She read out the syllables; some of them meant nothing, but some of them he could recognize.

"You have a good ear," he said. "You ought to be able to learn Spanish without much trouble."

It was as if he rebuked her for not learning Spanish; for not knowing more.

"I think I'll probably take it up," she said. "I've been taking French." She paused. "And piano and singing and dancing," she said.

He was not impressed. She went on.

"Then I've got dor-mi-lo-na, if that's anything," she said.

"It means—how do you put it—someone drowsy—sleepyhead."

"Oh...!" she said, staring at him.

"Does that ring a bell?" he asked.

It did ring a bell, like an alarum. But was Mrs. Condy Sleepyhead? Honey thought.

That one idea attracted a dozen others to it, so that it grew and grew and took on a solid form. If Mrs. Condy had been Lashelle's Sleepyhead, there was good reason for her to die. He surely had not wanted her on the same ship with Alma.

He hadn't wanted Alma to begin with. But she had come, and she had stayed. Two wives, were they? One of them had had to go. Captain

Lashelle wasn't on shore with the others, Honey thought. Alma said he'd gone back to get a jacket for her. He could have been there, shut in the bathroom, when I was in the cabin. He could have—

"What are you thinking about?" Michael asked, rather imperiously.

"About Mrs. Condy," she answered.

"I wanted to talk to you about that," he said. "I wanted to advise you—" He paused a moment. "To keep clear of that business."

"How?" she asked. "Just drop it, you mean?"

"Yes, I do," he said, with emphasis.

"I found her there dead—"

"You can't be sure of that," said Michael. "You didn't touch her, or—"

"She was dead all right," said Honey. It was a relief to talk like this, straight and hard. You didn't have to consider Michael's feelings. "Her eyes were wide open—and there were ashes all over them."

"She may just have been out, cold—"

"She was dead," said Honey.

"Well, nobody's going to believe that," said Michael.

"Do you?" she asked.

They looked squarely at each other.

"It doesn't make any difference what I believe," he said. "I'm advising you to drop this."

He was pretty imperious, pretty lordly. But she didn't mind that. He was anxious and worried, and it was on her account, she knew that.

"Whoever it was who killed Mrs. Condy is still around," she said. "I don't think that's so good."

"Well, look here! Suppose, just to please you, we admit that she was dead, there's no reason to think it was murder. Much more likely to have been an accident. A heart attack, maybe, or acute alcoholism."

"If it had been an accident," said Honey, "she'd still be there. Nobody'd have wanted to get rid of her."

He brought out a package of cigarettes, he lit one for her, and one for himself; there they sat smoking, with people going past them while they talked about a murder.

"All right!" he said, "Even if it was, you can't help Mrs. Condy now. You can't do any good. And you might do a lot of harm."

"How?"

"I don't want to tell you," he said. "In fact, I'm not going to tell you. But maybe you'll take my word for it that if you go on with this, if you manage to stir up a lot of trouble, you'll regret it."

"Do you realize," said Honey, "that you're advising me to let somebody get away with murder?"

"That's it," said Michael.

He means Weaver did it, Honey thought. That's the only thing he *could* mean. But he's wrong. He doesn't know Weaver.

Yet she, who knew Weaver so well, had thought that. It had been the first thing that had sprung to her mind, paralyzing her. Could there be something about Weaver she did not know, but only felt? Something that other people could see...?

No, she told herself. If Mrs. Condy was that—*Dormilona,* that ties it up with Captain Lashelle. He's the one. Look what he's done—what he's tried to do already.

Sleepyhead... she thought. That sort of fits Mrs. Condy. She had that way, as if she were walking in her sleep. She was so vague and so careless about how she looked. Maybe Michael found some clue that points to Weaver. Maybe Weaver went to her cabin to see her. He *was* sort of hypnotized by her. But he didn't kill her. He couldn't kill anyone.

"Will you keep out of it?" asked Michael.

She looked up at him again, and shook her head.

"I'm going to pin it on Captain Lashelle, she said, thoughtfully.

"My—God!" said Michael, staring at her.

She rose, and Michael with her.

"Well..." she said. "Do you feel like helping me?"

"I'm sorry..." he said. "I'm very sorry, but—no."

TWELVE

There was nothing sad or miserable in that refusal. Michael wasn't abandoning her, or letting her down; he was opposing her for what he thought was her own good.

He's as stubborn as a mule, she thought, glancing at his blunt, boyish profile. He was stubborn, and he was steady; he wouldn't change. You could count on him.

"Well... Au revoir!" she said with a smile, and went away.

At the foot of the stairs she met Mr. Basingly.

"Oh, Mrs. Stapleton," he said, "I was looking for you... How are you this morning?"

"Fine!" she said and flushed a little, wondering if he had heard of her breakdown last night. She was ashamed of that.

"I'd like to have a little cocktail party," he said, "If you and Mr. Stapleton are feeling fit...?"

"I don't know about Weaver..." she said.

"Sorry to put him in a cabin like that," said Basingly. "But later on, I dare say, we can do something better for him. There'll be people getting off at Trinidad."

"I see," said Honey.

She wanted to hide the surprise and the distress she felt. Basingly took it for granted that Weaver was going to remain in a cabin by himself; there was, apparently, no question of his returning to Honey. And what's the meaning of *that?* she thought. Weaver going off like that without a word to me. It's—pretty much of an insult.

"What's the number of his cabin, Mr. Basingly?" she asked. "I've forgotten."

"Oh, eighty-two," he said. "I'm sorry we couldn't do better."

"Well, we both know you've done the best you could," said Honey, standing straight and tall, the colour still hot in her cheeks. Mrs. Weaver Stapleton, she was.

"And—er..." said Basingly, "I thought perhaps you'd like to know... I mean you were a bit upset about Mrs. Condy. I thought you'd be glad to know that she's quite all right."

"I'd like to hear all about that, Mr. Basingly," she said, and he glanced at her quickly, a little startled by the sternness of her tone.

"Oh, certainly," he said. "I—naturally, after I'd heard what you'd seen, I looked into the matter. Y'see, earlier in the afternoon, Mrs. Condy came back on board, and told me she was leaving the ship. We arranged every-thing. She—" He paused. "In view of what you saw, I'm afraid I'll have to admit that she was a little—well... A bit unsteady on her feet, and so on, but she knew what she was doing. When she left me, of course she may have had a couple more. And she may simply have collapsed, for a time."

"But you think she's all right now?"

"Oh yes! I tried at first to find someone who'd seen her get into a boat. You've no idea how difficult a thing like that is. The man stationed at the gangway remembered having seen her go ashore, and come back. But he couldn't be sure whether or not he'd seen her into a boat here. Too much coming and going. I couldn't get any satisfaction. But at last I found a pas-senger who'd seen her and spoken to her on shore."

"Mr. Perez?"

"That's right—Mr. Perez."

"And he's the *only one?*"

He gave an uncomfortable smile.

"As it happens," he said, "Mr. Perez has had a message from her—a radio message from the island. He was good enough to show me the mes-sage. She's stopping at a hotel for a day or two, and then she's going to South America by plane."

"What hotel?"

"Er—" he said, and all his long, long years of passenger troubles came to his aid. "The Dominion Hotel, Mrs. Stapleton," he said with admirable courtesy.

"Thank you, Mr. Basingly," said Honey.

What Perez said, and the message Perez had got, convinced her not at all. He could have sent himself a message, and he could have told a lie. Indeed she was sure he had been lying. People believed him because they wanted to believe him; nobody was interested in what had happened to Mrs. Condy, just as nobody had been interested in what happened to Alma.

It was the first time she had encountered the full force of the world's laissez-faire. People, by and large, weren't cruel, weren't heartless; it was simply that they couldn't believe anything could happen. A shot in the night was a car back-firing; a cry for help was just somebody skylarking. Mrs. Condy lying on the floor with ashes over her face was only someone who had had too many drinks.

She had never been able to convince anyone that Alma was in danger. That had been bad enough. But this was worse beyond measure. This was the supreme injury to be done Mrs. Condy. She was to be denied even the dignity of death.

"No," said Honey, looking at Mr. Basingly.

"I beg your pardon?" he said.

"Mrs. Condy was *dead* when I saw her," said Honey.

It was as if a mask were wiped off his face, and he looked at her with a frank and brutal hostility.

"We can't have this, Mrs. Stapleton," he said. "We can't have the ship upset—the passengers alarmed. I went into that cabin myself and there was no one there. There was no trace of anything out of the way. It's a serious matter to start a rumour of this sort. If it goes any further I'll be obliged to take it up with the Captain."

"I think that would be a darn good idea," said Honey turning away.

But for all her valour, she was frightened. She did not know what powers the Captain of a ship might have; her faith in her own power was shaken. She had taken it for granted that the truth was obvious, that if you spoke in complete sincerity you would be believed. But it was not like that.

It—scares you, she thought. Why, even in court, even if you'd taken an oath, and were telling what you *knew* was true, maybe nobody would believe you. Maybe that happens—often... She could imagine how it would be to stand in court, a prisoner, most desperately and vehemently telling the truth, and looking into blank and unbelieving faces.

No! she said to herself. No! it can't be like that. The truth wins in the end. I know that *I'm* going to win, in the end—and to hell with that fine Mr. Basingly. She went on slowly down the stairs. To hell with the Captain too, she said to herself. Who's *he,* anyhow?

That made her feel much better. She stopped a steward and asked where Cabin Eighty-two was.

"D deck, madam," he said. "This way, madam Down the stairs, madam, and to your left."

D deck was inferior; it was hot down here, and there was a smell of oil and brass polish and disinfectant. It was a strange, a queer place for Weaver to be. And why had he done this? Why had he deserted her? She went along the alleyway, looking at the numbers; most of the doors were hooked open and she could see into dark little cabins. Eighty-six...

She stopped short there with a shiver of fear. For in that cabin was a horrible little brown head hanging up by its ropy, yellow hair. Like the one she had seen in Mrs. Condy's cabin.

I'm getting too jittery, she thought, and went on to Cabin Eighty-two.

That door was closed, and she knocked.

"Who is it?" asked Weaver's voice, and it seemed to her as if she had not heard it for a very long time.

"It's me," she said.

"Come in," said Weaver.

It was an inside cabin with no port; the electric light was turned on, and the fan was spinning at full speed, and Weaver in his dressing-gown sat in a basket chair, doing nothing at all.

"Er—close the door, will you, please?" he said.

And when she had closed it, a great embarrassment came over her, so that she stood there speechless. She could not ask Weaver why he had left her, why he was here in this dark and airless little cabin. And he, too, was embarrassed, he frowned a little, and cleared his throat, and rose.

"Sit down!" he said.

There were no other chairs, and he seated himself in the lower berth where he had to bend forward, his hands on his knees; he looked uncomfortable and unhappy.

"How are you feeling?" he asked.

"I'm all right, Weaver, thank you. How are you?"

"Not too well," he answered.

There was a silence, an unbearable silence.

"Have you got a cigarette, Weaver?" she asked.

He brought one to her; as he leaned over to light it, they did not look at each other. He went back to the lower berth, and sat down, and again he cleared his throat.

"I feel that it's necessary..." he said. "Necessary for my health to—be alone for the present."

A hot wave of colour rose in her cheeks, a tide of anger and shame and amazement rose in her heart. She sat still, and drew on the cigarette, and it all ebbed away; she felt no anger, nothing at all.

"I got this invitation," he said. "Basingly's asked us to cocktails in his cabin at six."

"Oh, did he?"

"I—we might as well go, don't you think? I mean—"

She waited, but he did not go on.

"What *do* you mean, Weaver?" she said evenly.

"I mean—" he said, "I hope you're not going to be—childish. I mean we—naturally we'll go here and there together."

"I don't want to go, thank you."

"I ask you to go, as a favour." he said. Her blue eyes were fixed on his face.

"To keep up appearances?" she asked.

"If you like to put it that way."

She went on smoking her cigarette. She had no clue to this behavior of his, and nothing could have induced her to ask him a single question. She scarcely cared what the reason was; the fact itself was enough. Her husband had left her. That was the supreme humiliation.

"I ask you, as a *favour,* to come to this party of Basingly's," he said. "There's no decent way of getting out of it. It's—simply making both of us conspicuous. You—you can't—"

"All right," she said rising. "I'll go. I don't care what I do."

"Don't say that!" he cried.

"That's what I mean," she said. "I don't care what I do."

She went out, closing the door behind her.

THIRTEEN

She went back to the big cabin on the deck above and put on her yellow bathing suit; she looked at herself in the big mirror on the bathroom door. And it seemed to her that her beauty was gone, and all the happiness and all the power it had given her. She was no longer a cherished and pampered creature; she was alone.

There were people in the pool; she swam around with them, and came out, and Mrs. Pruitt sitting on the hatch-cover called to her.

"Going ashore this afternoon?" she asked.

"I didn't know we were getting anywhere," Honey said.

"Three-hour stop at another island," said Mr. Lake. "Nothing to see, nothing to do."

"I don't know why you take trips," said Mrs. Pruitt.

"Don't you?" said he.

Their eyes met for an instant. Mrs. Pruitt was somewhere close to forty; she was not beautiful, not glamourous. But she had Mr. Lake roped and tied. She managed excellently; there was not a trace of possessiveness about her, she never asked him to do anything, she just went her own way, gay and amiable, and he followed her. I used to be pretty good myself, Honey thought.

"That Mr. Smith is strangely interested in you," said Mrs. Pruitt.

"Why is it strange?" asked Mr. Lake. "Personally, I'd call it very natural."

"Not from *him,*" said Mrs. Pruitt. "He's a man of mystery. I heard he was a detective."

"A detective?" Honey repeated, startled.

A detective standing on the boat deck outside Mrs. Condy's cabin...? It would be the most enormous relief to believe that, to feel that some trained and competent person was watching, observing, getting ready to act.

"He asked me questions about you," said Mrs. Pruitt, "and he's asked other people. I believe he thinks you're a spy."

"And a very fine spy she'd be," said Mr. Lake.

It was hard for Honey to keep her mind on what they said. The thought of Mr. Smith's being a detective was growing more and more important as she contemplated it. I've got troubles of my own, she thought, but nothing compared to Alma.

And she thought that now she would give all her attention to Alma's affair. Something had happened to her own life; what had seemed a structure almost too solid, almost like a prison, had collapsed, there were no walls left standing.

I'll never take Weaver back, she thought. Maybe he'll never want to come back, but even if he begged me on his knees, I wouldn't, I couldn't. I don't hate him, but I despise him. *He's* no gentleman. Everybody on the ship will know that he's walked out on me, and just about everybody will think it's because I've done something.

She took off her bathing cap, and the breeze stirred her light, glittering hair; the tropic sun came down in a fiery rain. Michael was standing by the pool smoking; she glanced at him, but very briefly. She was not going to think about him either. Only about Alma.

If Mrs. Condy *was* Sleepyhead, and Captain Lashelle's got rid of her, then maybe he'll lay off Alma. If his chief worry was having two wives around at once, the danger's over....

But the danger from a man like Lashelle could never be over; Alma could never be safe with him. Above all when she was so utterly unsuspecting. Had Mrs. Condy been equally trusting? There had been no expression of terror on her face, no expression at all, except perhaps a faint wonder.

The bugle blew, and everyone began to gather up towels and wraps and drift off, and Honey went too. It was strange to go into that big cabin, so neat, filled with sunshine, to be alone in it; she dressed, and it was strange to be going down to lunch alone. If any one asks me, she thought, I'll say Weaver's sick. They can think what they like.

I won't care.

Yet to walk into the dining saloon alone was the hardest thing she had ever had to do. She imagined an undertone of murmurs. Sh-sh-sh... Her husband's taken a cabin by himself. Sh-sh-sh... There must be some reason for that... He wouldn't do that for nothing. A man of very good family...

Basingly and Miss Bewley were sitting at the table; Basingly gave his cynical actor's smile, Miss Bewley smiled in her own way. Will she take Weaver's side? she thought. She's been awfully nice to me, but still she's a Weaver kind of person.

Basingly of course was an enemy, and a formidable one. Very affable he was to her now, and she responded in the same tone, but with an effort. She had, in the past, admired this type of behaviour on the screen, this suave conversation between enemies—with undercurrents. It seemed to her marvellously well-bred. But just now, she was not attracted by good breeding. She felt like being tough.

"You ought to go ashore, Mrs. Stapleton," he said. "If you drive up in the hills, there's a beautiful view."

So what? she thought. "Oh, is there?" she said.

"But it's such a very *brief* stop," said Miss Bewley. "I'm afraid, Mr. Basingly, that the *passengers* are so much less *interesting* to you than *cargo.*"

He gave a polite and meaningless laugh. And then Weaver appeared. He sat down at the table, he talked exactly as he always talked, he was attentive to Honey. "Steward, bring Mrs. Stapleton some chutney.... Is this fan blowing on you, Honey?"

All so well-bred, like a play. I thought I wanted to know people like this, Honey reflected. I thought I wanted a life like this. But I don't. I'd rather be eating in a diner with—a crowd of truck drivers. On went the pleasant talk, and she, insulted, injured, had to take her part.

And then along came Captain Lashelle, handsome and engaging, his dark-blue eyes dancing.

"Alma doesn't want any lunch," he said to Honey, in a low and confidential tone. "Afraid of gaining weight." He paused, smiling into her eyes. "I thought I'd better explain to you," he said. "You've shown so much interest in Alma."

He had an undisguised air of triumph; gay as a lark was he. And it seemed to Honey that everyone had triumphed over her, leaving her completely discredited and defeated. This was the nadir. Her pride, her spirit, her vital energy had deserted her; she sat in silence, not trying any more, not caring.

When she rose from the table, Weaver went with her.

"Do you contemplate going ashore?" he asked.

"I don't think so," she said.

"If you do..." he said, and paused in the alleyway leading to her cabin. He took out his wallet. "If fifty dollars—" he began.

"I—don't want it..." she said. "I don't want *anything*—ever any more."

He put the wallet back into his pocket with a gesture of formal elegance; he raised his eyebrows.

"Don't you do that!" she said evenly.

"Er—do what?" he asked.

"Don't you look like that," she said. "I don't know what you think you're—"

He turned and walked away, and after a minute she went on down the alleyway to the cabin. She locked herself in there and she cried, in great anger, and a still greater humiliation. If I had enough money, she thought, I'd get off this ship and get home, some way.

Standing at the port, she caught sight of a green island—she spun round on her heel and sat down in an armchair, hot, flushed, tear-stained; she could hear footsteps and voices from the deck.

"Oh, isn't it beautiful!" someone cried.

I wouldn't go out there for anything on earth, she thought. Michael's bound to hear about Weaver, about how my husband just walked out on me and got a cabin to himself. I don't feel like seeing Michael or anybody else. What's the *matter* with Weaver? What did he do it for? His 'health,' he said. And look at the way he said it. Why, you'd think I was—I don't know what. Just beneath contempt. He hasn't even bothered to make up a good lie.

Oh, if only, only I could get away. If I could get home.... She had stopped crying now; she lay back in the chair, limp, tired, so very hot. There was no breeze now that the ship was anchored; there was a feeling of stagnation, all stir and motion ceased.

Someone knocked at the door.

"Who is it?" Honey asked, sternly.

"It's the stewardess, madam," answered Mrs. Doakes's sweet, sweet voice.

"What do you want?"

"Mr. Stapleton says, will you meet him outside the Purser's office, madam, at six sharp?"

"Yes," said Honey after a moment.

It would be just too bad if I was 'conspicuous,' she said to herself. Suppose I should feel like being 'conspicuous?' Suppose I made a scene? I'd *love* to! I didn't know I had it in me, but that's how I feel. Right there, outside the Purser's office...

Weaver! Why have you deserted your wife? She imagined herself saying that, with low passionate intensity, she imagined how Weaver would look, and a slow smile came over her face. Weaver, my heart is broken. Heaven is my witness that never did I wrong you in thought or deed.

She began to laugh, thinking of that scene. She lit a cigarette and walked up and down the cabin with a hand on her hip. She saw herself in the mirror, and she hoped that she looked tough. Flaunting, coolly amused. She began to sing, and in French, too. Parlez moi d'amour.

Then she took a bath, a long one, and then she dressed in a long black silk skirt and a white ruffled blouse with little amethyst buttons. But still it was only five o'clock. Well, I'll go and see Alma, she thought. I haven't seen her for a long time.

She went out into the alleyway and knocked at the next door. There was some sound in response, a queer muffled sound; she waited and knocked again.

"Whaddyou *want?*" called Alma's voice.

"It's me," said Honey.

"Well—get *out!*" called Alma.

"Alma... Don't you feel well?" she asked "Alma—is anything wrong?"

There were stumbling steps and a crash and an oath.

"Alma! Alma, please open the door!" she cried, rattling the handle.

"What's the matter, Mrs. Stapleton?" asked Lashelle's voice beside her.

"Something's wrong with Alma," she said.

"There's nothing wrong," he said. "You—"

The door crashed open, and Alma stood there, barefoot in a pink satin slip, with blood running down her face, and her black hair wild.

"Get *out!*" she said to Honey.

Lashelle stepped into the cabin. "Excuse me!" he said, and closed the door.

The ship's whistle blew, and Honey pressed her hand against her mouth, leaning back against the bulkhead. What was that? she kept asking herself. What was that? What's the matter with Alma? What was it...? Why was she locked in there alone, with blood running down her face? What's he done to her?

Mrs. Condy had died. People did die. And nobody believed it, nobody noticed. I won't be—like that again, she thought. I ran away before—and that's why she's at the bottom of the sea. But this time...

She went away, past the square, and aft to the doctor's cabin; she knocked and he called, "Come in!"

He was sitting at his desk smoking. "And what's wrong now, Mrs. Stapleton?" he asked, not rising.

She was in a new world of rude and hostile people.

"It's Mrs. Lashelle," she said. "She's hurt herself."

"How?"

"I don't know. There was a cut—a wound—on her face. Please go and see her."

"Did she send for me?"

"Please go and see her."

"I asked you, did-she-send-for-me?"

"Look here!" said Honey. "I've told you that one of the passengers is injured. I'm going now to tell the steward and the stewardess, and anyone else I come across, that I reported the accident to you. If anything goes wrong, maybe you can laugh it off. Maybe."

"Where's the husband?"

"He's there. Shut up in the cabin with her."

"He's there?" The doctor rose. "Now Mrs. Mmmmmm..." he said with a very unconvincing benevolence. "You mustn't worry. Some little mishap, that's all. Very likely he cut himself when he was shaving."

"What?" said Honey, puzzled.

"Get a good night's rest," he said. "Don't worry your head about him."

He went past her to open the door, and with him went a fine aroma of whiskey.

"He'll be all right after a good night's rest," he said. "Nerves."

Honey went back to her cabin and rang the bell, and presently Mrs. Doakes came.

"May I help you, madam?" she asked.

"Do you look after Mrs. Lashelle?"

"Oh, yes, madam."

"She's hurt herself," said Honey.

"Oh, really?" said Mrs. Doakes with sprightly interest.

"I'd like to know how she's getting on," said Honey. "Will you go and ask, please?"

Mrs. Doakes rustled off, and Honey waited. It seemed a long time before Mrs. Doakes returned.

"Mrs. Lashelle is resting, madam," she said. "She's quite all right. Just a little bit tired, that's all."

"Did you see her?"

"No, madam. I spoke to Captain Lashelle. May I help you do your hair, madam?"

"It's done," said Honey.

She stood by the open port, looking out at the deep purple sky and the dark water, glad of the breeze that blew against her face. Maybe it'll have to be Michael in the end, she thought. I'll try some other people first, though. But I've got to see this through. It's not going to be like Mrs. Condy, this time.

That reminded her of a little half-formed idea she had had; she considered it a moment and it seemed good. She went along to the Purser's office, and the young Assistant Purser smiled happily at her.

"I'd like to send a cable or a radio or something," she said "To Puerto Azul."

"Oh certainly," he said, and pushed forward a pad of blanks.

"Mrs. Condy, Hotel Royal Dominion, Puerto Azul," she wrote. "Please wire me immediately about money you left in cabin. Honey Stapleton."

She lingered at the wicket, soothed by the young A.P.'s admiring politeness, and presently she saw Weaver, so neat, so distinguished in his dinner jacket, coming up the stairs.

"Very charming," he said. "This way—"

They were the first to arrive at Mr. Basingly's party; it was Weaver's lot in life always to arrive a little too early. But in a few moments Miss Bewley came, and she brought Mr. Smith with her. I'll try him, Honey thought. If he really is a detective, what could be better?

She went up to Mr. Smith, smiled up in his face, and he nodded his head as if she were doing well.

"It's an interesting trip, isn't it?" she said.

"Oh, quite!" he said, in his deep, lugubrious voice.

"It's the first trip I've ever taken."

"Really?"

"Have you taken this trip before?"

"Oh, rather!"

He was certainly not easy to talk to, but at least he was looking at her. If he'd just say something about having seen me up on the boat deck last night, she thought. But maybe he expects me to bring it up.

"You know you startled me last night," she said.

"Oh, sorry..." he said.

Her heart was beating fast; it was so important to do this right, to say the right thing in the right way, so that he would feel confidence in her. If he didn't know anything about what had happened to Mrs. Condy....

"Hello!" said Mrs. Pruitt, cheerfully.

She was looking incredibly smart in a short-sleeved pink sweater and a long skirt. She brought a new note into the gathering and Mr. Smith seemed interested. But he must not escape yet.

"Only there's one thing that's just about spoiling the trip for me," said Honey. "I'm so worried about Mrs. Lashelle."

"Really?" he said.

"I wish I could get someone to realize," she said. "Something happened to her. She's hurt."

"What's this? What's this?" said Basingly with the falsest sort of geniality. "Still worrying about Mrs. Lashelle? She'll be along any moment, Mrs. Stapleton."

"I'm afraid not," said Honey. "She—"

A boy came up to her with a tray.

"Martini, Manhattan, Daiquiri," he murmured, shyly.

Mr. Smith was moving away.

"Something's happened to her," said Honey in desperation. "There was blood running down her face."

Everybody heard that; all these polite people stopped talking, and looked at Honey. It was bad moment for her.

Weaver took her arm in a painful grip. "Honey," he said in a low and trembling voice. "You must *stop* this.... This is intolerable. You must—control yourself."

"My dear!" called out Miss Bewley. "Come and sit by me and tell me all *about* this."

She patted the sofa beside her; her little pointed face had a look of vigorous resolution. She was a friend.

"Come and tell me about Mrs. Lashelle, my dear," she said.

Honey sat down beside her, and the other people in the room began talking to one another, like people on a stage, directed to show animation.

"My dear," said Miss Bewley. "I know—"

Alma came into the cabin followed by the Captain.

FOURTEEN

"My dear . ." said Miss Bewley. "Never mind, my dear."

Alma was wearing the inevitable black dress, but with a beautiful diamond clip at the neck. She had her hair done on a different way, brought forward in an unbecoming scallop on one temple; she was paler than usual, and glaringly made up, with too much lipstick, too much mascara and eyeshadow, too much rouge on her high cheek bones. Her peasant stolidity, which had given her a sort of dignity, was gone; she looked vulgar now.

She began talking to Mr. Lake; Honey could not hear what she said, but Lake looked startled, and then amused; he laughed, and so did Alma. The boy came to them with a tray of cocktails, and she took one at random. And before she had tasted it Lashelle adroitly backed into her and knocked it out of her hand.

"Oh, sorry!" he said. "But anyhow it's time for dinner, I think."

"It is not," said Alma.

"I'm hungry," he said.

"Go and eat then."

"I don't want to go without you," he said, looking at her. Her dark and sullen gaze wandered, but came back to his face; his deep blue eyes looked and looked at her with a deliberate and imploring tenderness.

"I want a drink," she said.

"Later," he said. "Let's go now, Alma."

"Oh hell! All right!" she said, and turned toward the door, without having said a word to Basingly her host, without a glance at Honey. She staggered, and Lashelle took her arm.

It was an entirely convincing picture of a devoted husband shielding his wife from her own very unendearing weakness. And it was a defeat for Honey so complete that she was stunned. Mrs. Pruitt came and sat down beside her.

"Isn't she fearsome?" she said. "I saw a bit of sticking plaster under her hair."

"She ran into a door," said Mr. Lake. "Don't we all?"

"Well, anyhow," said Mrs. Pruitt, "nobody could ever believe that her husband beats her. She looks as strong as an ourangutan."

"Miaouw!" said Mr. Lake.

"It's not spite," said Mrs. Pruitt, "it's fear. She terrifies me."

"I'm glad you're afraid of someone," said Lake.

He and Mrs. Pruitt were looking at each other, and their conversation had again become cryptic, not to be understood by anyone but themselves. They were friendly and amiable, they had no intention of excluding Honey, they just forgot her. That's the real thing, Honey thought. They're not just crazy about each other; they *like* each other.

"Miss Bewley," said Weaver, "shall we take a turn on the deck before dinner?"

"Oh, *certainly!*" said Miss Bewley, and rose at once.

So that there was no one left at the party but Mr. Smith, and Basingly, and Mrs. Pruitt and Mr. Lake still looking at each other. The boy brought a tray of canapés, and Honey slowly picked out three.

"Another cocktail, Mrs. Stapleton?" said Basingly.

"No, thanks," she said. "But I'd like a cigarette, please."

She made up her mind to stay and stay. They can be just as nasty as they like, she thought. I don't care. I'm sorry Miss Bewley went away, because I like her. But I don't care. I don't care about *anything*. Only I'm still going to keep Alma from getting herself murdered. Just—as a matter of principle.

Mrs. Pruitt noticed the ghastly silence and took over; she started and kept up a nice little conversation, until the second bugle had sounded.

"Shall we go down?" she suggested to Honey. "Thanks for the party, Mr. Basingly. Ever so nice!"

His smile was wry as he stood in the doorway and watched his guests out of sight.

"Basingly's really afraid of Mrs. Lashelle," said Lake. "He told me she'd sent the Captain a note complaining about him. And she says that when she gets back to New York, she's going to sue everybody for everything."

"Well, you've got to admit that she's had a bad break," said Honey. "Losing her luggage—and that queer illness—"

"Would you call this another 'queer illness' this evening?" asked Lake, smiling.

"There's one thing," said Honey. "She's no drinker."

"She had a drop taken this evening."

"Maybe," said Honey. "And maybe she was drugged."

"Oh, darling!" cried Mrs. Pruitt. "I wish you'd get Mrs. Lashelle off your mind. It's—honestly, it's an obsession."

It's boring to everybody, Honey thought. But I'm going to keep right on, and some of it will stick. At the head of the stairway, she stopped, looking down into the dining saloon. It's *too* much, she thought. Sitting at the table three times a day with Weaver, and that Mr. Basingly—*and* Captain Lashelle.

She turned away and went back to her cabin; she rang the bell and Mrs. Doakes came.

"I think I'd like some dinner in here, please," Honey said.

"Some nice hot soup and some toast?" Mrs. Doakes proposed.

"No, thank you," said Honey. "Fruit cup, and chicken and vegetables and a salad, and some ice cream and cake."

Mrs. Doakes could think what she pleased about anyone with such an appetite dining in her cabin. She had to go and get all that; she cleared off the table and Honey sat down to it.

"Oh, by the way, madam," said Mrs. Doakes, in a lowered and confidential tone. "I heard from Parley the steward, that Mrs. Lashelle had quite a nasty fall."

Honey looked up quickly and saw Mrs. Doakes' face alight with joy.

"It seems she fell out of bed, madam," she said, "and cut her head on a flask of whiskey."

"I should think," said Honey, "that Parley could get into a lot of trouble, going around telling a story like that."

Mrs. Doakes was frightened.

"Oh, he wouldn't tell it to every one, madam," she said. "Just to me. And *I* know *you'd* never let it go any farther."

"No." said Honey. "I certainly won't."

It was a bad story, bad from every point of view. If it were true that Alma had been shut up there alone drinking; that was bad. And if it was not true, that was worse. It meant that Lashelle had found some new way to injure her.

I know Alma's a hellion, Honey thought. I know she's selfish and hard as nails, and all that. But that makes you all the more sorry for her. I don't believe she'd drink. She was saying how bad alcohol is for your figure and your complexion. It didn't help her any. She looked ten years older.

There was a tap at the door.

"May I come in, my dear?" asked Miss Bewley's voice. "But how very cosy you look! I was afraid that perhaps you weren't *feeling* well."

"Will you sit down, Miss Bewley?"

"Thank you, my dear, but I haven't had my *dinner* yet. I just wondered if you wouldn't come to my cabin for a little chat later on? Let's see... Nine o'clock, shall we say? It's number eight-*three*."

She's got something on her mind, Honey thought. She ate her dinner very slowly, and ate all of it, with a sort of defiant relish; for strong within her was the feeling that this was an interlude. The curtain had gone down after an act filled with violence and horror, and it would surely rise again upon something unimaginable.

A few minutes before nine she went down to D deck, to Cabin Eighty-three, a small cabin, and extremely crowded, with a big trunk in it, and two baskets bought on shore, a pile of books on the berth; there was a pleasant scent of powder and eau de cologne in the air, there was something indefinably cosy in the place.

"My dear, sit *down!*" said Miss Bewley. "You must try one of the cigarettes I bought in Puerto Azul. I bought them for my *nephews,* you know. There...!"

She lit a cigarette for herself, sitting on the lower berth and puffing in quick little gusts, with an air of jaunty nonchalance.

"My dear," she said. "I had quite a talk with Weaver."

"Yes?" said Honey.

"I'd never *met* him before," Miss Bewley went on. "But I'd *heard* about him, for years and years. He's not *sure* whether or not I knew this—this very *unpleasant* thing. He was trying to find out—*skirting* the subject, you know, but I was a perfect Sphinx."

"Something unpleasant, Miss Bewley?"

"I think you *ought* to know," said Miss Bewley. "Then you can do as you think best, my dear, about telling him or not."

She puffed and puffed at the cigarette, holding her chin up and half-closing her eyes to keep out the cloud of smoke.

"I met Weaver's mother once," she said, "some years ago. A very *intelligent* woman, with a quite delightful sense of humour. My cousin Evelyn Bewley had told me once that Weaver was tied to his mother's apron strings, but when I *met* her, I could see that it *wasn't* like that. He wouldn't let go of her apron strings; and it made her quite frantic. You hear so much about children trying to escape from the domination of their mothers, and of course, it often is like that. But you do see *quite* a number of mothers trying to escape from their grown-up children."

Her cigarette was soon finished with that desperate puffing; she stubbed it out in an ash tray.

"Weaver lived with his mother, you know, and he was most *courtly* to her. When she died he was in a dreadful state, so my cousin Stillman Portner told me. Stillman had been at Harvard with Weaver, and he really felt sorry for him. He practically shanghaied him off to Europe for a change of scene. Weaver was over forty then, and—"

She paused for a time.

"A friend of mine saw him in Budapest, having lunch with an *actress* in a big red hat," she said.

'You mean, he sort of cut loose, Miss Bewley?" asked Honey.

"That's exactly it, my dear. He—as Stillman put it—he had himself a time in Europe. I believe he was *engaged* to the actress, the one in the red *hat*. And of course he'd never taken any interest in women before, so that when something went wrong—I *think* she went off with another man—it was quite dreadful for Weaver. He came home, and he had a breakdown. He was in this place for months."

"What place, Miss Bewley?"

"It's called a rest-home," said Miss Bewley. "But Stillman told me it was chiefly for inebriates, you know, and people like that. Stillman said that most of the people there were really quite goofy—as he put it—and he felt it was *extremely* bad for Weaver. He said Weaver had completely lost heart; he was utterly wretched; and he was terrified that he was going insane. Stillman—the kindest creature—insisted upon taking him to our dear Doctor Da Costa, and Doctor Da Costa said there was nothing wrong with his *mind*. Simply his nerves. Psychological. But he did find a heart condition, and—-well, you can imagine, my dear. You can imagine the effect of telling *Weaver* to take care of himself!"

"Yes..." said Honey.

"In a way, I'm sorry for him," said Miss Bewley. "There he is, night and day, worrying about his heart, and avoiding any excitement or overexertion, and he lives in terror about anyone finding out about the rest-home. He imagines people would think he was insane—but *you* know what he's like."

"Yes," Honey said, surprised. "I didn't know about his heart. I wish he'd told me."

"But, my dear, when he wanted to seem so dashing...!"

"He's always getting excited," said Honey. "I suppose it's bad for him. But—" She pause a moment. "If he'd told me all this, he might have known I'd be—decent about it."

She paused again, trying to be sorry for Weaver, trying to understand and to forgive his shocking and public repudiation of her.

"If he felt he ought to have a cabin to himself," she said. "we could have started out that way. He needn't have done this without a word of explanation to me."

"He seems to think you wouldn't understand," said Miss Bewley. "He asked me to have a little talk with you. He asked me to tell you that he's willing to make very generous terms with you—"

"What?"

"That's what he said, my dear. He said—" Miss Bewley's bright little eyes were fixed steadily on Honey's face. "He said you were inclined to be hysterical and quite *violent,* and that he couldn't stand it."

"He said that?"

"My dear," said Miss Bewley, "he told me you were talking quite wildly last night. He said—I'd better tell you quite *frankly*—he said he didn't think you were quite responsible. My dear, he's *terrified* of you."

Honey sat motionless, gone very white, her eyes narrowed.

"My dear..." said Miss Bewley unsteadily, and glancing at her, Honey saw her lips trembling in an effort to suppress a smile. "My dear, I'm *sorry!*" she said, and began to laugh.

And Honey laughed with her, leaning back in the wicker chair and stretching out her long legs, laughing and laughing.

FIFTEEN

That laughter was a tonic for her; she waked in the morning feeling steady and strong, she lay in bed for a while, and it came to her that she was free. She could get up when she pleased, she could breakfast in here if she pleased, and when she pleased.

I don't feel like Mrs. Weaver Stapleton any more, she thought. I'll finish out this cruise, and then I'll go home, and things'll be as they used to be. I can get a job without much trouble.

The ship's whistle blew with that sound she hated, and looking out of the port, she saw a green island as if lying flat on the water, with little white houses, neat and toy-like. This is a British island, she thought. Sort of a thrill to go ashore here.

She was in a hurry now; she dressed and went down to the dining saloon, and there was Weaver. He rose.

"Good morning!" he said.

"Good morning, Weaver. How are you?"

"My digestion isn't satisfactory," he said. "Not at all satisfactory. I've seen this Doctor Lovejoy again, but he obviously doesn't understand the case."

"Why don't you see a doctor on this island, Weaver?"

"I don't think I'll go ashore," he said. "The heat doesn't agree with me. If you want to go, I've no doubt Miss Bewley will be glad to—arrange something."

For a moment, their eyes met, and in his she saw an uneasy and unhappy question; he was wondering, she thought. how much Miss Bewley had told her. But they could not speak of this; they could not say one simple or natural word to each other.

It's his fault, she thought. He's done this. I would have gone on trying. But he's broken up our marriage. He's gone back on me. It's all his fault.

But in her heart, she could not believe that. She returned, as always, to the brisk little sayings of her mother, familiar through her childhood. It takes two to make a quarrel. There are two sides to every question. There must he something to be said on Weaver's side. I suppose I've been sort of mean, in some ways. She thought about that. I threw my mink coat on the floor and kicked it, she thought. That honestly *was* violent. .

But she had no liking for self-analysis, and no patience for remorse; easier just now to forget Weaver than to forgive him.

But he was not disposed to be quiet this morning.

"Thank heaven that Lashelle woman hasn't come down," he said. "She's becoming more and more offensive. Why you should take it upon yourself to champion her in and out of season, I can't imagine."

"I think she's pitiful," said Honey.

"Pitiful," said Weaver, "isn't the word you mean. 'Pitiful,' my dear girl, means filled with pity. You mean 'piteous.' Or pathetic. Or moving." He tasted the omelette he had ordered, and pushed the plate away. "When I first met you, Honey," he said, "you seemed very anxious to improve yourself. You told me you learned a new word out of the dictionary every day."

"Well, I did," she said. "Only I don't remember all of them. And anyhow I only got as far as C."

"And you haven't any ambition now? You haven't spent half an hour reading on this trip."

"I've learned some poetry," said Honey. She put her elbows on the table and rested her chin in her hands, thinking. She had taken down a lot of those verses in shorthand and memorized them.

> "We are no others than a moving row
> Of Magic Shadow-shapes that come and go
> Round with the Sun-illumined Lantern held
> In Midnight by the Master of the Show."

"My dear girl!" he cried. "Have you been wasting your time on that preposterously hackneyed stuff?"

"I like it!" she said. "I love it."

Miss Bewley came along then, and the atmosphere changed. She was so cheerful, so friendly, yet so elusive.

"Oh, you're not *going* ashore, Mr. Stapleton...? Riquezas is such *a pleasant* island, *I* think. I spent a month here once in a little cottage, quite charming, but the electric light bill was *very* large.... Oh, good morning, Captain Lashelle!"

Lashelle looked wonderfully fresh and debonair, in a clean white suit with a blue silk handkerchief showing from his breast pocket.

"Good morning!" he said to everyone. "We're looking forward to a fine day ashore. I hear we're to have five or six hours, and Alma hopes to do some shopping."

That's for me, Honey thought. That's to show me how well and happy she is. All right! We'll just see....

She felt strong again this morning. She could not yet see any way to circumvent Lashelle, but she was sure that there was a way, and that she would find it. All alone, if it had to be so.

"Shall we go ashore *early?*" Miss Bewley asked. "In half an hour?"

She was so gay, there was so agreeable a stir on board, that Honey began to feel young again. She went out on deck; the ladder was down, and launches and row boats were plying back and forth, and in a boat directly beneath her two thin black boys in trunks were shouting at her.

"Mistress! Lady! T'row me money, lady! Lady!"

Someone beside her threw a coin, and the two boys dived into the clear, brilliant water; they swam around like frogs, one of them seized the coin, and they both came up and climbed back into the boat, melancholy and thin, shivering a little in that fierce sun.

"I shall throw more money?" asked Perez beside her. "It amuses you?"

"Well, no," said Honey. "I think it's sort of pitiful. Pitiable."

"They like to get some little money," said Perez, and threw a handful of coins down into the boat.

"Oh, sah! Thank you, sah! Thank you, mistress!" the boys called in their sad hollow voices, and Honey moved back away from that gratitude.

"I like to ask you somesing," said Perez. "May I take you to lunch? I know some place that is extremely nice."

"Thanks, but I'm going with Miss Bewley."

"Very good! I take Miss Bewley too. In this place they know me very well. They give me the best. You are going to have the most fine lunch."

There was a marked swagger about little Perez this morning; he was obviously pleased with himself.

"Come with me," he said coaxingly. "I am so nice. Also—" He looked over his shoulder. "Also I tell you somesing."

"Well, what?"

"Come to lunch, and I tell you. Somesing important."

"I don't know what you'd call important." He laughed.

"You think I only tell you how you are beautiful? No? Somesing else." His mobile face grew serious. "I like to give you some warning," he said. "Somesing pretty bad might come to happen. Somebody we know, you understand?"

He's such a little monkey, Honey thought. But she had no objection to his company, and there was a chance that he had something to tell. Miss Bewley appeared now in a green cotton dress, very full-skirted, with black butterflies appliqued on it, and a wide-brimmed green straw hat with a crown that rose to a peak.

"Miss Bewley," said Perez. "You permit me to take you and Mrs. Angel to lunch?"

Miss Bewley glanced at Honey, and Honey smiled.

"That would be very nice, thank you," said Miss Bewley. "But Mr. Nordstrom is coming with us."

"I invite him also!" said Perez. "Everybody! I take everybody to the Hotel Fernandez. I know very well Mr. Fernandez, and there they give me the best. Oh yes! I promise you they are very glad there, to see Joe Perez."

"Here's our launch," said Michael.

He gave Honey a sidelong glance, and no smile; he had an absent-minded air this morning. They all went down the ladder and got into a launch with a striped awning; off it went over the bright water. And it was somehow a gala day, a wonderful day.

"One time this island was Spanish," said Perez. "Then the French are taking it from them. Now it is the English. If you permit, we will drive to see where the pirates were coming in old times to get water. There were then very many pirates. Now there is only my good friend Don Carlos Fernandez."

He laughed at his little joke, very happy he was, and very active. As soon as the launch touched the jetty he sprang out and held out two hands to Honey.

"I will get a good driver," he said. "I know who is good here.... Hola, Percy!"

Percy was a portly Negro in spectacles and a belted khaki jacket; he smiled benevolently.

"Percy, we will see the beach of the pirates, eh?"

"Yes, sah," said Percy.

"We will pass the Hotel Fernandez," said Perez. It's awf'ly up-to-date there. If you would ever come back here, you would have a good time at the Hotel Fernandez, all right."

They drove through a busy little town with shops of British nonchalance; the dusty windows displayed the most paltry tourist junk side by side with articles of solid worth. The people, black and white, moved leisurely beneath the blazing sun, the traffic of cars, bicycles, and horse-drawn carts obeyed the gestures of the policemen in helmets with chin straps.

The exotic charm of Puerto Azul was lacking, yet Riquezas had a charm of its own, flat, without hills or cliffs, it had a certain melancholy wildness, wide sugar cane fields and straight long roads, and tidy little suburban villas, gay with flowers and vines.

"Hotel Fernandez," said Perez.

This was a building of dazzling white, with archways, balconies, a terrace, well-kept grounds and, in the back, a fine sandy beach where the sea ran in quietly. They drove past it, they drove for a long way. Perez in front, Michael between Miss Bewley and Honey, and that was also part of the interlude. At any moment somebody would speak, something would happen, and the hot, sunny peace would be shattered.

Mr. Perez's beach of the pirates was a wide stretch of sand where a sluggish little stream came down to the sea.

"You like to see?" he asked, and Honey got out of the car with him. But Miss Bewley and Michael stayed in the car. "I show you the swamp," said Perez. "I think that is an awf'ly funny word, that 'swamp.' " He repeated it; swamp, swamp, walking beside the tall girl.

They turned inland, and the little stream widened out into a basin of shallow and stagnant water flecked with foam, where mangrove trees had sent out their grasping and tormented roots. There was a rank ugly swamp smell here, and an oppressive steamy heat.

"The pirates were able to conceal the little boats in here," Perez said. "One time there was a woman pirate, very beautiful, with long, long hair. She was very passionate woman."

"That so?" said Honey, discouragingly.

"I like better a woman who is cold," said Perez. "Cold, cold, blonde—"

They stopped at the edge of the rank swamp, and the foam moved and eddied above invisible currents.

"I don' know how I will tell you this," he said. "Only don' laugh. It is somesing—true."

He took a package of cigarettes out of his pocket; Honey declined but he lit one for himself.

"Lashelle is angry with you," he said. "That bad sing."

"I guess I can bear it."

Perez was not looking at her.

"That's a bad sing," he repeated. "Please believe it."

"He can't do *me* any harm," said Honey.

"No?" said Perez.

"What could he do?" she asked, scornfully.

"Look," said Perez. "I don' know anysing. Only some little ideas I have.... Only Lashelle is aw'fly angry with you. Much better if you don't—bother him any more."

"Why don't you tell me the whole thing?" Honey asked gently.

"Me? I don' know anysing. Only you're such a nice beautiful girl.... You don' know what you're doing."

That was true. It had not occurred to her that she was taking any personal risk. She had deliberately let Lashelle see that she suspected him; she had done all she could to thwart him. Alma's danger had been terribly real to her, but she had felt perfectly safe herself. She had never even thought of Lashelle's trying to retaliate.

She thought of it now with surprise, and a curiously impersonal interest. Looking down at this dark and sluggish water, she thought of Mrs. Condy, lying now God knew where. She had seen Mrs. Condy, she had looked on death with her own eyes, sudden death. But she did not believe in any danger to herself. She could not.

There were all these people around, these important, confident matter-of-fact people. The sun was up in the sky, she was young and strong and immensely alive, and Lashelle was a figure in a nightmare.

"I'll be careful," she said, looking at Perez.

"You promise you won' bother him any more?"

"Did he tell you to ask me that?" she said.

"He did *not*. He only tells me you make trouble for him. This too, he said—"

"He said what?"

"Said you are a dangerous girl."

"That's funny..." she said half to herself. Only yesterday she had heard from Miss Bewley that Weaver was 'terrified' of her. And now Lashelle thought her dangerous.

"You promise me?" said Perez.

She shook her head.

"But why?" he said. "Why you do this?"

"I don't like the way he treats his wife," she said, slowly.

"That woman?" said Perez. "She is a tiger! She is... I have never seen a woman so rough. She is—she is a *beast*, that woman. Don' give yourself any worry for *her*. She has claws, that one."

He spoke with fury; it was plain that he had his own grudge against Alma. Like everyone else. Not once, not from one soul, had Honey heard a single word of friendliness or good-will for Alma.

Her arrogance, her ruthlessness, had isolated her.

"She's unlucky," said Honey.

"Onlucky?" he repeated as if startled.

"Miss Bewley's waving to us," said Honey, "we'd better go back."

"Please promise me first. I tell you, I don' like to mix myself in this affair, only I do it for you. It's—bad."

"I'll be careful," she said again, and started back toward the car.

Perez dismissed all his earnestness at once.

"Now to the Hotel Fernandez," he said. "We will get a good lunch there all right!"

"I think..." Miss Bewley murmured Honey, "that he must have some interest in the hotel, don't you?"

Certainly he had an almost possessive tone about it; he led them up on the terrace, pointing out the fine quality of the copper screens, he led them into the lounge, dim, lofty, pleasantly furnished in wicker and chintz.

"I'll just tell Mr. Fernandez," he said.

He returned presently arm in arm with a man as dark as himself, dressed exactly as he was, but much taller and heavier and more exuberant.

"My friend, Mr. Fernandez!" he said. " "Miss Bewley, Mrs. Stapleton, Mr. Nordstrom."

Mr. Fernandez shook hands with all of them.

"Suppose we adjourn to the bar?" he said. They sat at a table in a corner, and Mr. Fernandez was a king here.

"Bring five Carlitos," he said to the waiter. "A little drink of my own invention," he explained. "If you don't like it...."

"Your hotel wasn't built when I was here before," said Miss Bewley, and that aroused a quick interest in Mr. Fernandez.

"Oh, you've been here before?" he said. "Did you like it? It's made a difference to the place, having an up-to-date hotel like this, I think. We have dances here every Saturday, and other little entertainments."

"You must see the Casino," said Perez.

The drinks came and they were good.

"One more before lunch?" said Mr. Fernandez.

"Thank you, but no," said Miss Bewley.

Honey accepted the second one, and so did Michael.

"And while you're drinking," said Miss Bewley, "perhaps I can see the Casino."

She went off with the big Fernandez and the little Perez, and Honey and Michael were left alone. They had scarcely spoken a word to each other to-day, but Honey was in no hurry to talk to him or to think about him. She had a feeling that there was unlimited time before them; no haste, no urgency, he would not go away, or change.

The waiter set the drinks before them and withdrew.

"They're a pretty colour," Honey said.

"They are," said Michael, absently.

His face in profile had a look of sharpness, alert and anxious; after a moment he turned his head quickly and looked at her.

"D'you mind telling me what Perez had to say?" he asked.

"No, I don't," she answered, speaking in an even, flat tone. She did not want him to see how much that question pleased her, how much she liked his off-hand way. He took it for granted that she trusted him, and he trusted her.

"He wanted me to promise not to bother Captain Lashelle." she said.

"He's right," said Michael. "I'd like to ask you the same thing."

"Well, why?"

"It's a complicated business," he said. "For one thing, that little fellow's shaking down Lashelle. I heard him this morning. He told him in Spanish that he had to have twenty-five dollars to spend on shore."

"Well?" Honey said again. "That's not much of a reason for not bothering Lashelle. Doesn't it look like blackmail?"

"That's what I thought."

"But then—" she cried, leaning across the table. "Then don't you see...? It's another point against Captain Lashelle."

"Maybe," said Michael. "But there's something else. Perhaps I should have told you at the outset—but I didn't like to. I don't like to tell you now." He was silent for a moment. "Here it is," he said, and took a card out of his pocket. "When I went into Mrs. Condy's room with Basingly, I picked this up," he said, and handed it to her.

It was one of Weaver's correct and expensive visiting cards, and on the back was his tiny, clear writing:

"I shall be on the boat deck from three thirty on—hoping for an opportunity to explain this unfortunate misunderstanding."

She raised her eyes to his face and they looked at each other.

"Basingly saw it," said Michael. "He took it up and read it and put it down again."

"But this . ." she said. "This doesn't *mean* anything."

"It could lead to plenty of trouble," he said. "Questions and so on."

"I know. But you can't keep quiet about a murder, just to avoid trouble."

"It's up to you," said Michael.

They did not mention Weaver's name; they did not call each other by any name. They both avoided so much, repressed so much. Yet it seemed to Honey that they were speaking with a breath-taking frankness.

"It would take someone with a lot of physical strength to have got Mrs. Condy out of there," she said.

He let that go, and she thought it was because he knew something more. She had told him, in effect, that she was certain that Weaver was not dangerously involved. And by his silence, he was telling her that he did not agree with her.

"There's this," he said. "Once an investigation gets started you can't stop it. It will go on, to the finish." He picked up the card from the table, and tore it into pieces, and set them on fire in the ash-tray. And that was his way of telling her that he would hold his tongue. That whatever she did, he would stand by her.

SIXTEEN

It's up to you, Michael had said. He would help her, and stand by her, but he had no trace of the protective attitude she met with in so many other men. She was used to being treated as a precious and fragile creature. But Michael seemed to think she could make up her own mind, and choose her own road.

He had given her a warning, that was all. He thought she was on the wrong track; he thought Weaver was gravely involved, if not actually guilty. Little Perez had given her a warning of another sort. He had let her know it was dangerous for her to go ahead.

Sitting there in the dim, cool bar, she felt herself growing tougher and tougher. I'm going to get Alma out of this, she thought. Nobody else was at all concerned about Alma, just as nobody was worrying about Mrs. Condy. And just as Mrs. Condy had vanished off the face of the earth, so it could be with Alma sooner or later.

It's sort of fate, she thought. I'm the one that found Captain Lashelle's letter in the beginning, before we even sailed. I'm the only one that knows—all the little things. I can't make anyone believe me. Not even Michael. I'll have to manage by myself.

She thought, with a certain satisfaction, that at last she had made a start. Michael said she had started rumours. Perez said that Captain Lashelle was angry, and that meant he was frightened. I'll pin this on him, she said to herself. I'll make people realize that Mrs. Condy was murdered, and then I'll pin it on Captain Lashelle.

And what about Weaver? Well, if he's made a fool of himself about Mrs. Condy, I'm sorry. But he didn't kill her. He *couldn't* commit a murder, and then go and eat his dinner. I know what he's like.

But then she remembered how unlucky Weaver was. Everything went wrong with him. Suppose Mrs. Condy's death had been an accident, and he had been the sole witness to it? Or suppose he had even been responsible for it, in some Weaver way?

All right, she thought, but he couldn't have thrown her overboard. Not in a panic?

I'm going to read that note, she thought suddenly. It was probably very wrong, and a thing that even Michael would think highly dishonourable. But it's not going to hurt anybody, she thought, and before I go any further, I'm going to know all I can.

Again she raised her blue eyes to Michael's face.

"I'd like to get fixed up a little before lunch," she said, and rose.

A waiter directed her to the powder room. A neat little coloured girl in black and white uniform was in charge there; Honey smiled pleasantly at her, and sitting down in a pink brocade arm-chair she took from her purse the envelope addressed to Mr. Weaver Stapleton. I suppose I ought to steam it open, the way people do in stories, she thought. But I wouldn't know how to do that, and anyhow I'm not going to bother. I'll put it back in another ship's envelope, and copy the address the best I can.

The coloured girl was looking at her with a gentle, admiring curiosity—let her look. Honey tore open the envelope and took out the sheet of paper.

"Dear old Weaver-Beaver—"

Oh my gosh! she thought, shocked. And then a broad, slow smile spread over her face. It was awful; but it was funny.

"I got your card, but I don't think I'd better see you. I've suddenly decided to leave this ship. I don't like it. I think I'll go to Rio, or somewhere. I feel so low, Weaver-Beaver, and everything is so mixed up, isn't it? We'll meet again—somewhere. I *always* meet *everybody* again.

Don't come to my cabin. Be good. A rivederci.   Mimi."

Weaver had never got this note. That was part of his bad luck. And had he gone to her cabin? 'Weaver-Beaver,' she repeated to herself. Well, is that the sort of thing he likes? I always tried to be—well—more dignified than that. But if that's what he likes he'll be able to find somebody else. He can marry again. I can go to Reno—or maybe I could go to Mexico. I'd rather go to Mexico. All by myself. I'd like to see all those old ruined temples and things. I'd like—

She checked this train of thought, and sitting down at the dressing-table, she made up her face with leisurely care. I don't *think* I'll ever give Weaver that note, she thought. If he did go to her cabin she'd have told him about it. And if he didn't, what's the sense? It's very queer, the way I feel about Weaver. I ought to be furious at him. But I'm not. I'm just sorry for him.

When she returned to the bar, Mr. Fernandez and Miss Bewley and Perez had returned.

"*A perfect* hotel!" Miss Bewley said. "And the Casino is really a little *gem.*"

"You're too kind, Miss Bewley," said Mr. Fernandez.

He led them all to lunch in the palatial dining-room, and it was a fine lunch indeed. And Honey was aware that Mr. Fernandez was discreetly admiring her. After lunch he drove them in his own superb car to see the market, the statue of Nelson, and other sights not too interesting; Miss Bewley wanted to shop, and he left his car and his chauffeur at their disposal, and went off on foot, greeting the people in the street with royal etiquette, a half military salute here, a wave of the hand there, and for the elite, a courtly raising of the helmet.

It was late in the afternoon when they went back to the ship. Back to all that trouble, Honey thought. As a matter of course, she went in search of Weaver; it seemed the right thing to do. She found him stretched out in his deck chair, in white flannels and a brown jacket; he had his eyes closed against the dazzle of the setting sun; he looked elegant, grandly aloof, as if he were alone by his own fastidious choice.

She was sorry for him; honestly and generously sorry for him.

"Hello, Weaver!" she said. "Did you have a nice—rest?"

"Thank you," he said. "I'm afraid I did a foolhardy thing. My cabin was so intolerably hot that I went into the swimming-pool. I stayed in the water too long; I had quite a serious chill. Lovejoy says that I overexerted myself."

"I'm *sorry,* Weaver."

"This trip was a mistake," he said. "I didn't realize that the heat would affect me so adversely." He paused. "I hope *you've* enjoyed yourself," he said.

Weaver-Beaver, she thought. She tried to stop thinking that; it was mean.

"Well..." she said. "Shall we have a cocktail before dinner?"

"Lovejoy absolutely forbids any alcohol, any stimulants at all," said Weaver.

"Weaver, d'you think he's a good doctor?" she asked.

He looked at her with a faint smile.

"I'm afraid I do," he said. "I'm afraid I've changed my mind about Lovejoy."

"Why do you say 'afraid,' Weaver?"

"I hear that you have a very poor opinion of him."

"Who told you that?"

"It doesn't matter," said Weaver.

"No," she said, after a moment. "I guess it doesn't."

She could not see the motive for Weaver's air of spiteful triumph, but she did not care much. She went to her cabin and ran a bath; she was lying in it when the ship's whistle blew.

It's sort of sad, she thought. Leaving a place you'll probably never see again. It's sort of sad about Weaver and me, too. All of a sudden our marriage is—just nothing. We didn't even have a fight. Only when I really needed him, when I went to pieces about Mrs. Condy, he ran away from me. Calling me 'dangerous.' I'd be furious, if it wasn't so kind of sad....

Mrs. Doakes came in while she was dressing.

"May I help you, miss?" she said.

"Well, no, thanks," said Honey.

"I'll lay out your things, miss," said Mrs. Doakes, opening the wardrobe door. "Will you wear the green chiffon, to-night?"

"The brown and beige," said Honey.

Twice Mrs. Doakes had called her 'miss.' That was pretty fresh, but there was something new and strangely cosy about Mrs. Doakes to-day. It was as if she now granted Honey a new status, as if the Mrs. Weaver Stapleton she had warmly resented was now no more, and the cabin was now occupied by a girl, good-looking, but nobody much.

"And the bronze sandals?" asked Mrs. Doakes. "I really haven't the time to do what I'd like to do for my passengers, but with only two of us stewardesses for the whole ship—and there's one lady got on with a small baby, and there's an old lady that's as much trouble as a baby herself."

She was speaking now as a woman working for a living, and Honey could not help responding to that tone.

"Is the work very hard?"

"Some trips are worse than others," Mrs. Doakes answered. "And I must say this is one of the hard ones. The time I had clearing up that Mrs. Condy's cabin! And she left without even telling me... And Mr. Smith told me to collect everything she left, even the scraps in the wastepaper basket, he said—"

"Mr. Smith?"

"Oh, I went straight to the Chief Steward, miss, you can be sure of *that*. But he said it was quite all right, so I did just what Mr. Smith told me to do. I brought everything down to his cabin, the empty gin bottles and the hair pins, and a cheap little silver bracelet." She smiled. *"And* the book," she said. "Of course, I've picked up some Spanish, on these trips, although I must say you can do very well without it, if you know the right places. I'd heard of that book before. *Dona Dormilona.* It's—well! I wrapped it up in brown paper before I'd even carry it through the alleyway; it's that sort of book."

Oh God! Honey thought. Mrs. Condy had hair pins, and a little silver bracelet—like anybody else. She was *real*. And that happened to her.

Well, it won't happen to Alma, if I can help it. The rumours have started, and that's one good thing. And Captain Lashelle's being worried is another good thing. Only I don't want to waste any time.

> "The Bird of Time has but a little way
> To flutter—and the Bird is on the Wing."

She put on her two-toned dress, and went up to the smoke-room where she had arranged to meet Miss Bewley at six. There were a lot of people there, visitors from the island and the familiar faces, too; she sat down at the only vacant table, facing the doorway, to wait, and there she had a fine view of Alma's grand entrance. In white satin with diamonds in her hair, Alma came in, and she seemed glittering with triumph. She was beautiful. The long lines of her dress gave her a look of height and fluidity; she carried herself like a queen.

Lashelle and Perez followed her like courtiers. She crossed the smoke-room walking lightly, in gold sandals; Honey looked up at her with a smile. But Alma looked back at her with narrowed, scornful eyes, and sat down in a corner, the white satin spreading out on the floor at her feet.

What's happened? Honey thought. What's made her turn against me? Captain Lashelle? It must be. Where did she get that dress? And what made her look like that?

Doctor Lovejoy went over to her, and another man; there were four men standing about her now, and she leaned back smiling a little. Her face was best in profile with those black straight brows, the straight bold nose, the sharp angle of the jaw, that lift at the corner of her mouth was like a tiger's smile.

"Well, my dear," said Miss Bewley sitting down beside her. "I hear that Weaver had some sort of *attack* this afternoon."

She spoke with a satisfaction that Honey felt must not be encouraged.

"He seems quite miserable," she said.

"Oh, well, if you feel willing to kid him along, as my nephew says," said Miss Bewley. "I'm sure it's very *kind* of you, my dear."

They ordered their drinks and Miss Bewley glanced about her.

"Gracious!" she exclaimed. She was looking at Alma.

"She looks wonderful, doesn't she?" said Honey.

"Wonderful!" Miss Bewley repeated. "Oh dear me!"

"Why do you say that?" Honey asked.

"Because—but don't you get the same impression?" murmured Miss Bewley. "A *femme fatale...*"

"You mean you think something's going to happen to her?" Honey asked in dismay.

The ship's whistle blew, and a voice began to cry, "All ashore! All visitors ashore, please! All ash-o-ore." And the bugle began to play. It was a confusing, even an alarming medley of noise; the jaunty bugle, the sinister whistle, the hoarse and sorrowful voice. The engine-room telegraph rattled, and then in a moment everything was quiet, a light breeze came, stirring the dark-red curtains that hung beside the ports.

"Miss Bewley, would you mind if I just went out to take a look...?" Honey asked.

"By all means, my dear!" said Miss Bewley.

The little lighted town seemed floating on the sea. The low coast had merged into the dark sky, the island looked tiny and forlorn. She thought at random of what she had seen ashore, the Hotel Fernandez, the shops, and with startling clarity she thought of the mangrove swamp. The very smell of it came back to her, she thought of the brown stagnant water where the foam floated.

She shuddered so violently that she was startled—somebody walking over my grave, she said to herself. And then she was afraid. Where *is* my grave? she thought. Oh God! I hope not any place like that. I hope not at the bottom of the sea, like Mrs. Condy.

Perez had tried to make her believe that Lashelle was dangerous to her. What if he really was? What if she herself had been as blind in her way, as stupid, as headstrong as Alma? She had gone out of her way to defy Lashelle, to alarm and anger him. Even after she had seen Mrs. Condy dead, she had gone on, without so much as looking over her shoulder....

"You are dreaming...?" said the voice of little Perez beside her.

"That's right," said Honey.

"I weesh I could know what you dream of," he said, softly. "Only you are mysterious as the night herself."

"Yep," said Honey.

"I like how you say, 'yep.' " He repeated in a little bark, "Yep, yep, yep. You like a cigarette?"

"I would, thanks."

As he struck a match for her, she saw his dark and brilliant eyes fixed upon her.

"I will tell you somesing," he said in a low voice. "I don' like to mix myself in somebody else's business; only I know you like to know this. The love-birds are flying away."

"What d'you mean, Mr. Perez?"

"The honeymoon couple," he said. "They are going away to-morrow morning early, in a private plane."

"Going wh-where?" she asked with a slight stammer.

"Ah..." he said. "Who knows?"

"Just those two—alone?"

"Yes."

"Mr. Perez..." she said. She did not know how to talk to him, what tone to take. "Mr. Perez... Don't you think that's a bad idea?"

"It is badder than anybody knows," he said.

"Then—can't we stop them?"

"Not 'we,' " he said. "I can' do anysing."

"But *why* can't you?"

"I don' want to," he said, simply.

She laid her hand on his sleeve.

"Listen!" she said. "I don't think it would be safe—for Alma."

He said not a word.

"Mr. Perez, if you know anything against Captain Lashelle, please tell somebody—the Captain—the Purser. This is the time. Or tell me and I'll tell them."

"Me?" he said. "I don' know anysing. Only I think if you find some way to estop them, that's very good."

"You *do* know something! Mr. Perez, listen! Suppose anything happened to Alma, how would you feel then?"

"Senora," he said, laying his hand over hers, "I am a little fellow. I can' fight with big tigers. Here in this boat I am a foreigner. I say a word, and they bring some English, maybe some Yanqui policeman. Well, I don' like them."

"Tell me. I won't say where I found out."

"No," he said. "I can' take that chance. But you—you are young, beautiful, rich, you are North American. You say somesing, and everybody listens."

"All right then. What can I say?"

"I don' know. Only I hope you have success."

"Listen!" she said in desperation. "Suppose Alma—gets killed?"

"Well, that's too bad," he said. "But I like that better than *me* to be killed."

"You're afraid?" she said, with scornful amazement.

"I am," he said. "I am aw'fly afraid to go on any more in this affair."

She pulled away her hand, and he sighed.

"You think I am not very nice?" he said. "I leave you holding the bag? I am sorry. I am awf'ly sorry."

He made her a little bow and moved away.

SEVENTEEN

When Honey went back into the smoke-room, Mrs. Pruitt, and Mr. Lake and Mr. Smith were sitting with Miss Bewley. She gave them all a wide and photogenic smile, and sitting down turned her head to look at Alma.

Alma was drinking a champagne cocktail, and little Perez, back at her side, had one too. Doctor Lovejoy and the other man were still at the table, and Lashelle was facing her. Like a queen with her courtiers, in her white satin and diamonds, glittering and triumphant. And doomed.

This seemed to Honey so obvious, so glaring, it was incredible that nobody else saw it. The ill-starred bride who had so nearly been left behind, was coming now to the end of her brief honeymoon. There was no valid reason for Lashelle's taking her off in a plane, but he did not need to invent a reason. Nobody saw anything alarming, anything questionable in this, or in any of Alma's series of mishaps. Nobody was interested. She could go off with Lashelle to-morrow, and if she met with an accident, nobody would be disturbed.

Perez knew. And he had cared only just enough to give Honey a hint; not enough to involve himself. He could sit there and drink with her. Doctor Lovejoy who had seen her strange illness and her strange recovery could sit there quite untroubled.

She's not going with Captain Lashelle to-morrow, Honey said to herself. I'll stop it some way.

She thought again of Mr. Smith. Here he was beside her, and this was a chance not to be missed, for trying him out again. If he did turn out to be a detective...

She raised her soft blue eyes to his face.

"Can we see the Southern Cross from here?" she said.

"Oh, I think so..." he answered. "I think so."

"I'm crazy to see it," said Honey. "Won't you point it out to me, Mr. Smith?"

"Oh, er... Oh, yes..." he said.

"Let's step out on deck—" she began.

"Oh..." he said with a start. "Oh, sorry....My glasses... Another time... Without my glasses... Sorry... Excuse me... " And he rose in haste and went away.

Mrs. Pruitt began to laugh.

"He's terrified of you," she said.

"He needn't be," said Honey, briefly.

"He thinks you're trying to get someone to take a candid camera shot of you, with him," said Lake.

"And why should I?" demanded Honey.

"He's famous," said Mrs. Pruitt. "Something frightful happened to him in a jungle, poisoned arrows, or anacondas or something."

"Poor man," said Miss Bewley. "He has to take sleeping medicine *every* night, and he tips the watchman to come in every hour and see if he is *breathing* normally, and that nobody's robbing him. His cabin is directly opposite mine, and I'd *noticed* that somebody kept going *in* there all night in such *a stealthy* way, so I asked Mrs. Doakes."

"Oh, drugs, eh?"

"Oh, dear me no!" said Miss Bewley. "Mrs. Doakes told me what he takes, it's Somnol. A friend of mine takes that once in a while, and it's *not* a *drug,* Mr. Lake."

"He's a queer duck," said Mr. Lake.

"He's extremely *nervous,"* said Miss Bewley, with a hint of rebuke. "He went through this dreadful experience in the jungle—it was an alligator, Mrs. Pruitt, upsetting a *canoe.* And Somnol is really *not* a drug—"

"Oh, I know," said Mrs. Pruitt. "My doctor prescribed it for me a year or so ago when I was under a hideous strain. It's perfectly harmless—unless you take too much, of course."

The bugle blew.

"My dear?" said Miss Bewley; and she and Honey rose. As they crossed the smoke-room, Honey looked again at Alma, and their eyes met. This time Alma smiled, a superior and scornful smile, and turned away her head. You fool! thought Honey. You can't even be decent to someone who cares a little what happens to you.

Mr. Basingly was already seated at the table.

"I'm a bit early," he said, "but we'll reach Sainte Monique at daybreak, and that means work for me, y'know. A mixed cargo..."

"Will anyone be going ashore that early?" Honey asked.

"Mr. and Mrs. Lashelle," he answered. "They've chartered a hydroplane to take them to Madelena—heaven knows why. It's a Godforsaken place. Then they'll go on to Trinidad, and join us there."

Daybreak... Honey thought. In stories, that's the time people get shot; I don't know why. That's the time Alma's decided to go off alone with Captain Lashelle to a Godforsaken little island. She's a *fool....*

"That seems like a queer thing to do," she said, watching Basingly's face.

"Oh, passengers do queerer things than that, Mrs. Stapleton," he said.

"It would be terrible if anything happened to Mrs. Lashelle," said Honey.

"But my dear...!" said Miss Bewley.

"Such a lot of queer things have happened to her already," said Honey.

There was a brief silence, an uncomfortable silence; nobody liked to hear Alma's misfortunes mentioned; and then Weaver came to the table. A sort of desperation seized upon Honey. I'm going to make *somebody* listen to me and *believe* me, she thought. I'm not going to let that darn fool Alma go off with him at daybreak. I'll stop that, some way. I don't know how, but I will.

She had a great regard, and a growing affection for Miss Bewley, but she did not contemplate confiding in her. Her instinct was to turn to a man if she wanted help. Mr. Basingly's no good, she thought. And Mr. Smith definitely isn't a detective—Mr. Smith...

A new idea had come to her; an idea so outrageous that she rejected it. With an effort, she began to talk in the naive and amusing way Basingly liked; he and Miss Bewley were as benevolent toward her as if she were a good child.

But she had never felt less young. The Bird of Time has but a little way, she said to herself, to flutter—and the Bird is on the Wing. She tried to think of an excuse for leaving the table, but in vain, and then it came into her head that after all it didn't matter. While the others were taking their coffee, she rose.

"Excuse me," she said, politely.

Nobody can ask you questions, and nobody can stop you, if you just go.

D deck was very quiet; the doors on the alleyway were hooked open, the scent of warm oil and brass polish pervaded the air. Miss Bewley had said that Mr. Smith's cabin was opposite hers; then it was this one. A light showed behind the drawn curtain, but she had left him sitting at his table in the dining saloon, and after a moment's hesitation, in she went.

That coconut head hung on the handle of a drawer by its ropy hair, and she hated the thing.

But the cabin otherwise was perfectly matter-of-fact and tranquil, a little inside cabin with no port, no bathroom. Over the wash stand there was a cabinet, and that was the place to look. She opened it, and was confronted by two solid rows of bottles, most of them prescriptions with doctors' names on the labels. There was nothing for it but to begin at the top corner and go straight through. A teaspoonful three times daily after meals; one tablet as directed. One capsule every three hours.

Her heart was beating fast; haste made her confused, and she touched each bottle with her fingers to be sure of overlooking none.... If he should come in now... What's this? One teaspoonful at bedtime? Repeat in one hour if necessary.

She took that bottle out carefully, and went on along the second row. And there was a dark bottle labelled Somnol. She took the cork out, and looked at the capsules of a vivid metallic blue. Dose, 1 or 2 capsules as directed by physician. Somnol should be taken only under physician's directions.

She looked over her shoulder, and then shook three capsules into her hand. Her dress had a tiny triangular pocket on one side; she put the capsules into it and started to replace the two bottles; the Somnol bottle went into its place, she tried to fit in the bottle of liquid but her nervous fingers fumbled, shoved along the whole row, and the end bottle fell into the basin and smashed.

Oh, lord! she cried to herself, and snatched up a clean towel to gather up the broken glass. She glanced back over her shoulder, and Mr. Smith was standing there.

For a moment she was paralyzed. His eyes seemed to grow bigger and bigger; topaz eyes, clear as a cat's; she could not look away from them. But with an effort she managed a smile.

"I came in here by mistake," she said. "I'm terribly sorry.... You see, my husband's moved down to D deck, and I—came rushing down to get some aspirin, and I got mixed up about the cabins."

"Madam," said Mr. Smith, "it was no mistake. I know very well why you came."

"I'm terribly sorry..." said Honey. "Of course, I didn't see it was a mistake until I opened the cabinet. But I've got such a headache, I thought I'd see if *you* had some aspirin."

"Madam," said Mr. Smith, "you'll have a worse headache before long."

His topaz eyes were so big, so clear, so fierce. "Madam," he said, "I was Police Commissioner for the Interior Province of Tierra Montana for fifteen years, and you can't pull the wool over my eyes."

She drew a long breath to steady herself. "Then—" she said, "if you're in the police, won't you help me? It's about Mrs. Condy. About what happened to Mrs. Condy."

"Madam," he said, "I know all about Mrs. Condy."

"But then—"

"Mrs. Condy married my brother," he said. "He divorced her, and she was forbidden to continue using his name. But it's well known in this part of the world that she's Mrs. Somerville Smith. That woman haunts me, madam!" he cried. "Wherever I go, I see her, or hear of her. The last time I went to Rio, she was being held there because she had no passport, no papers. She loses her passport. She fills out declarations and so on, in an utterly haphazard way."

"Mr. Smith... She's dead."

"Madam," he said, "if I believed you, I should be greatly relieved."

"I saw her. I saw her lying dead on the floor her cabin."

"Madam," said Mr. Smith, "I have met your type before."

"What do you mean?" she cried.

"Your type," he said, "is well-known to the police everywhere. You are a sensation seeker. You'd stop at nothing, nothing in order to attract attention to yourself. I knew that, some time ago. And my original diagnosis has been amply confirmed."

"If you're in the police," she said, "you'd better—listen to me."

"Madam," he said, "there have already been many complaints against you. Doctor Lovejoy was prepared to go to the Captain, to charge you with a deliberate attempt to impugn his professional integrity."

"Mr. Smith—"

"And there have been other things," he said, glaring at her. "Madam, be warned!"

"All right!" Honey said. "You're a policeman, and I've reported a murder to you—"

He stood with his arm extended, pointing to the door. She looked steadily at him for a moment, and then she went past him out of the cabin.

EIGHTEEN

She had no doubts about her scheme, no scruples, no qualms. She waited outside the smoke-room for a few moments, but that was only to get her breath; then, moderately tranquil again, she went in, with her smooth artificial gait, her lashes lowered. She went straight to Alma, who sat drinking coffee with her husband and Perez.

"Can I take my coffee with you people?" she asked.

Alma resented that. But Lashelle sprang to draw out a chair for her, and Perez beckoned to the steward.

"I just heard you were leaving to-morrow," said Honey, "and I wanted to say 'bon voyage.'"

"Oh, it's just a little side trip," said Lashelle.

"It sounds terribly interesting," said Honey.

"You're going by plane, aren't you, Alma?"

"Yes," said Alma sullenly. She was stirring and stirring and stirring her black coffee, and that must mean that she had sugar in it. But it would not be much sugar, Honey thought. She had noticed how carefully Alma watched her diet.

"Now tell me about this trip!" she said, with an animated air very foreign to her.

"Well, it will make a little diversion for Alma," said Lashelle. "She's pretty fed up with this trip, and no wonder. I mean to say, losing her luggage, and so on."

"Can you do some shopping in this place you're going to?"

"That's what we hope," said Lashelle earnestly.

"That's a lovely dress you have on now, Alma."

"Think so?" said Alma. "It happens to be a nightgown."

Little Perez laughed.

"A nightgown, eh?" he said. "Then I think—"

Alma gave him a smouldering and scornful look, and he was silent.

"It's lovely on you," Honey went on. The steward set a small cup of coffee before her, and she dropped in a lump of sugar. And the three blue capsules. And she began to stir and stir and stir. The fluttering nervousness, the sense of dreadful haste and urgency had gone; she felt entirely cool and sure, and thrillingly alert. She was aware of everything, every sound, every gesture; she was ready, she was waiting for her chance. It would come somehow from somewhere. She stirred and stirred. Nothing gritty on the cup, no change in the dark colour. She took a spoonful and she could detect no taste but that of coffee.

She waited.

"Oh, *there* he is!" she exclaimed, looking at the doorway. The other three turned to there, and she pushed her cup toward Alma, and pulled Alma's cup toward her. It was done.

"It's Mr. Smith," said Alma. "What about it?"

"A funny thing happened," said Honey. "You know, my husband moved down to D deck, on account of his health. Well, I went down there after dinner to get an aspirin for my headache, and I got mixed up, and went into Mr. Smith's cabin by mistake. He came in and saw me there, and acted as if I was a criminal."

"I would not do that," said little Perez. "If you would come in my cabin, I would be aw'fly nice to you."

He's tight, Honey thought, glancing at him. But it was Mr. Smith she had to watch. He stood in the doorway, tall, thin, a little stooped, looking about him with a fretful frown. He caught sight of Honey and withdrew quickly.

Mr. Smith can't get me into any serious trouble she thought. What if he did find me snooping in his medicine cabinet? If it comes to a showdown between Mr. Smith and me, with the Captain or anyone else, well....

Alma was sipping her coffee from a spoon. Oh, drink it! Drink it right up!

"This coffee tastes queer," said Alma.

"It's Brazilian," said Perez. "I like very much."

"I don't," said Alma.

"You drink it four, five times, and you like," said Perez.

I *will* you to drink it! Honey said to herself. All of it. Take up the cup and drink it, and don't sip it out of a spoon. The label said one capsule, and another in an hour if needed. Mrs. Pruitt said it was harmless. The label didn't say poison. Oh, drink it!

But Alma didn't care for it; she kept tasting it half-heartedly. And they were silent, all four of them. Perez' black eyes had a dazed and confused look; he stared at Honey and Alma, and distant people, he had a vaguely demoralized air, his black tie crooked; he tried to talk but he could not. Alma did not try, she did not want Honey here and she made no secret of it. And Lashelle did not want her here either; he was restive, uneasy; his smile was mechanical, his remarks spasmodic.

"Pardon me, madam," murmured a steward at her elbow. "Cable for you, madam."

She took the envelope, but she did not want to open it here in front of these people.

"Excuse me just a minute," she said, and went over to a corner under a light.

"Mrs. Condy not registered here, regret no knowledge of whereabouts. Hotel Royal Dominions."

Well, she had expected nothing better than this. It might be another link in the chain, it might help a little to convince the hostile world that Mrs. Condy had gone upon a longer journey than they knew. But it was not of much importance now. She lit a cigarette, and stood pretending to read the cable over again with profound interest, for she was not anxious to go back to that table where she was so unwelcome.

But in the end, she went back and sat down there. She felt tired now, and battered; she made no attempt to talk. She was waiting for Alma to finish that coffee. And then I've got Captain Lashelle right where I want him, she thought. She glanced at him, and found him looking at her with a sort of dull intensity. As if he were planning something.

Let him, she thought. He can't know what I've done to Alma, and he can't stop me now. He's done for. He's not going to take her off in an airplane at daybreak.

"Finish your coffee, Hilary," said Alma imperiously.

And her little cup was empty. It was done.

"Get the check, Hilary!" she said in the same tone. "We ought to go to bed early."

"There's nothing to pay, querida," he said, and she rose.

"Good-bye!" she said, and moved away.

"Ay, ay, ay!" said little Perez, watching them as they crossed the room.

"Alma said her coffee tasted queer," said Honey.

"Como?" he said, startled.

"You heard her," said Honey. "She said her coffee tasted queer."

"Well, but maybe she don' like this Brazilian coffee."

"Suppose it was—something else?" said Honey, her eyes fixed on his face.

"But what?"

"Anyhow, you heard her say that," said Honey, rising.

He got to his feet with difficulty, and stood holding to the back of his chair.

"Please!" he said. "It's aw'fly bad if you say that."

"I'm going right now to say it to other people," she told him. "I'm going

to tell people Alma said her coffee tasted queer—and that I think she
looked queer."

"But, why, why, why?"

"You know why," said Honey.

"Oh, don'!" he cried. "You don' know how bad..."

"She's not going to get lost—like Mrs. Condy," said Honey.

"God!" he said, staring at her, his olive-skinned face grown grey. "How
you know *that?*"

"I know a lot," said Honey.

For a moment, she thought he was going to speak, to say something of
vital importance. But he shrugged his shoulders and sat down again at the
table.

Mrs. Pruitt and Mr. Lake were playing Chinese checkers, in a corner,
and Honey walked up to them; she asked a few idiotic questions about the
game which they answered politely, she tried to think of some clever way
to bring in what she meant to say; she was silent, and so were they, she
knew well enough that they were surprised by this intrusion.

I'm tired, she thought. I can't think up anything good. And she went at
it abruptly and clumsily.

"Didn't you think Mrs. Lashelle looked—sort of queer?" she asked.

"Queer?" said Mrs. Pruitt.

"Well, she said her coffee had a funny taste," said Honey. "And I
thought—she looked queer after she'd drunk it."

They were both looking at her in a way that made her feel like crying.

"She's hexed you," said Lake.

"You're *nice,* to worry so," said Mrs. Pruitt.

"Well..." said Honey unsteadily. *"I am* worried about her. Well... Good
night."

This was the hardest part of all, this was worse than stealing the tablets,
worse even than the strain of waiting for Alma to drink her coffee. She felt
like an outcast, she felt that people were beginning to dread the sight of
her, and the sound of her eternal refrain. I'm worried about Mrs.
Lashelle....

Just once more, she thought, looking about the smoke-room. It had to
be done. The suspicion had to be firmly planted, so that in the morning
there would be people to support her. Her plans were perfectly definite.
She was going to Alma's cabin early in the morning, to say good-bye. And
Alma would be asleep, so sound asleep she could not be roused.

And then I'll send a note to the Captain, or I'll see him if I can. I'll say

Mrs. Lashelle looked so queer last night after she'd drunk her coffee. So queer I mentioned it to people. I'll say right out in so many words that I'm sure her husband drugged her. And they *can't* laugh that off, because this time she'll really be drugged.

All the rest would follow, somehow. She was too tired to figure all that out. But once an investigation is started, Michael had said, you can't stop it. It would all come out, step by step, the missing luggage, the dormilona letter, up to Mrs. Condy's dreadful end. Just one more person, she told herself. She went down to the promenade deck feeling leaden with fatigue, and reluctant beyond all measure. Sitting in deck chairs, she found the Chief Engineer, and a sprightly and cultured youngish woman called Miss Shottery, and Michael, and she stopped before them.

The Chief Engineer was very pleased to see her, even if Miss Shottery was not.

"Taking a little constitutional?" he asked.

"Yes," Honey answered. "I took a lot of coffee, and I'm afraid it'll keep me awake.... Did you think the coffee tasted queer this evening?"

He gave one brief, loud shout of laughter like a bark.

"Never knew it *not* to taste queer," he said.

"I think it was all right," said Honey. "But Mrs. Lashelle seemed to think it tasted funny."

The Chief Engineer had risen, and he remained standing looking at Honey with a tightlipped smile on his lined and weather-beaten face. Miss Shottery looked out over the sea, and said not a word.

"Going ashore to see the sights to-morrow?" he asked.

"You bet!" said Honey. "Only I hope Mrs. Lashelle will be all right."

"All right?" he repeated. "Anything wrong with her?"

"I thought she seemed—queer, to-night," Honey said.

"Friend of yours?" he said, a little puzzled.

"In a way," said Honey. "I never heard of anyone having so many— queer misfortunes on a trip, did you?"

"Tell you the truth," he said, "I don't know much about the good lady."

"Oh..." said Honey looking into his eyes. "Well, do you happen to know anything about Mr. Smith?"

"Why?" he asked.

"Well, he doesn't seem very friendly," said Honey.

"He's been *sweet* to *me,*" said Miss Shottery.

"Oh, it's the young ones he's afraid of," said the Chief.

"But Miss Shottery's young!" said Honey sweetly.

He saw then that he had dropped a brick.

"What I mean is—" he said. "Smith's a very fine fellow—only—well, there you are."

"Is he really a police officer?" Honey asked.

"Retired," said the Chief. "Health broke down. You see, he was poisoned. Natives. They gave him something. Doctors couldn't find out what the stuff was. And now, why, they say the poor devil's a walking drug store. They say he's been given so much stuff, trying to cure him, y'know, that now he can take doses of this and that that would kill an ordinary person, and he never turns a hair."

"I see..." said Honey. "I see. Well.... Good night!"

She went away in haste, going nowhere, in a panic. If Mr. Smith had medicine that was unusually potent... If that label meant one or two tablets for *him*...? Enough to kill an ordinary person? To kill Alma...? Oh, *God!*

"What's wrong?" said Michael at her side.

She went over to the rail, and standing there, she told him what she had done.

"That was a good idea," he said.

"But—if I gave her—too much?"

"It was a bottle with the trade name on it," he said. "Not a special prescription."

"I'm afraid." she said. "I'm so afraid... All evening I kept thinking that she looked—doomed. I kept thinking it was the last time she'd ever look like that. And now..."

"Honey," he said, "if you'll go along to your cabin, and get to bed, I'll find out."

"You can't," she said. "It's too late."

"I give you my word I'll find out just how strong the capsules are, and how Alma's doing," he said. "And if there's anything wrong. I'll come and tell you."

"Michael..." she said. "Michael... I'm afraid."

"Take it easy," he said.

"I've done... I hadn't any right—"

"Look!" he said.

"Look at what?"

"At the stars," he said.

"What about them?"

"Well, they're supposed to help," he said. "They're supposed to make you feel very calm—and like a worm."

"They don't," she said.

"They don't me, either," he said.

They stood side by side looking over the quiet sea and the sky glittering with stars. Their hands were side by side on the rail, his bony freckled hand, hers narrow and delicate, with rose-tinted nails; they did not touch each other; they did not look at each other. But he was there.

"The stars do—sort of help..." she said.

"Will you go to bed then?" he said. "You're tired."

That was a mistake. With those two words, he gave himself away, all his pity and his tenderness; and his anxiety for her. She turned away quickly; and he did not go with her.

She went along the alleyway, struggling against a tide of tears. She opened the door and turned on the light. And the cabin was in mad disorder, clothes thrown about, jars and bottles broken on the floor; there was an overpowering smell of musky perfume in the air, her favourite perfume, wantonly spilled.

This was an open attack.

NINETEEN

She left the door into the alleyway open while she looked into the bathroom, and the two wardrobes. Then she closed the door and locked it and sat down on the bed.

A warning? she thought. It's pretty pointless. Pretty stupid. And still it was a blow. She sat looking at a pale-blue chiffon evening dress spangled with tiny silver stars that lay on the floor, and it had the look of a living thing stricken down. The scent of the spilt perfume made her a little dizzy.

A warning? she thought. Maybe he knows now that Alma's been drugged, and he's desperate. Well, he can't get in here. He can't do anything to me.

But Alma? The old panic rose in her. Alma was utterly helpless now. And if he were desperate... Take it easy, she told herself. Michael said he'd find out. I'll just sit here and wait. He won't let anything happen to her.

It was rather horrible here in the hot, brightly-lit cabin with the overpowering scent of perfume in the air. The fan spun steadily but it seemed only to lift the stale air, and let it fall again. It was like a bird flapping. The Bird of Time, she thought....

Michael will come and tell me, she thought, and stretched out on the bed in her long dress, with her ankles crossed. The door's locked. Nobody can get in. There are people all around; there's a watchman. If I rang the bell, somebody would come.

But in the next cabin, just on the other side of the bulkhead, Alma lay utterly helpless, and Captain Lashelle... What was he doing? What was he thinking? If I turned off the fan, I could hear better, she thought. It makes such a whirring noise.... There were so many other little sounds. The creak and strain of the ship, the steady rush of water along the sides, the drinking glasses on the washstand rattled. It seemed to her that the ship was moving very fast, rushing through the sea in the dark. And the Bird of Time fluttered on ahead.

A great white bird, struggling and fluttering; she could hear the beat of the mighty wings. They filled the room, they struck against the ceiling, the wind they made stirred her damp hair. She could *not* get out of here. She tried to get to the door, to find Alma, and warn her, but those grey beating wings barred the way. She tried to call out to Alma, to warn Alma. The Bird of Time...! But she could make no sound.

"Let me in! Open the door and let me in!" Alma was saying, knocking at the door.

It really was Alma. She opened her eyes, dazed from her sleep in the hot cabin, and it really was Alma's voice.

"Let me in!"

She got up and unlocked the door, and when Alma had entered she locked it after her. Alma all glittering in white satin and diamonds.

"It's so hot... " Honey said.

Alma was standing on the pale-blue dress.

"Sit down, Alma," Honey said; and Alma did sit down in the wicker arm-chair, with a sigh.

But what's happened? Honey thought. Haven't the capsules begun to work yet? The confusion of her dreams was still upon her; she sat on the edge of the bed looking at Alma stupidly.

"Alma," she said, "you've got your feet on my dress."

Alma did not move and did not stir.

With a shaking hand, Honey got out a cigarette and lit it.

"What's happened, Alma?" she asked.

"This is the pay-off," said Alma.

"I don't—"

"Why did you try to give me that poison?" Alma asked.

"Alma! It *wasn't* poison!"

"I saw you dropping those pills into my coffee. Did you want to kill me, *too?*"

Her voice had a hollow sound, as if it came from some depth that living creatures never plumbed. She sat, like an Egyptian figure, straight, two hands on the arms of the chair, her feet side by side on the blue dress.

"Alma, you ought to know—" Honey said, "you do know that I'd never do anything to harm you."

"I saw you drop those pills in my coffee," Alma repeated. "I changed cups with Hilary. Maybe he's dead now. I hope so."

She knew. She had the knowledge now that Honey had so desperately wanted her to have. And she would have been better without it. She would have been better, Honey thought, lying dead like Mrs. Condy.

"He's the only person I ever trusted," Alma said. "I gave him everything. I've been good to plenty of people, but I never trusted them. Not even my own mother. There were plenty of times when she tried to get money out of me—by lies—so that she could give it to my brother Carl. But just the same, I was good to her. I looked after her till the day she died. I've lent my sister money for those dam' arrogant brats of hers, money I'll never see again. I've been fair to the people that worked for me. But I never trusted them."

Honey sat down on the bed.

"I trusted Hilary all the way," Alma went on. "I got my life insured for him. He asked me to, and I did anything he asked. I got forty thousand dollars cash out of the bank before we sailed, for him to invest in a promotion in Trinidad. I'd have given him the eyes out of my head. He only had to ask. He didn't need to kill me."

What could you say to her? What single word of comfort was there for her?

"I've gone back over the whole thing," Alma said. "It's all clear now. He never meant me to sail. He stopped my trunks from coming. He got someone to make that telephone call, so that I'd miss the ship. He had the money I'd given him, he had my jewels. He was going to run away from me, the very day after we were married. But I came. And he killed me."

"Alma, don't!"

"It's the same thing," said Alma. "It was—I couldn't tell you. I'd never thought much about being happy. But I was happy with him. I felt I could learn all the things he'd want—the way to talk, the way to eat, and all that. I felt I could go ahead in my business—until I was the most successful woman in my field. I knew women went crazy about Hilary, but I didn't mind. I was proud of it. Because I thought he was mine. I thought I was getting better-looking. I thought... Then *she* came on board."

"Alma—"

"There's nothing *you* can say. The night she came on board, I found out. We'd gone to bed, and Hilary got up. He said he had a toothache, and he wanted to get some brandy. After he'd gone, I got worrying about him. I thought maybe he was in a lot of pain. I got up and got dressed and I went to look for him. The bar was closed, and the smoke-room was empty; just a few lights on. They were sitting in a corner. I went out on deck and I stood outside a window where I could hear. She wasn't someone he'd just picked up. They were lovers; you could tell that. He talked to *her* in a way he'd never talked to me. He told her to get off the ship at the next stop, and she'd hear from him when he'd got things cleared up. I knew what he meant."

"Alma, I know it's horrible, but—"

"Don't talk," said Alma. "Even then—even *then* I forgave him. I went back to the cabin and he came. I told him I knew, and he went down on his knees. He told me he'd married her, years ago, and she wouldn't give him a divorce. He promised to get rid of her. Only he had to play along with her, to keep her quiet, because he'd broken the law, committed bigamy. Because he wanted me so much. I believed him."

She was silent for a moment, staring at nothing.

"You can believe a thing—in a way," she said, "when you *know* it isn't true. He went down on his knees. He put his head in my lap. He said—"

She closed her eyes, and her lashes looked black as ink against her pale cheeks.

"I was comforted," she said, with a bleak simplicity. "He swore he was going to get rid of her." Her dark eyes flashed open. "D'you know what I did?" she asked.

"I—think so," said Honey.

"He was so sure of me, he was careless. I heard him talking to her the next morning. He said, 'I'll leave Alma on shore for a while, and I'll come back on board, and give you some money. You just wait for me, querida,' he said. He called *her* querida, too. 'I'll give you the money to get to Rio,' he told her, 'and I'll join you there as soon as I can.' He said he'd bring her five hundred dollars. Five hundred dollars I'd worked for. I gave it to him."

It seemed to Honey that she had never heard of a woman so wronged as this one, so brutally and utterly betrayed. She was beyond pity. She had nothing left to her.

"I gave it to him," she said again. "But before we went ashore, I took it back from her. We went to that place, and he said he'd go back on board and get me a jacket, so that I wouldn't catch cold. He went, and I waited, and after a while he came back. And I whispered to him in front of all those people: 'How did you find querida looking?' God! I wish you could have seen his face!"

"What?" said Honey, with a sort of child-like politeness. "I don't understand you."

"As soon as he went into her cabin and found her, he knew, all right."

"I'm afraid," said Honey, "I don't understand you."

"He told me you knew. He said you came into the cabin while he was there."

"I don't understand."

"What's the matter with you?" Alma demanded.

"I don't understand," Honey said again. She could not say anything else.

"He knew, all right. He dragged her out all by himself, and threw her overboard. Then he thought he could blackmail me."

I don't understand, said Honey but not aloud. She had to protect Alma, to save Alma. Alma was the victim. It couldn't be...

"Why did you want to give me that stuff?" Alma asked. "Did you want to get me out of the way so that you could meet Hilary in peace? You've got *your* husband out of the way."

"I—wanted to help you.... I didn't want you to go away with him—in an airplane."

Alma laughed.

"*He* wasn't looking forward to it, I can tell you that," she said. "It was my idea. He was so dam' frightened.... He knew by that time that his blackmail wouldn't work. I didn't care who knew. I had a right to kill that woman."

"It was—it was you, Alma?"

"I made her give me back my money. Then when she tried to get out of the cabin, I smashed her on the back of the head—with this."

She opened the big silver brocade bag that hung on her wrist and brought out a revolver.

"Then I threw ashes over her. Just emptied the ash-tray in her face. Killing her wasn't enough humiliation for her. I wanted him to see. I thought you knew."

"No..." said Honey. "No, I didn't know."

"I don't *know* if I can trust you or not," said Alma. "If I believed that story... What was it you tried to give me?"

"Just sleeping medicine. Just so you wouldn't go off alone with him."

It seemed to Honey that her words were light as thistledown, without force or direction. And her thoughts were like that. It was Alma who was in danger. Alma was the victim. Her mind held fast to that.

"If that's true," said Alma, and was silent again, looking down at the blue dress under her feet. "I came in here before, looking for you. I was mad then. I thought you'd tried to get rid of me. But it wasn't like that.... D'you mean that stuff won't kill Hilary?"

"No," Honey said. "No. It won't."

Alma rose.

"But if he died..." she said musingly. "If he died in his sleep, everybody would think it was from that."

"Alma!" said Honey, springing to her feet.

"Shut up!" said Alma. "That's all you have to do. You said you wanted to help me. All right. You have."

"Alma, you can't... You can't..."

"He's getting off easy," said Alma. "A couple of pillows over his face—"

"Alma, please—listen. Alma, that's—murder."

Alma turned toward the door, Honey ran to her and caught her arm as she turned the key. "Alma... Alma, don't!"

"Now, look here!" said Alma. "I can't live in the world with him. If I leave him, he'll blackmail me; and if I stay with him, he'll try to kill me."

"Tell the police that—"

"Oh, don't be such a fool!" said Alma. "All you have to do is to shut up. If you don't, you'll be sorry."

She started to open the door but Honey clung to her arm.

"No! You can't! I won't let you!"

Alma pulled away her clutching hand, but Honey seized her arm again. Alma took her by the shoulder, and hit her hard in the mouth, and flung her staggering back across the room. She fell, striking her head against the chest of drawers, and for a time she lay still, not unconscious, but dizzy and sick.

It was very hard to get up. She collapsed on the bed and closed her eyes until the spinning sickness passed. Alma was gone.

Now what? Now who...? Michael... Michael said... She went into the alleyway, and everything was so quiet. Maybe it was late. Her mouth was bleeding; she wiped it on the long sleeve of her dress. Maybe it's very late...

The square in front of the Purser's office was empty, the wicket was closed. There wasn't anybody.... She remembered where Michael's cabin was, and she went there and knocked, and then she opened the door. It was empty.

Now what? Now who...? Hurry... A pillow over his face.... And my fault... Hurry...

Weaver, she thought. Weaver will know what to do. Weaver will stop this. He'll know the right person to tell. Only why isn't there anybody left...? She stopped on the stairs to wipe the blood from her mouth again; the ship was moving, she could feel the vibration underfoot. But where were all the people?

She came to that alleyway on D deck, long and empty, covered with shining linoleum, smelling of hot oil and brass polish. It was such a long way to Weaver's cabin, and she was getting tired.... But hurry! Hurry!

She was out of breath when she knocked at his door.

"Who is it?" he called, crossly.

"It's Honey," she said.

"I can't let you in now," he said. "Not at this hour of the night. To-mor-row—"

"Weaver, open the door, please," she said, trying to speak quietly, and not frighten him. "It's very important."

"No!" he said. "Kindly don't disturb me. I'm not well."

For an instant she leaned her forehead against the door, because her head ached, because she was so tired, and almost in despair. But the sound of footsteps made her look up; somebody was coming, somebody who would help her. She stood waiting, and it was Alma, white and glittering and terrible.

"Weaver! Weaver, *quick!* Open the door!" she cried.

"I won't!" he shouted. "Go away!"

Alma was coming nearer and nearer, walking quietly and easily in her gold sandals. There was nowhere to run, and Weaver's door was locked against her.

"Weaver!" she cried once more.

But it was Michael who came out of a cabin opposite, followed by Mr. Smith.

"Go quick—and see—Captain Lashelle..." she said.

She slid down the door in a heap to the floor. Too tired...

TWENTY

Miss Bewley came out of her cabin.

"Good gracious!" she cried. and as Michael was helping Honey to her feet, Miss Bewley began to knock hard and fast on Weaver's door.

"Weaver Stapleton!" she cried, in a surprisingly shrill voice. "Open that door at *once!*"

"Oh, don't—" said Honey. "He—"

"Open the door this *minute!*" cried Miss Bewley. "Something terrible has happened."

"Stop her," Honey said to Michael. But the door had opened and Miss Bewley went into the cabin.

Michael took out his handkerchief and wiped off Honey's mouth, the watchman came hurrying around the corner, other passengers appeared

"Let's get out of this," said Michael.

"Go and see—Captain Lashelle," she whispered. "Quick!"

"All right," he answered. "I'll leave you in your cabin first."

She could not make any protest against that; she wanted so very much to escape from the sight of anyone, from the sound of any shrill, or angry or curious voice.

"Just sit down and smoke a pipe," said Michael, "and I'll go and see."

"Michael, she said she was going to kill him—while he was asleep."

"Well, I'll take a look," he said. "Here. You'd better keep this."

He put his handkerchief into her hand, and pressed her gently down into a chair. He went out, and she heard him knock at the door of the next cabin; she heard the door open. Her mouth hurt now, and her head ached violently.

It's all over, she thought. He's dead. And now they'll hang Alma. Alma's a murderess. They hang people in British places. They'll lock her up in jail, and then they'll take her to court. And she'll say everything wrong, everything to make people hate her. Everybody hates her.

She is a murderess, and it is right to hate her. Only I don't. I can't. She's too—unlucky.

That was the word she used, for an idea a little beyond her grasp. What can you do with the unlucky, the ill-starred, the people who can't win love? The clumsy, the blind, the infinitely unfortunate creatures who try to seize, to buy, to dragoon what can only be given? This was what she had felt about Alma from the beginning; that Alma had nothing and never would have anything.

She had seen what had happened to Alma. Step by step she had witnessed the atrocious betrayal, she had seen that poor, belated tenderness of Alma's exploited, she had seen her robbed, mocked. She could well imagine how it had been for Alma to hear that talk between Lashelle and Mrs. Condy. In one moment, everything was lost, her whole world had grown black and frightful. It would have been bad enough to learn, on her honeymoon, that her husband cared nothing for her, and never had. But to learn that he intended to get rid of her, to murder her...

She's not responsible, Honey thought. I know that what she's done is wicked and awful. But when they take her to court, somebody ought to explain what she's been through.

There was a knock on the open door, and Michael came in.

"Lashelle's all right," he said. "Sleeping very heavily, that's all."

"But, Michael...!" she said. "I'm afraid she'll—"

"Not now," he said. "Don't worry. She won't do anything now."

He stooped and picked up the filmy blue dress, and laid it over the foot of the bed.

I'll get Doctor Lovejoy to—"

"No, thank you," she said. "It isn't anything. Just a little cut."

"Shall I go away?" he asked.

"No, thank you," she said. "I'd like to tell you.... It was... You thought Weaver killed Mrs. Condy, didn't you?"

"I think he had something to do with it," said Michael bluntly.

"No," she said. "It was Alma. She told me so. It was—oh, it's so pitiful."

She began to tell him, as best she could, and he stood before her with his hands in his pockets and his head bent.

"You're a good advocate," he said.

"I can't—" she began, when Miss Bewley entered.

"My dear," she said, and sat down on the bed.

She looked very strange indeed, in a high-collared brown foulard dress with a Persian design in purple and white, her auburn hair dry as straw, was bushed up like a Hottentot's, her face, especially her nose was chalk-white with powder.

"My dear..." she said. "I *am* so sorry."

"Weaver?" Honey asked. "You mean he's sick?"

"My dear... It's my fault. It's *all* my fault!" said Miss Bewley beginning to weep a little.

"I'd better go and see him," said Honey, rising.

"My dear, no..."

"But you don't mean...?"

"My dear, I *do!*" cried Miss Bewley. "When I went into his cabin, he was alarmed...." She dried her eyes. "He fell down.... His *heart,* Doctor Lovejoy says. Of course you know how *timid* he was, and so worried about himself."

Honey looked at her sternly.

"It's all my fault!" said Miss Bewley, putting her handkerchief to her eyes again. "I *undoubtedly* frightened him to death."

He was gone.

Honey lay stretched out in the chair, her ankles crossed, her arms hanging loose. She had said she would like to be alone, and they had left her. She did not cry; she just thought about Weaver. It seemed to her that that was of the utmost importance, that was what she owed to him, and what he would want of her.

She thought about Weaver, and how courtly he had been to her mother. She thought about Weaver taking them to the opera; she thought of Weaver the day they bought the mink coat, and how he had sat in a chair and waited while she tried on one coat after another. She remembered the evening he had asked her to marry him and how beautifully he had spoken. She tried to remember everything like that.

The ship's whistle blew and the engines stopped. She raised her head and saw a pearly light in the sky outside the port. But she did not stir; she did not care.

I just want to go home now, she thought. And take Weaver home. That's what he'd want, I know. I *do* want to go home. I want to see Mother....

There was a very light rap at the door.

"Yes?" she said.

"It's me," said Michael's voice. "I thought perhaps you'd like to go on deck."

"No, thank you," she said.

Because it wouldn't be fair to Weaver.

"They're leaving," he said. "I thought, perhaps—"

"Oh . . *Who?*" she said, rising.

She went to the doorway and faced Michael.

"Leaving? You mean? You don't mean Alma?" she said very low.

"Yes," he said. "The hydroplane's coming now."

"But—she can't. I mean—but I told you."

"I know," he said.

She looked and looked at him.

"Well, do you mean you don't believe what I told you?"

"It's not that," he said. "Only I thought it might be better this way."

"To let her go?"

She could hear the drone of a plane now, and it brought back the sense of urgency that had so long been with her.

"I'll come," she said.

She did not know what he meant by this, or why he, who had never shown any great sympathy for Alma, was willing to let her go. Men aren't like that, she thought. They're generally much more sort of law-abiding and they want people to be punished, and so on. But I don't want Alma to be hanged. Maybe that's wrong, but I can't help it.

They went along the alleyway and out on deck. The plane was coming through the pale sky like a dark and rigid shadow; standing by the rail she saw it come down and cut through the water and lie at rest. A fresh wind blew, and in the grey world there was the thrilling expectancy of dawn. She too waited, not knowing for what. The ladder was down, with a row-boat waiting below beside it. There was no land in sight; nothing at all.

"Here they come," said Michael quietly.

They came. Alma first in her black dress, her mink coat over her arm, and after her came Lashelle in a white suit and a felt hat; he was carrying two bags. They turned, both of them, toward Honey, and in this twilight their faces were so pale. Lashelle took off his hat with a flourish; he smiled, a smile like a grimace of pain.

Alma did not smile, she did not speak. She started down the ladder.

"Michael...?" Honey said. And then with a rising insistence. *"Michael!* We can't let them go!"

"I think," he said, "that I'll speak to my father, later on. Get him to send a message on to Rio, for the police to hold whichever one arrives there."

"One...?" she said.

"Lashelle told me they've arranged to make two overnight stops," he said. "One in Trinidad, one in Cartagena—for his business affairs."

"And you think that only one of them will ever get to Rio?"

"Yes," he said. "That's what I think."

"But Michael! Michael, that's so horrible...!"

"It's the best way—for you," he said. "You wouldn't want to go into

court as a witness against Alma. You wouldn't want to be the one....
They're both guilty. They both have murder in their hearts. Let them go."

"But, Michael! It means—"

"What will it mean if you stop them? She'll hang, and he'll go free
because his murder didn't work. They're both guilty. Let them go. The one
who's left will be held in Rio."

She looked up at him in dismay and dread; their eyes met.

"They're going to get justice, Honey." he said.

The sun was coming up now, fiery gold above the horizon. The row-
boat came into a path of dancing glittering light where the sea was
turquoise blue. Alma and Lashelle were sitting there side by side, starting
off on the last lap of their honeymoon.

THE END

MIASMA

Elisabeth Sanxay Holding

CHAPTER ONE

DENNISON FINDS A JOB

Alexander Dennison made careful calculations before going to the little town of Shayne. He collected statistics about the population, the birthrate, the death-rate; he figured upon the probable percentage of accidents and illnesses, and, he was convinced that there was room for another doctor in Shayne.

So he rented a cottage there, engaged a woman to cook and clean for him, and hung out his shingle, and waited.

"Of course," he wrote to his fiancée, "the hard thing is getting a start."

He waited. His sign announced that his office hours were from 9-10 and from 2-4, and during those hours there he sat, in his neat little office. He felt that he could not smoke there; an odour of tobacco would not be seemly; he simply waited, looking out from behind the curtains at the tranquil street. When the office hours were over, he would go into the dismal little dining-room, and light his pipe, and read or meditate. And every day, rain or shine, he took a long walk, invariably leaving careful directions with his cook, if anyone telephoned, she was to say that the doctor was expected back at such and such an hour.

No one did telephone. In a month, he had just two patients. One was an errand boy with a cut finger; the other was a motorist passing through the town, who had sprained his wrist cranking his car. Neither of these was ever likely to return, or to recommend anyone else.

At the beginning of the second month, Dennison decided that he could do without a cook, and needed a house cleaning only twice in a week. By the end of that second month he found that he could do everything for himself. And he wrote to several steamship companies to ask if there were a ship needing a doctor. He spent his evenings making new calculations, covering pages and pages with neat little figures, trying to see how long he could hold on, on an impossibly frugal diet.

He was a lean and rather dour-looking young man, with a thin, intelligent face, and a stubborn mouth. He was not handsome, not at all amusing; his intelligence was more dogged and honest than brilliant. The girl he was engaged to told him that he must put himself forward more.

"You must mix with people, and make friends, dear," she wrote. "You must make connections. I am sure that is the only way to build up a practice."

He was ready to admit that her way might be a good one, but he saw no chance of trying it. He was too poor to belong to any club, and as nobody called upon him, he could not very well make overtures. What was more, he was not good at "mixing with people." He didn't want to do so. He was a doctor, and he wanted a chance to cure people.

His fiancée was strongly opposed to his idea of going on a ship.

"It simply means postponing our marriage indefinitely," she wrote. "If you do make two or three voyages, you'll have to begin all over again when you leave the ship. Alec, dear, do try to stick it out where you are. You know I don't want much. As soon as you are making even three thousand a year, we can get married, and I *know I* can help you."

Her letters filled him with a sort of rage, of impatience and misery. Of course, the poor girl didn't understand. She knew nothing about money; she lived in her father's house sheltered and protected; she could not imagine what it was to have nothing. Dennison was young and strong; he had no objection to enduring a good many hardships, but he had to have *something* to eat.

At last he had an answer from a steamship company; he went in to New York for an interview, and he was offered a berth on a little freight steamer. He asked for twenty-four hours to consider the offer, and went back to his cottage, with a heart like lead.

"I'll have to write to Evelyn," he thought, "and she'll think I'm a failure. Her father'll think I'm a failure. But I'm not! I'll do well enough, one of these days. Only, it takes time."

It was the dusk of a rainy April day when he got home. The chill drizzle had soaked through his thin overcoat; his feet were wet, he was tired, and he was hungry. But he accepted these discomforts as a matter of course. What really troubled him was the letter he must write to his girl.

"I'll have to offer to release her, that's all," he thought, "I can't ask her to wait indefinitely. Not fair to her."

And he thought of her as he had last seen her, at dinner in her father's comfortable house; such a pretty, gay little thing....

His cottage was dark, naturally. There was nobody there waiting for him. But, as he unlocked the door, he saw what he had never seen before—a note pushed under the door. He picked it up, and switching on the light, opened it.

"Can you call on Doctor Leatherby this afternoon?"

It was a disappointment for he had hoped it might be from a patient.

"Still," he thought, "this Doctor Leatherby may have a job for me...."

He scowled, reflectively. Before settling in Shayne, he had had a talk with the little town's chief druggist, who had given him friendly information about the other doctors in the place.

"And then there's Doctor Leatherby," the druggist had said, at the end. "But he's practically retired. Sees a few old patients in his office—makes two or three calls a day. But he hardly counts."

"And what does he want with me?" thought Dennison.

He was quite well aware of the number of discreditable jobs that could be offered to a young and needy doctor, and, perhaps because he was tired and hungry and unhappy, he had a sort of presentiment that this would be one of those jobs. It was too much to expect that a stroke of good luck would come just now, at the very last moment.

"I'll go and see him though," he thought.

So he locked the door after him, and set out again through the rain. He had looked in the directory for Doctor Leatherby's address, and he knew how to get to that street. It was a goodish walk, and he had plenty of time to meditate. And he did.

Doctor Leatherby's house surprised him when he reached it, it was so large and impressive, standing well back from the street, in well-kept grounds. He went up the drive, mounted the steps of a lighted terrace and rang the bell, and a manservant opened the door.

"I'm Doctor Dennison—" the young man began.

"Come in, please, sir!" said the servant, and ushered him into a room where a bright fire burned; a gracious and luxurious room, warm, softly lit, lined with books. Dennison walked over to the fire and stood there, downcast and grim, thinking of his own chilly and comfortless little house, and the supper of tinned herrings and bread that awaited him there.

"If Leatherby's got a job to offer me..." he thought, "but I don't see..."

The luxury of these surroundings did not reassure him. On the contrary! A retired general practitioner in a little place like this didn't usually live in such style. Moreover, he was inclined by temperament to distrust luxury; his own life had been a hard and lonely one, and he had little understanding of anything else. He was growing more and more dubious about this Doctor Leatherby.

"Well, we'll see!" he thought.

The sound of a leisurely footstep on the stairs made him stiffen to attention; he watched the doorway, unhappily expecting the entrance of some venerable quack. But the man who entered had no look of the quack about him. He was a stout man of perhaps fifty, with piercing dark eyes and a neat grey beard, a man of great personal dignity and authority.

"Doctor Dennison?" he said. "Sit down, if you please! I am Doctor Leatherby. I am obliged to you for calling."

Dennison did sit down, and waited.

"I shall come directly to the point," said Leatherby, in his unhurried fashion. "Will you smoke, Doctor Dennison?"

"Thank you," said Dennison, "not just now."

It was characteristic of him that he would accept nothing, until he knew what was to be asked of him

"I am not a young man," Leatherby proceeded. "I find it difficult to go out in all sorts of weather.

I need the assistance of a younger man. I have looked up your record, Doctor Dennison, highly creditable to you!"

"Thank you," said Dennison, briefly.

"I also, before approaching you, wrote to my old friend Professor Leeds, under whom you studied anatomy. And I received a most satisfactory account of you."

"Thank you," said Dennison again. He was not flattered by all this, because he was honestly, soberly aware that his record *was* good.

"You are just beginning to practice," Leatherby went on. "A difficult time for a young man without influence. And it occurred to me that you might find a connection with an older physician useful to you. I shall explain exactly what I shall ask from you, should you accept my proposal. I should ask you to live here, in this house, in order to take any night calls; and in bad weather, or in case I am indisposed, to take other calls; also to assist me at times with the office patients. I should offer you a salary of fifty dollars a week. It is not very much, but all your living expenses would, of course, be included, and I think the experience would be of value to you."

"Fifty dollars a week!" thought Dennison, whose shoes were nearly worn through, and whose bank account was below the minimum for checking accounts.

But he dismissed these considerations; that was not the right way to consider this proposal. If there were anything queer about this, anything shady...

"Is it a general practice, sir?" he asked.

"Very general!" said Leatherby, with a smile. "The usual things; nothing rare. But, I should say, a very valuable experience for a young man."

Dennison was silent for a few moments. He could see nothing amiss with the proposal; indeed it was a marvellous piece of luck for him. And he saw nothing in any way suspicious about Leatherby himself. In fact, he made a very favourable impression upon the younger man.

"And if I find anything, later on, that I don't like," he thought, "I can always quit." And glancing up: "Thank you, sir!" he said, "I'll be very pleased to accept your offer."

"Good! Then perhaps you'll dine with me this evening, Doctor Dennison, and we'll become better acquainted!"

With becoming gravity, the young man accepted, and returned to his cottage, in an odd mood. He was glad, very glad, of this chance, yet it depressed him. He tried to console himself by thinking of the salary, and of the invaluable experience he would gain, but it was no use. He did not want Doctor Leatherby's patients. He wanted his own. He did not want to give up his forlorn little cottage, and his independence.

But he certainly could not refuse this opportunity. He dressed in his best blue serge suit, and just before setting out, he ate the tin of herrings and several slices of bread, so that he should not appear shamefully hungry at Leatherby's table.

He was thankful presently that he had done so; for he sat down to the most perfect meal he had ever imagined; food exquisitely cooked, beautifully served, a vintage wine; not the sort of meal Dennison was used to, nor the sort of meal one would expect in the house of a country doctor.

They dined alone, in a fine old room, with candles on the table, shedding a pleasant light on damask and silver and delicate glass. The manservant waited on them; there was altogether an air of friendly ceremony, as if a dinner were a matter of importance.

At first Doctor Leatherby made an attempt to discuss various niceties of cooking, but he found Dennison wholly ignorant of the subject. He was silent for a few moments.

"You are welcome to the use of my library, Dennison," he said, at last, "I think you will find much to interest you there. Especially if you care for the classics."

Young Dennison never read anything but medical books and reviews, and for recreation, stories of the Wild West. But he thought it would be discourteous to say so.

"Thank you, sir," he said.

"In my younger days," Leatherby went on, "I wasted a good deal of time attempting a translation of Ovid. Until I realized how much better it had been done before I was born. Still, the work holds a peculiar charm for me. You know the Metamorphoses? You know the story—"

He went on to relate a certain metamorphosis. Dennison was not acquainted with it, and he found it somewhat startling.

"Well..." he said, embarrassed, "of course, I suppose people had different ideas in those days...."

"A different conception of life altogether," said Leatherby. "A richer and nobler conception, a harmony of body and spirit which has perished. In those days, men knew how to savour the pleasures of the body without grossness. They made even of drunkenness a divine thing. They sat, crowned with garlands.... Try this port, Dennison!"

"Thank you!" said the young man. He was impressed by Leatherby's talk and interested, but he was not convinced. He had seen plenty of cases of drunkenness in the hospital, and could recall nothing at all divine in any of them.

"*Carpe diem,*" Leatherby pursued, "to enjoy the day—that is the art of life. To savour and to delight in that which you actually possess; not to go hungry and thirsty with your eyes upon an impossible tomorrow. To enjoy the day."

"But sometimes you can't," said Dennison, thinking of people he had seen in the hospital whose days were all anxiety and pain, "when you haven't anything you can enjoy—"

"Ah!" said Leatherby. There was an odd note in his voice, and, glancing up, the young man saw a strange, steady smile upon the other's face. "We need not accept the terms offered us."

"I don't see—" said Dennison, with a faint frown.

Leatherby brought his fist down on the table with a crash.

"Some lives...!" he cried. "The suffering—the futility... the futility...! And we physicians are required to use all our skill to prolong even the most hopeless suffering!"

Dennison was startled and moved by this outburst. They were both silent for a time.

"I know," said Dennison, at last, "I've seen cases... But the thing is, sir...." He hesitated, because he was a little shy, but presently he went on, because he was honest and serious. "I think there's a purpose in suffering, sir...."

"We'll have our coffee in the library," Leatherby said, and led the way to the fireside, followed presently by the man-servant with the coffee service.

They conversed amicably for an hour or more, about the patients whom Dennison would see; then the young man took his leave; and went home through the rain.

The cottage was damp and chill as a vault; he kept on his overcoat when he sat down to write his letters; first to the steamship company, declining that job; then to Evelyn.

"Of course," he wrote, "this is a remarkable opportunity for me. I'll get just the experience I need. And out of that salary, I can save at least forty a week."

Then followed a page of his calculations; how he expected to save two thousand dollars in a year, half of which they would use for furnishing, and half for a little nest-egg. And *then*, with all the experience he would have gained, and all the connections he hoped to make, they could get married *then*. It was a sober and rather dry letter, the sort he usually did write, but at the end was one of those queer little outbursts which were, perhaps, one of the reasons why Evelyn liked him.

"A year seems a very long time, my darling girl. I am thinking this moment of your dear smile. I miss you so. I will do the very best I can. God bless you."

He went to bed, but not immediately to sleep. He had calculations to make, and he wanted to think about Doctor Leatherby.

"I can't quite make him out," he thought, "some of his ideas.... But, just the same, he's a fine man. Knows his job, too.... But these classics.... I never did very well in Latin.... That—that anecdote..."

He fell asleep, to the sound of the rain drumming on the roof, and he dreamed that he was lying on a couch, garlanded with flowers, listening to Doctor Leatherby, in a purple-bordered tunic, reciting something in Latin.

"Hasta. Hastae... Hastae," chanted the Doctor.

"That's the first declension," thought Dennison anxiously. "But I've forgotten... I don't know if he's making mistakes."

Then he knew, somehow, that Evelyn could hear, and he became badly worried.

"You'll be careful what you say, won't you, sir?" he asked. "There's a lady present."

"Hastam, Hasta," chanted the Doctor, and Dennison sat up, to urge him to be careful. And opened his eyes, to find the sun shining into his room.

CHAPTER TWO

DENNISON REFUSES ADVICE

Everything had marvellously changed during the night. Doctor Leather-by's house, which had in the dark impressed young Dennison as being of rather sombre magnificence, had in the morning an aspect generous and welcoming, and something less than magnificent. It was a brownstone house, with a brick terrace in front, and a colonnade, the roof of which formed a balcony for the first story, and on either corner rose an artless little turret, giving to the place the look of a neat little play castle. The lawn, sodden after the night's rain, was growing faintly green, the fine old trees were beginning to bud; the sky overhead was a pure, radiant blue, and young Dennison felt something of the thrilling promise of Spring.

Fifty dollars a week, he thought, for that was what his life had done to him. All his hopes, his dreams, had needed money for their fulfillment, and it had been so bitterly hard to get the money; money for his education, his medical training, for clothes in which to present a decent appearance.

And now his love required money. He couldn't have Evelyn unless he had money. So that all the delight in this sweet day, all the hopes of his young heart, were turned to that one object. The April wind blew in his face, and it bore the faintest, most exquisite fragrance of wet woodlands, and he thought:

"I'll have to get a pair of shoes, first thing."

He rang the bell, and the same man-servant admitted him, but now with a respectful trace of recognition in his mild, middle-aged face.

"If you'll step into the reception-room, please, sir," he said, "Miss Napier will explain everything."

And, thought Dennison, who might Miss Napier be? He followed the man down the hall, through a door at the end—and found himself in a dazzle and blur of sunshine.

It was a small room he had entered, with white walls and furniture, and at a desk sat a young woman in a white dress; her hair was bright as the sun, her white teeth flashed in a smile; the breeze blew in, making the curtains flutter; everything here seemed alive, vital and warm and stirring.

"You're Doctor Dennison?" she asked. "I'm Miss Napier. Doctor Leatherby's asked me to talk to you—about things."

He saw that she was wearing a nurse's uniform and the cap of a famous hospital, and she had risen, as was fitting for a nurse in the presence of a doctor. Yet somehow it embarrassed him a little.

"Sit down, please!" he said.

She did so, and he took a chair opposite the desk.

"Doctor Leatherby's not feeling well this morning," she said, "so if you can take the office patients—? Perhaps I can help you. I can give you their cards before you see them."

"Thank you," he said, in his stiff fashion, "anyone here yet?"

"Two," she answered, and handed him two cards, with the names, case-histories, and "remarks" neatly typed on them.

"Thank you!" he said again, and without another word, went into the lavatory to scrub his hands. When he went into the office, he found her standing there, waiting for him.

"Will you want me, Doctor Dennison?" she asked.

"I don't think so."

"There's the bell, in case you do," she said, and went out, into the little reception-room. He was conscious for a moment of a curious effect, as if the sun had dimmed a little; then his first patient entered, and he forgot all such fantasies.

There were five patients that morning, and they ranged in age from a small boy with a cut knee to be dressed, to a very old woman who want-ed a tonic. But whatever their age or condition, they had one thing in common; they all showed a candid disappointment at the sight of Denni-son instead of Leatherby. The old woman even told him how she felt about it, and expressed grave doubts as to the prescription he gave her. Denni-son found nothing in this to resent, though he was blunt enough himself, and he saw no reason why these people should like or trust him on sight.

When the last patient had gone, he went into the reception-room, where Miss Napier was knitting a scarlet jersey. She rose.

"Please sit down!" he said. "I want to ask you about charges."

"The boy doesn't pay anything," she said. "Mrs. Lacy—fifty cents. Mrs. Tyne, no charge, Miss Kerr, two dollars. Old Mrs. Milton, no charge. Most of them are poor people."

"Doctor Leatherby's very charitable..." said Dennison thoughtfully.

Miss Napier said nothing at all. It was, of course, quite correct for her to make no reply to his observation, yet, in a way, he wished that she would. He glanced down at her; she was looking at hint, and their eyes met. Her eyes were grey, and wonderfully clear and steady, and they were fixed upon him with an unequivocal appraisal. She was summing him up, and he knew it. He knew that she saw the frayed cuffs of his shirt, his faded neck-tie, his shabby boots; he felt pretty sure that she knew why he was here—because he had failed to win any practice of his own. The colour mount-ed in his dark face, but he didn't avert his glance, did not stir; he stood before her, not defiant, but with his own sort of pride. He had nothing to be ashamed of; let her look.

"Doctor Dennison!" she said, so abruptly that he started a little.

"Yes?" he asked.

"Doctor Dennison, if I were you, I shouldn't stay here," she said.

Because he was simple and direct himself, he was not inclined to impute subtle motives to other people. He saw in her grey eyes only an honest anx-iety, and he believed that she spoke in all honesty and good-will.

"'Why?" he asked.

"I don't think it's the right place for you," she said.

"Perhaps not," he answered. "But, just at present—"

She rose.

"I wish you'd go!" she said. "I can't—"

"Lunch is served, Miss!" said the man-servant from the doorway.

Dennison and Miss Napier were alone at the table, but the man-servant was there to wait on them, and, with an ease that surprised Dennison, the girl threw off her serious and anxious air, and talked to him as he had never been talked to before. Evelyn was a cheerful young thing; she laughed often enough; sometimes she teased him. But it was different. This girl made *him* talk; this girl, only by her smile, aroused in his lonely and cau-tious heart a friendliness altogether new to him. In his first glimpse of her, in the morning sun, she had seemed to him a creature somehow irradiat-ing life and warmth; and the impression remained. Their talk was quite professional, but she made him remember droll experiences he had had; for the first time in his life, he felt that he was being amusing. So that he actually forgot the curious thing she had said to him before lunch.

"There are three calls Doctor Leatherby would like you to make this afternoon," she said, when they had finished. "And now Miller will show you your room."

Dennison followed the man-servant up the stairs, and along the corridor to one of those little turrets, and opened the door. It was, to Dennison, almost an incredible room, round, with three windows looking out over the garden, luxuriously and charmingly furnished, and with a bathroom attached. After Miller had gone, he sat down in an easy-chair by one of the windows, and lit his pipe, with a little of the feeling of one transported here by a magic carpet. At the side of the bed was a table on which stood a carafe and glass, an ash-tray, and a blue-shaded lamp, suggestive of an ease unknown to him; there was a large chest of drawers, one drawer of which would hold all his worldly goods; the cupboard door was ajar, showing rows of hangers, and a low shelf for shoes. And near him lay his two bags, one quite new, with his instruments in it, the other shabby and battered, containing his personal effects. It was incredible to find himself here. And he did not care for the incredible. His alert and obstinate mind was uneasy.

"I don't see..." he said to himself, "five office patients—most of them not paying—and three outside calls.... Of course, he must have private means, to live in this style.... But why pay me fifty a week? No; I don't see...."

And it was his nature to want to see, to understand his position.

"This Miss Napier.... What did she mean? Advised me not to stay.... Why? She said she didn't think it was the right place for me—Well, why?"

He meditated upon this until his pipe was finished; then he washed, brushed his best blue suit and his hat carefully, and taking up his bag, went downstairs. He found Miller in the hall.

"The car is waiting, sir," said Miller.

"I don't drive," said Dennison, curtly.

"There is a chauffeur, sir," said Miller, and it seemed to Dennison that there was a sneer in his voice. He turned sharply, but he saw no expression at all upon that mild, middle-aged face.

So he went out, the door opened for him by Miller, a chauffeur in livery waiting for him, and a very smart little car.

"I'll have to get a decent pair of gloves," he thought, "and a new hat, and I need about everything new."

Sitting in that smart little car, he did not feel very happy. They stopped at the first house; the chauffeur jumped down to open the door, and Dennison, as he got out, was perfectly conscious of his own shabbiness.

"Is that what she meant?" he thought. "When she said it wasn't the right place for me, did she mean that I'm not—quite up to this?"

No, he could not think that.

"She's not that sort," he thought.

He made the three calls, and all the three patients were disappointed at the sight of him. The last one was pretty disagreeable.

"When I send for Doctor Leatherby, I want Doctor Leatherby," she said. "Not some young man, full of new-fangled notions."

Still, she allowed Dennison to look at her sore throat, and while he sat down, to write a prescription, he felt her sharp eyes upon him. He felt her looking at his frayed cuffs, his faded necktie, his worn shoes....

"The first pay I get, I'll buy a decent outfit," he thought.

And a new impatience filled him. He who had had to wait so long, to work so hard, to save so painfully—for everything he wanted, was annoyed now because he must wait six days longer for new clothes.

When he returned to Doctor Leatherby's, he saw a limousine standing outside the house. He thought that must mean a patient, so he hurried into the office. But the waiting-room was empty.

"Visitors," he thought, and hoped with all his heart that there would be no stranger at the dinner-table. Not until he had his new clothes.

He went out into the hall to go to his room, and at the foot of the stairs he met a woman coming down, a remarkably handsome woman, in a fur coat. She passed him without a glance, but he saw that her face was stained with tears.

"Not my business!" said Dennison to himself.

He had his foot on the stairs when Miss Napier's voice called, behind him, and turning, he saw her in the doorway of the library.

"May I speak to you a moment?" she asked.

He felt a singular gladness in turning to her; he went to her willingly. But as he drew nearer, he saw some change in her face, some cloud over it.

"Doctor Leatherby wanted me to ask you—" she began, and stopped.

He waited quietly. She was standing beside a massive desk, one slender hand resting on the polished wood, and he thought that against the background of richly bound books, in this solidly handsome room, she, in her austere white uniform, looked as incongruous as even he did.

"Doctor Leatherby thought you might want a week's salary in advance," she resumed. "He's written a cheque for you."

He felt his face grow hot, the more so because she too looked ill-at-ease.

"It's here," she went on, with her eyes averted. "But I thought that perhaps—if you weren't going to stay—you wouldn't want it."

"Why shouldn't I stay?" he asked.

She looked up at him now, with her direct and steady glance.

"Why shouldn't I stay?" he repeated.

She parted her lips, as if to speak, but said nothing, and he fancied he saw in her grey eyes a look almost of despair.

"I—don't think it will suit you," she said, at last.

"I'll try it," said Dennison, curtly.

"Doctor Dennison!" she said, "We had another young doctor last year...

I... I *know* it's not a good place for a young doctor—just beginning. There's no—scope here, you see...."

"You're mighty anxious to get rid of me!" thought Dennison, and his young mouth set in a hard line. "Just the same," he said, "I'll try it, for a while."

She picked up the cheque and handed it to him without a word; he took it without a word. He was angry, and bitterly hurt.

"There's probably some other fellow she wants this job for," he thought, "but I'm here, and here I stay."

He spent the rest of the afternoon in his room, reading a medical journal. When dinner time drew near, he washed, and brushed his hair, which was all the dressing he was able to do, and went down the stairs.

He strolled down the hall, in the direction of the office, and most casually glanced into the little reception-room, to see what Miss Napier might be doing. But instead of Miss Napier, he saw Miller there, sitting at her desk, and speaking into the telephone.   I

"The doctor will see you this evening at nine o'clock, sir," he said. "No, Sir.... Certainly, Sir.... No one else, sir."

He rose, at the sight of Dennison, with a respectful murmur.

"Making an appointment for me, Miller?"

"No, sir," said Miller, "for Doctor Leatherby, sir."

"I understand that Doctor Leatherby was ill."

"He's in the library, sir," said Miller, and Dennison fancied he heard in the man's voice a note of insolence. But there was nothing he could fasten upon, and, turning on his heel, he walked off to the library.

There he found Doctor Leatherby, in a dinner jacket, standing with his back to the fire.

"Ah!" he said, with his singularly agreeable smile, "I've plunged you—in media res. I'm sorry to have given you so little preparation. But I have an enemy...." He touched his heart. "Must be humoured at times," he said. "Now tell me how you got on."

They dined alone together and it was a dinner quite as good as the one on the previous evening, more like a feast, thought Dennison.

Again after dinner they went into the library for coffee.

"Did I tell you—?" said Leatherby, after he had lit a cigar, "that I always see certain patients myself?"

"No, sir, you didn't," said Dennison.

"'By appointment. Old patients—or persons particularly recommended to me. I have a little consulting-room upstairs."

"I see!" said Dennison.

But he did not see, and he did not like this.

"And, by the way," Leatherby went on, "as I am feeling so much better, I'll take the office patients tomorrow morning, so that you can have the forenoon free—for any business of your own. Shopping, and so on." He paused. "My sister comes home tomorrow," he said, "and that means an assorted variety of guests."

He smiled again, and his eyes met those of the younger man in frank kindliness. It was not possible to misunderstand him; he had sent Dennison that cheque, and now he was offering him an opportunity to spend it, so that he might be better equipped when the lady of the house returned. And Dennison could not but be touched by the delicacy and generosity with which the hint was given.

"I think," said Leatherby, rising, "that I'll retire now. If I don't grant myself enough rest, it's forced from me, and not too pleasantly. Good-night, Dennison."

"Good-night, sir!" said Dennison.

But he could not forget that Leatherby had an appointment at nine o'clock, and he made up his mind that he would have a look at this patient. At nine o'clock, he was in the library, and when the door-bell rang, he looked out into the hall, and saw Miller admit a portly, grey-mustached man. He saw him plainly then, and an hour later when he descended, Dennison saw him again. Saw upon his face an unforgettable look, a sort of desperate and dreadful resolution.

"This won't do!" thought Dennison.

CHAPTER THREE

DOCTOR LEATHERBY'S VIEWS

Dennison went up to his room, and lighting his pipe, sat down to think over all this. Two conflicting elements disturbed him. One was his profound instinct to mind his own business. If Leatherby chose to see patients in this unusual way, if he chose to pay his assistant out of all proportion to the work he did, that was Leatherby's business. Dennison had not been asked to do anything in the least discreditable or suspicious; he had legitimate and useful work to do here; that was his business.

But equally strong in him was the instinct to know, to understand. It seemed to him weak, and almost dishonourable, to go ahead blindly. If there were anything shady here, he ought to know it.

"That woman..." he thought. "She'd been crying. And that man to-night... He looked—queer. Damn queer... What do they come for? Drugs?"

But he could not believe that. The more he saw of Leatherby, the more he respected his dignity, his generosity, his learning. Even in this one day, he had seen how Leatherby's patients trusted and liked him; and when, at dinner, they had discussed the various cases, Dennison had heard from the older man advice he would always remember, for its sane, unflinching wisdom and humanity.

"No..." thought Dennison. "I'm inclined to be too suspicious—too cautious. Evelyn's told me that, more than once. Of course, if I do see anything that seems off-colour, I can quit. But I needn't be looking for trouble. Leatherby's not the sort of man to be mixed up in anything unethical."

Then, as was natural, his thoughts drifted toward Evelyn. He took a little snapshot out of his pocket, and looked at it. Such a pretty little face, such a gay and innocent smile! She looked at him out of the picture, as she looked at him in life, making unconscious enormous demands upon him, upon his patience, his energy, asking of him protection against the brutalities of life. Very well, he meant to meet her demands; he meant to take care of her. He would save his money, and secure a home for her, where, behind frilled curtains, her innocence and gaiety would be safe.

He felt within him the dogged strength and courage to do this, yet, sometimes, a great fear stirred in him. He would do for her everything possible, yet there was so much that was not possible, so much that one human being could never do for another. He remembered how pale, how dismayed she had been, when her dog had broken his leg. How was Dennison, with only his two hands, his fallible human brain, his pitiably fallible human heart, to keep from her every sorrow and anxiety?

He sat up straight, and knocked out his pipe.

"I'll do my best," he said to himself. "Poor little Evie...! I'll do my best."

Then he went up to bed, and to sleep, and waked in the morning to another sunny day. And the things that had so troubled him the evening before had a new look now. He had a cold shower, in that almost incredible little bathroom, he shaved, dressed, and went downstairs, not in a cheerful humour, for he did not know how to be cheerful, but in the mood of grim energy that sufficed for him. The first thing he saw, as he entered the dining-room, was Miss Napier's bright head, bent over her plate.

She was alone there, and this seemed to him a very awkward situation. She had wanted to be rid of him, and he had refused to go; probably she wouldn't speak to him now. And though he felt sorry, remarkably sorry, he was quite prepared for that. He had lived his childhood with an aunt to whom he was simply a responsibility and a duty; all his life had been a grim and lonely struggle; everything he had got he had fought for, and he expected no consideration from anyone else. The sight of her bright head, the memory of her transient friendliness, gave him a sharp pang of regret, but it never occurred to him that he could mollify her; he did not even venture to speak to her.

"Hello!" she said, glancing up.

He was dazzled to see that warm and radiant smile again, as if nothing had happened.

"Good-morning!" he said, briefly, as he sat down at the other end of the table.

"Isn't it a wonderful day?" she cried. "'Proud-pied April, dressed in all his trim, hath put a spirit of youth in everything.' Even in a trained nurse!"

He was entirely at a loss how to answer her, quoting poetry too, yet he wanted to answer. Something in her joyousness touched him.

"Yes," he said. "Very nice weather."

"And you're having a holiday this morning," she said. "Are you going into the city?"

"I thought of doing so," said Dennison.

"Would you do something for me, if you get a chance?"

"All right," he answered, in his ungracious fashion.

"I want another ball of wool," she said. "They haven't the right colour here. Would it be too much bother?"

"No," said Dennison. "I'll get it for you."

She gave him a bit to match, which he put carefully into his breast-pocket. And he could not have told why this pleased him so.

He had a few minutes talk with Doctor Leatherby before he set out.

"Don't hurry back," Leatherby told him. "I'm feeling very well to-day."

"Thank you," said Dennison.

It was a most unusual thing for him to feel as he felt this morning; he could have whistled, as he walked through the little town to the railway station. It seemed to him that he had never seen so gay and sweet a day, never felt in his heart such confidence and hope. He was not even troubled by the thought of spending all of this cheque, which was salary drawn in advance, too. In the train he made a list of what he would buy; two pairs of shoes, one of them patent-leather; four shirts, a dinner jacket and trousers and a dress shirt, six pairs of socks and a new hat. He knew well enough where he could buy these things cheaply, and he felt himself justified in buying them.

He could not remember a pleasanter day. With great care and deliberation, he made his purchases, and put them into a bag he had brought with him. Then he went to get Miss Napier's wool. He remembered that he had seen her knitting something scarlet; he liked it; he was curiously pleased to bring out the bit she had given and match it.

He lunched on Graham crackers and milk, agreeably sure of a good dinner that night, then he caught an early train back to Shayne, buying an afternoon newspaper to beguile the journey.

And on the front page, he saw a photograph of a face oddly familiar to him. He frowned, trying to remember when he had seen that portly, grey-mustached man before.

"Sudden Death of Prominent Banker. Lucian F. Manley Found Dead in Hotel Room"

Now he remembered. It was the patient he had seen last night.

"At eight o'clock this morning, alarmed at receiving no response to numerous telephone calls, members of the staff of the Hotel Ferris entered the room and discovered Mr. Manley dead in his bed.

"Doctors attribute the death to heart failure, due to over-work. Mr. Manley had been dead for probably nine hours when found.

"Mrs. Manley and Miss Sylvia Manley could not be reached this morning at their home in Asheville, South Carolina. Mrs. Manley has recently obtained a divorce, and the custody of their only child. The deceased was prominent in banking and financial circles—" And so on.

There was nothing really strange or startling in this, yet Dennison was both startled and unreasonably troubled.

"Dead nine hours..." he thought. "I saw him about ten o'clock.... He must have died almost as soon as he got home."

He could not forget the look he had seen on the man's face, that look of bitter and dreadful resolution. As if he had known.   .

His unusual mood of cheerfulness was gone now; when he reached the house, he wore his usual serious, almost dour look again, and in his head there stirred again the sense of uneasiness and distrust that had before assailed him. Miller admitted him.

"The Doctor's having tea in the library, sir," he said.

Dennison hesitated. Was he expected to join him? He had never in his life had tea in the afternoon; he didn't want any now.

But the unworthy thought occurred to him that if he did not go into the library, he would appear to Miller as one unaccustomed to these amenities. He knew that he ought not to consider for a moment what Miller might think. But he did. Setting down his bag, he walked into the library.

And he was immediately sorry, for Doctor Leatherby was not alone there. Miss Napier was there, and someone else, a cool, disdainful, dark lady sitting behind a tea-table.

"Ah, Dennison!" said Leatherby, glancing up. "You're back early—just in time for a cup of tea. Rose, this is my assistant, Doctor Dennison. Dennison, my sister, Mrs. Lewis."

Dennison bowed stiffly, and Mrs. Lewis leisurely inspected him.

"Will you have a cup of tea, Doctor Dennison?" she asked, in the clearest voice he had ever heard.

"Yes, thank you," he said.

For this lady awakened an immediate response in him. He resented her leisurely inspection, her voice, her indefinable arrogance; her manner seemed to set free in him a curious ease, almost a grace in his own manner. So that one looking at him might be put in mind of some Puritan, who, at an insult, reverted to a Cavalier. He sat down, accepted a cigarette, and lit it; he was almost debonair.

"We have had sad news," said Doctor Leatherby, "My old friend Manley.... You may have seen him here last night, Dennison?"

"I did," said Dennison. "I recognized his photograph in the paper—"

"In the paper?" Leatherby interrupted. "I wasn't aware... We had a telephone message... What did the paper say, Dennison?"

"I brought it back with me, sir," said Dennison "I'll show you."

He rose and fetched the paper from the table in the hall, and, as he returned, he glanced at Miss Napier. Her grey eyes met his steadily, her smile so welcomed him, that he felt at home here; he had come back—home—to this friend.

Leatherby took the newspaper, and read the article aloud.

"Heart failure!" said Mrs. Lewis.

Dennison looked quickly at her, saw on her face a chilly, regretful smile.

"That's one way of putting it," she said. "I suppose his heart did fail him, poor Lucian! He had more than he could endure."

"My dear Rose!" protested her brother. "The doctors..."

"No!" she said. "It's entirely too apropos."

"Rose!" he said, again, louder than he was won to speak.

"It doesn't happen like that," she went on. "People don't just die—at the very moment they most want to. They have to go on—and on—long past the proper time."

The pain in her voice startled Dennison, he looked from her to her brother, and he was disconcerted to find Leatherby staring at him.

Leatherby looked away at once, and addressed his sister.

"There'll be an inquest," he said. "If there's anything questionable, it will come to light.... And suppose it is so? His wife had left him; she turned their only child against him. Suppose in his loneliness and pain, he—opened the door and went out of this world? He leaves plenty of money. No one would suffer for his going. Do you blame him, Rose?"

She had lit a cigarette, and leaned back in her chair.

"It's not for me to judge him, Charles," she said, carelessly.

He turned to Dennison.

"Would you blame a man in that position, Dennison?" he said. "A man who had nothing left?"

"I shouldn't think it was right, sir," he answered.

Again Leatherby looked at him.

"You think life is to be preserved, even when it is worse than useless? When it is only a burden and a torment?"

It was never easy for Dennison to express himself, but when he was asked a direct question, he certainly attempted a direct answer.

"I don't think it's right to throw off burdens, sir," he said curtly. "It's cowardly."

"Perhaps you have never had any very heavy ones," said Leatherby, almost gently. "You might think differently if you saw someone you loved suffering, without hope or relief."

"If it was—" Dennison began, and stopped, thinking of Evelyn. "If it was the person I—I cared for most, I'd still say the same."

"That life must be prolonged at any cost?"

"At any cost, sir!" He made an effort to explain his attitude. "In the first place, sir," he said, "you can never say there's no hope. Things turn up .. . I... While there's life, there's hope."

This was one of those impossibly banal remarks which might well make a man of Leatherby's intelligence smile. But he did not smile. He rose, and as he passed Dennison, he laid his hand on the young man's shoulder.

"You're a good sort..." he said, half aloud, and went on, out of the room.

All this left Dennison very embarrassed and uncomfortable. He felt sure that Mrs. Lewis was secretly laughing at him, and he suspected that Miss Napier might be amused, though in a good-humoured way. Very well; let them be! When he was asked questions, he was going to answer, and he was going to say what he thought.

"Another cup of tea, Doctor Dennison?" asked Mrs. Lewis.

"No, thank you!" he answered, and obliged himself to look straight at her. But he found no trace of scorn in her handsome face; she looked only unhappy and tired.

And there came over him a plain conviction that he understood none of these people; that he spoke and acted in the dark, that he answered questions without knowing what they meant. There was something very wrong here; he had known it from the beginning.

He had to think about this. With one of his stiff bows, he withdrew, and went up to his own room.

"If that's Leatherby's idea," he thought, "that it's right to avoid suffering, then naturally he'd see nothing wrong in giving people anything that might relieve them. Anything at all. It's queer.... It's *damn* queer—the way he sees patients—by appointment—in that private room."

And if Leatherby gave his patients drugs, no matter how humane his purpose, how logical his reasons, Dennison would not be his assistant.

His eye fell upon his bag, which Miller had brought upstairs.

"I've spent that money," he thought. "Of course, I could pay it back, with what I have in the bank, and by selling my medical books and my watch, and so on.... But I don't want to be a fool. I don't want to throw up a good job unless I'm sure.... No! I've got to find out!"

How? It worried him intolerably. He took out his pipe, to light it, when there was a knock at the door. He opened it promptly, and found Miss Napier outside, in her hat and coat.

"I came to ask about my wool!" she said. "But perhaps—"

"I got it," said Dennison, and took the little package out of his pocket. "It's just the right colour, too."

"Oh, thank you!" she said. "That's awfully nice of you!"

"Just a moment, please!" he said. "Are you going out?"

"Going home. I live in the village, you know."

"May I speak to you a moment?" he asked. "I'd just been thinking about you.... Twice you've advised me not to stay here. I wish you'd tell me why."

She made no answer, and he saw a shadow cross her clear face.

"Miss Napier," he said, bluntly. "Is there anything wrong about Doctor Leatherby?"

She came into the room, and closed the door behind her. She stood within the circle of light from the lamp on his desk, and her hair beneath her dark hat was like a bright cloud about her face. She looked different now, not in uniform; she looked younger, more slight, and gentle; altogether lovelier.

"Doctor Dennison," she said, "I must tell you.... Doctor Leatherby is my saint. He is the most truly kind and generous human being I ever knew. He saved my mother's life when she was very ill—gave her ten happy years she'd never have had otherwise. And I think he saved my father's life, too, by helping him out of his horrible money troubles. There's nothing in the world I wouldn't do for Doctor Leatherby."

A curious little chill ran down Dennison's spine. Looking into her eyes, he saw something beyond his comprehension, something clear, yet fathomless.

"Miss Napier," he said, "you still advise me to go?"

"I still advise you to go," she answered, and opening the door, went out.

CHAPTER FOUR

MR. FOLYET ARRIVES

Dennison dressed himself in the dinner jacket—for the first time in his life, and descended the stairs. The fickle April day was ending in rain, a faint, soft rain, like tears of fatigue after too much laughter, after a day that had begun too gaily.

That was the way in which he regarded his own heavy spirits. There lingered in his mind, from his dour upbringing, a notion that somehow it was wrong to be happy, and that punishment would follow it. He had been happy that morning, and now he was not. That was right and proper.

"I still advise you to go," she had said.

Well, he had no intention of taking her advice or anyone else's. His hardy spirit had grown used to acting without advice.

"I'm not going to give up a good job without reason," he said to himself. "But I've got to find out. And if there is anything wrong—"

He was infinitely better housed and fed and served than ever he had been in his life; he was gaining every day in experience and assurance; he saw for the first time a prospect of freedom from financial worry, and a chance to save money for his marriage; if he had to leave here, he must renounce all this. Certainly he would not do that lightly.

The dining-room had never looked so charming; the table decorated with jonquils, with sundry little touches due, he supposed, to Mrs. Lewis. And she herself was charming, in a filmy, low-cut black frock and beautifully-dressed hair. She smiled on him with a sort of tired affability; there was no air of disdain about her now; she seemed to him only weary and preoccupied.

Yet she talked, as if it were a duty, and Leatherby responded, in a careless and aimless style of conversation which Dennison was quite incapable of sharing. He could answer questions, or ask them; he could, if required, give a clear and terse account of a case, of anything he had experienced, but mere conversation was beyond him.

He could not understand Mrs. Lewis. From time to time he glanced at her, and sometimes her careless eyes rested upon his face for an instant, almost without recognition. She was a handsome woman, young, too; twenty years younger than her brother, Dennison surmised; she was a courteous hostess. But she disturbed Dennison. She made him feel as if he were utterly unimportant, no more than a transient shadow in this house.

"There's to be an inquest the day after to-morrow," said Leatherby, breaking a long silence. "I'll be summoned to appear. I was one of the last persons to see poor Manley alive."

His sister looked up.

"Will they have to bring up all poor Lucian's—troubles, Charles?" she asked.

"Not likely," he answered. "If the doctors agree that he died from heart failure, that's the end of it."

"Was there something seriously wrong with his heart, Charles?"

"I don't know," said Leatherby, with a sigh. "He didn't come to me as a patient. He was my friend.... He brought a letter to show me—a letter from his daughter. It was the most heartless, the cruellest thing. She reproached him for his conduct toward her mother—which, of course, she knew nothing about—and she told him she would never see him again."

Another long silence followed, and all the time Dennison fancied that Mrs. Lewis was about to speak; he watched her uneasily, waiting for her unimaginable words.

But they did not come. The dinner ended, she rose, and Dennison rose, too. Leatherby had pushed back his chair, when Miller appeared in the doorway.

"Mr. Folyet is here, sir," he said.

His words were followed by an amazing stillness; he might have uttered some spell that froze the doctor and his sister to immobility. The man waited, as quiet as they, and Dennison looked on, trying to see....

"Shall I tell him, sir—?" Miller began, when Leatherby raised his hand.

"Wait!" he said, and turned his head toward his sister. What did his look mean, reproach, warning, anxiety?

"Charles!" she cried. "You know that I haven't—"

"My dear girl, of course!" said her brother, with an easy return to his dignified and kindly manner. "Show him into the library, Miller. Folyet was your predecessor, Dennison. He was here with me, a year ago."

Dennison felt a lively curiosity to see this man who had had his place, and left it. Mrs. Lewis was going down the hall ahead of them, with a quick, light step; she was hastening; yet when she reached the open door of the library, she stopped outside, and Dennison, who had come up with her, looked over her shoulder.

And looked directly into the eyes of a man standing in Leatherby's favourite place, before the mantelpiece, with his back to the fire. He was a slender young man, almost slight, with delicate, clear features and an olive skin, and a little dark mustache; he was, in Dennison's opinion, altogether too good-looking, theatrical, foppish.

Mrs. Lewis drew back into the hall, and her brother entered the room.

"Ah, Doctor Folyet!" he said, pleasantly.

"Not 'doctor' any more," said the young man, smiling. "I've given up the profession."

"It has its drawbacks, certainly," said Leatherby.

"But perhaps we'd better not discuss them before Dennison. He's just beginning; no use discouraging him, eh?"

He introduced the two young men to each other; they bowed, without offering to shake hands, and they all sat down. Presently Miller came in with the coffee; he brought four cups, but Mrs. Lewis had not returned.

"And what are you doing now, Folyet?" asked Doctor Leatherby, leaning back in his chair.

"Just looking about me," answered Folyet, cheerfully. Only his black eyes were not cheerful.

"Not settled down yet?" asked Leatherby.

"No," said Folyet. "Not yet. I find it hard—" he paused, "to settle down."

Again Dennison had a conviction that he was listening to a conversation to which he had no key. He sat back, smoking, watching the other two, as a man might look on at two swordsmen, not knowing if this were only a trial of skill—or if the buttons were off the foils.

Folyet lit a fresh cigarette.

"I read in the newspaper this morning—" he said, and paused, with his smiling mouth and his unsmiling eyes toward Leatherby, "—of Mr. Manley's—unfortunate death. So I came—" Again a pause, while he drew on his cigarette. "I stopped in —to offer my condolences."

"Remarkably considerate of you!" said Leatherby.

"Oh, not at all!" said Folyet. "I was interested in the—case."

"Case?" Leatherby repeated, with mild surprise. "Had Manley consulted you professionally?"

"No," said Folyet. "It's simply that these cases of heart failure interest me."

"Ah!" said Leatherby. "I see you haven't quite renounced the profession, Folyet! In fact, I find you singularly unchanged."

This was no fencing-bout; this was in earnest. Yet Dennison could not follow. He saw, floating before him, a thread, a clue to this, but he could not seize it.

"It's not—" Folyet went on, "exactly a professional interest. Perhaps it's idle curiosity."

"Very interesting..." murmured Leatherby, and smiled himself. "Are you living in New York now, Folyet?"

"At the present moment," said Folyet, "I thought I'd stop here in Shayne for a time. I was here so long—with you.... I've grown rather attached to the place. So I've got a room at the Eagle House."

"If you mean to stay in Shayne," said Leatherby, "stay here with us, Folyet."

The two men looked at each other, both smiling broadly. And Dennison was perfectly aware that Leatherby's invitation was a challenge.

"Very good of you," said Folyet. "But I couldn't think of bothering you."

"Certainly no 'bother', Folyet. In fact," said Leatherby, "I'd very much enjoy a visit from you."

"Well, in that case—" said Folyet.

Doctor Leatherby touched the bell, and Miller appeared promptly.

"Miller, kindly send Ames down to the Eagle House for Mr. Folyet's bags. And Miller!"

"Sir?"

"Tell Mrs. Lewis that Mr. Folyet will be stopping with us for a time."

Miller stood staring.

"Miller!"

"I beg your pardon, sir," he said, hastily, and turned toward the door.

"Just a moment, please!" said Folyet. "If the chauffeur's going down for my bags, may I go along with him? To settle up at the hotel, and so on."

"By all means!" said Leatherby. "Miller, let us know when the car comes."

Silence settled upon the three men after Miller had gone out. And Dennison's obstinate and hardy mind was working and working, trying to understand, to see, in a deepening fog. Something wrong here, something wrong.... Folyet insinuated—what? And Leatherby and his sister were dismayed by Folyet's coming; perhaps more than dismayed....

Dennison looked at Leatherby's fine, serene face. "No!" he thought. "No! I don't believe.... I can't believe...."

Believe what? He could not have told; only that there was rising about him a fog, a miasma of distrust and fear; he felt lost in it; no face seemed familiar and honest; there was no friendly light anywhere.

"The car is here, sir," said Miller, and Folyet rose and left the room. A moment later he appeared in the doorway, more theatric than ever, with his soft hat pulled low on his forehead, and the collar of his overcoat turned up.

"Any little errand I can do in the village?" he asked.

"Not for me, thanks," answered Leatherby, and a moment later the front door closed.

"Now if he'll just say something," thought Dennison. "Explain a little—"

But Leatherby did not speak at all. He lay back in his chair, smoking a cigar, with an expression half-ironic, half-melancholy on his face. Dennison could endure it no longer. He wanted, he must have, plain, blunt, words.

"This Folyet, sir," he began, "is he—?"

"Stop!" said Leatherby, and sat up, as if listening. Then Dennison heard, too; footsteps running down the stairs. Nothing in that; anyone might run downstairs, Mrs. Lewis, one of the servants. Running footsteps need not mean panic....

Leatherby rose and left the room, and Dennison got up, too. He had had enough; he meant to go up to his own room, shut himself up with his pipe, and try to understand. But standing where he was, though he could not see into the hall, he could hear.

"Charles! Charles! What are you doing?"

It was Mrs. Lewis's singularly clear voice, low-pitched now, and unsteady.

"I'm not doing anything, my dear girl," answered her brother, mildly. "You're—"

"Charles, you can't let Jeff Folyet stay here! Charles, don't you see—don't you realize? He's—your enemy, Charles!"

"My dear girl, I'm not afraid of Folyet."

"I am!" she said. "I am—afraid."

"But surely—"

"I don't understand," she said. "I don't want to understand. *I won't* know. But he means to hurt you, Charles. There's nothing he wouldn't do to hurt you."

"There's nothing he can do," said Leatherby, tranquilly. "You're overwrought, my dear girl. Certainly he made himself unpleasant last year, but it's not difficult to forget that sort of thing. In fact, the difficult thing—for me—is to keep old quarrels warm. Let him stay here if he likes."

"Charles, send him away, I beg you! He'll do you some harm, Charles! I know it!"

"Rose," said Leatherby's quiet equable voice. "He can't do me any harm.

Come, my dear girl, you're nervous and tired—"

"Not that," she said, with a sob. "I'm—afraid!"

"Come upstairs, and I'll give you a new book to read. Something interesting. Come along!"

Dennison heard their footsteps mounting the stairs; then a door closed above.

"What does it mean?" he said to himself, in a sort of despair. "I don't see...."

He must try to see. Mechanically he reached in his pocket for his pipe, but of course that homely article had not been put into the new dinner jacket. He helped himself to another cigarette from the box on the table, and sat down again.

"This fellow Folyet...." he thought. "What's he up to? Is he trying to insinuate that Leatherby knows—something more about Manley's death? What's his game? Mrs. Lewis says she's afraid of him... I don't see.... I think I'll wait here and have a word with Folyet when he comes back."

In the cottage he had got into the habit of going to bed early, and he was growing sleepy now. When the cigarette was finished, he sat staring at the fire drowsily; it would not matter if he fell asleep, for the least sound always roused him. He would hear Folyet when he returned.

"Of course, I can't make him talk," he thought. "But he may be willing to. I wish I were more—what you'd call diplomatic...."

The flames leaped up, red and splendid. Some day he would have a fire of his own, his own hearth to come back to at the day's end. And not be alone any more. Some day....

The sound of a light footfall behind him brought him wide-awake. It was Miller, taking away the coffee service. Dennison glanced at his watch, and was surprised to see that it was nearly eleven o'clock.

"Mr. Folyet come back yet?" he asked.

"He sent word to say he wouldn't return, sir," said Miller. "Shall I lock the windows now, sir?"

"All right!" said Dennison, absently, and rose. "That's queer," he thought. "Not coming back. . Well, it's none of my business!"

He nodded a good-night to Miller, and started up the stairs. And as he reached the dimly-lit upper hall, a door opened.

"Jeff...?" asked a low voice, which he recognized.

"It's Dennison, Mrs. Lewis," he said.

"Oh !" she said. "I thought.... Hasn't Mr. Folyet come back yet?"

"Miller says he's not coming back," said Dennison, and would have passed on, but she came out into the hall, and laid her hand on his sleeve.

"Doctor Dennison!" she whispered. "Oh, please tell me! Has—anything happened?"

"Happened?" he repeated, startled. "I don't—"

"Please, please tell me the truth!" she entreated. "Has there been—an accident?"

"I haven't heard of anything," he answered, looking anxiously at her white face. "Why do you think that? Miller only told me that Folyet had sent word to say he wouldn't return."

She made a visible attempt to control her agitation, to smile.

"It was—just a silly idea," she said. "I—I think I've been asleep and—dreaming. Of course there's nothing wrong. Of course! It's so stupid of me.... But one hears of so many—automobile accidents. Good-night! Please forget how silly I've been. You—won't mention this?"

"No, Mrs. Lewis," he said. "Good-night!"

But he did not forget.

CHAPTER FIVE

A LETTER FOR DENNISON

Dennison waked early, to see another bright day. He had had a long, sound sleep, he was well-rested, he was young and vigorous, and the sun was shining. Yet directly he opened his eyes, he felt again the oppression and disquiet.

His first impulse was to jump up, but he repressed it. So many things happened to interfere with his attempts to think over this situation; now he had an undisturbed hour, and he intended to make use of it. So, with his hands clasped behind his head, and his eyes upon the pure blue sky, he began.

"I don't know," he said to himself, "whether I'm not just a fool—whether there's really anything wrong at all."

He wanted very badly to think that, he wanted to throw off his anxiety, this curious feeling of foreboding. But he was too honest to do that.

"No, let's see," he thought. "One thing at a time. First, there's Miss Napier advising me to go. Well, good Lord! Nothing in that to mill over! She might have had a dozen good reasons. She may simply think I'm not the right man for the job. And anyhow, she doesn't seem to mind my staying. She's—"

His thoughts wandered to Miss Napier and her smile; he recalled them sharply.

"That's—immaterial," he thought. "Then, there are those patients that Leatherby sees upstairs.

Well, what of it? They come openly. He made no secret of seeing them. No reason why I should worry about that. He's known and respected in the place; not the sort of man for any underhand practice. Everything he's given me to do has been perfectly open and aboveboard.

"Now, that Manley affair.... Folyet certainly seemed to insinuate that Leatherby knows something about it. Folyet seems skeptical about the 'heart failure.' Well, suppose it was suicide? And that Leatherby knows it? And anyhow, who the devil is Folyet? No; there's nothing in this Manley affair for me to bother about. When you come to think of it, there's nothing in anything. I've go legitimate work to do here, and I can just do it, and mind my own business."

He stared at the sky.

"Of course there's one other thing," he thought. "What Mrs. Lewis said last night."

And that was the one other thing for which he could find no explanation that satisfied him.

"Why should she think there'd been an accident? And why didn't Folyet come back?"

He remembered how Mrs. Lewis had spoken to her brother.

"He is your enemy, Charles!"

And Leatherby had answered:

"Folyet can't do me any harm."

And then Leatherby's enemy had gone away—and had not come back....

Dennison sprang out of bed and hurrying into the bathroom, got under the cold shower. He began to dress with the same haste, but he could not be quick enough to escape that pursuing thought.

Why hadn't Folyet come back?

"I'll speak to Ames," he decided. "Just ask him about Folyet—and set my mind at rest. Of course, it's all nonsense...."

When he was dressed, he left his room, and went downstairs, quietly, as one feels compelled to move through a sleeping house. He drew back the bolts of the front door, and stepped out into the garden. And it was amazing to him, and wonderful, the beauty of this morning, made of clear and tender colours, the blue sky, the gay new green of the budding trees, the fragrance of damp earth and eager growing things.

Oppression and anxiety began to lift from his heart. No shadows here; here it seemed impossible to believe in fear and evil; they were nightmares that fled from the morning sun.

Up and down the drive he walked, hands in his pockets. The breeze blew cool in his face, but the sun was warm.

"Too early to see Ames," he thought. "I'll wait."

Everything could wait; all his thoughts could wait. He would just be alive for a little while.

Then, as he turned back at the end of the drive, he saw Miss Napier coming toward him from the house; all in the sun, her hair glittering, her white dress dazzling as snow, and on her face that wide, gay, generous smile. This brightness of hers always surprised him; it was a thing he could not understand.

On she came, and though he was so glad to see her, he would not hasten to meet her.

"Good-morning, Doctor Dennison!" she said, and he liked her manner, which was perfectly friendly, yet not lacking in the respect due to a doctor from a mere nurse.

"Good-morning!" he answered.

"I came to ask if you were ready for breakfast," she said. "Or shall I wait?"

"For—me?"

"Well, Doctor Leatherby very seldom comes down, and Mrs. Lewis never does. So there's only you and I," she explained.

Then he remembered.

"Unless Folyet comes back," he said.

"Folyet?" she cried. "Not—Jeff Folyet? Why should he come...?"

He could not escape the shadow, the fog. Even this girl, who had seemed to him a moment ago bright and clear as the daylight, was changed now, her candour obscured by this mystery so hateful to him. Something wrong—even with her. He stood before her, downcast, looking at his carefully-polished new shoes.

"Why did you think—he'd come?" she asked.

"He was here last night. He went off to get his bags. He said he was coming back—but he didn't."

"I'm glad!" said she.

This sounded like candour and he looked up at her hopefully.

"Why?" he asked. "Don't you like him?"

"It's not that," she answered, with a sort of reluctance. "He was always very nice to me while he was here. But—he just doesn't seem to—fit in."

Their eyes met.

"I don't understand," said Dennison. "As far as that goes, there are a lot of things here I don't understand. And I don't like that."

She was silent for a moment; then she looked straight at him.

"Doctor Dennison," she said, "there are lots of things I don't want to talk about—things I *can't* talk about. But it needn't make any difference, need it?"

"I don't see what you mean," said Dennison, puzzled.

"I mean we can be friends anyhow, can't we?"

A slow flush rose in his dark face, and he turned away his head.

"I thought you wanted me to go away," he said.

"I don't now, Doctor Dennison."

"Why?" he demanded, almost roughly. "I'd like to understand. What's made you change your mind?"

For answer she only smiled, a little uncertainly.

"You mean you want me to stay?"

"Yes. I'm sure Doctor Leatherby couldn't have anyone more trustworthy."

"That's as it may be," said the obstinate Dennison. "But I don't see—"

"Shall we have breakfast?" she interrupted, with respectful firmness.

"As you please," said he, and followed her to the house. As they entered the hall, they met Miller.

"Here's a letter for you, sir," he said.

With a great lightening of the heart, Dennison saw that the writing was Evelyn's. It could not have come at a better moment, this letter from his friend, his lover, the one person on earth to whom he was of any interest or importance. In this house he had felt more sharply than ever before how solitary he was, an outsider, completely shut away from other people's concerns. And here was a familiar voice to speak to him, a friendly little hand stretched out to him.

"Excuse me, please!" he said, and standing by the window, tore open his letter.

"Dearest Alex:" she wrote. "We are all so awfully pleased to hear of the really splendid place you have found. Dad says he thinks it is a simply wonderful opportunity for you.

"But, Alex, your letter was so *queer*. You didn't seem a *bit* enthusiastic. Dad and Mother both noticed that when I read it to them."

He frowned. She shouldn't read his letters to them, to anyone. He went on.

"And I know that Dad feels a little worried about you. He was so disappointed at your giving up your own practice—"

"Giving up my practice!" thought Dennison. "That's pretty good!"

"—and when he heard about your wanting to go on a ship, he was afraid you were just *a little bit* of a rolling stone. But I told him I was sure you'd settle down, Alex. You will, won't you? Even if you're not very enthusiastic about this new job, do try to stick it out. There are always *some* things we don't like about *everything*.

"You know, Alex dear, how willing I am to wait for you. But if you won't make a real effort, and put up with things, even if you don't like them, I can't see any end to our waiting.

"I went to Sonia's little dance on Wednesday, and I did miss you so. Though, of course, as you don't dance, you wouldn't have enjoyed it much. But I should have been so happy to see my dear, solemn old boy there.

"I'll have to stop now, dear, because it's time for lunch. I do so hope to get a letter from you soon, telling me you've made up your mind to stick to your present job, even if it doesn't just suit you, until you've saved up enough for us to have our own dear little home.

"*Lots* of love to my dearest boy, and don't mind my 'lecturing' a little. It's only because I want to help."

"Always

Your own

Evie."

Dennison folded up the letter and put it into I breast pocket.

"That's—that's damned unfair!" he said to himself.

"Sugar and cream in your coffee, Doctor Dennison?" asked Miss Napier.

"Any way you like, thanks," said Dennison, sitting down at the table. "A rolling stone... " he thought.

That phrase rankled intolerably; indeed, he resented the whole letter. He had no conception of Evie as his moral arbiter; he felt quite capable of looking after his own morals and his own career.

Certainly he needed no one to urge him to "stick to" a chosen course, or to endure difficulties. He didn't want Evie to help him, either. He was going to help her, going to work for her, shelter and protect her. All she had to do was to take what he could give.

He now caught sight of Miss Napier putting a slice of buttered toast quietly on his plate, and beginning to prepare another one.

"Look here!" he said. "Don't bother about that!"

"It's not one bit of bother!" she assured him, earnestly. "If you can just eat a good breakfast, Doctor Dennison—"

He glanced at her with a faint frown, and he saw upon her face such a look of kindness.... It occurred to him that everything about that girl was kind, her smile, her voice, her very hands were kind hands, strong and gentle.

But he was not accustomed to kindness, and it perturbed him.

"I'm not ill," he said. "I don't need—"

"Just this one more piece!" said Miss Napier. "It's whole-wheat bread. I can't help thinking it's a good thing to eat—though Doctor Leatherby doesn't believe in it. He doesn't believe in any sort of special diets. He says we're naturally omnivorous. Why, even in Mrs. Tisdale's case—"

Dennison had things to say about diet, and she listened to him attentively. He accepted another cup of coffee; he was not very observant of such matters, but he did notice that she had some very pleasing way of preparing it for him.

"I've heard Ledyard on diet in anemia," he said. "Nobody could listen to him and fail to be convinced. It's all on record, too. You can—" He stopped, surprised. "Was that nine o'clock that struck?" he asked.

"Yes, Doctor Dennison."

He rose hastily, but before he had reached the door, he realized that perhaps he was somewhat ungracious.

"Miss Napier!"

"Yes, Doctor Dennison?"

"You're—very kind," he said, stiffly, and paused a moment. "I don't quite see... " he said.

"I'm so glad that Doctor Leatherby has got *you* here," she said.

"I can't see that he needs me much."

"He does, Doctor Dennison."

He frowned again.

"Look here!" he said, abruptly. "These—private patients and so on.... Will you tell me, frankly, that you're perfectly satisfied that—"

"I'm perfectly satisfied with everything that Doctor Leatherby does," she said. "Naturally. You see, I'm going to marry Doctor Leatherby."

CHAPTER SIX

MRS. LEWIS OFFERS ADVICE

Here was something which could in no legitimate way affect Dennison. Miss Napier was clearly entitled to marry anyone she chose, and so was Leatherby, and it was none of Dennison's business.

Yet the idea shocked him beyond measure. There must be, he thought, something like thirty years' difference in their ages; and, more than that, there was some profound incompatibility which he could not formulate, but which was nevertheless patent to him. It was as if this were a contemplated marriage between two persons of different race, or different eras; as if some suave and polished Athenian of the age of Pericles were marrying a Viking's daughter.

"They don't belong in the same world," he thought.

He did not know what to do with himself this morning. Doctor Leatherby had not yet come down; there were no office patients, no calls. He wandered about, smoking, thinking his by no means cheerful thoughts. Sometimes when he turned in that direction, he caught sight of Miss Napier in the reception-room, knitting her scarlet jumper, the sun shining on her bright head. And he felt that everything was wrong. Everything.

"I won't answer Evie's letter yet," he thought. "Because I haven't made up my mind yet what I'll do. If I decide to leave here, I'll try to explain to her, and if she doesn't understand, I can't help it. 'A rolling stone....' So far, it's more as if I'd been trying to roll uphill.... So she reads my letters to her people, and they all discuss me.... Her 'dear solemn old boy', who doesn't dance.... How could I dance? What time or chance have I ever had for dancing? Or anything like that?"

He strolled down the hall and looked out through the glass of the front door at the garden, neat and bright in the sun.

"I didn't know I was 'solemn'," he thought.

The word was remarkably distasteful to him; it evoked the image of a pompous and tiresome young ass. Perhaps he was one.

"I certainly wasn't very—entertaining with Miss Napier," he thought. "She tried to be nice to me... Said something about our being friends..."

There came over him a great desire to be friendly; not to be "solemn," but to be easy, cheerful. To be happy.

He turned abruptly and strode down the hall to the reception-room. But when he reached the doorway, he did not know what to say, he did not know how to be friendly or happy. He stood looking at her with a constrained, tight-lipped smile. She laid down her knitting.

"No, don't get up!" he said. "This isn't—official. I just came to talk to you."

"Then won't you sit down?"

He entered, and seated himself on the edge of her desk; he searched his brain for something light and agreeable to say, and could find not a word. Yet the silence in the room was like balm to him; he felt so certain that she was not criticizing him, not condemning him.

"You know," said she, "I was so much interested in what you were telling me about Doctor Ledyard's theories of diet—"

"I've got his last book," said Dennison. "It's over in my cottage—little place I rented when I first came here."

"I know," she said. "I went there to leave the note from Doctor Leatherby. I *liked* that cottage!"

"I liked it myself," said Dennison. He was silent for a moment. "Look here!" he said. "If I get a chance to-day, I'll stop there and get you that book."

"Oh, thank you!" she said. "I don't think it'll be a very busy day for you. I'm pretty sure Doctor Leatherby's going to take the office patients. Shall I ask him?"

"All right!" said Dennison. Then he added, as if the words were being dragged out of him: "Perhaps you'd like to walk over there with me, this morning?"

"I'd love to!" she answered. "I'll just run up and ask Doctor Leatherby."

She went off, and Dennison remained sitting on the desk, waiting. And the moment she was out of sight, he began to remember the things he had for a moment forgotten. It was as if she dazzled him, so that he did not see clearly when in her presence.

"It's all right for us to go," she announced, coming into the room in her hat and coat.

But Dennison had been thinking.

"Look here!" he said. "Don't you think someone might enquire about Folyet? I mean—he may be ill, or something of the sort. He certainly intended to come back—and he hasn't."

"It's a good thing he hasn't," she retorted warmly. "He knows he's not wanted."

But Dennison remembered Mrs. Lewis's very strange question: "Has there been an accident?" As if she expected one.

"Still, it's queer..." he said.

His heart smote him at her anxious glance; he knew he was distressing her, but he couldn't help it.

"I'd like to ask Ames just what Folyet said," he went on. "Of course, it's not my business—"

"Why not?" she interrupted. "We'll speak to Ames as we go out. I don't mind asking him questions. You—" She paused, and looked at him squarely. "If you really think there's something 'queer'...."

"Well, I do," he said. And a curious relief filled him. For the first time he had been able to voice his vague suspicions bluntly, and instead of being angry, Miss Napier seemed to think him entitled to some sort of satisfaction.

"We'll ask Ames," she said. "I'll be glad for you to hear what he says. So that you won't—imagine things any more."

They found Ames in the garage; a very self-possessed young man, with the independent air of one who can always find a job.

"Morning!" he said.

Miss Napier's manner with him seemed to Dennison remarkable for its absolute rightness; sincere, straightforward, good-humoured. She asked him a few questions about the car, not from finesse, but out of politeness. Then:

"What did Mr. Folyet say about not coming back?" she asked.

"Folyet?" he repeated. "I ain't seen Mr. Folyet for a year."

"Didn't you drive him down to the Eagle House last night?" asked Dennison. "To get his bags?"

"Me? I was in N'Yawk las' night," said Ames. "To a show with the girl friend. That's where I was."

"Who drives the car when you're not here?"

Ames stared at Dennison.

"Well, Miller's got a driving license," he answered, "so's he could take out the car in an emergency. But believe *me,* it's an emergency all right for that guy to take the wheel. Was he drivin' last night? No one's never told me."

"I don't know," said Miss Napier, hastily. "Mr. Folyet called—and we thought that perhaps you'd driven him back to town. But it doesn't matter in the least. Very likely he got a taxi from the station."

With a smile, she turned away, and began to walk on, and Dennison moved so that he could see her face. And anger seized him at the look he saw there, such a guarded look.

"Doctor Leatherby said Ames was going to drive Folyet," he said. "And Miller came and announced that the car was there."

"What of it?" she cried. "I suppose Miller drove the car himself. There's really nothing very—sinister in that, is there?"

"Miller said that Folyet had 'sent word' he wouldn't return. As if he'd got the message from someone else."

"Well, what of it?" she cried again. She was angry now, the colour had risen in her cheeks, and her grey eyes were stormy. "What does it matter who drove Jeff, or where he went, or why he didn't come back?"

"I'd like to know," said Dennison.

"You're—ridiculous!" she cried.

They walked on in silence.

"I didn't mean to offend you," said Dennison at last.

For a moment she did not answer; then she turned toward him, with her utterly generous smile.

"I'm sorry!" she said. "I didn't mean to fly out at you like that. All about nothing, too. Down this street, isn't it?"

He had the key of the cottage in his pocket; he unlocked the door, and stood aside for her to pass. And as she entered, as she crossed his threshold, something stirred in his heart that he could not understand, some pain. It seemed to him that it was wrong for her to come here, that he had made some irreparable mistake.

He followed her into the little office; dust lay thick on everything; how small it looked, how poor and meagre, compared with Leatherby's.... He got the book out of the case, and showed it to her. And he wanted her to go now, this instant; it was somehow intolerable to him to see her standing here.

"May I see the house?" she asked.

"Nothing to see," he answered. Then he felt that he had been ungracious again. "All right!" he said. "This was the waiting-room, in here."

Here no one had ever waited. It was a dreadful little room, with chairs drawn stiffly against the walls. Then he showed her the dining-room, which had only a table in it.

"You see, I could bring chairs in from the other room," he explained.

Then the kitchen, equipped with a frying-pan, a coffee pot and a big tin saucepan.

He would not have taken her upstairs, but she began to mount unasked, and he followed, his heart heavy, ashamed of his poverty, his barren and unlovely life. Two of the upper rooms were quite bare; nothing in them but dust; the door of the third stood open, and he would not close it. Let her see, if she liked. There was an army cot in there, neatly made up, with a grey blanket on the foot, a chair, a shaving-mirror hanging on a nail. Nothing else.

She turned away with a sort of haste, and went down the stairs again, into the office.

"Well, you see..." he said. "Nothing much to look at here."

"I think it's a dear little house!" she cried, as if she were angry with him. "You could do wonders with it!"

"I thought that myself," he admitted. "For instance—"

He opened a drawer of the desk, and brought out a catalogue.

"Just to amuse myself," he said, "I picked out the things I thought I'd like. Curtains, and rugs, and so on. Nice, bright colours."

"Let's see," she said, looking over his shoulder.

"Why, what's the matter?" he exclaimed, for he saw her eyes brimming with tears.

"Nothing!" she said. "Only—I hope you'll get—every single one of these things. And the right girl to go with them."

"Thank you," he said, and could not trust himself to say any more. Her tears touched him so terribly; he would have given anything in the world to console her, but he knew nothing to do, could not guess at the reason for her tears. He stood, fluttering the leaves of the mail-order catalogue, for a long moment.

"You—you've beer very kind to me," he said. "I—appreciate it. I'm sorry if I've been—disagreeable. But I'm not used to girls." He paused. "Though I'm engaged—in a way," he added.

"In a way?"

"I mean, we're going to be married, if I ever get enough money."

"You will. I know you will, Doctor Dennison!"

"What makes you think so?" he asked, anxiously.

"Because you're clever and careful and—obstinate," she said, smiling. "You've got all the qualities to make you succeed."

It seemed to him the most wonderful thing that she should think that. Looking about the little office, a new pride filled him. After all, he had accomplished something, already; he had become a licensed physician, he had rented a house and bought some furniture to put into it. He had even a book to lend her.

"I'll get on, all right!" he thought.

They walked back together, talking a little about Ledyard's book. In the hall they parted, Miss Napier to go to the reception-room, and Dennison to go upstairs. He turned to look after, saw her white dress vanishing through the doorway—

"Doctor Dennison!" said a low voice.

He turned abruptly, and saw Mrs. Lewis coming out of the library.

"Yes, Mrs. Lewis?" he asked.

She drew nearer to him, with a leisurely step, and a faint smile on her face.

"You've been out with Hilda, haven't you?" she said. "It's rather difficult to speak.... You won't want to believe me.... I've seen it happen before."

"I don't quite see—" he began, frowning.

"You don't see at all!" she interrupted, still smiling. "It's a pity. I wish you hadn't come here at all. I wish I could persuade you to go."

"I'm sorry," said Dennison, stiffly. "But unless Doctor Leatherby's dissatisfied—"

"Oh, he's not!" she assured him. "He likes you. So do I. Only, if you will stay—" She drew close to him. *"Don't* be so blind!" she said, very low.

"What do you mean?"

"Don't let Hilda Napier make a catspaw of you."

"What do you mean?" he asked, again.

"She's a splendid girl," said Mrs. Lewis. "But she has her own ends to serve. And she'd do anything—simply anything—to get you on her side."

"Her—side?" he repeated, white with anger.

"She's done the same thing before," Mrs. Lewis went on. "She's very pretty, and naturally, if she sets out to attract you and win you over—"

"She hasn't," he said, curtly.

Again Mrs. Lewis smiled.

"Anyhow, I've warned you," she said.

CHAPTER SEVEN

"LOOKS LIKE A MURDER"

Of all possible roles to play in this world, that of catspaw was most offensive to Dennison. He would have preferred to see himself as a sinner, anything rather than a dupe.

"But it's not true!" he thought. "She's not like that. 'Setting out to attract me—win me over'... It's not true!"

He remembered her in the cottage, the tears in her eyes, all her kindness to him this morning.

"It's a lie!" he said to himself. "She's not like that!"

But he could not help remembering things he had heard and read of the unscrupulousness of women, especially when their affections were concerned. They had, so he had been told, a code of their own. She might feel justified in anything she had done. Perhaps all her friendly interest in him, her kindness, her smiles, even her talk about Ledyard's book, had had a subtle motive?

"No!" he said to himself. "She's not like that."

He sat in his room, smoking, waiting restlessly for lunch time to come.

"When I see her again—" he thought.

When he saw her again, he would look at her dispassionately, critically; he would read her soul in her face. And he could not be utterly deceived; he was not a fool; if he studied her, he would know....

At one o'clock he went downstairs, and in the dining-room he found Doctor Leatherby and Mrs. Lewis, as well as Miss Napier. They sat down at the table, they talked, and Dennison listened with dismay to those amiable, polite voices.

He knew there was a shadow lying dark upon this house, yet no trace of it was reflected upon any of these faces. Leatherby was, as usual, dignified, courteous, and urbane. Mrs. Lewis, who an hour ago had spoken so cruelly of Hilda Napier, now talked to the girl easily and pleasantly. And in Hilda's clear face he could read nothing, nothing at all.

"Does she—love Leatherby?" he thought.

He did not know, he could not know. Her way of loving, he thought, might be different from Evie's; not indulgent and cheerful, but tragically tender. And there might exist for a man a love not like his conscientious affection for Evie.

"I don't know..." he thought, with an unusual humility. "I don't know much—about anything."

He felt deeply depressed, and that angered him. He could not endure to feel ignorant and helpless. If he didn't know much, then he must learn. And if he could not—yet—read human hearts, at least he could find out what was going on about him.

"I'd like to know why Folyet didn't come back," he thought. "I'd like a talk with him."

The thought of Folyet obsessed him strangely.

"I want to see Folyet again," he thought, and made a plan.

When Mrs. Lewis rose from the table, he followed her dutifully into the library, but he did not stop there. Unobtrusively he slipped out and went back toward the dining-room, for a match-case he had purposely left behind.

He was at all times deft and light in his movements, and now he went more quietly than he realized, for neither Miller nor parlour-maid heard him coming down the hall.

"Well, that's what I heard, anyhow!" the girl was saying defensively.

"You hear too much," answered Miller, severely.

"I can't keep my ears shut, nor my eyes, neither," said she. "The grocer's boy told me himself he heard their bill hasn't been paid for three months and it's mounted up something fierce."

Dennison had now reached the doorway. He saw Miller standing, leaning one elbow on the sideboard, while the girl cleared the table; a pretty girl, if somewhat sulky. He would have spoken, only that the girl's next words checked him.

"That's why I was real glad to hear Mr. Manley'd left him something handsome."

Dennison stood where he was, very still.

"Where'd you hear that?" asked Miller. He spoke severely, but he looked at the girl complacently.

"I heard Mrs. Lewis telephoning. To that Mrs. Francis. 'I'll be able to help you out, dear,' she say, 'because poor Lucian's left a hundred thousand dollars to Charles. And you know Charles'll be glad to help you.'"

"You shouldn't listen," said Miller. "And anything you do hear, keep to yourself. You've got a good job here, Jessie. But if I find you gossiping, out you go."

"I don't gossip!" she retorted, indignantly.

"Don't put those spoons back in the plate-basket!" said Miller. "Anything that's been on the table goes out to the kitchen to be washed, used or not used. And I don't like you making those stars in the saltcellars. It's vulgar."

Dennison came into the room.

"I left a match-case—" he said.

"Here it is, sir!" said Jessie, eagerly.

"Thanks!" said Dennison, dropping it into his pocket. "And by the way, Miller—"

"Sir?" said Miller, turning back from the door.

"You drove Mr. Folyet down to the Eagle House last night, didn't you?"

"No, sir," said Miller.

Something intangible in the man's tone made Dennison uncomfortably aware that he had no business to ask questions. But he went on.

"Didn't he go back to the hotel?"

"I couldn't say, sir."

"He left here in the car. Weren't you driving it?"

"Yes, sir. But Mr. Folyet asked me to set him down at the corner of the boulevard, and he told me to say to the Doctor that he wouldn't return."

Miller's voice and glance were steady and composed, yet Dennison was quite convinced that he was lying.

"All right!" he said, briefly, and went off, back to the office. "No!" he thought. "Folyet meant to come back. Something prevented him. Mrs. Lewis expected some 'accident' to happen to him.... No; this won't do!"

The thought of Folyet obsessed him; he was haunted by that handsome, bitter face with smiling mouth and unsmiling eyes. And he thought:

"Suppose something has happened to him, and nobody bothers to find out? Or nobody wants to find out?"

Then a most simple and obvious idea occurred to him. He put on his overcoat, took up his hat, and looked in at the door of the reception-room.

"I'll be back before office-hours, Miss Napier," he said. "I'm just going down to the town."

He set off, at a rapid pace, filled with a queer sense of urgency; went in haste, as if he wished to escape from something.

"I'll ask at the hotel," he thought, "just to set my mind at rest. I'll find out there where Folyet is—perhaps I'll find him there."

His mind needed to be set at rest, for it was unduly active now. He remembered all sorts of things.... So Manley had left a small fortune to Doctor Leatherby? And Leatherby, living in luxury, could not pay his bills...?

"Servants' gossip!" cried Dennison angrily to himself. "None of my business."

He tried to plan what he would say to Folyet if he found him in; what excuse he could offer for such an unwarrantable visit. And because his nature was not subtle and his mind not trained in finesse, he could think of nothing better than that match-case again.

"I'll ask him if it's his," he decided. "I'll say I thought he left it in the library last night."

He strode into the lobby of the Eagle House, and up to the desk.

"Mr. Folyet in?" he asked.

"No, sir," answered the clerk. "He checked out last night."

"What time?"

"I don't know. I'm not on at night. But the night-clerk told me Mr. Folyet telephoned in—some time—and said he was called away unexpectedly and that he'd send someone to get his bags and pay the bill."

"Are his bags still here?"

"No, sir. Man came to get them this morning, and settled up."

"What sort of man?" asked Dennison. Then, at the sight of the clerk's expression, he realized that his questions must seem extraordinary, and he added: "I—I wondered if it were his—his brother—"

"More like his father," said the clerk. "Elderly man—thin and sort of frail."

"Thanks!" said Dennison, and went out again.

Very well; why shouldn't Folyet be called away unexpectedly? Perhaps when he had told Leatherby he would return, he had forgotten some important engagement, only recalling it later.

"No reason to think there's anything wrong," he said to himself, as he walked back to the house.

He mounted the steps and rang the bell. As usual, Miller opened the door.

"There's a call for you, sir;" he said.

But Dennison made no answer. Before his eyes stood a man who very well fitted the hotel-clerk's description—elderly man—"thin and sort of frail"...

"I'm getting morbid!" he thought, impatiently. "There are hundreds—thousands of men to fit that description.... All right, Miller!" he said, aloud, and went to Miss Napier, to ask about the call.

"It's the Templeton boy again," she told him. "And Doctor Leatherby says will you please stop at the Eagle House and ask if Mr. Folyet's coming back here?"

He glanced at her quickly, but she met his look with a wide, school-girl smile. Evidently she didn't see anything amiss in this request. But he did.

The obvious, almost the inevitable thing for Leatherby to have done, was to telephone the Eagle House and make his enquiry. Why should he ask Dennison to go?

For a moment he considered telling her that he had already been there, and what he thought. But he decided against it. Not because he distrusted her, but because of a strange pity that seized him at the sight of her.

"I won't worry her," he thought. "She's so young.... So young to marry a man of Leatherby's age.... She—" He turned away his head. "Anything I can do for you? "he asked. "Any more wool to get?"

"Well..." she said, "if you're going to the Eagle House—if it wouldn't be too much trouble to stop at the stationer's next door...? They have a special sort of almond bar—"

"Yes, I will!" said Dennison, unreasonably touched. "I'll be glad to. I will!"

"Thank you ever so much!" said she. "And here's the money."

He took the coin she held out to him, because he thought she might be offended if he protested; he put it into his pocket and went out.

"She's nothing but a kid..." he thought.

The idea of the future wife of Doctor Leatherby, the epicure, wanting an almond bar....

The car was not at the door, and he strolled across the lawn to the garage. Ames was just putting on his coat.

"Sorry, Doctor!" he said, cheerfully. "But I bin runnin' the vacuum-cleaner over them cushions. Gosh! Looks like a murder been done in that car—"

"*What!*" cried Dennison.

Ames laughed.

"Maybe it's not that bad," he said. "Only I found a handkerchief, all blood, stuffed down behind the cushion—"

"Let's see it," said Dennison.

"I didn't keep it," said Ames. "It went in the incinerator, with the rest of the rubbish. It was all tore up, anyway."

Dennison's mind was working rapidly.

"What makes you think I'm responsible for the handkerchief?" he asked, with a very good assumption of careless amusement.

"Well, Doctor Leatherby hasn't used the sedan for a week," said Ames, grinning. "Don't worry, Doc! I won't give you away!"

He made more jokes upon the topic of doctors and their supposed victims, and Dennison responded with a readiness that surprised himself. For the dominant idea in his mind was, that Ames must not suspect anything amiss. Not yet. Not until he had time to think this over.

He sat back in the car. The handkerchief "all blood" must have been left in the car last night, when Miller had driven Folyet—somewhere. Two persons could explain its presence: Miller and Folyet.

"Shall I ask Miller, squarely?" he thought. "Or would it be a mistake to let him see that I suspect anything?"

It seemed to him that it would be a mistake. He did not trust Miller, and he did not like him.

"No," he thought. "The thing for me to do is to try to find Folyet. If I don't—"

If he could not find Folyet?

He had reached his patient's house now, and directly he crossed the threshold, he forgot Miller and Folyet, forgot everything except his work. He gave all his attention to the sick boy; even when he was in the car again, his mind was busy with the case for some time.

Then, with a jerk, he came back to that ugly and threatening problem.

"I must find Folyet," he thought. "All this has got to be explained."

He did not care now how "ridiculous" he might appear to anyone. If the whole thing turned out to be a mare's nest, very well, let everyone laugh at him. But he meant to make sure.

"Looks like a murder been done in that car—"

They were turning into the driveway of Leatherby's house, and in the afternoon sun the little turrets threw long black shadows across the lawn. And his heart sank at the thought of entering there again. He wished he might turn his back upon this tangle of doubt and fear, and walk off into the world, free as he had been before. With empty pockets, with only his clever, supple surgeon's hands and his obstinate, alert mind, but free....

Only, of course, he was not free. There was Evie to think of.... And the thought of Evie reminded him of something else.

"That bar!" he said, aloud.

"What?" asked Ames.

"I forgot something. Take me back, will you, to the stationer's next to the Eagle House?"

The obliging Ames swept round the drive and out of the gates again, back to the town, and Dennison entered the stationer's.

Twice the stationer's wife asked him what he wanted, before he answered her; he stood looking down at the case of sweets, with a pain in his heart he could not understand. He had, upon special occasions, brought boxes of chocolates to Evie, ornate boxes, trimmed with ribbon. He saw some of

these in the case before him, and he wished so that he might take one to
Hilda Napier.

But he knew it would not do. She must have just what she asked for;
only that one little almond bar. And he scrupulously paid for it with the
very coin she had given him.

CHAPTER EIGHT

THE INTOLERABLE DREAM

Dennison's mind was a dogged, straightforward one, and he took the plainest course first. That evening, when he was taking coffee in the library with Doctor Leatherby and Mrs. Lewis, he began. He said exactly what he had planned to say.

"Can you give me Folyet's address, sir?" he asked. "I'd like to get in touch with him."

Leatherby smiled.

"An interesting type," he said. "A remarkable fellow, altogether.... No; I don't know where he lives. I never did know exactly where he came from. Somewhere in New York.... Do you happen to know, Rose?"

"No," said Mrs. Lewis, coldly, without glancing up.

"I'll ask Miller," said Leatherby, and rang the bell. "Miller, have you Mr. Folyet's address?"

"I have one he gave me last year, sir," answered Miller, promptly, and going off, came back in a moment with an address written on a piece of paper, which Leatherby glanced at, and handed to Dennison.

"I've been expecting him back," he said. "But he's rather erratic...."

These ready answers, this air of obliging unconcern, perturbed Dennison. It was like a wall that he could not climb, could not see beyond, a wall that shut away Folyet. .. .

Leatherby had begun to speak again, addressing his sister now, in his easy, quiet voice.

"I heard this morning that the Wallings have got their divorce," he said.

"Oh, what a pity!" said Mrs. Lewis. "I went to their wedding—only three years ago. And they seemed so happy."

"They were happy," said Leatherby. "For two years. There's nothing melancholy in that, my dear girl."

"It's so sad that it didn't last."

Leatherby smiled again.

"They're young," he said. "They can both experience that sort of love again."

Dennison glanced at him sharply, uneasily. For he had an idea that Leatherby was talking for him; he felt that somehow he was being assailed, and must make a defense.

"You believe in divorce, sir?" he asked.

"Naturally," said Leatherby. "With the modern conception of marriage."

"There isn't any 'modern' conception of marriage, Charles," said his sister. "Young people are just as they've always been. They start life together so confidently—so sure they're going to be happy—"

She stopped, and fell silent, her dark eyes sorrowful.

"And generally they are happy—for a reasonable time," said Leatherby. "But that in itself is a modern idea; the idea that marriage should be based upon what you call 'love'—a passion, a passing fancy. That its purpose is the personal happiness of two persons. If you admit that basis—that people marry to be happy, then when they cease to be happy, the marriage should be dissolved."

He lit a fresh cigar.

"The ancients had another point of view," he went on. "The home was sacred to them, and passion had no place in it. A man did not marry to indulge a fancy, but to establish a home, and carry on a tradition. The notion of romantic love was unknown in those golden days. And unimaginable. A wife was chosen for other qualities than physical charm. She remained in the home, in a position of unassailable dignity and honour."

"And loneliness," said Mrs. Lewis.

"Not at all. She had her children, her friends, her duties."

No one replied to him. Dennison was uneasy, and displeased. Leatherby's words about marriage sounded austere and noble; the honoured wife sheltered in the home.... But behind the words lay a thought which the young man could not quite seize, yet which offended him. There was something unwholesome here, unsound, basically wrong.

"Damned if I'd like a marriage like that!" he thought. "A wife shut up with her children and friends and duties.... There ought to be—comradeship—"

He moved restlessly.

"Miss Napier—" he thought. "That wouldn't suit her."

Mrs. Lewis rose, and wished them good-night. For a time Leatherby talked to Dennison about certain cases, then the young man too retired. But he did not sleep well that night.

In the morning, before breakfast, he shut himself into the office, and telephoned to the address he had got from Miller. And he was told that Folyet had left there a year ago, and had given no forwarding address. He was not surprised nor especially disappointed; he had not in his heart expected to trace Folyet so easily.

But too much time was being wasted, and he had to do now what he was most reluctant to do. He entered the dining-room, where Hilda Napier sat waiting for him, and after exchanging a greeting—

"Do you happen to know where Folyet lives?" he asked.

He asked it casually, and he had a little explanation ready, to account for his interest. But he never made it. He was astounded, shocked by the girl's behaviour. Her face grew white; she looked at him for a moment in undisguised fear; then, with an effort, she smiled.

"No, I don't," she said.

And he did not believe her. Her smile itself was a lie; strained, frightened, uncertain.

"I must find out," he said, looking steadily at her.

"But why?" she asked. "He—I'm sure you didn't—like him. He's not the sort of man you'd like.... He—he made trouble here."

"I've got to find him," said Dennison.

She was silent for a moment; then she looked up at him.

"Oh, please don't!" she entreated. "It's so much nicer without him! Do let sleeping dogs lie! Did I make your coffee right for you yesterday? Or shall I put in a little more hot milk?"

He saw now how a man might be made a catspaw of; saw that a man might be willing, glad, to close his eyes. Her distress so touched him, she was so lovely, with her troubled eyes, her uncertain smile; it was so hard not to yield to her and make her happy again.

But he would not even pretend to yield.

"I'm sorry," he said.

So he was, sorry for everything, sorry to see her grow silent, retreat from him, sit at the table and not speak again, and not look at him. Sorry to think that she knew—something, at least, and would not trust him with her knowledge.

He wanted time now to think what he must do next, but he got no time. There were an unusual number of patients in the morning, and after lunch there were several calls to be made. The last of these was far out in the country, and he was thankful for the long drive and the solitude.

"I think," he said to himself, "that I'll get one of these private detectives. Simply tell him to trace Folyet. I needn't give him any reason. Or, if I do have to, I'll say—well—that Folyet owes me money. Then, if I find there's nothing wrong, there's no harm done. But I've got to know. And know now."

The patient he had to visit was a singularly difficult old man, who demanded a good deal too much attention from Dennison. And got it, for

Dennison was very young and serious. It was dusk when he left the farmhouse; he was tired, and he felt somehow defeated by the cynical old man. And there, outside the shabby picket fence stood the smart little car, with Ames in his uniform; the headlights were turned on; in the twilight they had a magically softened radiance; there was altogether a dreamlike quality about this moment. He was to get into this car and be driven luxuriously home, to put on a dinner-jacket, to sit down to an exquisite dinner....

The memory of other twilights rushed over him, rainy dusks, when he had been far more weary than this, and had had nothing before him but a meagre dinner in a dairy-lunch, and a return to a dismal little furnished room. He thought how long it would take him to attain his present standard of comfort by his own efforts; how many years and years it would be before he could have a car like this, a room, a dinner such as Leatherby provided him.

Leaning back in the car, he felt that he had not appreciated before the delight of this swift and easy transit. He thought of his room, with the lamp lighted, that easy-chair, that perfect bed, that glittering bathroom. He thought of dinner, eaten with heavy silver, from fine china, the woodfire in the library; Mrs. Lewis in evening dress, all the charm, the dignity of that life.

And he clung to it, with all his heart.

"If I can live like this for a while," he thought, "it'll do me all the good in the world. That's what I need. I've knocked about so much I—I hardly knew what that style of living meant. I thought I didn't care. Thought I'd be satisfied with a cheap little house, cheap furniture, a cheap life altogether. It's not right for a man to be satisfied with so little."

Well, he wouldn't be satisfied again. This was what he wanted, this life. He lit a cigarette, and sighed with relief. This was so good....

His glance fell upon the sturdy shoulders of Ames, driving the car steadily through the Spring dusk. What had Ames said...? "Murder"... Ames had spoken that word.

"Rot!" said Dennison to himself.

And for the first time in his life he deliberately shut a door in his mind, deliberately refused to see what waited his attention.

"All rot!" he said, again. "There's nothing really wrong here. Couldn't be, with people like this. I've been trying to make a mountain out of a molehill. I'd better mind my own business."

When he got back to the house, Miss Napier had gone home, and he was not sorry. For some reason he did not want to see her just now. He went up to his own room, turned on the light, saw again all the delicious comfort and tranquility. There was time for a pipe before he need dress; he sat down in the arm-chair, and took the leather tobacco pouch from his pocket.

Then he noticed on the table before him an envelope propped against the lamp; he reached for it, found it addressed to himself and opened it.

"My dear Dennison

The inquest on my friend Manley is to be held to-morrow morning at half past ten. That would mean an early train from here, and you may have noticed that early rising is not one of my virtues. So I am going in to town to-night; if you need me, telephone me at the Regal Hotel.

And there is one little service I shall ask of you. I rather expect a patient to stop in this evening for a tonic I have put up for her. Will you be kind enough to go to my consulting room and, in the safe there, you will find a small bottle. There can be no mistake; it is the only bottle there. The combination is set for the letters t-i-n-s-e-l. Then please wrap this bottle in a bit of paper and give it to Miller, who will hand it to the patient, if she calls.

I shall be with you in time for dinner to-morrow; perhaps for tea.

Faithfully,

Charles Leatherby."

"That's—queer..." thought Dennison, staring at the letter. "Queer—to keep a bottle of tonic in a safe. And if he wants Miller to have it, why not give it to Miller himself?"

Because someone had been watching him, and he could not get to the safe...?

"No!" thought Dennison, angry at the unbidden thought. "Nonsense!"

He rose instantly, and went out of the room, down the corridor in the direction of the consulting room. All the doors were closed; everything was quiet. Was anyone watching him now? Let them!

He had not yet caught so much as a glimpse of this upstairs consulting-room, and the sight of it surprised him. It was so serene and beautiful, filled with things which even his untrained eye could recognize as rare and exquisite. There was no sign here of the physician's business, not even a desk; only an inlaid table on which stood a bowl of opal glass filled with tulips.

He went direct to the safe, walking softly among the treasures, turned the dial to the proper letters; the thick door opened; he saw in there on a shelf a little vial; he put it into his pocket and reclosed the safe.

Then, as he was leaving the room, a great reluctance came over him. What was this which he had undertaken to do? What was in this bottle?

"None of my business!" he said to himself.

Returning to his room, he dressed, in that new dinner-jacket, and went downstairs. There was no one in the library, and he occupied himself by examining some of Leatherby's books. There was one, bound in scarlet leather and gold, which attracted his eye; and he drew it out and turned the pages idly. There were pictures in it—what pictures! He put it back hastily, feeling a sort of uneasiness that he had looked at such obscenity.

"Probably it's a—a sort of curiosity," he thought.

"Good-evening, Doctor Dennison," said Mrs. Lewis's clear voice behind him.

He greeted her with a new amenity he was beginning to acquire, but with constraint, for somehow it seemed to him wrong that she should be in the same room with that book.

They sat down to dinner alone together. At first he was silent, lost in his own thoughts, but happening to glance up, he caught Mrs. Lewis looking at him with an odd expression of appeal. Of course she expected him to talk. And, to please her, he tried.

Her response was almost pathetic. She was skilled in this game; she could make so much out of his rather stilted remarks, ask him questions he could answer, give to their talk a very charming air of spontaneity.

He had at first thought her disdainful, but not now. He felt now that what he had thought disdain was pure sorrow; she was indifferent in her manner not through pride but because of some secret preoccupation; he saw her as fragile, affrighted, forlorn.

"Worried about her brother?" he thought. "Or what?"

He was not likely to find out. They went into the library for their coffee, and Mrs. Lewis lit a cigarette, sat there until it was finished. Then she rose.

"If you'll excuse me..." she said. "I'm so tired.... Good-night, Doctor Dennison."

"Good-night!" he answered.

After she had gone, he remained standing for a few moments before the fire. He rather missed Leatherby and his conversation.

"This inquest..." he thought; then frowned impatiently. "None of my business!"

He turned down the hall, thrusting his hands into his pockets, and as he did so, he felt the little bottle. He went on, into the office, and sitting down at the desk, took it out of his pocket and looked at it. It was an ordinary half-ounce chemist's bottle, filled with a clear green liquid; the colour was unfamiliar to him; he removed the cork, and the smell was unfamiliar to him. He poured a few drops on the back of his hand, and tasted it, and the taste was utterly strange to him.

"What is it?" he thought. "I know most of the ordinary drugs well enough. But this... Why did he keep it in a safe? And no label... I don't see..."

He leaned back in his chair, staring with a frown at the bottle.

"There's something queer... " he thought. "I don't like this...."

He covered his eyes with his hand, and sat that way for some time. Then his hand fell listlessly, and he looked up, and a smile came over his face.

"After all, what does it matter?" he thought. "What a wonderful colour that green—with the light on it... Like the—cold Northern seas...."

Like the sea at the foot of an iceberg. Looking down into it, he could see for miles, all crystal clear, the water brightened like a jewel as the sun shone through it, and at the bottom, tiny figures of women with flowing hair, swimming leisurely about.

"The mermaids!" he thought, and a thrill of ecstasy shot through him. "I never knew they were real."

He had never known before what marvels there were in the world. Raising his eyes, he looked into the heart of the iceberg; he saw there spears of trembling light, ruby red, sapphire blue, a fierce, glowing green so lovely that tears rose in his eyes.

And overhead, in the unclouded sky, came a flight of rosy birds with eyes like jewels, going by in an endless stream. He wanted to see them closer, and without effort he rose into the air. And the delight of that, the exquisite lightness of his body and soul, that went drifting up into the pure sky... He flew...

The sweet air blew against his face; there came to him the very perfume of paradise, a perfume that ran through his veins like a new, strong current of life. He had never been alive before, with this thrilling ecstasy of power and joy. He rose higher, above the sea.

But the birds were going. He tried to hurry after them; he wanted to touch, even with one finger-tip, that plumage of rose and white, but they rose higher, and he could not follow. He was growing heavier. He saw them winging straight to the golden portals of the sunset; he struggled in anguish, panting, tears running down his face; he clutched at the feathery clouds, and they crumpled in his hands. He was sinking, through a sky grown chilly and grey; his foot struck against the iceberg, and a bitter pain stabbed him. He was falling, limp and helpless, upon the smooth ice, so cold...

So cold... He opened his eyes, found himself sitting at the desk, with his head on his arms, and a dreadful oppression on him. He closed his eyes again, in an intolerable longing to get back to that colour, that perfume, that light, pure joy. But it was gone, all gone; there was nothing left but a monstrous blackness, like endless corridors down which tiny specks of light whirled giddily and were quenched.

He opened his eyes and sat up; his head was spinning.

"I've been—dreaming," he thought, dully.

What dream had ever been so bright? There were still tears on his face, and a desolate ache in his heart.

"If I could have that dream again—" he thought. And thought that the world about him was dust and ashes, grey and cold, and nothing was lovely but that lost dream.

His head was beginning to clear a little.

"What's the matter with me?" he thought. "I never fall asleep like that—never dream like that."

He looked at his watch, looked again, stared, with growing dismay. An hour gone? He had sat here dreaming for an hour?

"Never did such a thing in my life," he thought. "I don't see..."

He lit a cigarette, but the taste of the tobacco sickened him, after the ineffable perfume and clear air of his dream. A wave of sorrow rushed over him; he dropped his head on his arms, forlorn and desolate, longing for his lost paradise.

"Not feeling quite fit, sir?" murmured a voice in his ear.

With an effort he raised his head and saw Miller standing beside him.

"No..." he said. "Never mind..."

"May I assist you upstairs, sir?"

The man's face seemed veiled in a haze, his voice very distant. And it seemed to Dennison that he saw something moving on the desk, something crawling, like a snake...

The strangest thing was happening inside him. It was as if there were two Dennisons, one sick and shaken and confused, and the other, firm and stern, trying to break some chain of steel. That other Dennison knew that what moved along the desk was Miller's hand, that while Miller murmured respectfully to him, his hand was stealthily seeking something.

"Stop!" said Dennison.

"Yes, sir," said Miller. But now his fingers had closed about something. It was the bottle of green liquid.

"Put that down!" said Dennison. He was struggling in a fog, fighting desperately against his own terrible listlessness and confusion, and it was growing better for him.

"Excuse me, sir," said Miller, "but I believe Doctor Leatherby wished me to give this medicine to a patient—"

"Put it down!" said Dennison.

No one must touch that bottle. Why...? He could not tell now, but he was sure that he was going to know, soon. It was coming to him... Now he had it. His dream had come out of that bottle—and it was beyond all measure dangerous and evil.

"Put it down!" he ordered.

"Excuse me, sir," said Miller. "Doctor Leatherby's orders... I'm afraid you're not quite yourself, sir—"

There was an unmistakable sneer in his voice, and picking up the bottle, he turned away. For an instant Dennison was unable to move; then, with a monstrous effort, he broke through his lethargy, got up, lurched forward, and caught Miller by the shoulder.

He tried to twist away, but Dennison held him fast.

"Give it to me!"

"No!" cried Miller. "That I won't!"

In a sudden gust of fury, Dennison struck at him, a wild blow. But it found its mark; Miller pitched forward, lay face downward on the floor, quite still. Dennison stooped and picked up the little bottle—

The office door-bell rang.

CHAPTER NINE

"MRS. SMITH"

Carefully, even with a sort of considerateness, Dennison lifted Miller's limp legs out of the doorway, and closed the door on him.

"Can't take any patients in there—just now," he reflected, and believed himself to be profoundly reasonable, wise and cool. Yet he staggered a little as he went down the hall, and he quite forgot to turn on the light. And it was difficult for him to get the door open.

"Well?" he asked.

Immediately a hand seized his sleeve, and a woman's voice, terribly agitated, whispered:

"I've come, Doctor! I've come... I've made up my mind! Give it to me!"

Startled, he snapped on the light; the woman before him drew back, ghastly white, staring at him.

"My God...!" she faltered. "I thought—"

He recognized her now; it was the woman he had seen once before, coming down the stairs, with tears on her face; a dark, handsome woman, beautifully dressed. But so white now, with such dilated, brilliant eyes.

"Where is Doctor Leatherby?" she demanded.

"He's away," said Dennison. "I'm taking charge of his patients. Is there—?"

'He knew I was coming!" she interrupted. "Did he leave—something for me? He promised! He knew—"

"So she's the one!" thought Dennison. "She's come for that bottle. Some drug, of course... But the effect—"

A wave of nostalgia swept over him, of terrible longing for his dream; he stood looking at the woman with blank eyes. Then, as it ebbed away, he felt the sharp wind from the open door blowing upon him, bitter, but wholesome, driving away the fog of confusion.

"By the Lord!" he thought. "It's—damnable!"

"There's a bottle for me," the woman went on. "He promised me... Look for it, please. Look upstairs, in his room. Look everywhere—"

"Was it—medicine?" asked Dennison slowly.

"Yes! Yes, of course! Won't you look—?"

Dennison was silent. And he made up his mind that for no consideration would he give the unlabelled, unknown liquid to this desperate creature. Not unless he knew what it was, and why she wanted it.

"If I only had a little time to think—" he said to himself. "I'm taking a good deal upon myself—a great responsibility. That stuff may be something new I've never heard of—some remedy—some palliative. The thing is, have I any right, when I don't know—"

He did know. More deep-seated than reason was his utter conviction that the liquid was dangerous and evil. He looked again at the woman.

"I'm a qualified physician," he said, carefully. "You needn't hesitate to talk to me…. Perhaps I can help you. Is that—medicine for yourself?"

She looked at him; her eyes narrowed; he saw, plain in her face, the swift, tormented calculation going on in her mind. She was studying him, his youth, his inexperience, his stubbornness. And, according to his nature, he endured her scrutiny with hardihood. Let her look! His brain was growing clearer every moment.

"No," she said, and there was an almost incredible change in her tone; she spoke softly and sorrowfully. "It's for my husband. He's suffering so…. If you could only find—what Doctor Leatherby left for me…"

"I'll come to see your husband," said Dennison, promptly.

"No!" she cried. Then, with an effort, spoke gently again. "It would only worry him to see a strange face. Doctor Leatherby knows all about him. The medicine he left is the only thing—please find it for me!"

Suppose it were true? Suppose that bottle contained medicine important, necessary for a suffering man?

A suffering man—a grey-haired man, lying face downward on the floor.

"Did I really knock down Miller?" he thought, frowning. "Or was that part of the—dream?"

He had to find that out at once, and he wasted no time in thinking up any plausible excuse.

"Just wait a moment, please!" he said, civilly enough, and turned away, leaving the woman standing in the open doorway. He had an unpleasantly vivid image of Miller, limp and still in the lamplight…

But when he opened the door, the office was empty, neat and tranquil.

"I—imagined it—dreamed it," he said to himself. "It couldn't—"

"Doctor!" said the woman's voice, at his side. "Please give it to me, and let me go!"

"I can't," said Dennison. "You see, I don't know what the—medicine is… I'll have to see the patient."

"Don't you think Doctor Leatherby knows his business?" she asked, with a faint frown.

"I don't mean it that way," said Dennison, deliberately. "But Doctor Leatherby's not here, and there's no label on the bottle. I won't take the responsibility of giving a medicine I know nothing about to a patient I haven't seen. It may not even be meant for your husband. I'll—"

"So you have it!" she interrupted, smiling again.

He realized that he had rather given himself away, but after all, it didn't matter. She was not going to get her bottle.

"You'd better come with me," she said, abruptly.

"To see your husband?"

"Yes. Perhaps after you've seen him, you'll be convinced. You'll bring the bottle with you, of course."

"Where do you live?"

"My car is here," she said. "I'll take you, and send you back."

"Very well," said Dennison.

Still he hesitated for a moment. He felt that he ought to let Miller know he was going out, yet he was very reluctant to see Miller just then.

"If I did knock him down," he thought.

"Come, please," said the woman, with a frown.

He rang the bell and waited. What if Miller didn't answer?

"Did you ring, sir?" asked Miller's voice from the doorway, bland and remote. Dennison glanced at him, and saw nothing amiss in his appearance; simply an elderly man with narrow shoulders and a pallid, inexpressive face.

"I'm going out, Miller, to see a patient. What's the name, please, and the address, so that I could be reached?"

"Mrs. Smith," said she, with no attempt to make the lie convincing. "On Main Street."

"Very well!" thought Dennison. "But I'll find out more than that before I've finished."

He stepped into the passage to get his hat and coat, and out there he smiled to himself. Because this curious affair was a challenge to him, and he accepted it with grim satisfaction.

He had picked up his bag, when a sound arrested him; he stood motionless, straining his ears, but he heard nothing more. He could scarcely be sure that he had really heard even that—heard a whisper from the office.

He re-entered quickly and quietly, but the woman was there alone, looking at herself in the mirror of a vanity-case.

"I'm ready!" said Dennison.

She brushed past him, out of the office, down the, passage, and threw open the door. It was a sharp, windy night; as he followed her down the path, he shivered a little.

Her car was waiting at the gate; she got in without a word; he followed her and she set off at once. She drove well enough; her hands on the wheel were steady; she never turned toward him, never spoke. And Dennison was equally silent, trying to see where they were going.

They went through Shayne, past the railway station; so far the way was familiar to him. But after that, he was quite at a loss; they turned up one dark country road after another; twice they crossed railway tracks, once they ran for a time along a wide boulevard, empty, well-lighted, lined with woodland. He could not tell now in what direction they were going; he saw nothing in the dark that might serve as a landmark.

After a drive of roughly three-quarters of an hour, they turned in at a driveway, and stopped before a large house with a facade of lighted windows. The woman got out without a word, mounted the steps of the terrace and taking a key from her handbag, opened the door.

"No servants?" thought Dennison.

The house was blazing with lights; it was richly furnished, well-warmed, yet directly he entered, he felt its desolation.

"In there!" she said, pointing to a door. "Wait in there!"

It was a small room with a harp in it, and a cello in a case; a charming room. But it did not charm Dennison. He stood near the door, with his hat in one hand and his bag in the other, his shabby overcoat still buttoned, and waited, watching the hall, down which the woman had vanished.

He did not hear her step on the thick carpet, or any sound at all, until she spoke behind him, and turning, he saw that she had entered through a curtained doorway at the end of the room.

"I don't think you've told me your name," she said, smiling.

"Dennison," he said.

"Doctor Dennison," she went on, gently, "I admire your conscientiousness. You want to feel sure that this medicine is really meant for my husband. And if I offer to pay for the bottle, that will convince you how certain I am that it's the right medicine." She held out a roll of bills. "There's a hundred dollars here. No! Please. It's not a bribe!" She smiled again. "I'm only trying to convince you that I *know* it's meant for me. Otherwise I shouldn't want it so much, should I?"

"I'm sorry," said Dennison.

"You mean you won't give it to me?"

"I'd like to see the patient first."

"It would only disturb him—"

"Then let me speak to his nurse, please."

She came closer to him.

"Doctor Dennison," she said. "I'll give you a thousand dollars for that bottle."

"It's not for sale," said Dennison.

"I'll give you five thousand," she said. "Now. In cash."

"I'm sorry," said Dennison. "But I can't give it to you."

She seized his arm.

"I'll give you anything I have!" she cried. "Ten thousand—twenty—all my jewels. See!"

She pulled off two rings and threw them on the table, and tried to unclasp her pearl necklace with trembling fingers.

"No," said Dennison, "it's no use."

He had seen this mad eagerness before, these sudden changes from threats to cajoleries; he had seen this desperation—in drug-addicts. And he pitied her.

"Mrs. Smith," he said, "you're—not very well. A little overwrought. I'm perfectly willing to give you a hypodermic—to quiet your nerves—"

Her eyes dilated; she stared at him with a wide, mirthless smile.

"I—" she began. "No... Perhaps, after all... You'd better—see the patient. Just wait, please."

Again she went out of the room, leaving him standing by the table, looking down at the glittering little heap of jewels and the roll of bills.

"Poor devil!" he thought. "Poor devil! It's a crime—it's a damnable thing—"

A chill ran down his spine like a trickle of ice-water; the hair stirred on his scalp. For behind him he heard a sound like nothing he had ever heard before; a sound without a name. It was like a cry of frightful effort, smothered into an inhuman, bestial groan.

He turned stiffly. The sound came from behind the curtains that hung across the doorway through which the woman had come. There must be a room there, and someone—something—in it....

Again it came, that stifled, atrocious sound. He drew a long breath, and took a step forward.

"Stop !" cried the woman's voice behind him.

But he had to see now. He strode forward, and pulled aside the curtains.

There, lying on a couch, with wrists and ankles bound, and a handkerchief tied over his mouth, lay Folyet. For one instant Dennison looked full into those sombre black eyes—then something struck him on the back of the head and he dropped like a log.

CHAPTER TEN

EMPTY

He opened his eyes. He knew that he opened his eyes, yet he saw absolutely nothing. An intolerable blackness was before him. He lifted a shaking hand, held it before him, and still saw nothing.

"Am I—blind?" he thought.

His head ached agonizingly; he felt nauseated, helplessly weak. And filled with a horror of this darkness. He moved cautiously; he felt that he was sitting up, with his head resting against the corner of something. Of what? He raised his arm, with a great effort, and his fingers touched a roof. A roof above him, a wall on one side... He stretched his arm to the other side; he felt another wall. He was in a box... A box... A—coffin?

A cold sweat broke out on his forehead; he flung out his hand wildly—and his knuckles struck against the smoothness of glass.

"Now, see here!" he said to himself. "Keep cool. You're not dead. If you're shut up in—something, you can get out. If you keep cool."

He tried to rise, but his head struck against the roof, and he sank down again, half-fainting with the pain. There was no room in this place to move. He was shut up, helpless, in utter darkness....

"Hold on!" he said to himself. "Keep cool! Let me think.... If I only had a light—"

He put his hand into his pocket; there were matches there, his pipe, a fountain-pen, old familiar objects that sent a thrill of relief through him. He struck a match—and laughed aloud at what he saw.

His box, his coffin, was simply the inside of a small closed car.

He lit another match, and looked for the door-handles. They were gone.

"All right!" he thought. "Plenty of windows."

They were so fastened that he could not move them. He clenched his fist and struck the one nearest him. But the glass was thick and he was weak now; there was no result but bleeding knuckles.

"Just the same, I'm going to get out," he thought. "I want—a breath of air."

A sort of madness seized him; a fierce, desperate craving for a breath of fresh air. But he fought it down, fought against the faintness and nausea that assailed him. He waited a moment with his eyes closed, until his heart was beating more quietly.

"Now, let's see..." he said to himself.

He could not break that thick glass with his fist, nor with a pipe or a fountain-pen.

"I'll kick it," he thought, and lay down on the seat.

The first kick, misdirected, struck the side of the car, but the second one struck the window, and exerting all his force, he sent a third one crashing through the glass. He heard it fall tinkling on to a hard surface. Then he took off his shoe, and chipped away the glass about the jagged hole until the frame was fairly clear.

He had to rest for a while after that. Then he discovered that the window was too small for his shoulders to pass through.

"Just the same, I'm going to get out," he said aloud.

He got one leg over the sill, groped until his foot rested on the running board; then he got his other leg out. Then, as he stood there, bent over, with head and shoulders still inside the car, the pain in his head turned him faint. He set his teeth, and fought it down.

In a nightmare of slow, agonizing effort, he twisted his shoulders in the narrow opening; bits of glass still clinging to the frame tore his face; slowly, patiently, he twisted sideways, got one arm out, his head, the other arm, and slipped down, half-unconscious on the running-board.

When he recovered, he lit another match, and found himself in a cement garage. He caught a glimpse of an electric light switch, and another match brought him staggering across the floor to it.

The light that flooded the place gave him immense relief; he had no longer the sensation of struggling in a hideous dream. All this was perfectly real and comprehensible. He was simply shut in a garage. The double doors were locked, the window was locked—but on the inside. He pushed back the catch and opened it, and the chill air blew in his face, exquisitely fresh and pure. A thin drizzle was falling; it refreshed him unspeakably; he stood leaning out, the rain falling on his throbbing head, and drew in greedily the scent of the wet Spring night. He could think now.

"Someone knocked me on the head," he reflected. "Just when I saw Folyet. That was—real, wasn't it?"

He knew it was real, yet the memory of Folyet's sombre eyes had the quality of a dream. He put his hand up to his head, and found the hair stiffened with blood.

"Did she do that?" he thought. "Mrs. Smith...?"

He could not think clearly, but there was coming back to him that sense of urgency, of great and pressing responsibility.

"I've got to find Folyet," he thought, as he had thought so often during the past days. "I can't leave him there—like that."

He had little trouble in getting out of the garage window, but he did have trouble in keeping on his feet. Where was he, and where should he go? He saw nothing before him but a glade of young trees, visible in the light that streamed from the window; beyond this bar of light was only blackness.

"But there must be a road in front of the garage," he thought.

Half-leaning against the wall, he got round the corner. There was no light here, but his eyes were accustomed to the dark, and he discerned a gravel driveway. Hard to walk, when his head reeled so.... But, every road leads somewhere... And the chill rain refreshed him.

Now he saw a light through the trees. Where there was a light there would probably be a human creature, and he could get a drink of brandy, a cup of coffee, anything to revive him. He staggered on, and, at a turn of the driveway, he saw before him a big house, blazing with lights.

"The same house!" he thought, and stopped.

Perhaps it was not quite reasonable to go back to the house where he had been knocked senseless, to ask for assistance...?

"But Folyet's there," he thought. "Tied up... I can't leave him like that."

He leaned against a tree, frowning in the effort to collect his confused thoughts.

"I ought to get the police," he thought. "Perhaps there was a telephone in the garage... I didn't notice... I can't go back... Not now... Better go forward than back."

He could never remember afterward what he had meant to do, what he had imagined he could do, alone, sick, unarmed. The only definite idea in his mind was that he must find Folyet. He had known that for a long time.

He did not even attempt to go cautiously. He stepped forward into the path of light that shone from the windows, and, stiff and clumsy from weakness, mounted the steps of the terrace. He stumbled over a wicker chair and had to wait a moment to recover himself; then he went forward and rang the doorbell.

He heard it ringing inside the house, but no one came. Strange, wasn't it, that a house so blazing with light should be so silent?

He tried the handle, and the door opened easily. And he walked in. He closed the door behind him and stood leaning against it, dazzled by the light. Then, as he was about to move, he heard a sound, a door closing softly upstairs. A footstep.

He went forward to the foot of the stairs, and looked up with dismay at the flight which seemed to him endless.

Hard job—to get up there..." he muttered.

He set his foot on the bottom step. The footsteps were coming nearer. He raised his head—and looked into the face of Hilda Napier. He saw, and was never to forget, the terrible look on her face.

And she screamed, a cry that pierced his head with an intolerable pain. Something she was holding fell from her hand and rolled down the stairs.

Weakness and confusion fled from him instantly. He straightened his shoulders; he looked at her with a sort of stern wonder.

She came running headlong down the stairs. "Oh, what has happened to you!" she cried.

"Nothing," he said. "It doesn't matter. Where's Folyet?"

"Folyet?"

She was standing now on the step above him, so that her head was a little above his, and the sight almost stopped his breath from pain. She was so lovely, in her pallor, her fair hair in disorder—and so guilty. That was sheer terror in her eyes.

"Oh, what has happened to you?" she cried, again.

"It doesn't matter," he repeated. "Where's Folyet?"

"But he's not here—"

"I saw him here."

"Then he's—gone. Please, Doctor Dennison, let me attend to you. You're hurt!"

"I'll get over it," he answered, curtly. "But I must find Folyet—"

"He's not here, Doctor Dennison. I promise you he's not here."

"I'm sorry," said Dennison, "but I'll have to look."

"Let me attend to you first. That cut—"

He saw the tears spring to her eyes.

"What are you doing here?" he cried, in anguish. "Won't you explain—?" Again that shadow crossed her face.

"I—I heard that Mrs. Smith was ill—and I came—"

His steady glance never left her face, but she was not looking at him.

"She's—very ill," she went on. "There's a nurse with her now—"

"Now?" he repeated. A nurse, who did not appear after that scream?

"Yes. So—there's nothing for me to do. I was just going home. Doctor Dennison—won't you come too?"

"Is there a doctor in attendance?"

"Oh, yes. Doctor Leatherby came—"

"He was here to-night?"

"Yes. Miller telephoned into the city for him, and he drove out. He sent for Miss Horton, from the hospital, and he's asked Doctor Peters to look in in the morning."

She spoke with a miserable attempt at casualness, and smiled. And at the sight of that terribly anxious smile something crept over him like a fog, rising, chilling him to the marrow of his bones. He *knew* that she was keeping something from him, trying to banish from her eyes and her voice something he must not see.

"And Folyet?" he asked.

"I don't know anything about him. I haven't seen him. He's not here, Doctor Dennison. Won't you please come back to the house with me and let me dress those cuts?"

"I can't go—yet," said Dennison.

She was silent for a moment.

"Doctor Dennison," she said, at last. "If I ask you—as a favour to me—to come away with me now...? If I—give you my word that there's nothing you can do here—?"

He could not endure to look at her.

"I'm sorry—" he said.

"You *won't* come?"

"I cannot," he said. "I saw Folyet here—"

"Where?"

"In a room, behind the music-room."

"We'll go there and look," she said. "And when you see that he's not there, you'll come away, won't you?"

"No," said Dennison.

"We'll just look!" she said, with a pitiful attempt at brightness. "May I pass, please?"

He stood aside, and she went by him. Suddenly she stooped, and he stooped too and caught her wrist.

"No!" he said.

She straightened herself, and her eyes met his.

"Please...!" she said, faintly.

He did not answer, only stood looking down at the object which had dropped from her hand and rolled down the stairs. He knew it well enough. It was the bottle for which Mrs. Smith had offered so great a price. And it was empty.

"It's—mine," she said.

He released her wrist.

"Very well," he said. "Then take it."

CHAPTER ELEVEN

THE HOUSE BLAZING WITH LIGHTS

He saw her pick up the bottle, saw her put it inside her blouse. He knew that she was going to tell him nothing. And he was going to ask nothing. Without a word he turned away and walked into the music-room.

It was empty, perfectly neat and peaceful. He crossed the room and drew back the curtains, looked into the room where he had seen Folyet. It was empty.

"You see—" she said. "Now won't you please come?"

He shook his head. He went back along the hall to the next room, a fine, lofty drawing-room, brilliantly lit. And empty. He went into the dining-room; the remains of a meal stood on one end of the polished table, and the room was empty. The kitchen, neat as a pin, was empty, the pantry, all the closets.

He came back to the stairs. But, before he reached them, the girl sprang ahead of him and barred the way.

"You—mustn't go up there, please!" she said. "Mrs. Smith is—resting. You—can't disturb her. There's a nurse with her—"

"I'll just speak to the nurse."

"No! No, Doctor Dennison! You—you have no right... No! Please!"

"I am going up," said Dennison.

"I beg you not to go!"

"Why?"

"Because—it would disturb her. Because—she's resting. I—Doctor Dennison! Won't you trust me?"

"I'm sorry," he said, gently, "but I can't."

"Can't—?"

"No," he said. He spoke carefully, anxious to say exactly what he meant. "I think you've been—misguided—"

"You're wrong!" she broke in, vehemently. "I'm not 'guided' at all. I'm acting on my own responsibility—entirely. I ask you to come away now—for my sake. I thought—"

She stopped suddenly. But she had said enough. She had thought that what she asked, he would do, for her.

And he knew then what her power was. He thought that a man might be glad to give his very life in service to her heart-stirring young beauty and valour. Looking into her worn young face, pity and tenderness so seized him that he could not speak.

And anyhow, what had he to say? He *could not* do what she asked. There was something horribly wrong here in this brilliant house, and he could not turn his back upon it.

She read that in his face, and moved aside.

"I'm sorry," he said again.

She made no answer. Half-way up the stairs he turned, to see if she were following, but he saw her in the hall below, leaning against the wall, with her hands over her face, like one in utter despair.

The upper hall was brightly lit too, and lined with closed doors. He knocked upon the first one, and getting no reply, opened the door and entered. He took a step forward—when before him he saw an appalling figure, a ghastly face, streaked with blood, with dazed, staring eyes.

"Stop!" he cried, threateningly.

The figure did not stir, and he realized that what he saw was his own image in a mirror.

"This won't do," he thought.

If Mrs. Smith, if anyone were still in the house, he could not present himself in this condition. There was a bath-room opening out of this room; he went in there and washed his hands and face, and the cuts that still bled.

Then he returned to the mirror that was over a dressing-table and picking up a brush, smoothed his wild hair. His collar was past doing anything with, but he re-knotted his necktie and once more wiped away the blood from the cuts.

"That's the best I can do," he thought.

It was a purely mechanical impulse that made him pull open the top drawer. He badly needed a clean handkerchief, and all his life clean handkerchiefs had come from a top drawer. Sure enough, there were plenty of them here. He took one out, and shook it open. And he saw, marked in ink on the border—J. Folyet!

It gave him a shock. It was as if, until now, he had half-hoped he was dreaming, and was suddenly made aware that the dream was reality. It was no dream; Folyet had been here.

He went out of the room in haste, entered the next one, the next, handsomely furnished rooms, lit by lamps with soft-coloured shades, all neat, all empty, all of them with the strange, impersonal air of hotel rooms. There were no trifles left about, no signs of occupation. On every door he knocked and there was never an answer, never a sound.

He knocked on the door of the fourth room, expecting no answer, and getting none. He turned the handle, and, to his surprise, the door opened upon blackness. It was utterly dark and still, with the night wind blowing in from an open window.

He struck a match and found the switch near the door; he turned it, and a dim little lamp sprang alive.

He saw a nurse in white uniform, sitting in a chair with her hands clasped in her lap. She did not stir; she sat there, monstrously indifferent to light or darkness. He strode across to her, and found her breathing calmly. He touched her on the shoulder, and she did not move.

"Nurse!" he said, sharply.

But the sound of his voice did not trouble her, sitting with her hands clasped in her lap. Nor did it trouble the woman lying on the bed.

It was "Mrs. Smith," lying there in a sort of innocent grace, her dark hair loose on the pillow, and a little drowsy smile on her lips. He touched her hand, and it was cold, and her heart had stopped beating.

There was a carafe of ice-water on the table; Dennison dipped a towel into it, and flicked the nurse's face. She sighed and stirred. He pressed the dripping towel against her face, to the back of her neck; her heavy lids fluttered, and she stared up at him vaguely.

"Nurse!" he said.

She was coming awake now.

"What...?" she asked. "I—I've been asleep...?"

Dennison did not answer, and his silence frightened her. For a moment she sat staring up at him, at his pale, blood-stained face.

"What—is it...?" she faltered.

"Your patient's dead," said Dennison.

She was wide-awake enough now, and horror stricken. She rose to her feet and ran to the bedside; then she turned to Dennison with a blanched face.

"I didn't know... " she said. "I didn't know... Are you—one of the family?"

"I'm a doctor," he answered.

"Oh!" she cried. "Oh, Doctor! I *never* did such a thing before! I don't know how it happened... I—just dropped off... My record—"

"Who's in charge of the case?"

"She was Doctor Leatherby's patient. He sent for me. But he was called out of town, and Doctor Peters was coming in the morning."

"Get Doctor Peters on the telephone."

She went to the telephone that stood on a desk in the corner, and asked for a number.

"Doctor Peters? Miss Horton speaking.... Doctor Leatherby's patient has ceased breathing... Yes, doctor."

She hung up the receiver, and stood before Dennison, very straight, but with a trembling lip.

"Sit down!" he said. "What servants are there?"

"None, Doctor. Mrs. Smith was on her way to Asheville. She only stopped in here for the night."

"You mean she was alone in the house?"

"Yes, Doctor. She told me she hadn't intended to stay overnight. She'd just meant to stop and collect some things she'd left here. But she was taken ill with a heart attack. She was in bed when I got here, and she looked—very bad. Doctor Leatherby warned me—" Her voice was unsteady. "He said she might go, suddenly, or she might take a turn for the better. He said there was nothing to be done, but to give a stimulant if she seemed to be sinking, and to ring up Doctor Peters. Oh, Doctor! I don't *know* how I could have fallen asleep! I never—"

"Never mind that," he said, not unkindly. "What time did you come here?"

"About half-past eleven."

He glanced at his watch; it was now a little after three.

"Who else has been here to-night?"

"Nobody but Doctor Leatherby."

"Nobody at all? You're sure?"

"Yes, I'm sure, Doctor. And I'm *sure* I haven't been asleep long. I never did such—"

"All right. When did Doctor Leatherby leave?"

"A few minutes after I got here. He was in a hurry. He only stopped to give me directions. He seemed annoyed because the patient wouldn't go to the hospital. I—I'm sure I only closed my eyes for a moment—"

"She hasn't been dead long," said Dennison. "Not more than half an hour. You can tell Doctor Peters that when he comes."

"Aren't you going to wait here for him, Doctor?"

"I don't know," said Dennison.

She stared at him, taking in more fully his strange appearance.

"Doctor! You're hurt!"

"An accident," he said. "A motor-accident."

He turned abruptly, left the room, and went downstairs. Once more he went through that house blazing with lights, and once more he found no one. Hilda Napier had gone.

CHAPTER TWELVE

WHAT DOCTOR PETERS SAW

Dennison paced up and down the hall as if it were a cage; up and down, as if he were driven.

And he was encaged, and he was driven.

"No!" he said to himself. "I don't know anything. I won't know. I—I wash my hands of the whole thing."

Then he remembered someone else who had said that, nineteen centuries ago; someone else who had washed his hands of a responsibility—and was accursed.

A man might fight on the wrong side, and still be honest. But a man who takes no side at all, who strikes no blow, is contemptible. And Dennison was a born partisan and fighter; his ancestors had died, to bear witness to their grim faith, and he could not shut his eyes, could not stand apart.

Very well then; which side?

"The nurse was drugged," he thought. "She doesn't know what happened—who came into the room. The woman was scarcely cold, and— No use shutting my eyes to things... I saw no one in this house but— Hilda. She had that bottle—and it was empty."

He could have groaned aloud, in his pain and dread.

"If she'd trusted me—told me," he thought. "I could have helped her. But now—"

Now how was he to help her? Doctor Peters was coming, was on his way. And he would see. The nurse drugged and the woman dead.

"She wouldn't trust me. She took away the bottle, so that no one would know. She tried to keep me out of that room. If she had, perhaps no one would ever have suspected anything. The nurse would have waked up. She would have thought that she'd simply been asleep, and for her own sake, she'd have said nothing. And Mrs. Smith would just have been dead—of heart failure."

Like Manley.

As far as Dennison could see, there was no sign whatever of Mrs. Smith having died of anything but natural causes. If one did not know that the nurse had been drugged, did not know of the bottle, had no information of Manley's exactly similar death....

"Leatherby was here to-night," he thought.

Well, what of that?

"There's no reason to suppose that the stuff in that bottle was—poison," he thought. "It may just have been used to drug the nurse, so that someone could—commit a robbery, perhaps. Why shouldn't Mrs. Smith have died of heart failure?"

He wanted to believe that.

"It might easily have been that," he thought. "Someone may have drugged the nurse, in order to get hold of—of some important papers."

That was not so horrible a crime. Even if it were Hilda Napier who had done that.... Hilda, creeping into the room where a woman lay dying, drugging the nurse, seizing what she wanted, and creeping out again, leaving the woman to die untended—?

"No," he said to himself, "it's not possible. She couldn't do that. She's not like that."

Suicide, then? Suppose Mrs. Smith had killed herself? What was there against that theory?

A suicide, who sent for a doctor and a nurse? If she had wanted to kill herself, and if the contents of that bottle could cause her death, she could have swallowed it, then and there, in the music-room, after he had been struck down unconscious.

And who had struck him? He found it hard to believe that a woman could have the strength for such a blow. Still it was possible.

But it was not possible that she could have carried him out to the garage. Not she alone.

And Folyet? Nowhere, in any theory, could he find a place for Folyet. Where had he gone?

Doctor Peters was coming, and he would of course demand an inquest and Doctor Dennison would surely be cited to appear. He had found the woman dead. He would be questioned.

"I'll say nothing—about Hilda!" he cried to himself. "No one can make me speak!"

He could, if he chose, keep silent about the bottle, about the presence of Hilda in the house. But he could not keep silent about Folyet. And if that came out, what else might not follow? Suppose Folyet were found somewhere in the house—dead?

He had a vision of the inquest, of Hilda questioned, bullied, threatened....

"She may be misguided," he thought. "She may be reckless—foolish... But nothing she has done can be really wrong."

Her face rose before him, her grey eyes that he had seen shining with tears, her smile, he remembered her kindness.

"What can I do for her?" he thought.

If he could only talk to her, make her trust him....

The door-bell rang. Too late now; there was no chance to see her, to make a plan. Someone from the outside world had come, and this monstrous thing must be made known.

With bitter reluctance he opened the door, and there was Doctor Peters, a brisk, self-possessed little man in eyeglasses, with a grey mustache.

"Hello!" he said, staring at Dennison. "And what have *you* been doing to yourself?"

"Automobile accident," said Dennison, briefly. "It's nothing."

Doctor Peters took off his overcoat.

"Let's see.... You're working with Leatherby now, aren't you? You've been looking after this case?"

"No," said Dennison. "The patient was dead when I got here."

"Hmn... " said Peters. "Well... Leatherby prepared me for this. Told me she was likely to go. He rather specializes in these heart cases, doesn't he? Personally, I don't like 'em. Tricky... Well, I'll go up now."

Dennison led him up the stairs, through the brilliant, silent house, and they entered the room where the dim lamp burned. Miss Horton rose; Peters nodded to her, and approaching the bed, made a brief examination.

"When did this happen, Miss Horton?"

"About—half an hour before I telephoned to you, Doctor Peters. I—I was sitting here—" She glanced at Dennison, but she could read nothing in his face. "I—I didn't hear anything. I—didn't know the patient had ceased breathing until—this doctor came in."

She was flustered and miserable, ashamed of her unprofessional lapse into slumber, waiting for Dennison to tell. But he said not a word, and Doctor Peters took no notice of it. He asked a few more questions about the patient's condition, which she answered intelligently.

"Any of the family here?" he asked.

"No, Doctor Peters. She'd just stopped in here for a few days—"

"Have you notified them?"

"I don't know anyone to notify, Doctor."

"Ask the servants. They'll know."

"There aren't any servants here, Doctor."

"What!" he exclaimed, with a frown. "D'you mean to tell me you were alone in the house with this patient—patient in a serious condition?"

"Doctor Leatherby wanted her to go to the hospital, but she refused. He said he'd send over one of the servants from his own house, but I said I thought I could manage till morning. It was late then—and there was very little to be done for the patient. He said he'd send someone early in the morning."

"Do you know how to get in touch with any of her family, Dennison?"

"No," said Dennison. And he thought to himself: "Now it's coming. He's beginning to see. He must see. This woman dead here, like this. Alone, no servants...."

"Hmn..." said Peters. "That's awkward... Somebody must be notified. Somebody ought to have been notified before... But Leatherby'll know. I'll speak to him on the telephone. Regal Hotel—ring it, please, nurse. Hmn... Well, I don't know... I don't see how I can give a certificate. Never saw the patient before... How about you, Dennison? Did you ever attend her?"

"No," said Dennison.

Doctor Peters stood looking down at the woman, and stroking his grey mustache.

"Now he sees," thought Dennison.

"Little irregular..." Peters went on, half to himself. "But after all... Leatherby turned the case over to me. Perfectly plain case. I dare say—"

"Doctor Leatherby's on the telephone, Doctor."

He took up the receiver.

"Leatherby? Ha...! Yes, Peters... Well, your patient's gone... Yes... Yes, I dare say I can certify. You'll notify the family—friends? Good! Yes, I'll look after that... No, Leatherby, I don't see any need to call in anyone else. This young Doctor Dennison's here... Long-standing case—under your care... Nurse was here... No peculiar symptoms. No... You saw her this evening. I suppose this was to be expected? Very well; I'll certify. Good-bye!"

He turned to the nurse.

"Doctor Leatherby wants you to ring up Freeman's. They'll take charge of the funeral arrangements. And he'll notify her family out in Denver. Body's to be removed to the undertaker's parlours. You'll wait until they come, of course. Well! Nothing more I can do. Too bad!" He sighed. "Young woman..." he said. "It's a pity. People live too hard and too fast, these days. Well...! Goodnight!"

Dennison preceded him down the stairs, waited while he put on his overcoat. And it seemed to him that somewhere in the lighted house a voice would speak. Someone *must* speak. Something must warn Peters that something horrible had happened here. Couldn't he feel it in the very air?

"Well, good-night!" said Peters. "You want to look after those cuts of yours, young man. *You* ought to know better than to neglect that sort of thing. Get that nurse to fix you up... Poor Leatherby's upset—losing another patient... It's a pity—young woman like that. Good-night!"

The door closed behind him. He had gone, and no one had spoken. Dennison himself had not spoken.

"I can't!" he thought. "Not until I've seen Hilda. What in God's name shall I do? *Where is Folyet?*"

It seemed to him that he could endure no more. The miasma of vague doubt and dread which he had felt in Leatherby's house had followed him here, had risen now to a dense, stifling fog. He could not breathe in it. He opened the front door, flung it back with a crash, and stood inhaling the cool night air.

Still this same night, that had no end. Only a few hours ago that he had tasted that green liquid and had had his dream. Still this same night in which the desperate woman had come to him, that he had accompanied her here, had been assaulted, imprisoned, escaped. Still this same night in which he had at last found Folyet, and lost him again, had found that desperate woman dead, in the dark. Still this same night in which he had seen that awful look on Hilda Napier's face. A night with no end, in which he had endured everything.

"Doctor!" came an anxious voice behind him. "You're not—going, are you?"

It was Miss Horton, half-way down the stairs.

"I heard the door open," she said. "I—I hoped you wouldn't be going, just yet."

"All right," he answered. After all, it wasn't quite decent to leave her alone here. "I'll wait."

"Doctor..." she said. "I'd like to thank you for—not saying anything about—my falling asleep like that—"

He stared at her so strangely that she felt nervous. For he could not believe it possible that she suspected nothing. Didn't it even enter her head that she had been drugged?

"No..." he thought. "I suppose things like that don't enter people's heads—"

"Doctor!" she said. "You look— Won't you let me dress those cuts for you?"

He thanked her and went upstairs with her; she had a few simple dressings in her bag, and she bandaged his head deftly. Then he went downstairs again, to stand near the open door where the chill, clear air blew in, because he could not endure this fog. And his weary mind went on and on, trying to understand, trying to piece together the grotesque facts he knew into some rational design.

This woman had died like Manley. They were both Leatherby's patients. Leatherby had profited by Manley's death; was he to profit by this one too?

"Folyet would probably know," he thought.

Folyet had come to Leatherby's house, and obviously he had known something about Manley. And Folyet had not come back. Instead, he had been here, gagged and bound.

Very well; here was a theory. Leatherby had got rid of Folyet, because he knew too much. Then he had poisoned this woman, and Hilda Napier had tried to help him by removing the bottle. That fitted the facts, fairly well. The only incongruous elements were—Leatherby and Hilda. It was utterly impossible to think of her conniving at a murder, and equally impossible to think of Leatherby's committing one.

"Folyet ..." he thought. "If I could only find Folyet—"

He sat down in the hall, and leaned his head on his hands.

"I'm—tired," he thought. "Perhaps I'm making too much of things."

And he tried then to make a theory which would minimize everything. His own injury? The woman had been a drug-addict, mad for her drug; she had struck him down and got the bottle away from him. Then perhaps she had taken an overdose and died. Perhaps the nurse had inadvertently taken a dose, a small dose. And Hilda was only trying to avert a scandal. Doctor Peters was satisfied; the nurse was satisfied; why shouldn't he be?

But Folyet? Always he came back to Folyet. Nothing could explain Folyet's presence here.

It was early in the morning when the men came to take away all that was left on earth of that most unhappy woman. Dennison stood on the terrace, watching them go, in the gay, glittering freshness of the Spring morning, and for the first time, anger stirred him, an austere, impersonal anger. If a supreme crime had been committed against her, if she had been murdered, was she to be taken off like this, buried and forgotten, and no one to protest? She had been young and beautiful, was no one to protest?

He passed his hand over his forehead. He had made himself as presentable as he could, but still the men had stared curiously at him, with his haggard face, his bandaged head.

"You must be tired, Doctor," said Miss Horton, behind him. "I'll make some coffee—"

"Not for me, thanks," he answered. "If you'll just telephone for a taxi, please—"

For his fatigue had reached such a point that he no longer wished to rest, to eat. He thought only of getting back to the house and seeing Hilda Napier. He *must* speak to her before he saw anyone else.

The taxi came and he started down the steps.

"But, Doctor!" cried Miss Horton. "Your hat and coat!"

"I've—lost them—" he said, with difficulty. For the earth was rocking wildly; the light of the sun was so fierce that he could not see at all. One step, another, another... He reached the top of the steps, and stopped, swaying.

Miss Horton put her hand under his arms and helped him down and into the cab.

"Thanks!" he said.

"Shall I go with you, Doctor? Shall I bring you out a little brandy?"

"No, thanks!" he answered, and managed to smile. Women were so kind...

His head ached horribly from the jolting of the cab, but he felt a little better, sitting there, with the air blowing on him, moving at last, going somewhere.

"When I've rested a little, I can think better," he said to himself.

Suddenly a new idea came to him.

"Driver!" he said. "What was that place I just left?"

"What?" asked the driver, startled.

"That house—whose house is it?"

"It's the old Bates house. I dunno who has it now."

"What's the name of the place—the town?"

The driver was still more amazed. Not before had he encountered a "fare" like this one, hatless, with a bandaged head and a cut face, helped into the cab by a nurse in uniform, and now asking the name of the place from which he had come.

"Clearbrook," he answered.

"How far from Shayne?"

"Twelve—fifteen miles."

Dennison felt in his pocket to see if he had enough money for so long a trip. And his hand encountered a roll of bills, secured with an elastic band. He brought it out cautiously and looked at it. It was the hundred dollars the woman had first offered him for the bottle.

Returning it to his pocket, he leaned back in a corner of the cab, filled with a strange sorrow. In his exhaustion he could not quite grasp the thought which so oppressed him; only that the beautiful and desperate woman was gone. Folyet was gone. And he himself was lonely beyond all measure, as if he had lost everything....

The cab turned into the driveway, and before him he saw Leatherby's house, the curtains fluttering at the open windows, the morning sun shining warm upon it. Here was the source of all this pain and evil; from this house had emanated the fog of suspicion and fear—and death. It seemed to him that the shadow of it fell upon him now, cold and black.

He paid the driver with the last of his own money, and, still giddy and weak, mounted the steps and rang the bell.

Miller opened the door for him. He said nothing; his face expressed no surprise at the certainly extraordinary appearance of Dennison.

"There are two patients waiting, sir," he said.

Dennison stared at him, astounded at the idea of being expected to go on—after all this. As if nothing had happened. But his professional instinct asserted itself. If there were patients here, they must be seen.

"Very well," he said. "I'll be down—in a few minutes. You might send me up some coffee—something to eat."

"Yes, sir," said Miller.

With an inward sigh, Dennison began to mount the stairs, slowly, with immense difficulty. To see patients, to take up his life again at once, without even time to think...

"After a cold bath and something to eat, I'll feel better," he thought.

He reached the upper hall, stood for a moment, breathing fast; then he turned in the direction of his own room.

The door of the room next to his stood open. And in there, leaning back in a chair, smoking a cigarette, he saw Folyet.

CHAPTER THIRTEEN

DENNISON IS DISARMED

"Folyet!" he cried.

Folyet turned his head.

"Ha! Doctor Dennison, I believe?" he said, in excellent imitation of Peters' manner. "And how are we, this morning?"

But Dennison was not able to accept the situation with this admirable coolness.

"Folyet..." he said. "I don't understand... How did you get here?"

"Why, by train and taxi, my dear Dennison," answered Folyet, with a look of mild wonder. "How else? I've been in New York, on business—for the last day or so, and—"

"'That's no good," Dennison interrupted. "I saw you—"

"The last time you saw me," said Folyet, "was here, in the library, taking coffee with you and Leatherby."

"No!" said Dennison. "You know damned well that wasn't the last time. I saw you last night—"

"An error," said Folyet, gently. "I'm afraid, Dennison, that you're too imaginative. I've sometimes even feared—" he paused, and went on, in a tone of deep compassion. "I've sometimes feared—that you—take drugs, Dennison."

Dennison started angrily, and was about to speak, but something in Folyet's expression deterred him. Those sombre black eyes were fixed upon him in a look he could not fathom. He was well aware that in a duel of words he was no match for Folyet, and he had an uneasy feeling that he must be careful, very careful.

Yet he was certainly not going to be shut up like this.

"I mean to find out what's happened," he said.

"Nothing's happened," said Folyet.

There was a moment's silence.

"Nothing's happened," Folyet repeated. "Nothing at all. And, my dear colleague, if you imagine you've—seen things, my earnest advice to you is—to forget them. Forget everything."

"That's not my way," said Dennison.

"I advise it," said Folyet, "for the sake of—other people. Who might be distressed—by your imaginings."

"Do you mean to tell me," said Dennison, "that you think you can hush up a thing like this? Why, man, you're crazy! There are half a dozen people—"

Folyet rose, and crossed the room, standing directly opposite the other.

"Dennison," he said, "you're a nuisance."

"I'm going to be more of a one, before I've finished," said Dennison.

"If you try to make trouble—" said Folyet, "you'll be sorrier than you've ever been in your life."

"Is that a threat?" asked Dennison.

"Take it any way you please," said Folyet. "Only try to get this into your head. If you stir up muddy water, the first one to suffer will be Hilda Napier."

"Leave her out of this!" said Dennison.

"Just what I'm suggesting," said Folyet. "All you have to do—is to mind your own business. If you imagine you've seen things, forget 'em."

"No," said Dennison. "I won't." And without another word, turned away and went into his own room.

What he wanted above all was a chance to think, to decide upon the attitude he would take. Above all, he must take no step that might bring trouble to Hilda Napier.

"I must see her," he thought. "I can't do anything until I've seen her."

He deliberately put from his memory the look he had seen on her face; he refused to think that perhaps she would not speak. He would remember only other moments, when he had seen her in the sun, seen her with that joyous, candid smile.

He turned on a bath, and while it was running, he shaved; when he came out of the tub, he found an excellent breakfast waiting for him on a tray. He ate in haste, troubled by the thought of those patients downstairs who had waited so long; then he re-bandaged his head as best he could, dressed, and went down.

He had not crossed the hall before he began to suspect....

He felt too well, far too well; he had a sensation of floating down the stairs, a sort of gay and careless vigour ran through his veins.

"I've been drugged!" he said to himself.

He stopped short, to deliberate with himself. "There was something— probably in the coffee," he thought. "I'm—not myself.... Perhaps I'd better go back—to my room...."

But his hand was quite steady, his brain felt clear, amazingly clear. He thought that anyhow he could attend first to those two patients; indeed, he felt that he could do anything in the world. His sense of vigour and power increased.

"I've been drugged," he thought, "but even at that, I'm a match for any-one in this house. They thought they'd put me out of the way—but here I am! By Heaven, here I am! I'll see these patients first. I'm a qualified physician. I'm more than that. I'm a born doctor."

He laughed softly to himself.

"There's not a blamed thing I can't do!" he thought. "Nothing! It's not so easy to get *me* out of the way.... I'll see these patients—then I'll look into this little mystery of 'Mrs. Smith.' Give me half an hour undisturbed, and I'll get to the bottom of it. I'm a born detective. Everyone here is against me. All right; let them be! I don't need any help. *Nothing* I can't do."

He went into the office, and the first patient came in to him. He could not see her very well; she seemed so small and far away. But his brain was wonderfully clear. When she began to talk, it seemed to him that at once he could grasp every detail of the case.

As soon as he opened his eyes, he was conscious of a lapse of time. He was lying in bed; through the window he could see the blue and sunny sky, but he knew it was not morning. He knew something was wrong. He looked at his wrist-watch; it had stopped at half-past twelve.

He sat up, and was at once aware of a miserable nervous weakness. He felt exhausted, and at the same time horribly restless. His head ached; he yawned and yawned.

"What's this?" he thought. "Have I been ill?"

It was easy to believe that. He had a vague impression that he had been lying here for hours, days. He raised his hand to his aching head, and felt a fresh bandage there, skillfully applied. He kicked off the covers in a sort of weak fury, and as he moved, broke into a profuse sweat.

"I won't—stand this!" he cried, aloud.

He swung his feet to the floor, but it was quite impossible to rise.

"I won't—" he began again, in a voice shaken with rage, when the door opened, and Mrs. Lewis entered.

"Oh, Doctor Dennison!" she cried, dismayed. "Please lie down—at once!"

He was startled to see her, and considerably embarrassed.

"Thank you..." he muttered. "But I—If you'd mind handing me my dressing-gown from the closet—"

"Oh, no!" she said. "Please lie down! You mustn't think of getting up."

"Yes, I must," he said, struggling with a violent irritability. "I will get up. Please hand it to me."

She came over to him, and laid her cool fingers on his forehead.

"Do, please lie down!" she entreated, with an anxious little smile. "I'll sit here beside you. Shall I read to you?"

He stifled his anger with a great effort.

"No, thank you. I'm not ill. I'm going to get up —if you'll kindly go away."

"Doctor Dennison," she said, gravely, "I'm afraid you don't realize.... You've been ill. You mustn't think of getting up. My brother left orders that you must be kept very quiet."

"Ill?" he repeated. "Your brother left orders—? He's been here, then? Look here! What day is this?"

"I won't talk to you unless you lie down."

He lay back on the pillows promptly.

"What day is it?" he repeated, with growing dread.

"It's Monday."

"Wait!" he cried. "Wait.... Monday! It was Saturday...."

It was coming back to him now.

"Where is Doctor Leatherby?" he said. "I must see him."

"He's out. But he'll be back presently."

"Then—Miss Napier."

"She's not here."

"Then Folyet. I *must* see Folyet!"

"Please don't get so excited!" she said, earnestly. "It's so bad for you. My brother and Mr. Folyet have gone to a funeral. They'll be back soon—"

"Whose funeral?" he demanded.

"A patient. A Mrs. Smith. Please stay quiet—or I'll have to call Ames."

"I've been lying here since Saturday?"

"You've been ill," she said, evasively.

"How ill? Unconscious?"

"I—yes, I think so...."

"You're not telling me. You're keeping something back. I've got to know. Have I been unconscious?"

"Oh, really I don't know!" she said, distressed. "My brother and Doctor Peters have been looking after you. Doctor Peters wanted you to be kept quiet this afternoon, and I said I'd look after you—"

"Look here!" he interrupted. "Thank you very much—but I'm not ill now. I know what I'm doing. Please believe me. I've got to get up—at once."

"No," she said. "You must wait until my brother comes home."

"I can't," said Dennison.

His strength was coming back to him, and with it a grim resolution. He must see Peters at once, if possible before that unhappy woman was buried. There was no shred of doubt now that a crime had been committed and an attempt made to keep him out of the way. But the attempt had failed. He was not out of the way. He sat up again.

"Mrs. Lewis," he said, "I can't explain now—but it's a matter of urgent importance.... I'll have to ask you to go, please. I've got to dress—"

She crossed the room and rang the bell.

"Why did you do that?" he demanded.

"Because I can't manage you," she said. "You're—very unreasonable, Doctor Dennison. I'll have to call Ames."

"Better that way," thought Dennison. "He'll listen to me."

So he lay quiet and waited, and presently Ames came into the room on tiptoe.

"Aw' right, Mrs. Lewis!" he whispered. "I'll set here a while."

"You'll remember, won't you, Ames?"

"Trust me!" said Ames.

Dennison waited until the door closed behind Mrs. Lewis.

"Ames!" he said, sitting up. "I want you to help me."

"Sure!" said Ames, affably. "You jest lay down and take it easy."

"I've got to go out—at once."

"Aw' right. Tell that to the Doctor when he gets home."

"Now, see here!" said Dennison. "I'm not a fool, Ames. I'm a doctor myself. I know what I can do. I tell you I'm perfectly able to get up and go out. I want you to get me a good stiff drink of brandy or whiskey—"

"Maybe you do," said Ames. "But I'm not goin' to."

"What's the matter with you?" demanded Dennison. "If you won't do what I tell you, then get out."

"Nope!" said Ames. "You done enough harm awready."

"Harm? What are you talking about?"

"I don't see why it should be kep' from you," said Ames, severely. "I think you'd ought to know. If it wasn't for Doc Leatherby, you'd be down in the gaol, right now. He said you'd forget the whole thing when you come to your senses, but I think you'd ought to be tole. You ought to realize what it leads to—takin' that dope. And you a doctor, too."

"Give me a cigarette!" said Dennison.

"I do' know..." said Ames, dubiously. "Well, nobody didn't say not to...."

He brought a crumpled pack out of his pocket and handed it to Dennison, who lit one without delay, and leaned back on the pillows, smoking.

"All right!" he said, after a moment. "What did I do?"

"You gave a ole lady a prescription that could of killed her," said Ames. "Only the Doc found out in time. You was crazy with dope Saturday. I seen you myself, sitting on the window-sill of the office, talkin' to yourself.... Doctor Leatherby, he was darn nice about it. He tole me it's terrible easy for a doctor to take that stuff. You get tired and wore out, and you got to keep goin', and you got the stuff handy. He says you could be cured, all right. I hope you'll—"

"He sent for Doctor Peters?"

"Sure. I heard 'em talking about you. Doc Peters, he says he seen you in a patient's house, with your face all cut up, actin' funny. And a feller I know drives a cab, he says he brung you back here Saturday without no hat or coat—and you asks him what was the house you come out of. Didn't know a thing you were doing. Well, I'm sorry," said Ames. "I liked you when you first come here. I hope you'll quit."

A strange smile came over Dennison's face, a smile of bitter amusement. After all, he had been put out of the way, in a remarkably effective fashion. He was thoroughly, irretrievably discredited. No one would believe anything he said now.

He imagined himself going to Doctor Peters with his tale of the nurse who had been drugged, of Mrs. Smith's efforts to secure a drug from him, of his own breakfast having been drugged. It made him smile again, it was so typically the maundering of an addict.

He imagined himself going to the police, he, the disgraced, the discredited, making accusations against a man of Leatherby's standing. Leatherby would bring forward that prescription, and everyone concerned would deny everything. He would have only his unsupported statement.

"It's damned clever!" he said, aloud.

"What is?" asked Ames.

"See here!" said Dennison. "I don't know if it's any use telling you that I'm not a drug-addict. That the whole thing's a frame-up—a plot to shut me up, because I know too much."

"Rave on !" said Ames.

"I've got a hundred dollars here," said Dennison. "You can have it, if you'll get me a drink and send for a taxi."

"That'll do," said Ames. "No more o' that. I was tole to keep you here, quiet. And you'll stay here."

"All right. Then telephone for Doctor Peters."

That evidently disquieted Ames.

"What for?" he asked. "Doc Leatherby'll be back in a little while."

Dennison reflected for a moment. If he could get Ames to the telephone, with his back turned, he could jump at him, overpower him, and get out.

"He's a pretty husky lad," he thought, "and I'm not at my best—but I can try. I've got to get out of here—somehow—anyhow."

"I feel an attack of delirium coming on," he said. "I know what I'm talking about. Remember I'm a doctor myself. If you don't get Peters at once, you'll be sorry."

Ames frowned in perplexity.

"How do I know it's true?"

"All right!" said Dennison. "You can take the responsibility of refusing."

"I dunno..." said Ames, very unhappy.

Dennison lay back and closed his eyes. With his pallour and his bandaged head, he certainly looked very ill....

"Aw' right!" said Ames. "I'll tell him what you said." He rose, and to Dennison's great surprise, went out of the room.

Like a shot, Dennison was out of bed. He went to the door; Ames had locked it on the outside. He went to the telephone; it was disconnected. In desperate haste, he began to dress, putting on his trousers and jacket over his pajamas, shoes on his bare feet. He had lost his overcoat and hat on that memorable night; he could find nothing now but a very old raincoat and a cap. He heard footsteps in the hall....

Opening the window, he climbed out on to the little balcony. He thought that he might be able to climb down the lead pipe he had noticed there.

"Hi!" shouted Ames, slamming up the window.

No time for climbing. He swung over the railing, hung by his hands for an instant. The fall stunned him for a moment, but the ground was soft from the recent rain. He staggered to his feet—and he saw a little car coming down the drive, with a girl at the wheel.

"Evie!" he shouted.

CHAPTER FOURTEEN

AN ALLY

Evie stopped the car with a jerk.

"Alex!" she cried. "What—!"

He climbed in beside her, just as Ames came running out of the office door.

"Quick, Evie!" he said. "Round the drive and out at the gates. Quick!"

The little car sprang forward. Ames ran across the lawn to cut them off; he ran into the middle of the drive, shouting "Stop!" But Evie swerved aside on to the grass, shot past him, out through the gates and down the highway in a cloud of dust.

"First turn to the left!" said Dennison.

She took the turn neatly.

"Straight ahead!" said Dennison. "I'll tell you when to turn again."

"All right!" she said. "But I'd like to know where we're going."

Dennison did not answer. He glanced sidelong at her, and his heart sank. Her charming little face wore a look of firm displeasure; she was shocked.

"Well?" she demanded. "Aren't you going to tell me why you were jumping out of a window—with no collar on and your face all scratched?"

"There's such a lot to tell..." he murmured. "Hard to know where to begin."

"I should think it might be," said Evie.

They drove on for a time in silence.

"I suppose," she said, at last, "that you've lost your job now."

"Lost my job..." he repeated, stifling an impulse to laugh. "Yes—in a way—I have."

"I was afraid of that," said Evie. "I could see from your letters that you were awfully discontented."

"It's a little more than that " said Dennison.

Again there was a silence.

"Are you going to tell me, Alex?" she asked.

He hesitated. He knew her to be absolutely loyal and trustworthy—and after all, wasn't it her right to know?

"Evie..." he said, "are you willing to promise to keep a secret from—everyone? I mean—even your parents?"

The severe look fled from her face; she glanced at him with a little frown of distress.

"Oh, Alex!" she cried. "From Mother and Daddy? They trust me to tell them everything. I always have. They're so dear and wonderful to me—"

Dennison felt like a brute and a villain.

"I know," he said. "But there are some things—If you were my wife, Evie, there'd be things I'd tell you—in confidence"

"But I'm not your wife," said Evie.

Another silence, while she drove steadily ahead.

"If you'd rather not tell me—" she said.

"It's only because it concerns—someone else," said Dennison.

"A girl?" asked Evie.

He was astounded by that question. How could she possibly know, or even suspect such a thing?

"You know," Evie went on, "something's changed you, Alex. I could tell by your letters."

"You've changed," she repeated.

And he could not deny it. He had changed. How was he not to change, after all that happened to him? There had been a time, and only a little while ago, when Evie had seemed to him an entirely superior creature; she read books, she went to concerts, she had an assurance in social matters that had impressed him. But to-day she seemed to him incredibly young, intolerant, unversed in life. He felt that in this little time he had grown years and years older; he felt battered and worn in comparison with her fresh youth. And bitterly experienced.

"I'm sorry," he said. "I'll try to be different, Evie."

She said nothing to that.

"Alex," she said, after a time, if you want to tell me what's happened, all right. I *will* promise not to tell anyone. Ever."

He was touched. and somehow abashed by her words.

"It's not the sort of thing you ought to hear, Evie," he said.

"Don't be silly, Alex!" she said. "This isn't 1860. I guess there isn't much you can tell me that I haven't heard before. You know Daddy's a lawyer, and he talks to me about all sorts of cases. Go ahead."

So, in a curt, matter-of-fact way, he began. He told her about the patients that Leatherby saw upstairs, told her of Manley's death, of Folyet's coming, of what he had heard Mrs. Lewis say to her brother.

"And when Folyet didn't come back, I began to be—uneasy," he said. He told her of the enquiries he had made at the hotel, of the blood-stained handkerchief Ames had found in the car, of his own resolve to employ a private detective.

"But then things began to happen," he went on, and told her, as well as he could, about the green liquid he had tasted, the dream he had had, about Mrs. Smith's coming, and his leaving the house with her.

"But Alex!" she protested. "How could you have been so stupid? Couldn't you see, from the very beginning, that there was something wrong?"

He frowned, impressed.

"In a way, I did," he said. "As soon as I set foot in Leatherby's house, I—I *felt* something wrong. It sounds like rot, but I did."

"Go on!" said Evie.

He told her all that had happened in Mrs. Smith's house that night; how she had tried to bribe him, how he had caught a glimpse of Folyet, gagged and bound, how he had been struck unconscious and had come to his senses in the closed car; how he had got out, and gone into that house blazing with lights, how he had found Mrs. Smith and the nurse.

"Alex!" she cried. "How horrible!"

"I know," he said. "And somehow the most horrible part is, that Doctor Peters saw nothing wrong when he came. The nurse saw nothing wrong. Evie, Mrs. Smith is being buried to-day—and no one has said anything."

"And you haven't said anything either. You've just let it go on."

Then he told her what had happened to him.

"I was drugged, of course," he said. "But I can never prove it. I'm—discredited. That story of the prescription I wrote—if Leatherby or Folyet choose to bring that up against me at any time—it would ruin me professionally."

"And you're not going to fight? You're going to let yourself be ruined?"

He did not answer for a moment.

"I don't know," he said, slowly. "I don't know what I'm going to do, Evie. I'm going to find out the truth—if I can. But—I may not be able to use the truth, if I learn it. Left turn here!"

They entered upon the boulevard now.

"Who is she, Alex?" asked Evie.

He realized with a start that he had not once mentioned Hilda.

"She's—a trained nurse," he said. "She's engaged to marry Leatherby. She's been—kind to me. I shouldn't like to—cause her any trouble."

"And you mean," said Evie, "that just to spare her feelings, you'd let *murder* go unpunished?"

He winced at the word.

"Perhaps it wasn't—that," he said. "There's no proof—"

"But if you find out that it was murder?"

"Good Lord!" he exclaimed. "After all, I'm not the public executioner.

I'm not obliged—Evie—if there was someone who'd been—kind to you, you wouldn't—"

"I'll just tell you this, Alex," she said. "If it was the person I loved best in the world, *still* I'd want justice to be done."

Her pretty mouth shut like a steel trap; she looked straight ahead of her; then the little car shot forward, down the empty boulevard, at a breathtaking speed.

"Daddy's taught me that," she said. "Not to put myself and my own feelings—not to put anything in the world ahead of justice."

"There are some things better than justice," said Dennison to himself.

"Where are we going, anyhow?" asked Evie.

"I thought I'd go to Mrs. Smith's house. There must be someone there in charge. I thought I'd make enquiries—try to find out someone who'd take an interest in what I've got to say. I'm pretty well certain that her name's not Smith. If I could find out who she really is, it would be something. You see, it's no use my going to Peters now. He'd think I was—raving."

"What about the police?" said Evie.

"I don't want to go to the police—yet," said Dennison.

Evie said nothing to that, and Dennison found the silence uncomfortable.

"New car, isn't it, Evie?" he asked.

"Yes," she said. "Daddy gave it to me this morning."

"You must have been pleased."

"Yes," she said. "I was."

Her taciturnity was curious, for as a rule she was very enthusiastic upon the subject of motor-cars. But Dennison was not in the mood to ask questions; he had enough to think of just then.

"There's the house!" he said, abruptly.

Evie stopped the car a little way up the road.

"You know, Alex," she said, "you look pretty weird."

"I suppose I do," he admitted.

"You look like a tramp," she pursued. "Nobody'd be likely to answer questions from you. Just look!"

She opened her vanity-case and held the mirror before him, and he saw in it his scratched, unshaven face, no collar, that cap pulled low on his forehead.

"I didn't realize—" he said.

"You can't go in," said Evie. "I'll go."

"But you wouldn't know what to say."

"Yes, I should!" she said. "Anyhow, you can't, Alex. I'll find out as much as you could, and maybe more."

"I don't—" he began, but she jumped out.

"Don't leave the car a minute!" she said, and set off across the road to the entrance of the house, a slim, erect little figure, sturdy and valiant, in her close-fitting yellow hat and her very short skirt. And somehow the sight of her hurt him terribly.

She went up the drive; he saw her mount the steps and ring the bell; then someone opened the door, and she entered.

"Somebody there, anyhow," he thought. "But she's such a kid...."

Evie had left the car in a pleasant spot, drawn up by the roadside; the sunlight filtered through the budding branches of the trees, and a soft and steady breeze blew. In the pocket of his jacket he found a package of cigarettes; he lit one, and leaned back, to think.

"My bag must be in that house," he thought. "And my overcoat and my hat. Lord knows if I'll ever see them again. I've lost—a lot. I've certainly lost my job—as Evie said. I'll have to start all over again."

But why should that so painfully oppress him? He was young and strong and very confident of himself; he was inured to hardships. He reasoned with himself.

"Of course, if I don't get my bag back, that's a pretty heavy loss—all my instruments. Perhaps I'd be entitled to keep that hundred dollars, but I won't. I—couldn't. I don't want it. And then there's that money I got in advance from Leatherby. If I take every cent I've got in the bank, and sell my books, I can just about pay that off, and get a few instruments. The cottage is paid for till the end of the month.... I can wear that straw hat I had last summer, and I can manage without an overcoat."

Yet he felt desolate, robbed of everything. Life stretched before him, bleak and sunless.

"Evie'll have to wait a long time," he thought. "Well, I can't help it."

He remembered what she had said. "And you're not going to fight?"...

"I ought to be angry," he thought, surprised. "I've been treated badly enough."

But he could not be angry just then; he was only unhappy. He lit another cigarette and lay back, looking up at the bright sky. Then the sound of a door slamming violently made him start; turning, he saw someone running down the steps of the terrace, a slight, grey-haired figure which he recognized in a moment as Miller. At the same moment a window opened upstairs, and Evie leaned out.

"Stop him, Alex!" she cried. "He's locked me in!"

Dennison jumped out of the car. Miller, running headlong, had not noticed him before, now, seeing him, he stopped, wavered, and turned back.

He had a good start of Dennison, and he ran with the speed of fear. But he was elderly and short-winded, and there was nothing before him but the house. He had no chance of escape.

Suddenly he dodged round the corner of the house. Dennison increased his speed, and as he turned the corner, saw the man dart in at the back door.

Dennison was after him, almost on his heels. But the door was locked. The kitchen window was open on to the porch, though, and Dennison climbed in. He heard footsteps running along a passage, and he followed. A door banged in his face. He opened it, and saw the man running up the stairs, bent almost double. He was after him so closely that he heard the other's gasping breath. He almost had him, when Miller plunged through an open door, slammed it after him, and a key turned in the lock.

"Come out of that!" shouted Dennison.

"Excuse me, sir," came Miller's trembling and breathless voice, "but I can't see—as you've—any right—"

"Open the door, or I'll break it down!" said Dennison, and gave it a vigorous kick.

"Don't do that, sir!" cried Miller.

Dennison gave another kick. The noise was shocking in the quiet house, but somehow it relieved him. He wanted to make a noise, he wanted to make trouble. For so long he had been in the dark, with no enemy whom he could see, with nothing tangible to fight. And here at last was someone who had run away from him, someone who resisted him.

"All right!" he cried. "Here goes!"

And a well-aimed kick split the lower panel.

"Oh, don't!" cried Miller, piteously.

Then the key turned in the lock, the door opened, and Hilda Napier faced him.

He could not speak, he could do nothing but look at her. She was pale, her blue eyes looked hollow; she was strange to him, unfamiliar in her dark dress, terribly remote.

Behind her stood Miller, in his shirt-sleeves, and somehow the absence of his decent livery wrought a curious change in the man; he seemed smaller and meaner, his pallid face was smudged, as if he had wiped away tears with a grimy hand; he was trembling and breathless, but he was defiant.

"You're a bully!" he cried. "You knocked me down once.... Don't you come near me! Miss! Don't let him!"

"Please, Doctor Dennison," she said. "Please don't—interfere."

"I'm sorry," he said, "but I've got to speak to this man."

"No," she said, almost inaudibly.

He could not bear to look at her, standing there to defend so mean a rascal. He turned to Miller.

"What are you doing here?" he demanded. "I'm going to know—if I have to choke the truth out of you."

"Miss!" cried Miller, shrinking back. She stood blocking the doorway.

"Doctor Dennison—!"

"If you'll go away, please," said Dennison, "and let me speak to this fellow alone—"

"Don't you do it, Miss!" said Miller. "He'll kill me!"

She looked steadily at Dennison.

"No," she said. "He's here—by my orders. He came—to do something for me. I can't let you—worry him."

"Is that the truth?" asked Dennison.

"It's the truth," she answered. "I told him to come. I'm responsible for anything he's done."

"If I let him go," said Dennison, "will you—-explain?"

"No," she said.

There was a silence. And somewhere down the hall, Dennison heard a muffled knocking at a door. That must be Evie.

He looked at Hilda Napier. Let her see what was in his face.

"He can go," he said, briefly, and turning went down the hall in the direction of the knocking. It came from a room at the end of a wing. The key was on the outside; he turned it, and Evie fell against him.

"I've got them!" she cried, in triumph.

He stared over her shoulder at the room that was filled with smoke.

"That's nothing!" said Evie. "I caught that man burning a perfect mass of papers and things in the grate.... He told me to wait downstairs in the drawing-room—but I didn't like the look of him. I came upstairs after him, and I caught him in here. He was frightened out of his wits when I spoke to him. He bolted out of the room, and locked the door behind him. He'd made a pretty good blaze, but I threw a rug on top of it and put it out. And I've raked out some things. .. . Alex! You'll never guess! Who do you suppose your 'Mrs. Smith' was? Alex, she was Folyet's wife!"

CHAPTER FIFTEEN

"ANYONE BUT JEFF"

She stood before him, her face alight, a crumpled mass of papers in her hand.

"It's the first step!" she said.

The first step where, along what road, to what end? To justice, no doubt, to the punishment of wrong-doers and of those who dared affront justice by aiding wrong-doers. Justice was blind, and held a sword, and that sword would surely and terribly fall upon Hilda Napier. ... .

"Alex!" said Evie.

He looked up at her, found the light of triumph gone, and a very grave look on her little face.

"Alex," she said, "is Folyet a very handsome man?"

"Why, yes..." he answered, puzzled. "I suppose he is. Why?"

"I'm sorry..." she said.

"But why, Evie? I don't understand."

"I'm sorry," she said, again, and fell silent, looking down at the papers she held in her hand.

"Let's see what you have there, Evie."

"They're—terrible," she said slowly. "It must have been terrible for her when she read them—and for him, when he wrote them."

She looked up at him, and the compassion in her face filled him with a vague fear.

"Let me see them!" he said.

With an effort she resumed her usual cool and assured manner.

"First there's this," she said. "Do you recognize the picture?"

She shifted the papers and held out to him a charred passport, made out for Denise Folyet, aged thirty-one, wife of Geoffrey Folyet. He did recognize the photograph at once.

"Yes," he said. "That's Mrs. Smith."

"Then here— They're not in order, but it doesn't matter. Read this."

He took the letter from her. The black, bold writing began at the top of the page; there was no salutation of any sort, no date.

"If you tell her, I'll deny it to your face. I'd be very pleased to perjure my soul—only I haven't any soul left. I know I've lost her for ever and ever, and she was all the soul I had. She was everything good and sweet in life.

But even if I've lost her, she shan't know what I've done. If you tell her you're my wife, I'll tell her *any* lie. She'll believe me. She's sorry for me.

Let me go. For your own sake, let me go. I tell you again that I love her and I hate you. Let me go—or you'll be sorry.

Folyet."

"Evie!" said Dennison. "We shouldn't read these. They're private letters. It's—"

"They've got to be read—by someone," said Evie. "There's the key to the whole thing in them. Read this!"

She handed him another letter. He held it for a moment, thinking, or trying to think, still oppressed with that vague fear. But if other people were going to know, then he must know. He began to read.

"Dear Denise," it began. "Can't we come to some half-way decent arrangement? I will admit my share of the blame. I'll take all the blame. Make your own terms. I'll agree to anything. I'm making money now. You can have it all. Only let me go. I don't want to hate you. But if you make me—I'm a damned good hater.

You'll see, pretty soon, what I'm going to do to Leatherby. I'm going to ruin him, as he ruined me. He took her away from me. He 'advised' her against me. She was beginning to love me then, but she listened to him, because she's been taught to listen to him. He kicked me out of Paradise into Hell.

I can't get back. But I'll drag him down. You'll see your benevolent and dignified friend in the dock. She'll see him there. No more banquets for him.

Don't make me hate you, too. You'll regret it, if you do. Divorce me and let me go.

Jeff."

Evie handed him another letter, and another, and reading them, Dennison could evoke the image of Folyet's handsome face, with his sombre eyes and his gleaming smile. The letters were all alike, all blazing with hate, all reckless, savage and bitter. He had hated that woman who had been his wife. And he had loved—

"You see, don't you, Alex?" asked Evie.

"See—what?"

"He killed her."

"He couldn't have. I saw him tied up and gagged—"

"But you know that he got free, some time. Alex, can't you see, in these letters, how he felt?"

"Yes," said Dennison. "But—"

"He didn't want her to tell—someone—that she was his wife. So he tried to stop her. But—that someone did find out, and tried to help him. Alex, *don't you see?*"

Folyet had killed his wife, and Hilda Napier had tried to help him. She had taken away the bottle which might have incriminated him. She was here to-day, helping Miller to destroy all evidence of the woman's identity. Because she loved Folyet.

In his letters Folyet had written of someone whom he loved, who was beginning to love him, and whom Leatherby had "taken away" from him. Folyet had done this hideous thing, and she was shielding him. "She's sorry for me," he had written. She must be more than sorry....

And now justice would pursue Folyet, and whether or not he was overtaken, it would be the same. Shame and suffering for Hilda Napier.

He sat staring before him at nothing. He had forgotten Evie until she spoke.

"Alex," she said, "I'm—s-sorry for you—"

"For me, Evie?"

Then he was sorry that he had spoken. Her glance of grave compassion was intolerable; he turned away from her, went over to the window and looked out. Amazing that the sun was shining, the sky blue, all the Spring world serene and bright.

She too had been serene and bright. He remembered her as he had first seen her, in the sunshine; as he had last seen her, worn, pallid, her lovely youth clouded. Very well; let her be guilty. Let her love another man, let her turn away from himself as if he were her enemy. It could make no difference. She would be with him all his days.

"Alex," said Evie, "I'm sorry—but something will have to be done. We ought to question that man."

"M-Miller?" asked Dennison.

"I thought it was Miller. Yes. He'll have to answer—"

"He's—gone," said Dennison.

"Alex, how could you let him go? He was here, trying to destroy evidence—"

"I let him go," said Dennison.

"I see..." said Evie, slowly. "I see... "

Dennison spun round on his heel.

"I'm not a policeman!" he cried. "It's not my business to hound—" He stopped short.

"Very well," said Evie. "It is my business."

"It's not. You—"

"Alex," she interrupted, "what are you going to do, anyhow?"

"I don't know—yet. I've got to think...."

"All right, then think," said Evie.

And what he thought was this: that Evie had come as if she were destined to come, that the mills of justice were already beginning to grind, and he could not stop them.

"I've got to see Miss Napier," he said.

"She's gone," said Evie. "I saw her go down the hall a few moments ago, with her hat on."

"Then—I'll see Folyet. I'll tell him what we've—found out."

"Tell him?"

"Yes. I'll just warn him—before I go to the police."

"Of course you realize that he'll get away?"

"Let him," said Dennison, briefly. "If he can. I suppose I'll have to tell what I know. But I'm not Folyet's judge and executioner. Will you drive me back now, Evie?"

"To Doctor Leatherby's? You know what they did to you, Alex—"

"No one's going to bother me now," said Dennison.

Without another word, Evie set off down the corridor, and he followed her, down the stairs, and out of the house. Evie climbed into the car, and he got in beside her, they drove down the quiet, shady road, and turned the corner, into the boulevard. And there, before them, he saw Hilda Napier walking along with her easy, unhurried gait. Again she was in the full sunshine, as he had first seen her, but there was such a difference now. He thought he had never seen anything so lonely as her slender figure.

Evie slowed down.

"Want a lift, Miss Napier?" she called, cheerfully.

"No, thanks!" answered Hilda, quite as cheerfully. "I've got my ticket on the train."

They smiled at each other, and Evie drove on. And Dennison thought to himself that he would never be able to understand any woman.

All the way back Evie talked of nothing but the car. She displayed an intelligent knowledge of every detail, and Dennison responded to the best of his ability. It was, he thought, the least he could do for her.

How strange it was, to be going back to that house with Evie! They turned in at the drive, and he saw before him once more the lawn, the turrets, the windows that had in so short a time grown so familiar to him.

"It's the last time," he thought.

For inevitably he must leave here. He did not know what part, if any, Leatherby had had in the death of Folyet's wife. He did not know if it had been by Leatherby's orders that he had been drugged. But certainly Leatherby's "medicine" was evil and dangerous; certainly Leatherby lay under grave suspicion.

In his letters, Folyet had said that his sojourn in Leatherby's house had ruined him. It was easy for Dennison to believe that now. He remembered how he himself had felt, driving home in the dusk, last week. He too had been learning to love this life of dignified luxury, had been learning to cling to it.... He had had a rude enough awakening, though. He had lost everything now.

"Are you just going to walk in," asked Evie, "as if nothing had happened?" She smiled. "If you could see yourself!" she said.

This disconcerted him more than he cared to show. He had forgotten his unseemly appearance.

"It can't be helped," he said.

"I'll come in with you, Alex. I'll wait while you pack your things."

"I'd rather you didn't, Evie."

"I want to," said she, and that settled it.

They went up the steps, and he rang the bell, hoping with all his heart that he could get to his room and make himself presentable before he met anyone. The parlour-maid opened the door, and gave a little gasp at the sight of him. He frowned.

"Doctor Leatherby home yet?" he asked.

"Yes, sir. He and Mr. Folyet came in about half an hour ago."

"Where's Mr. Folyet?"

"He's gone, sir."

"Gone? Where?"

"I don't know, Sir. He sent for a taxi—"

"Does anyone know where he's gone?"

"Mrs. Lewis might know, sir. She's in the library."

Again he forgot his disreputable appearance, and he forgot Evie, too. He threw his cap down on the hall table, and went into the library.

Mrs. Lewis was sitting in a low chair, facing the empty hearth; at the sound of his step she turned, and started nervously. He had a fleeting impression that she looked ill, white and drawn, but he was too much occupied with the matter in hand to be checked by that.

"Mrs. Lewis," he said, "if you'll please tell me where Folyet's gone—"

"Folyet?" she cried. "What do you want with him?"

"It's very important that I should see him—"

"Why?" she demanded, her clear voice rising. "Why do you have to trouble Mr. Folyet?"

"It's important," Dennison repeated, trying to speak quietly and reasonably. "If you'll please tell me—"

"I shan't," she said, and turned back toward the hearth.

A wave of exasperation swept over Dennison. It seemed to him that for an incredible time he had been trying to catch up with Folyet; he was always catching a glimpse of him, and then losing him. It was as if Folyet fluttered ahead of him like a will-o'the-wisp, as if Folyet alone held the key to all that tormented him.

"Look here!" he said. "If you won't tell me, I'll have to go to the police."

She looked back at him over her shoulder, with a face drained of all colour.

"The police—for Jeff..." she faltered.

"He's involved—" Dennison began.

"Involved!" she said. She rose to her feet, resting one hand on the back of the chair. "Involved! He's suffered enough. Let him alone!"

"I can't," said Dennison. "Something's happened—"

"You mean that woman's death?"

"Yes."

"Then you've found out that she was his wife?"

"Yes," said Dennison, surprised. "Did you know?"

"He told me to-day—just now. She's dead. You can't help her. Can't you let him alone? What good can you do by dragging out that miserable, unhappy story? Let him alone!"

Dennison stood there, grim as fate.

"That woman died in extremely suspicious circumstances," he said. "Her death must be investigated. There—"

"You don't think—you can't think—that Jeff—" she began, and stopped, looking into his face with a dreadful anxiety. "Why should you think—it was—Jeff? Isn't there—anyone else...?"

"Yes," he said. "There is someone else—who ought to be cleared."

"You mean Hilda?"

That name sent a tremour through him

"You—you can't want her to suffer," he said. "Tell me where Folyet is."

"No!" she cried. "I'll never tell you, never! He's gone. He won't come back. He's suffered enough." She covered her face with her hands.

"God help me...! Anyone but Jeff..." she said.

CHAPTER SIXTEEN

MRS. LEWIS SPEAKS

She sat down again, one trembling hand playing with the pearls about her neck.

"It's my fault..." she said. "I should have seen.... I know he has faults—but all his faults might be virtues.... If I'd only seen...."

She looked up, with tragic, tear-filled eyes.

"I was so stupid..." she said. "So cruel.... I listened to Charles. I thought he knew—and that's the one thing he doesn't know. He can be generous beyond anyone else, and so kind.... But he can't understand love. He talked to me about Jeff, and I listened to him. I sent Jeff away."

"You?" thought Dennison. "Then it was you—and not Hilda? Not Hilda that Folyet wrote of?"

There came back to him that curious question Evie had asked. "Is Folyet a very handsome man?" And Folyet was handsome, with that theatric charm which was perhaps irresistible to a woman. It had happened often enough before in the world that a woman has loved a man who cared nothing for her. So lonely she had looked, walking down that road....

She might have believed that Folyet had done that thing, and had tried to shield him. There was no doubt that she had tried to suppress all evidence of the woman's identity. Out of pity? Out of—love?

"Men never understand," Mrs. Lewis went on. Tears were running down her cheeks, but she paid no heed to them. "Jeff did the worst thing he could have done. He tried to turn me against Charles. He told me—he'd found out—something horrible.... Of course I wouldn't listen. I told him I hated him for saying that. I thought I did. I—tried to hate him. I told Charles to send him away."

Her voice broke; she was silent for a moment.

"Charles never meant to—hurt me so," she said. "He's always meant to help. No one else can know how good he is, how generous. There are people—patients—friends—who bless his name. He'd do anything, give anything, to help. He's been so good to me. My parents died when I was a tiny girl, and all my life Charles has been everything to me. I have never heard one unkind word from him. I have never asked him for anything, and not got it. My marriage wasn't—happy. I don't know what I should have done, then, without Charles. I have never turned to him, and found him anything but generous and noble and kind. And his kindness isn't like other people's. He never blames, never judges. He just helps. He doesn't give only money, but his time and his strength and his wonderful sympathy. You must have seen. You must have heard how people speak of him."

"Yes," said Dennison. "I've heard."

"And no one must judge him!" she cried. "You mustn't judge him according to your point of view. He sees things differently. If he's ever done—harm, it's because his ideas are too far above other people's. He didn't mean to hurt Jeff so. He liked him. He meant to help him. It was my fault...."

Again she was silent for a time. Her tears had stopped now; there was in her face an immeasurable sorrow.

"I didn't know until to-day what Jeff did then," she went on. "He told me to-day. When he was sent away from here, he was desperate, reckless. And he turned to—someone else. A woman he didn't love—or respect—a woman more reckless than himself. He married her—the very week after he left here. And then, almost at once, he was sorry.... He wanted her to let him go, but she would not. And—he's not patient. He's not always kind—or just.... He was unhappy, and he tried to believe that it was all Charles's fault. He made up his mind that he'd injure Charles, that he'd make me see that Charles wasn't— what I thought him. He never could have done that! Even if—"

She stopped for a moment.

"Whatever Charles has done," she said, "he felt it was right to do. No one must judge him." Her face grew almost stern.

"It was wrong of Jeff," she said. "It was cruel and wrong. Only, he's suffered so.... He thought he'd found out—this horrible thing, and he came back here. He meant to make me see.... But that woman—his wife—spied on him. When she learned that he'd come here, she followed him. She was mad, desperate because he wanted to get away from her. She telephoned to Miller. You see, she was a patient of Charles's, and she knew Miller. She told him that Jeff had come here—to make trouble. And Miller would have done anything to stop that. I want you to understand that Charles knew nothing of this. Nothing! When Jeff got into the car to go to the hotel, Miller hit him on the head with something and stunned him—"

"I see!" said Dennison. What Miller could do once, he could do twice. He too had been hit on the head and stunned.

"No, you don't see!" she said, with a sort of vehemence. "You can't. I'm trying to tell you. After that, Miller drove him to his wife's house—a furnished house she'd taken so that she could be near here—to spy on him.

"At first she pretended to be reasonable. She persuaded him to stay there, to talk things over, to arrange about their—separating. Miller went to the hotel to get his bags, and Jeff stayed, because he believed her.

"But after a while he saw how it was. She told him the truth then, that she'd never let him go. And he said he would go, and she might do whatever she pleased. She must have telephoned to Miller again, for he came—that night—"

Dennison stood as if rooted to the spot. Their eyes met.

"It was her idea!" she cried. "Hers—and Miller's. Nobody else—"

There was another silence.

"She gave him something, in a glass of wine," she went on. "When he came to his senses, he was tied and gagged. And she told him she was going to get—poison—to kill him.... Then she went out and left him alone in the house, for a long time. He knew she meant what she said. You can think—how it was for him."

Again their eyes met, in a strange and dreadful look.

"It was Charles who set him free!" she said. "Charles untied him, and gave him something to revive him. Jeff told me what Charles said to him. 'I'm sorry, Folyet. If I have done you any harm, I ask your pardon. You must do as you think best, but I shall bear you no ill-will, Folyet,' Jeff remembered the very words. I've remembered them. Now don't you see...?"

"No," said Dennison, half-aloud.

For he could not "see" yet. Only some monstrous thing that was forming in his mind.

If the woman had gone to get poison for Folyet, where had she gone? She had come here, to Leatherby's house, for the bottle which Leatherby himself had left for her.

Again he looked at Mrs. Lewis, again their eyes met, and they could not look away from each other.

"No!" she cried, as if he had spoken.

But he had not spoken; he could not speak. Only his eyes asked those questions he could not put into words.

What was the "horrible thing" that Folyet had found out about her brother?

"Jeff has gone away," she went on, still answering what he had not asked. "He promised me he would—say nothing more. It's all over, finished. You see that, don't you?"

All over and finished? That desperate woman had been buried and was now to be forgotten, never avenged?

"It can't be like that," he said, aloud. "What do you mean?"

He did not know how to explain. Simply, he *knew* that it could not be like that. Let he himself hold his tongue forever, let Folyet be silent, let Hilda keep her secret, still someone would speak. What had happened that night in the house blazing with lights could never be buried deep enough.

"Now," said Mrs. Lewis, "now that I've told you, you'll let Jeff alone?"

"I can't," said Dennison. "Folyet knows something—   "

"He'll never speak!" said she. "He's gone. He'll never come back. Your— police will never find him. They'll only bring disgrace and misery on— other people. Oh, why can't you go away? Haven't we all enough to bear?"

"It's too late now. Someone else knows who the woman was. Things have got to go on. Whatever Folyet knows, he'll have to tell."

"He won't! He won't—ever! I tell you—I've sent him away—again! I know I love him now—but I've sent him away—in all his misery and bit- terness. I've sacrificed him—again!"

Her growing agitation alarmed him; she was losing control of herself, her eyes were dilated, her lip trembled, her voice had risen to a pitch that made him wince.

"See here!" he said, in a tone purposely cold and brusque. "You'll have to face things, Mrs. Lewis—"

"I have!" she interrupted, wildly. "I have—faced things. Didn't I listen to Jeff call my brother a *murderer*—?"

The sliding-doors that led into the dining-room rolled back with a crash, and Miller entered.

"And that be damned for a lie!" he said.

He held in his hand a bit of chamois with which he had been cleaning the silver, and he twisted it, as if he were wringing a neck.

"You ought to be ashamed to say that—to him!" he said to Mrs. Lewis.

"Here!" interposed Dennison.

"Don't you interrupt!" said Miller, savagely. "Look here!"

He put the bit of chamois into his jacket pocket, and with a sort of fum- bling haste, brought out from another pocket a little automatic. But his aim was steady enough, directly at Dennison's face. "I nearly did for you, twice before," he said, "and this time I'll finish it."

"Then you're a fool," said Dennison. "You'd have to pay for it—in a way you wouldn't enjoy."

"I'm no fool!" said Miller. "Doctor Leatherby wouldn't let anything happen to me. I've served him for twenty years and he wouldn't let anything happen to me. If I was to shoot you down in the public street, he'd find a way to get me out of it. Did anyone ever get anything against him those other times? They did not! And what's more, they never will."

"Miller!" said Mrs. Lewis, faintly. "What are you saying?"

"That's all right," said Miller. "He's not going to make any more trouble. Who cares what he thinks? I got the best of him twice before. Once out at Mrs. Folyet's house—only I didn't hit him hard enough. He gave me a fright that time! Doctor Leatherby told me to go back and let him out of the garage and bring him back here, careful. He wouldn't have needed much care by the time he reached here, I can tell you.... But he wasn't there. I went up to the house, and I see him talking to Doctor Peters. 'The game's up!' I says to myself. I tried to telephone to Doctor Leatherby, but he'd given orders at the hotel that he wasn't to be disturbed till morning. All night I was thinking the police would be here. And in the morning, in he walks! Into a trap. All I meant to do then was to give him something to keep him quiet until Doctor Leatherby got back, but I don't know enough about those drugs. The doctor says that what I gave him was enough to kill any ordinary man. But he's tough! Nothing but a bullet will do for him."

"Miller!"

"Well, why not?" demanded Miller. "If you was in a jungle, and a tiger come in front of you, and you shot it, you wouldn't call that murder, would you? It's the same with human beings. If anyone's dangerous, they ought to be put out of the way. There's very few people can understand Doctor Leatherby's ideas. I'm not an educated man, but he used to talk to me sometimes. Life isn't anything sacred. He's told me the world would be a better place if a lot of people—people that can't be cured and all—could be put out of the way. He's said to me, more than once, that only about one life in a thousand is of real value in the world. Like a tree, he said; the tree of human life needs pruning—better to have a few perfect blossoms than hundreds of poor ones. I can understand that. My father was a gardener in the old country."

It seemed to Dennison horrible and pitiful to hear Leatherby's words on these lips, to hear Leatherby's "ideas" used as this man's justification for his acts.

"Miller!" said Mrs. Lewis. "Doctor Leatherby only said things like that—"

"Excuse me, Miss Rose," said Miller, "but he meant them. Now, take the case of Mr. Manley—that that Folyet was prying into. I've given that a lot of thought. I want to understand the doctor's point of view. I figure it out this way. The doctor, he thought that in Mr. Manley's hands all that money did no good to anyone. He knew Mr. Manley was very unhappy. He thought he'd be better dead, and that he could use Mr. Manley's money to the advantage of a great many people. And he had that way of making death absolutely painless. More than painless, beautiful."

His eyes sought Mrs. Lewis's face with a sort of appeal, but she looked hard, blank, as if a door had closed in her mind, as if she could not really hear any words he spoke.

"The doctor never talked to me about—that," he went on. "But I found out, because I thought I could help him better if I knew. Nobody else suspected, but I knew. Every patient that died of 'heart failure' had got one of those bottles first. One day when he was out, I went up to his consulting room. I'd found out the combination of his safe and there was a bottle. I poured out some of the contents and filled it up with water. What I'd taken out of the bottle I put into a saucer of milk and fed it to a stray cat. The poor little beast began to purr. She stretched herself out, and in the middle of her purring, she died. I was sorry. I'm very fond of animals. But I wanted to know. And when that Folyet came snooping around, I was glad I knew, so that I could help the doctor. I saw that Folyet was getting suspicious. I would have got rid of him easy. I'd have poured the stuff down his throat and held his nose till he had to swallow. Only the doctor came, and let him go. I don't understand that."

"Then I must explain," said Leatherby's voice from the doorway. "For I really have only one murder to my credit."

CHAPTER SEVENTEEN

THE ETHICS OF DOCTOR LEATHERBY

He stood there with his usual kindly smile on his bearded lips, dignified, courteous, serene as usual.

"I must apologize," he said. "I have been listening for some time. And it seems to me necessary to explain my ideas a little. Miller, hand me that gun, please. Thank you. No, don't go! I should like you to stay and listen. I should like you to understand."

"I don't care, sir!" cried Miller. "What I say is, that anything you do is right. If there's any trouble, I'll stand by you, sir."

"Sit down, Miller," said the Doctor.

"But—Mrs. Lewis, sir—"

"'Mrs. Lewis has no objection," said the doctor, glancing at his sister. But she did not move, did not stir; she sat with that same blank look on her face, as if she no longer heard. Miller sat down on the edge of a chair in a corner; Leatherby took his accustomed armchair; only Dennison remained standing.

"I do not, as a rule, recognize any necessity for justifying my acts," Leatherby proceeded. "I am accountable to no one. Even if I had been fully aware of Folyet's peculiar theories, I should not have troubled to refute them. I should have allowed him to go on—to make charges against me which would have brought disgrace and ridicule upon him and done me no real harm. Who would have credited the wild tales of a young man I had been obliged to dismiss? He had no proof. He never would have had any proof."

He paused, to light a cigar. He held out his case to Dennison, but the young man shook his head.

"I am going to explain now—to you, Dennison," said Leatherby, "because a misapprehension on your part would trouble me." He smiled. "And it will be difficult," he said. "There is no bridge between us, no common ground. It is the stern Calvinistic point of view, opposed to the classic, and they cannot exist in the same world. I could never convert you, Dennison. I don't think I should like to, if I could. I have a profound respect for your character."

"Very good of you, sir..." muttered Dennison, very much taken aback.

"I should have liked you to sit at my feast," said Leatherby. "I have enjoyed it, Dennison. I have found life rich and exquisite. But you have your own nourishment—some unquenchable spring... I don't know..."

His voice trailed away, and he sat looking absently before him for a time. Then with a slight start, he recalled himself.

"As I have said, I do not feel obliged to justify any act of mine. Whatever I have done has been actuated by pity. By an intolerable pity for human creatures—the tormented playthings of the gods. What I have seen in our world, Dennison! The pain—the utterly futile pain... And you can't feel that? You can't feel that a poor, tortured creature can properly seek *any* relief?"

"It's my business as a doctor to give people what relief I can," said Dennison. "But—"

"But what, Dennison?"

It was hard for the taciturn Dennison to speak, to bring out in the presence of this man so superior to him in intellect his own plain, stark ideas. But he did speak.

"There is some suffering that can't be evaded, sir," he said. "It ought to be faced."

"Why, Dennison? Why face a life that is all bitterness? If there is no peace left?"

"I don't set so much value on peace," said Dennison. "I don't know that it's such a good thing."

"The man who lives at peace with himself lives like a god, Dennison."

"I don't want to live like a god," said Dennison. "I'm a man. I don't expect anything but a man's life. If it's hard, then it's my job to put up with it—if I can't make it better."

Leatherby leaned back in his chair.

"Dennison," he said. "Dennison, you're very eloquent."

"Eloquent?" said Dennison, flushing. "I don't make any claim—"

"I mean what I said," Leatherby interrupted, with a shadowy smile. "'Almost thou persuadest me'— Almost—but not quite. No; I hold to my idea that a man's life is his own, and that if he wishes to fling it back into the faces of the gods who have mocked him, he is free to do so. As Miller told you, I have found a way to make death easy and beautiful. That is my gift to my fellow-creatures."

"I—don't quite see—" said Dennison.

"I gave death to anyone who really wanted it," said Leatherby. "I tried all other means first, always. I was willing to give my time, my sympathy, my money. But when I could do nothing more—when I was faced by ills and sorrows that were incurable, I gave death."

"Do you mean—?"

"I investigated every case. And only when I found life really intolerable did I consent to give my gift. To Manley, for instance. He had nothing left. His wife and daughter had left him; his health was failing. There was nothing before him but loneliness and grief. So I gave my remedy to him."

"He—knew what it was?"

"Knew? He begged for it—in anguish. My poor old friend.... He took it away with him as the greatest treasure ever discovered. I saw him at the inquest, and he was happy. There was a look on his dead face he had not worn in life for twenty years."

"You—you sold this—for money?" said Dennison.

"Put it that way, if you like. Once I agreed to give it, I expected the recipient to contribute everything possible, so that I might go on with my work. They gave only what they chose."

"How did anyone know they could get—this from you?"

"I told them. At the end, when there was before me some fellow-creature in the very extremity of suffering, without hope, then I would say that there was an open door."

"Were there—many?" asked Dennison, very low.

"It doesn't matter," said Leatherby. "The responsibility is mine alone. It does not weigh upon me. Only, I see now that there was a flaw. A serious flaw..."

The shadowy smile left his lips.

"I did not reckon sufficiently with human weakness," he said. "I can see now that what happened in this case might have happened before. But I give you my word that the possibility had not occurred to me. A woman came to me—a woman at the end of her tether. She was a drug-addict and incurable, because she had no will to be cured. Her marriage was unhappy; her life was a living hell for her. She asked me outright for something—anything—to put an end to her miserable existence. She came again and again, and at last I promised relief and freedom to her. But she deceived me. She wanted death, not for herself, but for someone else."

"For Folyet?"

"For Folyet. I did not realize how she hated him. I cannot understand hate. I have never felt it. She meant to kill Folyet, but you would not give her the bottle. So she decided that you must be forced to give it up. She got Miller to help her. Poor Miller! He saw in Folyet a danger to me which never really existed. He thought Folyet could destroy me. And he was ready to destroy Folyet. He would have helped that madwoman to pour death down Folyet's throat, only that I came in time."

He paused.

"It is pitiful," he said. "It is pitiful and terrible to think of Hilda. She had been greatly troubled by Folyet's disappearance. She knew of his marriage, and she wanted to keep that knowledge from Rose. She had questioned Miller, but he would tell her nothing. And that night, as if by some ghastly jest of the gods, she went to Folyet's wife, to see if she could get news of Folyet. She came there, in time to see..."

Again he paused.

"Before he left this house, Miller telephoned to me. He was frightened, panic-stricken. He told me that you were going with Mrs. Folyet, and that you would find Folyet there. I had not known of that before. And I had not understood Miller's point of view. That was—another flaw.... When I learned that Folyet was in that house, and that you were on your way there with her, I feared that there might be trouble. But I never suspected what was afoot. I hired a car and drove out there at once. Fortunately it took Mrs. Folyet and Miller a long time to get you out to the garage. They had not had time to attend to Folyet. I arrived in time. I set Folyet free, and I sent Miller home. Then—I faced the woman who had deceived me. I told her that she was not fit to live. I told her that she would either drink what she had meant for Folyet, or I should kill her with my own hands."

"Charles!" cried his sister. "No...!"

"If she had lived," said Leatherby, "she would have been a menace to everyone. She would have made Folyet's life unbearable. She would have caused misery and humiliation to you, my dear. She was the only one who really knew my—call it my secret—and she could have ruined me. And she was not fit to live. She knew that—and she drank. I knew that there would be at least two hours left to her, and I telephoned for a nurse from the hospital. I naturally wished to give a natural appearance to the event. I offered the nurse a glass of wine in which there was a sleeping-draught. I calculated that she would sleep until morning, and then would not care to mention the wine. She has that type of mind. I was afraid that Mrs. Folyet might talk—wander in her mind, and, what is more, I did not wish the death known until the morning. I wanted time for Dennison to be released and myself to return to my hotel in the city. I telephoned to Peters; I spoke of it as an ordinary case to him, and I knew he would take it so. I had told Miller to return later and release Dennison, and I went back to the city, feeling no uneasiness. It seemed to me unlikely to the point of impossibility that anyone would enter the house that night. And, unhappily, my poor Hilda came. She found the door unlocked and she entered. She found the nurse asleep and Mrs. Folyet—talking....

"I had left the empty bottle in the room. As you knew about it, Dennison, it seemed to me wiser to make no mystery about it. I could say it was medicine I gave her for her heart. It leaves no detectable trace; there would have been no way of connecting it with her death.

"But Mrs. Folyet told Hilda. The effect of that drug is to produce a condition which I can describe only as bliss. The patient's mind remains clear, though exalted; toward the end, the patient sinks into a peaceful sleep, in the course of which death occurs imperceptibly. A true euthanasia.... Hilda unfortunately came upon Mrs. Foylet during the stage of exaltation. She talked to Hilda, showed her the bottle, told her how glad she was to die, how grateful she was to me for putting an end to her sufferings."

He was silent for a moment.

"Poor Hilda! She came into the city, to my hotel, with that empty bottle. I had given orders that I was not to be disturbed on any account until morning, and she had not enough money to go back to Shayne and return in the morning. She sat in the waiting-room at the Grand Central all night; then at eight o'clock she returned to the hotel. She really believed that she was 'saving' me from the electric-chair. I assured her that I was in no danger. I tried to explain my ideas to her, my theory of life. But she could not understand. She recoiled from me as if I were a criminal."

For the first time Dennison saw upon Leatherby's face a look of weariness, of disappointment, of age.

"She is above all things loyal and grateful," he went on. "I was able to render considerable assistance to her parents during their lifetime, and she will never forget that. But she cannot understand. My point of view, my conception of life, are horrible to her. She is so young.... She is too young.... I should have known.... Only gratitude...."

Dennison thought of her, sitting all night in the waiting-room, with her empty bottle, determined to save the man who had been kind to her parents, enduring Heaven knew what agony of disillusionment and terror. Her admiration for Leatherby had been so profound, so faithful.

"Of course," Leatherby resumed, "Hilda will say nothing. She is here now—" Dennison started, "—completing the records, finishing the work which I invented for her. And she is at this moment sending announcements to my patients that you are taking over my practice."

"I—I cannot!" said Dennison.

"You are over-squeamish," said Leatherby, with a smile. "The patients are quite untainted by my philosophy. They are all anxious to live as long as possible, in no matter what circumstances. I am giving them your former address; you must be there at two o'clock for your office hours. It is not a highly lucrative practice, Dennison, but it is a nucleus...."

The door-bell rang and Miller rose like an automaton, sidled respectfully around the room to the door.

"We are at home to no one, Miller," said Leatherby. He rose. "Hilda will say nothing. Miller will say nothing. Folyet has gone and will not return. And you, Dennison?"

Dennison said nothing.

"I shall take my sister away," Leatherby went on. "We shall travel. We shall take up our lives again in some new place. And I shall never again give my gift to anyone. I promise you that. Will you keep silence, Dennison?"

Still Dennison did not answer, for he could not. A terrible struggle was going on in his soul, and it was reflected in his face....

Then from the hall outside came Miller's voice, in a cry of fear.

"Doctor Leatherby, sir! *Look out!*"

They all turned toward the door. The curtains parted, and Evie entered, with Folyet.

CHAPTER EIGHTEEN

VALE!

Mrs. Lewis rose to her feet.

"Jeff!" she cried. "Jeff! You promised.... Traitor...!"

She sank into her chair again, and Dennison moved nearer to her, alarmed by her appearance. Fragile, high-strung, she had had more than she could well endure.

But Folyet was before him; he strode across the room and stood beside her chair.

"I couldn't help myself," he said, with his bitter smile. "I'm a captive."

"But who is this?" asked Leatherby.

"I'm Evelyn Curtis!" said Evie.

She spoke almost with a snap. Her short hair was ruffled under the little yellow hat, her cheeks were flushed, and there was on her pretty, childish face a look steely and implacable. Her father was a stout man in spectacles, and Evie was a pretty young girl, but she looked very like her father now. The district-attorney of his town, he was, a notable prosecutor. And at this moment Evie was every inch his child.

"And what can we do for you?" asked Leatherby.

Standing beside him, she looked very small and slight, yet she had the air of one well-armed; she glanced toward Folyet as if she held a gun at his head.

"I've brought him back," she said. "When I heard the servant say he'd just gone, in a taxi, I went after him, in my car. I thought he'd probably gone to the railway station—and he had. I saw someone waiting on the platform that looked like I thought he looked, and I went up to him and asked him if he were Mr. Folyet. And he said, yes. I made him come back."

"What could I do?" Folyet asked Mrs. Lewis. "She showed me half-a-dozen letters of mine—she threatened to take them to the police. And that would have meant an investigation. You see...."

Never had Dennison imagined Folyet ill-at-ease, but he saw him so now. Evidently he had found Evie too much for him.

"And I'd forgotten her!" thought Dennison, in wonder. "Entirely forgotten her."

"Who are you?" asked Mrs. Lewis, looking up at the girl. "Why are you interfering?"

"I'm interfering, because nobody else will," said Evie. "There's been a crime committed, and everyone else wants to hush it up. But I won't!"

"Evie!" said Dennison, sharply. "You gave me your word—"

"I said I wouldn't tell the things you told me. All right, I won't. But I can tell the things I've found out for myself, I can take these letters to the police and tell them that that poor woman was buried under a false name. I can prove who she really was—and that she'd been threatened. That ought to be enough to start something."

"Evie—" Dennison began.

"No, Alex!" she interrupted. "You won't do anything, and they all know that. They're just making a fool of you. Look what they've done to you! You've been knocked unconscious. You've been drugged and slandered. And now I suppose you'd just go meekly away. But I won't keep quiet! Whoever did that horrible thing is going to pay for it. And I don't care who it is!"

He looked at her, impressed by something very fine in her. It was true that she did not care what happened, who suffered, so that the wrong-doer was punished. Dennison thought of her letters to him, in which she had kindly and firmly reproached him for his various shortcomings. It was her nature and her training to do this. She was her father's child. She was not tolerant, not understanding, but she was utterly honest and fearless.

"What do you want?" asked Mrs. Lewis, faintly. "What do you mean to do?"

"I mean to know the truth," said Evie

"That's a large order," said Folyet. "Does anyone know The Truth? Is there any absolute Truth—"

"It's no use talking like that," said Evie. "Someone killed that woman. And someone's got to pay."

"Do you think I did it?" asked Folyet.

"It seems to me very likely," said Evie, coolly. "Considering what I read in those letters."

A curious silence followed her words, a silence that was like a wall of resistance against her. And she felt it; she knew that no one in this room wished her to know the truth.

"I think you did it," she said, "and I think that girl—Hilda—helped you."

"No," said Leatherby. "That's quite a mistake."

"She was there this morning, burning up papers—destroying evidence—"

"Quite a mistake," Leatherby repeated. "I think you will have to be told."

"Charles!" cried Mrs. Lewis.

"My dear," he said, "it's inevitable. You can see that. Hilda cannot be accused in this irresponsible fashion. And Folyet cannot keep silent now, in face of those letters. It's inevitable." He turned to Evie, and looked down at her with his kindly smile. "I killed Mrs. Folyet," he said.

Dennison pitied Evie then. She had hitherto been sustained by the excitement of the chase, the most thrilling game in the world. But now it had grown real, starkly real. She had announced her principles; now she was confronted with their implications. She had said that whoever had done this thing must pay—and here was the man.

The flush faded from her cheeks, leaving her white as a little ghost, but she stood her ground valiantly.

"Perhaps you're just saying that—to shield someone else," she said.

"Ask Dennison!" he answered, still smiling.

She turned to Dennison.

"Alex...?"

"Yes," he said.

Evie's eyes were fixed upon his face with something like desperation. She looked toward Mrs. Lewis, who lay back in her chair with her eyes closed, at Folyet beside her, his hand resting lightly on her shoulder. She was to have no help from anyone. She must make her own decision.

"All right!" she said, a little unsteadily. "Then—you'd better come with me—and tell Daddy the whole thing. He'll know what ought to be done."

"No doubt he will," said Leatherby, courteously. "And now.... Folyet, you will look after my sister?"

Folyet stood up straight; the mask of bitterness and mockery fell from him.

"I will, sir!" he said.

"And Dennison...?"

"I—I'm sorry, sir... " said Dennison.

"No need for that, Dennison. I am not a young man any longer; many of my friends have gone. I have been sitting almost alone at my banquet; the lights are going out, one by one, the garlands are withered. I am not sorry to go through the open door."

"I'm sorry, sir... " said Dennison again, and held out his hand.

Leatherby took it in his firm clasp; then with another glance at his half-unconscious sister, he turned toward the door.

"Wh-where are you going?" asked Evie.

"I am going—to get ready," he answered.

Mechanically she followed him into the hall, stood there watching him as he mounted the stairs. Dennison came out to her, and as Leatherby vanished from sight, he became aware of the sound of the typewriter from the reception room. Hilda was there....

Leatherby had meant so well and done so ill. Like a miasma, his ideas had spread through this household, poisoning everyone—except Hilda. He thought of her in her white uniform, the honourable livery of her fine calling, she so anxious to help, so faithful, so kind. She alone had been untouched; she alone had been able to move and breathe in this air and be unaffected by it.

But sorrow and shame had come to her, too.

"What will she do now?" he thought.

That was not his problem. There was nothing in the world he could do for Hilda Napier, nothing he could say to her....

"He's taking—an awfully long time... " said. Evie.

Her voice sounded forlorn; turning, he saw her sitting on the hall table, such a youthful figure, so shockingly incongruous with the task she had undertaken.

"She'd be sorry," he thought, "if she'd ever let herself be sorry for anything she did."

A rattling volley against the glass of the front door startled him; he walked over there and stood looking out at the sudden Spring shower. Leatherby had thought that happiness should be the one aim of life, but he was wrong. A man could live without happiness....

"Alex!"

"Yes, Evie?"

"He's taking such an awfully long time to come down again I..."

Dennison said nothing. He knew that Leatherby would never come down those stairs again alive; he had known it all the time.

"Alex !"

"Well?"

"You—look so queer...."

Her eyes widened; she came nearer to him. "Alex, tell me!"

Still he would not answer, and she caught him by the shoulders and tried to shake him, in her great and sudden fear.

"You wanted a death for a death," he said. "Well, you've got it."

"You mean—he's killed himself?"

"Does it matter? Or can't Justice be satisfied without the whole show—the judge in the black cap, and the newspaper stories?"

Without warning she began to cry.

"You're as hard—as nails!" she sobbed. "I always knew it! You will have your own way—always. Mother saw that, long ago. She *knew* we'd never get on."

"Evie!" he protested.

"I came out here this morning to tell you," she went on. "I could see by your nasty letters that you didn't really care one bit if we didn't get married for a hundred years."

"That's not fair, Evie!"

"I know it's not," she answered, unexpectedly. "I ought to be ashamed of myself—to try to blame you when I—I've met somebody else.... I came to tell you this morning—but when I saw everything so *miserable* for you— I made up my mind not to tell you, ever. I thought I'd marry you and do—the best I could for you—as long as—everything was so—miserable—for you—"

"But, Evie! Do you mean—?"

"It wasn't the—real thing—with us, ever," she said, with a sob. "Alex, I'm—*darn* sorry...!"

He put his arm about her shoulders, but she slid away, and shook her head. She dried her eyes, and looked back at him, with more tears already over flowing.

"I'm going!" she said.

"But what about—?"

"I just can't stand any more!" she cried. "I never thought anything could be so—terrible.... *I'm* not a policeman, either. I'm—just a—girl. I want to go home! Oh, I want to go home!"

The door closed after her; through the glass he saw her running in the rain to her car.

He turned back, down the hall, to Hilda.

THE END

If you enjoyed this title, you might enjoy the following from

Stark House Press

Storm Constantine

0-9667848-1-2

CALENTURE

by STORM CONSTANTINE $17.95

Fantasy novel set in a world of floating cities.

0-9667848-0-4

THE ORACLE LIPS

by STORM CONSTANTINE $45.00

Signed/Numbered/Limited Edition hardback collection of the author's stories.

0-9667848-3-9

SIGN FOR THE SACRED

by STORM CONSTANTINE $19.95

Novel about the search for an elusive messiah.

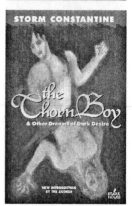

0-9667848-4-7

THE THORN BOY & OTHER DREAMS OF DARK DESIRE

by STORM CONSTANTINE $19.95

Nine voluptuous, erotic fantasies.